TOTAL POWER

Also by Vince Flynn and available from Center Point Large Print:

The Survivor
Order to Kill
Enemy of The State
Red War
Lethal Agent

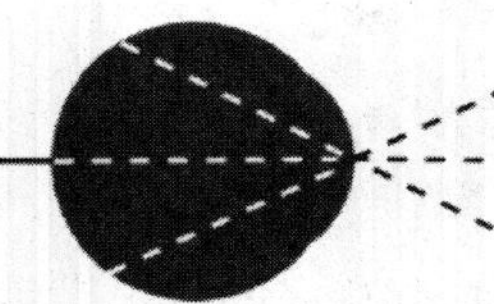

VINCE FLYNN

TOTAL POWER

A MITCH RAPP NOVEL BY KYLE MILLS

Center Point Large Print
Thorndike, Maine

This Center Point Large Print edition
is published in the year 2020 by arrangement with
Atria Books, a division of Simon & Schuster, Inc.

The text of this Large Print edition is unabridged.
In other aspects, this book may vary
from the original edition.
Printed in the United States of America
on permanent paper.
Set in 16-point Times New Roman type.

ISBN: 978-1-64358-725-7

The Library of Congress has cataloged this record
under Library of Congress Control Number: 2020944484

ACKNOWLEDGMENTS

It's hard to think of all the people and events that put me on the path I've taken: my first-grade teacher, Mrs. Burnside, who stoked my desperate need to know where Dick and Spot would run next; the seventh-grade librarian who offered her bemused encouragement when I chose James Clavell's weighty tome *Shogun* for my book report; even the swim coaches who demanded that I spend my youth staring at the bottom of a pool with nothing to do but create elaborate fantasies in my head.

More recently, I've been lucky enough to be surrounded by some of the most talented people in the business. Vince's editor, Emily Bestler, and his agent, Sloan Harris, are there for me just like they were for him. Simon Lipskar and Celia Taylor Mobley keep the business side humming along. Lara Jones handles the details that constantly get away from me. Ryan Steck lends me his unflagging passion and unparalleled knowledge of the Rappverse. David Brown, already the marketing master, has turned his creativity up to eleven in the time of COVID-19. My mother and wife provide early criticism and remind me when Mrs. Burnside would be disappointed in my grammar. Rod Gregg spends an inordinate amount of time helping me understand the ins and outs of firearms. No small task, I assure you.

Finally, to all of Vince's fans who continue to stick with me. It's hard to believe that this is my sixth Mitch Rapp book. *Total Power* would have never happened without your continued support and enthusiasm.

AUTHOR'S NOTE

The most terrifying thing about writing this book was how little I had to make up. Between actual historical power outages, government assessments of power grid vulnerabilities, and official estimates of the casualties that a long-term outage would generate, much of the book wrote itself. Having said that, things like the details of how attacks would best be carried out and specific locations of critical infrastructure have been purposely obscured or fictionalized.

TOTAL POWER

PRELUDE

Near Fayetteville
West Virginia
USA

A light mist condensed on Sonya Vance's windshield, turning the forested mountains around her into smears of green. Clouds had formed beneath the bridge she was driving across, dense enough that it looked like they would catch her if she jumped.

Tempting.

A vehicle appeared on the empty road behind and she examined it in the rearview mirror. A pickup streaked with rust and listing a bit to one side. She slowed to let it pass, examining the young couple and toddler inside. Nothing to suggest a threat. But then, that was how the game was played.

When her last name had still been Voronova, she'd been taught that everything was a threat. Every kindly old woman could be hiding a blade or vial of poison. Every car could be a tail. Every innocuous knickknack, light fixture, or television could be a recording device.

Those lessons seemed impossibly remote now. After so many years, even the proper pronunciation of her real name was a challenge that demanded a few stiff drinks to accomplish with flourish. But not vodka. Never vodka.

She'd been born in the Soviet Union to a mother she knew only from a yellowed file presented to her in her mid-teens. It had depicted a hard, bony woman with deep-set eyes that suggested a life of addiction. According to the file, she'd been a thief and a traitor. Perhaps even a murderer. A vile creature willing to do whatever was necessary to get her next fix.

Over the years, Voronova had come to question whether the woman was really her mother or if that same file had been given to everyone in the program. A lie calculated to foment horror, guilt, and gratitude in whoever heard it.

She'd been taken from a Romanian orphanage so dystopian that visions of it still came to her in nightmares. Apparently, government testing had discovered early indications of exceptional intelligence and a strong probability that she would grow up physically attractive. Excellent traits for a sleeper agent.

She'd spent the rest of her youth in a purpose-built town in northern Russia surrounded by children just like her. They'd been raised on a steady diet of English instruction, Western music, and Hollywood movies—all put into ideological context by their ever-vigilant political officer.

Many of the others seemed to be genuinely passionate about the endless lectures on the evils of capitalism, the inevitable chaos of democracy, and the absurdity of God. Her enthusiasm, though, had been largely feigned. The bare minimum necessary to get her in front of the latest Tom Cruise movie.

The Soviet Union had fallen in 1991 when she was still a girl, but the program had continued. The message became less ideological and more nationalist, but it didn't really matter. She was young and it was all she'd ever known. Like most kids, she'd wanted to please the adults around her, to avoid punishment, and to watch *Top Gun*.

She'd been twenty-two years old when she finally crossed into the country she'd spent her life studying. The memory of the experience still clung to her mind. The smell of it. The light of its sun. The warmth of its people. It had felt strangely like . . . home.

And so it had been for the last sixteen years. She'd turn thirty-eight next month, assuming she managed to live that long. Her survival was something that she'd taken for granted until a call had come in over a hidden app on her phone. A call she'd convinced herself would never come.

The GPS built into the rental car's dashboard demanded that she turn off the highway and she felt a surge of adrenaline not befitting a secret agent. But she wasn't a secret agent. She was a moderately above-average computer programmer who worked out of a cramped basement flat in Washington, DC. A city that was only a few hours behind her but that right now felt like it might as well have been in another galaxy.

She suddenly felt completely lost, disoriented to the point that she thought she might have to pull over to the side of the road. What was she even doing here? Everything she'd been told she was fighting for was gone. Russia was now a capitalist country run by a dictator and his court of absurdly wealthy oligarchs. The SVR didn't even pay her. What money she had came from coding.

Despite those observations, she obeyed her GPS's orders and turned onto a steep secondary road. Above all others, *that* was the lesson that had been beaten into her. Follow orders. You are nothing. A machine cog that either performs its function or is torn out and replaced.

When the pavement ended, the GPS got confused and began endlessly recommending a U-turn. Voronova shut it off, focusing on the dull hum of the motor and vague slosh of mud beneath the tires. She knew where the critical turn was. But not much else. She was to meet a lone male at a cabin situated near the end of the deteriorating track she was traveling. She was to listen to what he had to say, probe him for any additional information that might be pertinent, and report back to Moscow. The only clue she had as to the subject matter of the meeting was her superiors' demand that she familiarize herself with the US power grid—a project she'd spent the last five days immersed in. Other than that, only one thing could be said for certain: the person she was on her way to meet was important. The risks of activating an agent like her weren't something Moscow took lightly.

The building started to appear, ominous in the mist. It was a basic A-frame that probably dated back to before she was born—a strange teepee of peeling logs and asphalt shingles, fronted by a large porch. Predictably, the shades were drawn, but a little light bled around the edges.

Voronova was carrying a knife in her boot, but that was her only weapon. She hadn't fired a gun in almost twenty years and her combat training since arriving in the United States consisted entirely of her Thursday night kickboxing class.

She felt the fear growing in her and it wasn't difficult to pinpoint its contradictory causes. First, the most likely: the SVR had decided that people like her were more risk than reward and the house contained an assassin charged with solving that problem. The second was perhaps even more terrifying: that this was a legitimate operation and she was going to survive it.

After being activated, would it be viable for her to stay in the United States? Would she be called back to Russia? And if she was, what the hell would she do there? Go to work in an SVR office building? Continue coding for US companies? Work at the new Kentucky Fried Chicken on Red Square? How would she reintegrate into a country she'd never really integrated into in the first place?

Voronova parked and grabbed a jacket from the passenger seat before stepping out in the rain.

Only one way to find out.

Everything seemed on the up-and-up, but it was hard to know that for sure when the Russians were involved.

He'd been the one who had dictated the location for this meeting and his iPhone, connected to various cameras in the area, showed nothing suspicious. Pocketing the device, he turned his attention to a gap between the windowsill and shade. He wasn't sure what to expect, exactly. Maybe a supermodel with one of those big fur hats? An East German shot putter with a tight bun and breath that smelled like borscht?

The woman coming up the steps, though, looked disappointingly normal. Mid-thirties, with a curvy figure poured into snug-fitting jeans. She had the hood of her coat up, but that didn't fully hide her attractive, no-nonsense features and a lock of blond hair blown across her forehead.

Mostly, though, he was amazed that she was

actually there. He'd spent the last six months trying to set up this meeting. It had taken hundreds of anonymous exchanges over the Internet to prove that he was real and that he had something they wanted.

Finally, the day had arrived.

When she reached the porch, he pulled away from the shade and wiped the sweat from his palms. The time spent chatting up the Russians was actually just a drop in the bucket. It had taken more than five years of relentless work to get him here. But really it was much more than that. In truth, his entire life had been leading him to this place, this moment. And while he believed neither in God nor destiny, he did believe that this was his purpose. That he was meant for greatness. Terrible greatness.

The rattle of boots on the deck was followed by a knock that was more timid than he'd expected.

When he opened the door, she stepped in and pulled her hood back. The hair was indeed blond, but with dark streaks. A little edgy, but fitting with features that leaned just a little Asian. Up close, she was hotter than at a distance. Maybe she was there to ply him with her feminine wiles? Not necessary, but certainly welcome as a fringe benefit.

He realized that they'd been looking at each other for an uncomfortably long time but wasn't sure what to say. Maybe he should have insisted on some code like in the movies. *The wind whistles through the trees.* And then she'd reply with something like *it comes from the frozen north.*

In the end, she was the first to speak.

"What do you have for me?"

No sexy Russian accent. She sounded like she was from DC.

"What do you know about the power grid?"

"More than most. But it's not my area of expertise."

He examined her stylish down coat. "What is? Fashion?"

Her smile was polite, with just a hint of distaste. It wasn't the first time he'd seen that expression on a woman's face. Or the hundredth.

"Killing people and disposing of their bodies," she responded.

He resisted the urge to step back, trying to discern whether she was joking. Her face had become a dead mask. The only thing she wasn't able to hide was that she clearly didn't want to be there.

"Then I'll keep it simple," he said, trying to regain the upper hand. "It's been called the world's biggest interconnected machine and that's probably pretty close to the truth. Call it seven thousand power plants, fifty thousand substations, and two hundred thousand miles of transmission lines."

"When I said it's not my area of expertise, I meant I couldn't run the grid or fix a broken transformer. Not that I didn't know what it was. Now why did I come all this way? I hope not to listen to you recite a Wikipedia page."

He felt his mouth go dry and covered by walking to the refrigerator for a beer. The landlord had left a six-pack of Bud as a thank-you for renting the place in the off-season.

"What you don't know is that it's a miracle that it even works. It's made up of more than three thousand different utilities, and it's governed by more different state and federal organizations than you can count—most of which barely communicate with each other. A lot of the infrastructure is over forty years old and some has been running for the better part of a hundred. It's an incredible balancing act. Despite all the different components, the demand and supply have to be perfectly matched. When you plug in your hair dryer, the grid has to add just that much power. When you turn it off, it has to shut down that power or move it somewhere else."

"Sure, it's complicated, but the fact is that it *does* work. Almost flawlessly. And it has for a long time. A lot of it's also redundant. If any piece—or series of pieces—fails, they can route around them until they're repaired."

"Flawless and redundant," he said incredulously. "You've been drinking the Kool-Aid, sweetheart. Think about it. In 2003, we had one of the biggest blackouts in history. Fifty-five million people suddenly lost power. Why? An attack by your friends in Moscow? A nuclear bomb? Geomagnetic storm? Nope. Some power lines in Ohio brushed an overgrown tree. That's it."

"There were other factors that kept them from—"

"Exactly!" he said, pointing at her with the neck of his beer. "That tree should have tripped an alarm, right? Some power company you've never heard of should have seen the problem and routed around it. But there was no alarm. Why? Because of a little software bug. A minor glitch that caused a cascade that shut down the whole Northeast."

"Whatever," she said, clearly unimpressed.

"That wasn't a planned, malicious attack, lady. It was a tree branch and a coding error. Now imagine the possibilities of a conscious, coordinated effort. How much damage could be done? How long would it take to get things back online?"

"I don't know."

"No? I do."

"So, you're saying that you've figured out how to take out a portion of the US grid and keep it down for a while? It seems—"

"I've figure out how to take down the *entire*

US grid and keep it down for a *year*. Maybe even permanently if you figure that after about six months there wouldn't be anyone left alive to work on it."

Her expression went from unimpressed to skeptical. "That's a lot easier said than done. Like you just told me, tens of thousands of moving parts—a lot of them independent from one another."

He smiled. "I'm glad you say you know something about the grid. That way you'll have some inkling of what you're looking at."

"I don't understand."

He pointed toward a laptop on the kitchen table. "Go ahead. Check it out."

Sonya Voronova leaned back in the kitchen chair and stared blankly at the computer screen. After almost forty-five minutes of examination, she'd come to the conclusion that this scrawny sleazebag might actually be telling the truth. Not only did everything seem to be there; it seemed to be there in gory detail. High-resolution photos of more than a thousand critical substations. Comprehensive schematics of transmission systems including their interconnectivity and weak points. Analysis of software security issues in all the major power companies as well as many of the smaller operators. Exhaustive evaluations of transmission line vulnerabilities—from ones that were too close to trees to ones that had poor seasonal access to ones that were beyond their useful life.

And she'd barely scraped the surface of what was on this asshole's laptop. The quality and sheer volume of the data was astounding. Maybe a little too astounding.

The obvious question was whether it was all bullshit. But even compiling that much convincing bullshit would have been a monumental task. Why bother? He'd have to know that Russian analysts would go through it with a fine-toothed comb before any wire transfers were made.

"The key to taking down the US grid isn't in the hardware," she said, speaking aloud for the first time in almost an hour. "Sure, blowing up some critical substations could do a lot of damage. But it wouldn't last. The key is SCADA—the supervisory control and data acquisition systems. You'd have to be able to get that level of access in literally hundreds of separate utilities. And just trashing their systems wouldn't be enough. You'd have to get control. Force their computers to provide fake data to cover up real damage, overload systems, and shut down safeguards." She turned toward the sofa he was sitting on. "That kind of access just isn't doable. Sure, you could get into a few utilities the normal way—phishing attacks and such. But hundreds? No way in hell."

"No way in hell?" he said, pushing himself

off the sofa and approaching. When he stopped in front of her he slid his fingers down one side of her hair. She was too stunned to react other than to just stare. Was this his idea of a come-on? Here? Now? The very idea of touching this creep made her stomach roll over.

“You heard me,” she said, scooting her chair back and moving her hair out of reach.

He frowned in a way that suggested he thought she was part of whatever payment he was looking for. “Then it’s weird that I’ve already done it.”

“What do you mean? Done what?”

“Put malware on the computers of nearly every power company in America.”

“Bullshit.”

By way of an answer, he leaned over and used the touchpad to navigate to a long list of hyperlinked utility companies. “Go ahead. Knock yourself out.”

She watched him walk back to the sofa and fall into the worn cushions. After staring at him for a few seconds, she turned back to the laptop and followed a link to Exelon, America’s largest electric company. The log-in page immediately auto filled and she was in. Ten minutes of navigating suggested that she didn’t just have access to relatively unimportant areas like accounting or personnel. She had command and control authority that would allow her to do whatever she wanted.

She continued through the list at random, accessing both major utilities and tiny ones serving limited areas. Every time, the password manager auto-filled the log-in and she found herself with unfettered access.

Finally, she used a sleeve to wipe her fingerprints from the laptop and closed it. Her research for this meeting had focused on the technical aspects of the grid, but there had been no avoiding information on what would happen if this kind of attack were ever carried out. Society relied on electricity for everything. Food production. Transportation. Health care. Heat. Refrigeration. America was like a finely tuned watch—incredibly effective as long as every single gear was turning. But if even one failed . . .

"Well?" the man said, pulling her back into the here and now.

"Well what?"

"What do you mean, *well what?* Is it something your government would be interested in or not?"

"It's possible," she said.

"Time is of the essence, sweetheart."

"What do you want for it?"

He laughed, but it came off as more of a twisted giggle. "I don't give a shit about your rubles. I just want to see America sent back to the Stone Age. And if it's going to happen, it needs to be now. A consulting firm has been working on a plan to upgrade and secure the grid for six years and they're finally going to present their findings this week. If the government's smart enough to implement their recommendations, this thing gets a whole lot more complicated."

She contemplated him, trying to maintain an air of calm that she didn't feel. "You're telling me you want us to *act* on this?"

"Didn't I just say that? I mean, I could do the computer stuff myself, but to really bring it off like I designed, I'd need a team of people to take out some physical infrastructure. Not a lot—just a few critical substations spread out across the country. You have people who could pull that off without breaking a sweat. The truth is that none of the substations I need destroyed even have a guard. Mostly just chain link fences. I figure Russia has bolt cutter technology, right?"

She winced at hearing the word *Russia* spoken out loud.

"Why?"

"Why what?" he said.

"Why would you want something like this to happen to your own country? To your own countrymen?"

"What's it to you? Are you on board or not?"

She remained silent, but her expression must have hinted at her uncertainty.

"Who better than you?" he said. "NATO's pushing you. The world's big economies are squeezing you. Renewables are going to trash your resource-based economy. And straight-up wars just aren't feasible anymore. You can't roll your tanks across Kansas. Hell, you know that better than anyone. You're the kings of asymmetrical warfare. Why screw around trolling Americans on Facebook when I'm willing to hand you the equivalent of a million-megaton nuke? And the US won't even be able to retaliate because they won't know who did it. By the time they figure it out, they'll be busy chasing possums so they have something to eat. Now's your moment. To the bold go the spoils, right?"

"Russia is a responsible member of the international community," she said, sounding a bit naïve even to herself. "Our goal is to be capable of defending ourselves against US aggression. This could help us do that and I imagine we'd be willing to pay handsomely for—"

"I'm already rich."

Voronova nodded thoughtfully. It was time to punt and get the hell away from this freak. "I'm afraid I'm not authorized to start World War Three. But I'll relay everything we discussed to my superiors and they'll get back to you."

"When?"

"Soon, I would imagine."

"You're not the only person I'm talking to, you know. The Chinese are interested. So are the Iranians and Cubans. And there are more than a few terrorist groups who would give their left nuts for what’s on that computer. But, like I said, you’re my first choice. America’s existential enemy. It’s hard not to appreciate the historical symmetry of that, you know?”

CHAPTER 1

Madrid
Spain

When the plane finally began to descend, Mitch Rapp turned to the window and examined the grid of runways and buildings that made up the Madrid-Barajas airport. A delay in Cairo had put his flight three hours behind schedule, but that was the least of his problems. It had taken him almost a day longer than expected to clean up one of the Saudis' many messes in Yemen and he was now a full day and a half late arriving.

Sayid Halabi was rotting in the Somali desert thanks to Scott Coleman, but much of the elite team the ISIS leader had assembled was still on the loose. The men had significant expertise in everything from social media to spec ops to science and had scattered throughout the world. Now, though, they seemed to be re-forming under the leadership of a former Iraqi army captain. He was no Sayid Halabi, but he was tough as nails and motivated as hell.

Their targets and strategy going forward was largely unknown, but what was certain was that they weren't going to just crawl under a rock and die of old age. They were looking to inflict some pain before they finally met Allah.

Rapp coughed into his hand and checked it for blood. There hadn't been any for months, but it was a habit that was proving hard to break. He'd managed to prevent Halabi from smuggling a deadly pathogen across the Mexican border, but had contracted the disease in the process. The docs still seemed surprised that he was alive. And, in truth, so was he. He'd spent longer than he cared to remember with machines breathing for him and, at its worst, death would have been preferable. As far as he was concerned, the next time a bioterror threat raised its ugly head, the fucking FBI could handle it.

The wheels touched down, but Rapp stayed in his seat as the other passengers prepared to disembark. He turned his phone back on and scrolled through the texts, searching for anything that suggested his impending operation had run into a snag. Nothing. As of that moment, it was still a go. His plans for a shower, steak, and some shut-eye before the briefing, though, definitely weren't.

Once the plane was more or less empty, he slung a small pack over his shoulder and started up the aisle. The crew near the door gave him a quizzical look as he approached and he reflexively turned his face away, mumbling the expected thanks.

Rapp had spent most of his adult life seeking anonymity and his current state wasn't helping that quest. His dark hair hadn't completely regrown and was in the uncontrollable stage between short enough to behave and long enough for gravity to take control. Thankfully, his beard had come back more quickly, effectively obscuring his lower face and leaving only his sunburned nose visible below mirrored sunglasses.

What really made him stand out, though, was the dust. It was still clinging to every part of him from his trip across Yemen and Saudi Arabia. The loaded Range Rover he'd been promised had been on fire when he found it and there hadn't been a lot of other options. So, instead of making the trip cradled in leather and caressed by air-conditioning, he'd made half of it in the back of a dilapidated pickup and the other half by motorcycle.

The jet bridge and corridor beyond were empty, already cleared of passengers hurrying to secure a good place in the passport control line. He kept a leisurely pace, walking toward a sign pointing him left, but instead passing through a door marked NO ENTRY. The alarm that was supposed to sound didn't and he was met on the other side by an impeccably dressed Spanish woman.

"I trust your flight was a good one," she said in more than acceptable English.

"Fine, thanks."

"We have a car waiting and I fear I'll have

to take you straight to your meeting. As you requested, there is food, water, and a clean change of clothes in the back seat. Also, you'll find a brief that will bring you up to date on the situation."

"It's good to see you again, Mitch."

Jordi Cardenas, the head of Spain's national intelligence agency, held out a hand and Rapp took it. "Good to see you, too. We appreciate the assist."

"It's very much our pleasure," he said, leading Rapp into a windowless conference room. The men around the table were ones Rapp had known for most of his career—Scott Coleman was at the far end and his top operators had taken the chairs closest to him. Claudia Gould, the woman Rapp lived with and who also happened to be Coleman's logistics director, was standing near a large screen hanging on the wall. Rapp gave them all a silent nod and took an empty seat that wouldn't put his back to the door.

"Okay, I think we're all here," Claudia said with a French accent that had become a bit less pronounced over the last year. "Let's get started."

The screen came to life with photos of a number of Middle Eastern men as well as a few squares containing silhouettes with question marks inside. "We're in the dark as to the identities of three of the people in Sayid Halabi's inner circle and we have very little intelligence on which of his enforcers are still alive. What we do know is that Muhammad Nahas has taken over leadership." She pointed to the screen. "This is the only existing photo of him, taken by the US Army when he was a member of Iraqi special forces."

It had been cropped to focus on the man's intense eyes and hawklike nose, framing out the smiling American and Iraqi comrades that had been visible in the original. Perhaps fitting in light of the fact that they were all dead now. Nahas had purposely led them into an ambush that only he survived.

"Based on what we know from US Army records and people who fought with him, he's an extremely disciplined and well-trained soldier. Smart, and well respected, but not necessarily a man who commands the kind of devotion Halabi did. Also, he's not the big thinker that Halabi was. Based on Internet activity we've intercepted from the group, they haven't yet formed any concrete plans. They're talking about everything from a 9/11-style attack, to a sarin gas attack similar to the one carried out in Japan. There's also discussion of more far-fetched operations like poisoning a water reservoir. Overall, it comes off a bit like . . ." She paused for a moment to search for the right term in English. ". . . spitballing."

"Is Nahas the target?" Scott Coleman asked.

"Unfortunately, no. We haven't been able to find him." She zoomed in on another of the on-screen photos. This one depicted a clean-shaven, bespectacled man in his early thirties. Middle Eastern descent for sure but he had the look of someone who'd lived a comfortable life in Dubai or Kuwait City.

"*This* is the target. Hamal Kattan. He doesn't look like much, but he was actually a key person in Halabi's orbit. His educational background is in physics but he seems to be knowledgeable in pretty much anything relating to technology. A renaissance man who Halabi relied on to keep him connected to the modern world."

"He looks soft," Rapp said.

"That's probably an accurate assessment. He wasn't particularly religious in school and his parents are secular Jordanians also involved in the sciences. The overall impression is that he was looking for a purpose in life and Halabi gave it to him."

Rapp knew the type better than he wanted to—people who bought a copy of *Islam for Dummies* on their way to join ISIS. Some were looking for excitement or a sense of brotherhood. Others for power or to get laid. Still others just wanted to get bloody and make other human beings suffer. And finally there were the ones like this little pissant—aimless bastards in search of the meaning of life.

The slide changed to a picture of Kattan walking down a narrow cobblestone street, head down and collar up against what appeared to be a stiff wind.

"This was taken yesterday in southern Spain. Granada to be precise."

"What's he doing here?"

"Meeting with like-minded jihadists, it appears," Jordi Cardenas interjected. "We've been following him and we're getting all kinds of interesting information on his friends."

"But you're not moving against them," Rapp clarified.

"No. Not until you give us the go-ahead."

Rapp nodded and motioned for Claudia to continue her briefing.

"The day after tomorrow, Kattan is scheduled to fly from Granada to Washington, DC, via Barcelona and New York."

"Do we know why? Entering the US is a pretty big risk," Rapp said.

"Based on our wiretaps, he's going there at the orders of Muhammad Nahas to meet someone. It's possible that Nahas is going to be at this meeting as well."

Rapp perked up at that. He'd love to put a bullet between that son of a bitch's eyes. "What do you mean by 'possible'? How possible?"

"We don't know. The communications have been vague on that point. Call it fifty-fifty."

She switched slides again, bringing up a seating chart from the airplane Kattan would be taking from Granada to Barcelona. She used a laser pointer to indicate an aisle seat near the left wing. "We've arranged for the target to be sitting here."

"Does he have anyone watching his back?" Coleman asked.

"We aren't sure yet," Cardenas said. "We just found out about his flight yesterday and we're working around the clock doing background checks on the passenger list. So far, we have one strong possibility—a young Muslim male originally from Morocco but living in Seville now. He's taking a train to Granada and catching that flight to Barcelona, but not continuing on to the US."

"Will you have looked at all the passengers before the wheels on that plane go up?"

"Absolutely. If there's anyone else suspicious, you'll know about it before you board."

Scott Coleman let out a long breath. "It's a lot of moving parts, Mitch."

"Maybe one of the most complicated ops we've ever done," Coleman's sniper Charlie Wicker agreed. "And here we are two days out, still wondering if the target has backup."

Rapp nodded.

"We all know it'd be easy to snatch Kattan off the street, but when he goes missing, his network's going to find out. We'd have a few hours at the most to question him before they scatter and everything he knows goes stale. If we can do it in a way that makes them think he's dead, then we might actually have a shot at completely decapitating what's left of ISIS."

"What about weapons? If he has an escort, how are we going to know if they're armed?"

"We're in the process of quietly upgrading the security in the Granada airport," Cardenas said. "We should be able to find any significant weaponry going through."

"Can I assume we're not going to do anything about it?" Joe Maslick said.

Rapp shook his head. "If we take one of them down in security—"

"Their network's going to know," Bruno McGraw said, finishing his sentence for him.

"Right."

"So we're going to get on a plane with an unknown number of terrorists carrying an unknown number of weapons and try to take them alive."

"That about covers it."

"Bullets and planes don't mix," Coleman pointed out. "Remember Azerbaijan?"

Rapp remembered it a little too vividly. "Look, I understand that these aren't our normal operating parameters. We're going to be in a confined space thirty thousand feet off the ground, working with people we have no experience with, and relying on crap intel. I'll do what I can to mitigate the risks, but if the wrong thing on that plane gets shot there's not going to be much to do but bend over and kiss our asses good-bye. Anyone who wants to sit this one out should do it. It's the smart move and I'm not going to hold it against you."

None of the men at the table even bothered to look around. They were in. They were always in.

Rapp leaned back in his chair. "All right, Claudia. Give us what you've got."

CHAPTER 2

Moscow
Russia

"Kremlin in your language means *fortress inside a city,* but most people don't know this."

Sonya Voronova scanned the strange architecture of Russia's seat of power, feigning interest and shivering from the cold.

"The palace you see over there used to be the czar's residence but is now the home of our president Boris Utkin . . ."

She allowed the man to press against her as he spoke, not only for appearances but for the warmth. Otherwise she ignored him, turning her attention to the snow cascading from steel-gray skies.

He was about her age, broad shouldered and good looking. They'd ostensibly met in a bar the night she'd flown in and later retreated to her hotel room a few blocks away. To anyone watching, she'd be a single female tourist looking to have a good time and he'd be a Russian local willing to provide it. As always, the truth was very different. To the degree that truth even existed in the life that had been foisted on her.

"It's beautiful," she said when she noticed he'd

fallen silent. And it was. But what it all meant for her was a mystery. She'd been ordered back to Moscow to give a personal report of her meeting with the man in West Virginia. Why? Secure channels were abundant in the modern world.

She wondered if she'd ever see America again. If her life would end here in a country that felt as foreign to her as it did to the tourists around her. And if that was to be her fate, would it come at the hands of the beautiful young man next to her?

Whatever was going to happen, it turned out that it wasn't going to happen there. After an exhaustive review of Russian history and architecture, they wandered back to the road, grabbed a bite from a street vendor, and hailed a cab.

She was thankful to be out of the wind, but despair set in when the driver used his cell phone to report that she was on board and to provide an ETA. Part of that despair came from the fact that she had to strain to understand his Russian over the background noise. The rest came from watching the engaging smile of the man sitting across from her fade into a blank stare.

"Where are we going?" she asked in English.

Predictably, he replied in his native tongue. *Their* native tongue. The one-word response translated roughly as *elsewhere*.

The outer office was nondescript and governmental, and had the same stale tobacco smell as the cab. A stout woman sat behind a desk on the far side of the room, working on a computer but also watching to make sure Voronova wasn't up to any mischief.

Her despair had withered into something more like resignation—an emotional state that the Russians had elevated to an art form. She knew she had to keep her wits about her but having no idea what she was about to face made preparation impossible. In light of that, she grabbed a magazine and squinted at the Cyrillic writing it contained.

Just over an hour passed before she was ushered through the door at the back. Despite the chill she couldn't seem to shake, sweat broke across her forehead as she entered. Her handler was nowhere to be found. Instead, she was faced with not only Pavel Kedrov, the director of the SVR, but with the president of Russia himself.

"I understand that your meeting with our contact was successful?" Kedrov said, while Boris Utkin silently appraised her. She felt utterly naked and wondered if it would have been more comforting to have worn a uniform instead of the jeans, sweater, and down jacket of an American tourist. Maybe. But what uniform? She'd never been an official part of the Russian military or even the KGB. She'd never been an official part of anything.

"It was, sir."

"He's made some very bold claims. What's your assessment of them? Does he actually have anything that might interest us?"

"I believe he has the ability to do what he says."

The surprise registered on both of their faces and they gave each other a look that she couldn't quite read.

It seemed to her that men—particularly men like these—were little more than children. They could never fully escape their schoolyard thirst for power and notoriety. They craved it. Fought for it. Sometimes died for it. The ones who possessed a great deal—like Utkin and Kedrov—became intoxicated and wanted ever more. The ones who didn't have it—as she suspected was the case with the man in West Virginia—endlessly romanticized it. Led by males like this, it never ceased to amaze her that humanity had survived long enough to crawl down from the trees.

"This seems extremely unlikely to me," Utkin said.

"Me as well," Kedrov agreed. "We've spent a great deal of money and effort penetrating the American power grid with results that are, at best, uneven. Certainly blacking out portions of the country for a limited time is achievable, but a long-term shutdown of the entire system? Are you sure you wouldn't like to reconsider your response, Sonya?"

She found herself paralyzed. Telling them what they wanted to hear was the only hope she had of returning to her modest life in Washington. But what were those magic phrases? The ones that would get her on that plane?

"I don't think I do, sir," she heard herself say. "The amount of information he has is incredible. As is the level of detail. He also has full access to the mainframes of nearly every power company in America."

"He told you that?"

"He *showed* me that. He let me use his computer to enter various systems. I chose at random and got into every one I tried."

"At what level?"

"I had command and control access. He also says he's uploaded malware to all those systems and that he can activate it at any time."

"Did you confirm this as well?"

"It wouldn't have been practical. But with the level of penetration he has it would be a trivial matter. I see no reason not to take him at his word."

Again, they looked at each other.

"Did he tell you how he achieved all this?" Utkin said.

"No, sir."

"And you didn't press him on the issue?"

"Those were not my orders."

Utkin looked over at his intelligence chief.

"The path seems clear. If this man has that kind of information on offer, we'll acquire it." He turned his attention back to Voronova. "What does he want?"

"For it to happen, sir."

"Excuse me?"

"He isn't asking for money or anything else. Apparently, for his plan to work, he needs a small group of well-trained saboteurs to operate in concert with his cyberattack. He believes we can provide those saboteurs. But if we refuse, he made it clear that he's talking with other parties."

"You're telling me that he asked for no financial compensation?" Utkin said incredulously.

"None," she confirmed.

Utkin leaned back in his chair and ran a hand over his mouth. "Your people have gamed this, haven't they, Pavel?"

"The ramifications of a widespread, long-term power outage on America?" He nodded. "It would be carnage. On par with a large-scale nuclear strike."

"And the worldwide effects?"

"More difficult to predict," Kedrov said. "You're talking about taking the US completely off-line for the foreseeable future. They account for almost a quarter of the world's economic activity."

"But we're less reliant on them than many other countries."

"Unquestionably. We're a resource-rich, relatively independent country. Still, there would be serious—"

"But if we knew the attack was coming and no one else did," Utkin hypothesized, "could we position ourselves to weather the storm and come out ahead of our enemies?"

"In any tragedy there's opportunity," Kedrov said, sounding a bit hesitant. "But it's likely that we'd be facing a worldwide depression. Not something that's so easy to weather. Even from an advantageous position."

They seemed to have forgotten she was there and all Voronova could do was look on in disbelief. In the time since her meeting in West Virginia, she'd done some research into the potential effects of a massive grid failure in America. Kedrov's choice of the word *carnage,* if anything, was an understatement. How could these men be even considering something like this?

It reminded her of a joke told by one of her instructors so many years ago. It was about a peasant farmer whose neighbor saves enough money to purchase a goat. The peasant asks God to put right this injustice and God answers, asking what the peasant wants him to do.

Kill the goat.

According to her instructor, that one joke explained the Russian people better than all the history books ever written. The fall of America could only harm Russia. The question these two overgrown toddlers were debating was whether others would be harmed more.

Of course, they could have spent their time and resources making Russia a prosperous, respected, and productive country in its own right. But that was too difficult. Instead, they'd sink the boat containing all of humanity because they believed their life vests were the most buoyant.

"America is as weak and fractured as it's been in more than a hundred years," Utkin said. "So this comes at an interesting time."

It was a true statement. The front-runner in the recent US presidential election had committed suicide, throwing America's politics into even more turmoil than usual. The eventual winner was a largely unknown quantity and conspiracy abounded. Polls suggested that almost half of Americans supported the idea of a new election, but there was no constitutional provision for one. Perhaps the era of American democracy was coming to an end. Perhaps they would finally fall back into the oddly comfortable embrace of a de facto dictator like Utkin. Certainly, that would be of great comfort to the men whispering in front of her. Nothing frightened autocrats more than a successful democracy.

She strained to make out their increasingly hushed conversation but her rusty language skills made it impossible. Or maybe that wasn't it at all. Maybe she just didn't want to know.

Finally, Utkin rose, brushed past her, and disappeared through the door. His body language suggested that his involvement in the meeting was done.

In front of her, Kedrov removed his glasses and examined her. When their eyes met, his expression had morphed into one of vague disapproval.

"You've put us in a very difficult position, Sonya."

A hint of fear escaped the façade she'd constructed but he dismissed it with a casual wave of the hand. "I didn't get to where I am today by shooting my messengers. Now tell me. What's your opinion? You've lived in America for years. What would happen if the American people were faced with an attack like this? If the average citizen got a taste of real desperation and suffering, would they turn to a leader of strength? Someone capable of providing order and security?"

"It's possible," she admitted.

He nodded and contemplated her again, this time staring at her leather boots and ending with her knit hat.

"What should I do with you, Sonya?"

Taken by surprise by the question, she found herself unable to answer. What she wanted was to go home and die of old age without ever being called on again. But was that wise? Based on the less-than-scientific research she'd done, she calculated her chances of surviving a long-term US power outage at pretty much zero. On the other hand, the thought of trying to build a new life in Russia was somehow even more terrifying than the thought of dying of cold or hunger in her basement flat.

"I only want the privilege of serving my country, sir."

He nodded in a way that suggested he wasn't buying her sudden patriotism. "Then you'll go back to the US."

She gave a short nod. It wasn't reassignment to Paris or Rome, but it also wasn't a basement cubicle in Novosibirsk or a bullet in the back of the head. In her line of business, that was about as much of a win as you were going to get.

"Do I have orders, sir?"

"What kind of orders?"

"Would you like me to investigate this man? Based on how extensive his knowledge is and the fact that I know what he looks like, it's possible I could identify hi—"

"You'll do nothing."

"But it could help Russia in its preparations," she said, daring to push a little. "We would be able to—"

"No," he said with utter finality. "At this

moment, he's a nameless man with information that we declined. We haven't communicated with him since your meeting and based on what you've told us today, we will never do so again. Our only concern is ensuring that there is no trail that leads back to us."

"But, sir, what if he was also telling the truth about having other countries and organizations interested? It doesn't seem so far-fetched. If we—"

"Enough!" he said, his voice rising almost to the level of a shout. "Perhaps I'm making a mistake sending you back, Sonya. Perhaps you've become a little too sympathetic to your adopted country."

"No, sir. It's just that—"

"The Americans are very good at making enemies both from within and without," he said, cutting her off again. "It's their responsibility to defend themselves against those enemies. Not ours."

CHAPTER 3

Federico García Lorca Airport
Granada
Spain

"Gracias," Rapp said, handing a ten-euro bill to the woman at the cash register. She doled out his change and he wandered off to find a place to sit in the cafeteria. Only about half of the tables were full and he managed to secure one with a decent view of the people coming through security.

Jordi Cardenas and his people had delivered beyond all expectation, assembling detailed dossiers on every passenger and quietly upgrading the airport's security. No one was getting so much as a squirt gun to the gates without them knowing about it.

Based on the information they'd gathered, there were three solid suspects in addition to the primary target, Hamal Kattan. All were youngish Middle Eastern men on trips that seemed out of the ordinary for them. One was terminating in Barcelona while the other two were continuing to the United States on the same flight as Kattan. A fourth man—from Pakistan—was a possibility but probably less than fifty-fifty. He had a history of international travel and was headed to Paris, where he had an apartment rented for the next two weeks.

Rapp gnawed off the edge of his ham sandwich and watched the people clearing security. Kattan and his likely escorts were already through and had spread out in the gate area on the other side of Duty Free. A group of Asian tourists was causing a bit of chaos at the X-ray machine but, with the help of their frazzled guide, finally pulled it together. They were followed by some annoyed travelers who appeared to be local. Finally, the Pakistani appeared.

Rapp kept working on his sandwich as the man put his roller on the conveyor and passed through the scanner. None of the security people displayed any more interest in him than they had in the Spaniards that came before. Behind the scenes, though, high-tech images were being uploaded to Langley for analysis.

After retrieving his carry-on, the Pakistani made a beeline toward the cafeteria. Rapp turned, watching him in windows that the darkness outside had converted into mirrors. His gut said that this guy wasn't involved, but he wasn't certain enough to bet anyone's life on it. His team would keep as close a watch on this Pakistani as they did the others.

The possible terrorist moved out of view and Rapp turned his attention to his own reflection. His beard had been trimmed into something more respectable than his normal look, which Claudia disparaged as "man raised by wolves." His unruly hair had been corralled and green contacts were irritating his eyes. The straightforward disguise was rounded out by enough subtle foundation to lighten his deeply tanned skin.

He'd resisted that last one, but it was hard to complain. In order to camouflage Joe Maslick's 280 pounds of muscle, they'd had to put him in a fat suit that expanded his girth to the point that he barely fit in a premium seat at the front. The pièce de résistance, though, was Charlie Wicker. Claudia's sense of humor probably had something to do with the fact that she'd decided to go with a gay theme. Whatever the motivation, it worked. No one would peg the diminutive American poured into lemon-yellow jeans as one of the most dangerous men in the world. The other two had gotten off relatively easy. Bruno McGraw naturally looked like an American tourist and Scott Coleman's blond hair and language skills made it easy for him to pass as German.

The music in Rapp's earbuds faded and a moment later was replaced by Claudia's voice. "They're all through. Jordi's people couldn't find any weapons on Kattan or the Pakistani. Two of the other men appear to be carrying custom firearms disassembled to fool the scanners. The third has a knife built into the frame of his carry-on. Take a look at your phone."

Rapp pulled up an email attachment that

depicted the Airbus A320's seating chart. The tangos were marked in red with a symbol indicating the weapons they carried. His team's positions were noted in green.

"We did the best we could to seat the targets in good strategic positions, but Fred had the final word."

The Fred she was referring to was Fred Mason, Rapp's go-to pilot on any mission he could persuade him to participate in. The man could fly or fix anything from hang gliders to 747s and had nerves of steel. He'd be flying the plane that night and had seated the tangos where they would do the least amount of damage if they managed to get off an errant shot. It was an inexact science, though. Modern planes were crammed with critical wires, fluid lines, and computer circuits.

The intercom announced Rapp's flight and he tossed what was left of his food before heading to the gate. They'd added another flight that was going out ten minutes before his and the boarding area was jammed with people trying to figure out what line they were supposed to be in.

Kattan elbowed his way back from the bathrooms, coming close enough that Rapp could pick up on his nervousness. He was clutching a laptop case like it was a holy relic and there was a bead of sweat running down his cheek. The little prick wanted to play secret agent and now he was discovering the weight of that game.

• • •

Kattan put his ticket back in his pocket and pushed his way into a small room crammed with other passengers. The chaos of boarding had been amplified by the fact that the airline had for some reason added a flight that was going out nearly simultaneously with his. The weather had taken a turn for the worse and apparently the tourists who flocked to the ancient city of Granada were now trying to escape before the forecasted snowstorm hit.

He, on the other hand, was going to America to evaluate the claims of a man who said he had the ability to destroy the US power grid. It was likely a wildly exaggerated claim, but the information the anonymous Internet poster had provided was unquestionably intriguing. Whoever he was, he was very different than the other voices on jihadist sites—men willing to die for the cause but not capable of doing much more than driving vehicles into crowds or detonating homemade explosives.

A door on the other side of the room opened and the people flooded outside, rushing through the freezing rain toward a plane some hundred meters away. Kattan put his laptop case beneath his jacket and went for the stairs at the back of the aircraft. Out of the corner of his eye he could see one of the escorts Nahas had provided, but resisted the urge to look at him.

Once on board, he took his seat next to a sturdy young woman with short blond hair and an even shorter skirt. She smiled at him as he shoved his bag beneath the seat in front of him and then went back to scrolling through pictures of herself on her phone.

The crush of people fighting for overhead space gave him an opportunity to look around unnoticed. One of Nahas's men was out of sight near the back of the plane. Another was in the aisle ahead, still trying to reach his seat. The last was sitting three rows back next to a little gay man.

The woman next to him kicked off her red heels and closed her eyes. The top three buttons of her blouse were undone, revealing intermittent flashes of a lacy bra. He looked down at the tan skin of her chest for a moment and then turned away.

Western whore.

CHAPTER 4

Capitol Complex
Washington, DC
USA

John Alton's eyes moved from the deep blue carpet to the portrait of some old white guy hanging on the wall. The hearing was now into its fifth hour and the number of congresspeople in attendance had dwindled to six. A few had never even bothered to show up, leaving their elevated seats occupied only by the relevant name plates.

Witnesses consisted of an endless parade of government regulators, military personnel, and power company executives—all with their own self-serving agendas and all completely clueless as to what they were talking about. The man currently in the hot seat was the head of a large West Coast utility company. He'd spent the last fifteen minutes crying a river over how even the slightest change to the regulatory environment would absolutely decimate his ability to provide power to millions of customers.

His personal net worth? Around a hundred million dollars. Poor guy. How would he make ends meet if he had to update his twenty-five-year-old computer systems and put eight-dollar padlocks on the gates of his electrical substations?

He finally stopped whining and kissed a little congressional ass before ceding his seat to Alton's boss. Janice Crane ran the Department of Energy's Office of Cybersecurity, Energy Security, and Emergency Response, and had been put in charge of assessing the vulnerabilities of America's power grid. It had taken almost five years, but the report was now all but complete. Twenty-eight hundred pages of detailed technical analysis that she had only a basic understanding of. In fact, it had been Alton's one-man consulting firm and its myriad subcontractors who had compiled the data. As she'd requested, he walked up the aisle and settled into the seat behind her.

Davis Graves, the congressman overseeing the hearing, dispensed with the normal niceties. "We've heard a number of perspectives from a number of people, Ms. Crane, and I'm sure we're all interested in your thoughts since it's your department that created the report. And it's quite a doorstop, isn't it?"

Crane leaned into her microphone. "I wish it were shorter, sir. But we uncovered a lot of vulnerabilities."

"I have to admit that I find the tone of this report a bit hysterical," the man continued. "And it seems that many of the people who've testified today agree. There are threats everywhere, Ms. Crane. I could get hit by an asteroid right now. But I don't think America should pay for an asteroid shield over the head of every one of its citizens. How much money and effort should we put into protecting ourselves against every potential threat that *could* happen but never has?"

"With all due respect, sir, I don't agree. For instance, a number of US energy companies were recently targeted in a cyberattack called Dragonfly. In many of those incursions, the hackers were able to access the companies' networks and gain operational control. What I mean by that is they had the ability to take over parts of our grid. They could reroute power, trip breakers—"

"But they didn't," another congressman interrupted.

"Excuse me?"

"You tell us that they had all this power, but they didn't *use* it. And because of this, we should put an incredible burden on power companies to protect themselves from this kind of non-attack."

"Again, sir, I disagree. It's like saying that we shouldn't protect ourselves against an opposing army probing our defenses because they haven't bombed us yet."

The congressman opened his mouth to respond, but she ignored him and kept talking. A condescending smile played at Alton's lips.

Janice was feeling spunky today. She must have doubled up on her latté at lunch.

"If you want an attack that was carried out, you don't have to look any further than the Metcalf substation in California. A single perpetrator managed to take out seventeen transformers with just a rifle. The—"

"And what was the effect of that attack, Ms. Crane?"

"Power outages were limited because the utility was able to divert electricity from other—"

"And how many substations do we have?"

"Excuse me?"

"You said this man did damage to one of our substations. How many are there in the US?"

She glanced back at Alton, who mouthed the answer.

"About fifty-five thousand, sir."

"So, he managed to temporarily damage one fifty-five thousandth of our power generation capacity and caused a few people to lose power for a couple of hours."

"The problem is the attack had indications of being a dry run. A proof of concept. And the perpetrator's never been caught. This didn't turn out to be a serious issue because it was only one minor installation. Based on our analysis, though, a coordinated attack on only a handful of critical substations could take down the entire US grid."

"When you say a handful, how many do you mean? A hundred? A thousand?"

Again, she turned to Alton. This time he just held up fingers.

"Nine, sir."

The congressman laughed. "Nine? We have fifty-five thousand substations and you're telling me that the loss of nine could put the entire country in the dark?"

"That's correct, sir. In fact, it was that realization that prompted Congress to request the vulnerability report that we're talking about now."

"I've experienced blackouts," another congressman interjected. "In fact, I lived through the blackout caused by Superstorm Sandy. And while I agree it was a serious incident, even combined with a hurricane, it wasn't quite the Armageddon you suggest."

"Sandy was by no means a worst-case scenario, sir. With storms, there's advance warning and the damage is random as opposed to targeted. Further, that blackout only affected a portion of a single city for a few days. A coordinated attack could conceivably put the entire country in the dark for more than a year."

Graves actually laughed at that. "Again, the hysterical tone of your report rears its ugly head. In the incredibly unlikely event that nine of our substations were simultaneously destroyed, why wouldn't we just fix them?"

Alton didn't bother to hide his widening grin. These people were complete fucking idiots. And worse, they were complete fucking idiots who thought they were geniuses. The most dangerous kind, but just the kind the American people loved to vote for.

"There are very few manufacturers of this type of equipment and most of them are overseas. Also, it can take over a year to build one—they're designed custom for every application. And if that were the case—if it took a year for us to get the power back on—it would be . . ." Her voice faded for a moment. "It really would be the Armageddon you mentioned earlier."

"Oh, come on . . ." the man said. "I feel like that's just inflammatory language, Ms. Crane. We're trying to have a reasonable conversation here and I don't appreciate it."

"Years ago, a congressional commission estimated that if the power went out for one year, ninety percent of our population would die. I think the use of the inflammatory language is warranted, sir."

He rolled his eyes. "Everything's a disaster to you people. You're a regulator, so you regulate. You create these wild scenarios and tell us that everybody's going to die so you can expand your own authority. You—"

Alton tried to control his snickering, going so far as to cover his mouth, but it was impossible.

When the congressman noticed, he fell silent and stared directly at him. Alton looked around and discovered that every eye in the half-empty gallery was fixed on him. Expressions ranged from confused to stunned. The look on his boss's face, though, was more a mix of fury and terror.

"Is something funny?" the congressman asked finally.

Alton considered his response for a moment. The fact was that he'd completed the job he'd been contracted to do and his pockets were already lined with embarrassing amounts of taxpayer money. What was this asshole going to do? Fire him? A little late for that.

"Frankly, yeah," he said finally. "Let me ask you a question, Congressman. What would you do?"

"Excuse me?"

"Let me set the scene. You wake up and you have no power. No light, no heat, no air-conditioning. Restaurants basically give away all their food in the first couple of days of the blackout because of the loss of refrigeration. Within another day or two every grocery store in America is completely empty. And because the blackout is nationwide, none are being restocked. Food production relies on electricity. And transportation relies on gasoline, which in turn relies on electric pumps. And don't wait for FEMA or the National Guard to bail you out, because they don't have any power, either. First responders have stashes of supplies, so they'll be up and running, but those stashes aren't going to last long. They'll barely have time to free the people stuck in elevators before they have to start worrying about their own survival. And that's just the pleasant stuff. In a few more days, the water pressure is going to start to fail. So you're living in the middle of DC, you've got only the food in your pantry, your toilets don't work, and nothing's coming out of your tap. What do you do?"

The congressman looked like the top of his head was going to explode. "The American people are the most capable and resilient in the world. More government isn't the answer to everything. They'd pull together—"

"And do what?" Alton interrupted. "Bring you a sandwich? Maybe carry away the bucket you and your family are shitting in? Let me tell you what—"

"Perhaps we should move on," the congressman on the far right said. He had recently announced his retirement and was no longer beholden to the idiots the Founding Fathers knew better than to allow to vote. Maybe he would have something intelligent to say, but Alton was doubtful.

"Any way you look at it, this is a serious issue," the man continued. "So why don't we talk a little about what we can do to keep this gentleman's scenario from playing out?"

"Thank you," Crane said, clearly anxious to move on. "As has been pointed out, this is a pretty extensive report, but I think I can summarize our findings and get you out of here before midnight. We need a massive upgrade to our grid and the integration of significantly more renewable energy, which is intermittent, but less vulnerable to being taken off-line for long periods of time. We need to harden the physical security around our critical infrastructure. And finally, we need to create, build, and stockpile universal recovery transformers that can be used to quickly replace damaged ones. The ultimate goal, though, would be to heavily distribute our energy production and match it to critical areas. So, food manufacturing plants, fire stations, and water treatment facilities, to name only a few, would have their own generation and storage capability. Eventually, we'd like to see those capabilities move to an individual level—solar panels on people's houses, batteries in their basements, and the like. The technology is getting to where this is absolutely feasible if the government takes a leadership role."

"And what would all this cost, Ms. Crane?"

"The implementation of our minimum recommendations would run around two billion dollars. A full upgrade would climb to more like five billion."

"Are you joking?" Congressman Graves said,

trying to regain control of the hearing. “These are businesses. Where is all this money going to come from?”

“I would imagine through increased rates to customers.”

“The American people are already struggling to pay their bills and now you want me to make it impossible for them to heat their homes?”

Alton let out a low groan. What a load of horseshit. The American people couldn’t buy thousand-dollar cell phones and big-screen TVs fast enough. What was it about politicians that made them behave like everyone in the United States was half starved? Had they not noticed how fat people were?

“Security!” Graves said, pointing down at Alton. “Remove that man!”

Whoops. Apparently, that groan wasn’t as low as he’d thought.

The retiring politician held a hand out, stopping the security guard before he could even make it to the aisle.

“Who is this gentleman?”

Janice Crane leaned reluctantly into her microphone. “John Alton, sir. He’s the energy consultant that took the lead in creating the report that’s in front of you.”

“So, would it be fair to say he’s an expert on America’s power grid?”

“I’m afraid so, sir. In fact, it would be fair to

say he's *the* expert on America's power grid."

"You seem frustrated by this process, Mr. Alton. Would that be a fair characterization?"

Crane shot him an icy stare, but he didn't really give a shit. She couldn't do anything for him anymore. And even if she could, pretty soon it wouldn't matter.

"Yeah, I'd say that's fair."

"Would you care to explain why?"

"Because this is coming. It's not an *if,* it's a *when* and *how bad*. A few years ago, in order to pull off something this big, you'd have needed a major state actor—Russia or China. Now we're at the point where a minor power—say, Iran or North Korea—could probably get it done. If we don't do anything to protect ourselves, a few years from now we're going to be looking at the possibility that a teenager with a laptop could put half the US in the dark. So, the chance of us suffering a serious attack on our grid is pretty much a hundred percent. And what are we going to do about it? Nothing. We're going to blow all the money that we could use to secure it on a new paint job for one of our aircraft carriers. Which, in the unlikely event that America ever engages in another major naval battle, would immediately get taken out by a hundred-thousand-dollar missile."

"So, you're an expert in military affairs, too?" Graves interjected.

"I'm an expert in *common sense*. Why would Russia or North Korea get into a drawn-out shooting war with us when they know we have the largest military in the world? Wouldn't it be a lot smarter to hit our grid, kill ninety percent of our population, and leave us unable to retaliate because we don't actually know for sure who attacked us?"

"As much as I don't like Mr. Alton's disrespectful delivery," the congressman on his way out said, "it's hard not to sympathize with his conclusions. America won World War Two. We went to the moon. By comparison, upgrading and securing out grid seems trivial. And if the stakes are only half as high as this report says, five billion seems like a bargain."

Not surprisingly, a heated discussion ensued. On one side, a retiring politician who now had the luxury of actually giving a shit about what happened to America. And on the other, an entrenched politician who only worried about getting the utility companies to give him enough campaign funds to convince the sheep to vote for him again.

Alton watched silently, happy to finally get a little entertainment after being stuck in this hearing all day. Humans really were just monkeys throwing feces. They'd grandstand for a while and then make a few backroom deals that led to absolutely no action at all.

In any event, they couldn't say that he hadn't warned them. He'd told them exactly what was going to happen and wrote thousands of pages on how. You could bring a human to water, but you couldn't make him drink. The unfairly maligned horses that were the subject of the original proverb, on the other hand, were smart enough to know a good thing when they saw it.

CHAPTER 5

Over the Sierra Nevada Mountains
Southern Spain

"I'm sorry," the flight attendant said in a pleasant Spanish accent. "We're out of Coke. Can I get you something else?"

"Water," Rapp said.

"Sparkling or still?"

So many decisions.

"Sparkling."

She dropped a lime and some ice in a cup and handed it to him along with the can. A moment later, she'd moved on to the passengers behind.

With his sight line clear again, Rapp was able to take in the plane's cabin. He was in an aisle seat located near the back. One of the Arabs armed with a gun was sitting directly in front of him. The tango with the knife was six rows ahead sitting next to Charlie Wicker. Coleman was two rows ahead of that, kitty corner to Kattan. The other gun toter was one row ahead of Kattan, covered by Bruno McGraw in the seat next to him. Maslick was squeezed up front, keeping an eye on the Pakistani.

The calm before the storm.

They leveled out and the seat belt sign went off,

prompting the tango in front of him to get up and head for the bathroom. Rapp resisted the urge to crane his neck and follow the man's progress, instead looking across the people seated next to him and out the window into the darkness. At this point, they were over a rugged and largely uninhabited part of the Sierra Nevada mountain range. Below the cloud layer, rain had reportedly turned to snow, providing a perfect environment for the operation he'd planned. And if things went wrong, a little fresh powder might soften the impact when they plummeted from the sky. If it was deep, maybe they could scrape up enough of him to put in a coffin.

Within ten minutes from the seat belt sign going off, three of the four suspected terrorists had gone to the bathroom and returned to their seats. Tellingly, all had taken their carry-ons. The exception was the Pakistani near the front of the plane. He'd stayed put and his carry-on was in the overhead, providing further evidence that he wasn't involved. Not that it mattered. When the shit hit the fan, the Pakistani would find the better part of three hundred pounds of fat-suit encased muscle coming at him at like a freight train.

The music faded from his headphones and Claudia's voice came on. He played absently with the thick cord leading to his satphone as she spoke.

"Spanish intelligence was dead on. Mitch, the guy in front of you now has what looks like a fully operational gun strapped to his left ankle. Charlie, yours has a knife in the same place. Bruno, the man next to you has a gun on his right ankle. Mas—your target is reading a romance novel on his Kindle. No weapons that we're aware of. Scott, the target's still unarmed. His computer is under the seat in front of him in a courier bag. I've looked at the specs of that specific bag and it doesn't provide a lot of protection. So, don't step on it or anything. We need it undamaged. Is everyone a go?"

Rapp nodded subtly, a gesture that would be picked up by the many cameras placed throughout the plane. Clearly all his men had given the same affirmative signal because a moment later Fred Mason's voice came on—first in mangled Spanish and then in English.

"It looks like we have some turbulence ahead, so if you need to get up, now's the time. In a few minutes I expect to have to turn on the seat belt sign."

A woman across the aisle from Rapp got up and opened the overhead, shoving a coat aside and digging into the exterior pocket of her suitcase. Ahead, a couple of guys who looked like they'd had a rough night in the Granada bars were clowning around filming each other with their cell phones.

The woman managed to find what she was looking for—a quart-size bag of sundries—

but quickly discovered that the top wasn't fully sealed. A shower of Chapstick, Tic Tacs, and who knew what else cascaded to the floor. She swore under her breath and then dropped to all fours, gathering them together as the other passengers moved their feet out of the way. When she started reaching toward the leg of the tango Rapp put his tray up and unfastened his seat belt.

At first, it looked like things were going to go easy. She'd retrieved her travel-sized deodorant and seemed like she was going to return to her seat. Then she froze, staring at the place where the terrorist's pant leg met his ankle.

"Oh my God! He's got a gun!"

And then all hell broke loose. People leapt from their seats, turning to look at her as she fell onto her butt and started desperately scooting away from the armed man.

Rapp managed to stand but found himself being jostled on all sides while terrified people invaded the aisle and shrieks filled the confined space. A gunshot sounded and the screams grew in volume as he was shoved over the seat in front of him. The man sitting next to the tango was thrashing around, trying to unbuckle his seat belt, and Rapp came down awkwardly on his head.

The terrorist was more agile than he looked and had gotten to his gun, which was rising quickly in his left hand. Rapp managed to clamp down his wrist and redirect the weapon toward the overhead luggage bins. It went off, once, twice, three times, punching holes in the plastic and showering them with sparks as one of the reading lights exploded.

Hamal Kattan heard the screamed warning and his body flooded with adrenaline. He twisted in his seat and looked back down the aisle. The man he knew only as Malik was reaching for his ankle as a woman sitting in the aisle pedaled away from him. Passengers throughout the plane were leaping to their feet and he saw the man behind Malik get pushed forward over the seats. Four rows back, he saw another of his men reach for a knife. The gay man in the adjoining seat had fallen into him, interfering with his effort to get a grip on the hilt.

Various gunshots rang out but it was impossible to know from where. He turned to look at his man in the seat in front of him, only to discover that he'd fallen into the aisle and was being trampled by fleeing passengers.

Kattan clawed at his seat belt, bile rising into his throat. He managed to free the clasp just as the plane lurched right. The blond whore trying to escape the middle seat was thrown across his lap, trapping him. A moment later she was straddling him, her face only inches from his as she screamed and tried to escape to . . . where?

"Help me!" Kattan yelled to his man lying in the aisle, but it was pointless. Two people had fallen on top of him and a number of others were trying to climb over the pile of writhing bodies that had been created. The shifting weight of the passengers caused the plane to lurch again, throwing the woman in his lap forward against him.

"Get off of me!" he shouted, and swung a fist awkwardly toward her. It connected with her nose, snapping her head back and causing blood to start flowing toward her ample cleavage. She swooned and fell forward again, smothering him with her dead weight.

"Stand down!"

The command was a deafening shout coming over what sounded like a megaphone. A moment later, everything went still.

Kattan was utterly confused as to what was happening. He pushed the woman's limp body back against the seat in front of him. In the aisle, the people piled on top of his man stood and returned to their seats, leaving him bound hand and foot with zip-ties.

"Is anyone hurt?" someone yelled behind him. "Speak up!"

He twisted around in time to see a bearded man with piercing green eyes walking up the aisle.

"We've got a broken arm up here!" someone said.

"Serious?"

A different, heavily accented voice answered. "It's nothing, sir!"

The green-eyed man nodded and paused, looking down at the corpse of one of Kattan's men. His body was leaning into the aisle, held in place only by the seat belt stretched across his lap. The knife he'd been carrying was buried in his neck and blood was still pouring from the wound.

He looked at the gay man next to the body. "Way to go taking him alive, dipshit."

"Sorry, Mitch."

"Is the plane okay?" he shouted to no one in particular.

A voice purred a response over the intercom. "This is your captain speaking. Thanks to all the carry-on luggage being full of Kevlar, we're expecting an on-time arrival and suggest you sit back and enjoy the flight. We know you have your choice of airlines and, as always, appreciate your business."

The man in the aisle scowled.

Kattan faced forward again, as though it were still possible to hide in the crowd. When he did, he saw that the woman on top of him had regained consciousness. She brought a manicured hand to her damaged nose and then looked down at the blood on her fingers. A moment later, she was glaring furiously into his eyes.

"Asshole!"

The last thing Kattan saw was the glint of a diamond ring as her fist arced toward his face.

CHAPTER 6

Over the Sierra Nevada Mountains
Southern Spain

"Is he good?"

The man's arm had been straightened somewhat and was now immobilized against his chest. Rapp didn't know his name but did know he was on loan from Japan's intelligence apparatus. Everyone else on the plane except the terrorists and the apparently innocent Pakistani had similar stories. All were borrowed from the operational wing of one of the world's intelligence agencies, selected because they could be made to look like tourists and because they were nuts enough to volunteer for this shit show.

"Yes, sir," the medic said. "He'll need a couple pins when he gets home, but in a few months he'll be right as rain."

Rapp clapped the injured man on his good shoulder and headed to the front of the plane, where the first few rows had been cleared.

Hamal Kattan was still in his seat, but now with two full rolls of duct tape wrapped around him. His torso was anchored to the seatback and his forearms were pegged to the armrests. Even his legs had been immobilized, with everything below the knee hidden behind the gray-silver material. The only thing he could move was his head and that was lolling back and forth as he slowly regained consciousness.

Time was of the essence, so Rapp sped the process by swinging the back of his hand into the man's cheek.

A string of spit rolled from Kattan's mouth and his eyes fluttered, straining to focus. He jerked when he came fully awake, thrashing weakly in the few millimeters the tape would allow.

Then he started shrieking. The piercing sound was dampened by the white noise of the plane's engine and the storm outside, so Rapp just sat on the armrest across the aisle and let him scream. By the time the CIA man had poured a tiny bottle of whiskey over some ice, Kattan was running out of breath.

Rapp took a sip of his drink as the man's terrified eyes fixed on him.

"What is this? I'm injured!" He nodded toward the crimson stain on his silk collar. "I'm bleeding."

"You're fine," Rapp said. "It stopped a while ago. You've got a nice gash on your cheek, though. About three karats' worth by the look of it."

"Who . . . Who are you?"

"Let's talk about you instead. Why are you and your friends going to the US?"

The calculations started behind his eyes, but they took longer than they should have. A complete amateur—clearly selected by ISIS because of his technical expertise, not his combat experience or mental toughness. That was going to make the night go a hell of a lot smoother.

"My friends?" he said finally. "I don't know what you're talking about. I'm traveling alone. I remember someone started shooting. Then everyone panicked. That's all. That's all I remember."

Rapp just sipped his drink.

"I'm going to America on vacation," Kattan added hastily. "To tour Washington, DC, and New York."

Rapp pointed to the man's laptop, which was open and running on the seat tray to the left. "Then you won't mind giving me the password."

Kattan's response was again delayed, but this time the lull was shorter. "What right do you have to ask me for that? It's my private property."

Rapp nodded. "I know you took a pretty good shot to the head, but they tell me you're a smart guy. I want you to look around and tell me what you think's happened here?"

"I . . . I don't know. There were terrorists on the plane. The passengers stopped them . . . You must think I'm with them. But it's not true! I'm—"

Rapp held out a hand, silencing the man. Then he brought up a video on his phone, turning the device so Kattan could see. It depicted some passengers clowning around in front of a woman crawling on the floor. Suddenly she shouted "He's got a gun!"

Rapp cut to different video and watched it for a moment before showing Kattan. It depicted Fred Mason putting the A320 through multiple dives steep enough to cause anyone who wasn't wearing a seat belt to float weightless. "Is your situation becoming clearer?"

"No. I—"

"Then let me spell it out for you," Rapp said. "We goaded your friends into shooting and then faked a crash. Once this video is edited, we'll start releasing it, saying it came from a phone recovered by rescue workers. No one will ever question the story that someone spotted your friend's gun, he shot something critical, and the plane went down."

"What? Why? Why would you—"

"Because everyone's going to think you're dead, Hamal. That means I get to do whatever I want to you and the information you give me won't go stale for a very long time." Rapp pointed to the laptop again. "Password?"

"I want to talk to a representative from my embassy."

Rapp took another sip of his drink, feeling it burn the inside of his cheek. He'd bit it when he'd come down on an armrest after one of Mason's dives. To his left, a young man with a queasy expression appeared from the bathroom. Marcus Dumond was a genius with technology but his abilities as a field agent were pretty much nonexistent. When he'd been ordered to take part in this operation, he'd actually teared up. None had rolled down his cheeks, though. As far as Rapp was concerned, that was progress. A few years ago, he'd have resigned and made a break for the parking garage.

"He's awake," Dumond observed, though the act of speaking seemed to add to his nausea. He scooted into the seat with the laptop.

"Password," Rapp repeated.

"I'm innocent!" Kattan shouted, starting to show a glimmer of backbone. "This is an illegal action and I demand to speak with someone from my embassy."

Rapp poured what was left of his whiskey on the man's hair and then set it on fire with a lighter he'd retrieved from his pocket.

Dumond jerked away from the flames and instinctively poured the soft drink he'd been sipping over the man's head. "Come on, Mitch! I can't take the smell of burning hair right now. I'm barely holding my food down as it is."

Kattan whimpered quietly as the sugary fluid ran down his face and mingled with the blood on his collar. The skin of his scalp was largely undamaged but much of the hair covering it was a singed mess.

"Let me make this as clear as I can, Hamal. If I don't get that password in the next five seconds, I'm going to go to the galley, get the dullest plastic spoon I can find, and use it to saw off your right testicle. We have a good medic on board and he tells me that other than the incredible suffering, you'll be fine. Once he stops the bleeding, then I'll start on your left one. And if it turns out you're tougher than you look, no problem. I have all the time in the world to work on you. Weeks. Months. Years, if necessary."

"Give him the password," Dumond pleaded. "If I have to sit here and watch him cut your balls off, I'm going to puke."

"I—" Kattan started, but then fell silent. When he spoke again, he seemed to have lost what little strength he'd managed to conjure. "It's Dark Destiny 4822."

Dumond tapped it into the keyboard. "I'm in."

"Good decision," Rapp said. "Now, why are you going to the US?"

"To meet someone."

"Who?"

"I don't know his name."

Rapp turned toward the galley, where Joe Maslick was wolfing down what looked like a plate of cannelloni. "Mas! Give me that spoon."

"No!" Kattan shouted. "Stop! Why would they tell me his name? I'm not even sure they know it. He's someone who contacted us over the Internet."

"Why would you be going to meet someone no one knows?"

"Because of his expertise."

"Expertise? In what?"

When Kattan didn't answer, a tomato-sauce-covered spoon came flying through the air. Rapp caught it without taking his eyes off the man.

"America's power grid!" Kattan blurted, as his eyes locked on the plastic utensil.

"What about it?"

"How to take it down."

"I'm not buying it, Hamal. You're telling me that ISIS sent its top tech expert all the way to the US to meet with some electrician? Are you really committed to keeping your balls? Because if so, I'm not feeling it."

CHAPTER 7

CIA Headquarters
Langley, Virginia
USA

Rapp pulled his Dodge Charger into underground parking, causing the roar of the engine to echo through an embarrassingly large portion of the structure. He'd tried to convince his mechanic to quiet it down but the man insisted the supercharged V8 sounded "awesome" and refused. In the end it was easier to turn up the stereo than argue.

As was his custom, he skipped his designated space and parked in a random empty one. Even with the heavy security imposed on the CIA's campus, parking in a space with his name on it seemed inordinately stupid. The reason he'd lived long enough to make as many enemies as he had was that he never underestimated them.

Rapp killed the motor and got out, setting the state-of-the-art security system before heading for a private elevator. Finding excuses not to come to headquarters was a game he played at a near-professional level, but sometimes even he lost. Unfortunately, this was one of those times.

The trip to the seventh floor was quick and

he went straight to the executive suite when the elevator doors opened. After exchanging a quick greeting with one of Irene Kennedy's assistants he pushed through the door leading to her office.

"Thanks for coming," she said, striding across the carpet to give him a quick kiss on the cheek. "I know it's not your favorite thing to do."

He shrugged and glanced over at Marcus Dumond, who was sitting on a sofa with a computer on his lap.

"Where do we stand?"

"Using Kattan's computer and the information he gave us, I've been able to access the chat rooms ISIS was using to communicate with this electrical grid guy," Dumond said, holding out some papers. "These are transcripts of some of the more interesting exchanges I've come across."

Rapp and Kennedy sat and scanned the pages while Dumond continued. "There's a lot of bickering going on within what's left of ISIS because of the lack of a big, overarching vision. Now that they've pretty much given up the idea that they're going to build a caliphate across the Middle East, their leadership is refocusing on figuring out how to hit America."

"And by leadership, you mean Muhammad Nahas," Rapp said.

It was Kennedy who answered. "Correct."

Rapp nodded. While very different than his predecessor, Nahas was not a man to be dismissed. He'd received training from American troops and served in the Iraqi special forces before turning to ISIS. Since then, he'd not only directed a number of unusually well-executed terrorist attacks in the Middle East, but also managed to hold Halabi's inner circle together after the man's death.

"Nahas's ability to execute is pretty clear. Our guys have been on both sides of that—they've worked with him and then found out what it's like working against him. The thing with Nahas, though, is he's not creative. We've talked about this before. He's a meat-and-potatoes suicide vest kind of guy."

"That's our analysis as well," Kennedy said. "Unfortunately, he might have found a muse." She indicated to Dumond, who continued the thought.

"A guy who goes by the name PowerStation sprung up in the ISIS chat rooms a while back and they've been having increasingly detailed and secure conversations with him."

"So, what's PowerStation have to say?" Rapp asked.

"That he knows how to take down the entire US electrical grid and keep it down for more than a year."

"My understanding is that's easier said than done. And talk is cheap on the Internet."

"You have no idea," Dumond said, shaking his

head incredulously. "But this guy is different. He hasn't given away too much, but it's been enough to make it clear that he's not just some basement dweller throwing around fancy jargon. He's got expertise and a lot of it."

"And that's who Kattan was coming to meet?"

"Yeah. ISIS has been trying to get a face-to-face meeting with this asshole for a long time and he keeps blowing them off. A few days ago, he suddenly changed his mind and agreed."

"Why?"

"Based on some other comments he's made, we suspect that ISIS is just one of the groups he's trying to sell his expertise to," Kennedy said. "And they don't seem to be his first choice."

"So, everyone else he's gone to has turned him down."

"That's our best guess. In fact, when he agreed to a meeting, he made a circumspect comment about hoping that ISIS wasn't as useless as the Russians."

"You think he took this to the SVR?"

"I imagine he tried. Whether he would be able to actually make meaningful contact with them is hard to say. Either way, I think we're presented with an interesting opportunity."

"Which is what?"

"With Kattan out of the picture, it seems likely that they're going to have to delay their meeting long enough for ISIS to bring in another technology expert. And now that we have their communications . . ."

"We might be able to get a time and location," Rapp said, finishing her thought.

"Exactly."

Rapp put his feet up on the coffee table and considered that for a few moments. "The clock's ticking, though. How long can we keep the plane crash story alive? Eventually, someone's going to figure out that there's no wreckage and no bodies."

"We're doing everything we can. So far, the weather's cooperating with blizzard conditions in what we've designated as the crash site. Responders supplied by Jordi Cardenas will start filtering pictures of snow-covered wreckage to the press tomorrow. And, at least for now, we're on reasonably solid ground withholding the names of the victims until all the families can be notified. So far, no one's asking *if* it happened—only why."

"Except the conspiracy theory sites," Dumond corrected. "But they can be handled. We have people on those twenty-four/seven leading people away from the idea that it was faked and putting more interesting theories out there. The theory that the Spanish military shot it down and is covering it up is getting a lot of traction. And, of course, there's always the UFO angle. That stuff never gets old . . ."

CHAPTER 8

Centerville
Virginia
USA

Here it comes.

John Alton watched his boss's approach through the interior windows of his office. Her face was devoid of expression and her gait supernaturally steady, as though her wedge heels were floating above the carpet instead of sinking into it.

After years of working with Janice Crane at the DOE, he'd come to know her body language like the back of his hand. She was pissed as hell, but was going to maintain the calm reason that made her so popular with the people she worked with.

Well, the *other* people she worked with anyway. As far as he was concerned, her grasp of technology was tenuous, her oh-so-inclusive management style was cloying, and her goody-two-shoes sense of duty was downright irritating. On the other hand, she always paid his exorbitant consulting fees on time. So, no point in complaining too much.

She entered and closed the door behind her, smiling vaguely as she pushed a button that lowered the shades. Comfortably isolated from the outside world, she dispensed with her normal pleasantries and took an uninvited seat in front of his desk.

"I assume you know why I'm here?"

"No idea," he replied, deciding not to give an inch. He'd been hired to analyze the vulnerabilities in America's power grid and devise ways to fix them. Not kiss ass. Not play politics. And now he was on his way out after having done his job beyond all reasonable expectation. Fuck her and the wedge heels she rode in on.

That vague smile again. She knew she was being played but refused to let it show. "I thought we might take a minute to talk about your performance at that congressional hearing."

"You wanted me there to back you up with facts and I did."

"Like always," she said. "Your ability to keep all this information cataloged in your head never ceases to amaze."

There was a hint of sarcasm in her voice, but it wasn't justified. What she was saying was one hundred percent accurate. After a couple of years at MIT, even his professors had started to struggle to keep up with him. He'd initially planned on staying for a master's, but it became clear that there wasn't anything left for them to teach him. Instead, he'd graduated a year early and immediately started a consulting company specializing in electrical utilities. Now, fifteen years later, he was a millionaire many times over. He had a huge house in a ritzy neighborhood. He had a Porsche Cayenne and a loaded Corvette. He had a mansion overlooking the ocean in Mexico. Basically, everything other people dreamed of, but couldn't get their hands on.

The cell phone next to his keyboard chirped and he glanced down at the incoming text notification. Its origin caused a brief jolt of adrenaline, but he managed to hide it. "Well, thank you for that, Janice. Now if you don't mind I've got a lot of—"

"I'm not done."

"No?"

"No."

Crane leaned back and examined him. He stared back with equal intensity. In truth, she wasn't a bad-looking woman. Early forties, with a curvy figure and blue eyes behind stylish glasses. Kind of like one of those aging strippers who get hired to show up to a birthday party disguised as an IRS agent. A few threatening words about your mortgage deduction, then off comes the blouse.

He'd made a few advances early in their relationship, but she'd backed away. It was a common thread in his life. Women were intimidated by him. They always had been, going all the way back to high school. And now, with all the success he'd had in life, the effect was even more powerful.

A slippery bunch, the fairer sex. On a grand scale, they couldn't get much done. But they were masters of the mind game.

"The first draft of the report is done, but that isn't the end of it, John. The politicians, power companies, and lobbyists are going to want to put their spin on it. We need to figure out how to mitigate that. You worked really hard on this thing and have done an amazing job. Don't sabotage it. If these politicians get their backs up, they'll bury all your years of work just out of spite."

"I'm not a child psychologist and I don't actually work for the government, Janice. I have a very specific written agreement with the DOE and I don't remember stroking politicians being part of it."

She nodded thoughtfully but didn't immediately speak. Another notification sounded on his phone but there was nothing he could do about it. Not until this woman got her ass out of his office. And at this rate, that might not happen until sometime next June.

"Wouldn't you like to see some good come of all your effort?" she said finally. "I mean, I agree one hundred percent with you. An attack like this is coming. And even if it's only moderately successful, think of how many victims there will be. Think about *who* they'll be. Sick people. Children. The elderly. I don't know if you're close to your parents, but mine aren't as young as they used to be. I can't imagine how they'd get through a disaster like this."

In fact, he'd never known his father and his mother had died years ago. Not that it had really mattered to him—they'd never had any real connection. She'd had very little education and had spent her life working an endless string of low-level jobs. Her ability to understand the incredibly gifted son she'd given birth to had been nonexistent and she'd started distancing herself pretty much from the day he was born.

Crane seemed to realize that the heartstring tugging wasn't working and shifted strategies. "If you don't care about anyone else, what about yourself? Because if an attack happens, it's going to affect you, too. Even the nicest Corvette and biggest mansion don't count for much if you can't heat or put gas in them."

The familiar tone from his phone sounded again and his stomach clenched. If she wouldn't end this pointless meeting, he would.

"Okay, Janice. I admit it. I might have been a little out of line in that hearing. But like I said, I don't work for the government. You might have built up a resistance to this bullshit over the years, but I haven't. After five hours watching the theater of the absurd, I snapped."

"I haven't built up a resistance," she said through another forced smile. "But I've learned to pick my battles. And to avoid frontal assaults."

"Fine. You're the expert. Just tell me what you need and I'll give it to you. Maybe I don't always show it, but I *do* think this is important. If I didn't, I wouldn't get so frustrated, you know?"

Crane nodded and—thank God—stood. "I appreciate it, John. We'll talk later."

She left the door ajar and he didn't bother to close it before snatching up his phone.

It wasn't the Russians.

Not surprising, but damned disappointing. After his meeting with their little hottie secret agent, they'd gone completely silent. Even still, he maintained a glimmer of hope that they'd decide at the last minute to nut up.

That was better than the Chinese, though—they'd never even responded to his overtures. Same with the Cubans. He'd had a little more success with the Iranians but they'd turned out to be too afraid of ending up in a full-scale war with the United States to follow through. And then there were the North Koreans. He couldn't even figure out how to get to those assholes.

Surprisingly—and somewhat dangerously—it was ISIS that was coming through. They weren't worried about retaliation, political clusterfucks, or jeopardizing their place in the world order. And, after working anonymously with them over the Internet, they were proving far more capable and organized than they got credit for.

Alton checked the crack in his door before pulling up the encrypted text thread. It seemed strange to communicate so openly, but there was very little to fear from the idiots he worked with. That had been evident since the beginning of all this.

And what an interesting beginning it had been. The whole thing had started as a lark. When he'd taken the contract and started diving into details of the power grid, he'd been stunned at the lack of security. When he'd breached the firewalls of his first few power companies, it had been in the interest of probing for weaknesses and creating safeguards. The same had been true of his initial review of America's physical power infrastructure and its similar lack of security.

Initially, the code he'd uploaded to the power company servers had been benign—little more than a practical way to demonstrate flaws. Eventually, though, the malware had become more sophisticated, as had his investigation of the connections between substations.

He could still remember the exact moment his life had been transformed. Two years into the project he'd managed to get a worm to spread through more than half the country's power companies. It was in that split second that he realized he could really do it. He had the access and tools to put the whole of America in the dark and keep it there. With little more than a wave of his hand, he could send the world's most formidable country back to the eighteenth century.

The congressmen like the one he'd just been grilled by thought they had power, but they didn't even know the meaning of the word. If they were good at begging for money and telling people what they wanted to hear, maybe they could get people to vote them into a fancy office. From there, they could go to endless meetings that accomplished nothing, get good tables in mediocre DC restaurants, and have sex with moderately attractive interns. But they couldn't change anything. Hell, they'd be lucky to get a memorial plaque put on some bridge in the middle of nowhere.

Alton scrolled to the most recent ISIS text. As always, it was short and to the point.

Meeting must be delayed.

He stared down at it, feeling his chest tighten uncomfortably. If there was one thing he despised, it was unexpected changes. And, in truth, he had no desire at all to come face-to-face with these terrorist psychos. The Russian meeting had been exciting, but reasonably safe. They were professionals and that made them relatively predictable. ISIS was pretty much on the opposite end of the spectrum, but he didn't have the luxury of keeping them at arm's length. While the Russians were all ability and no motivation, the Arabs tended to be the opposite. They'd need hands-on guidance to pull off his plan. And while the additional risk was a little disconcerting, the idea of being personally involved was strangely exciting. It made the whole thing feel so much more intimate.

Why the delay? he typed.

None your affair was the immediate response.

He rolled his eyes and tapped out a reply.

Then go fuck yourself.

He tossed the phone on his desk and began digging through one of his drawers in search of a file he'd misplaced. Predictably, another chime sounded after less than a minute.

Our technology expert was on the plane that crashed in Spain. We have to bring in another.

The vague tightness in Alton's chest cinched down to the point that he suddenly found himself unable to breathe. That plane crash was complete bullshit. 4chan was completely lit up with all the incongruities and unknowns. Anyone with half a brain would see through the lies in less than a minute. But most people didn't have half a brain. Hell, most people still believed the United States flew to the moon in a time when math was done on a slide rule.

That the official story about the crash was bullshit had always been self-evident. The question was why the cover-up?

Now he knew.

CHAPTER 9

Southwestern Virginia
USA

The rain had eased, now more fog than precipitation. It combined with temperatures in the low thirties, coating the dead leaves beneath Rapp's feet and the empty branches they'd fallen from. Moving silently was virtually impossible, but it didn't matter. Other than a deer he'd spooked about an hour ago, the dark mountainside seemed devoid of life.

The Sunset Motel became visible after another twenty minutes of picking his way down the slope, matching perfectly the detailed surveillance photos he'd seen the day before. In the end, it was a fairly simple structure—basically a straight two-story building with outdoor staircases and walkways. The parking lot in front had a small diner on its northeast edge but it would have closed hours ago around 9 p.m.

Probably a third of the exterior bulbs were burned out, but they still provided enough illumination to make out six cars and one semitruck in the lot. Despite that, no light was bleeding around shades covering the back windows. It looked like all the guests were asleep.

Based on the Agency's monitoring of ISIS communications, Muhammad Nahas and his replacement technology expert would be meeting the enigmatic PowerStation there tomorrow morning. Three adjacent rooms had been reserved with a prepaid credit card that the eggheads back in Langley hadn't been able to trace. The assumption was that the primary targets would meet in the middle room with security flanking them in the others, but it was impossible to be certain.

Rapp closed in on the edge of the tree cover, trying to move as quietly as possible over a surface that had turned crunchy as temperatures continued to fall. Finally, he stopped, standing motionless for a good five minutes as he tried to pick up movement or anything else out of the ordinary. Satisfied there was nothing, he jogged across twenty yards of open terrain to the back of the motel.

They'd been able to confirm that room seven wasn't in use and Rapp slipped up to its rear window. There was a gap wide enough to accept the blade of his pocketknife and he used it to flip the latch. Getting the window to actually move proved a little more challenging, requiring him to throw almost his entire weight against it. Once it was open an inch, the contents of a small can of WD-40 made the rest of the job a hell of a lot easier.

He climbed inside, sliding awkwardly onto a countertop with a hole where the sink had once been. After closing the window, he eased down to the floor, finding it covered with what were probably pieces of acoustic tile that had fallen from the ceiling. The stench of mold was overwhelming as he felt his way through the darkness and into the main part of the room. After skirting a bare mattress on the floor, he went to the front window and peeked around the curtain. Nothing unusual.

And that wasn't just a carefully created illusion. It was real. There wasn't enough traffic flow in and out of this rural motel to absorb even one or two operators. They'd stand out like sore thumbs—particularly if they stayed more than one night. This wasn't a place you lingered in. It was a lumpy mattress you fell onto when you got too tired to drive anymore.

He stripped off his outer jacket, leaving the goose down layer beneath. The first electrical outlet he tried was dead but the second worked well enough to keep his phone charged. Less than a minute after he turned the device on, it began to vibrate subtly.

"Go ahead," Rapp said, picking up on a Bluetooth earpiece.

"My tracker says you're in," Claudia said.

"Shouldn't you be asleep?"

"The bed's too cold without you. I built a fire in

the bedroom fireplace. It's hard to believe we've never used it before. It's so romantic! How are your accommodations?"

"There's no fireplace," he said settling onto the mattress.

"And no running water."

"Yeah."

"Well, not the worst place you've ever stayed. And it's not for long. I'll put a nice Guinness stew on the stove for when you get home."

He nodded in the darkness and pulled a piece of quiche from his pack. The old saying was that real men didn't eat it, but these homemade snacks were one of the benefits of having a French girlfriend. No more MREs and PowerBars.

"Did we get the surveillance cameras placed out in the parking lot?"

"Absolutely. Bebe got there around eight o'clock and set up four. Two in her car—it's the Dodge minivan out front—one on the second-floor walkway, and one on the front of the diner."

Bebe was Bebe Kincaid, a plump, gray-haired woman who was the most unlikely employee of Scott Coleman's company, SEAL Demolition and Salvage. She was a little nuts, but as long as she stayed on her meds, she was the best surveillance operative in the business. Not only did she have an honest-to-God photographic memory, she was also extraordinarily bland—her features, her figure, even the way she moved. Hell, Rapp had known her for more than a decade and even he'd have a hard time pulling her out of a police lineup.

"What about the target rooms?"

"Audio, but no video."

Rapp launched the surveillance app on his home screen and a light-adjusted, high-definition view of the exterior appeared. It was incredible what technology could accomplish these days. When he'd started out, equipment this good cost millions and weighed hundreds of pounds. Now it was the size of his thumbnail and could be bought online.

He swiped through the feeds for all four cameras, analyzing the angles and coming to the conclusion that they were exactly what he needed. Bebe had come through again.

"What about my backup?"

"Bruno and Mas are at a campground twenty miles to the east. At dawn I can get them into the woods pretty close to you. Scott and Wick are standing by at a hotel in town. In an emergency, their response times are going to be fairly long but from a surveillance standpoint, they're in good position."

The hope was that an emergency situation wouldn't materialize. They weren't there to generate any fireworks. The goal was to just record the meeting and then put a tail on the attendees. With a little luck, they'd be able to ID their entire network.

"Okay," he said, putting on a black stocking cap he fished from his pack. "Then I guess we wait."

"And I know how much you like doing that," she joked.

"Yeah."

"I wish you were here, Mitch. Anna and I were drinking eggnog next to the tree earlier, trying to guess what our presents are. She's dying for you to open the one from her."

"I wish I was there, too," he said, honestly. A little eggnog, a crackling fire, and a shower big enough for two seemed pretty attractive. But not as attractive as the image of tracking these pricks back to their cells and putting bullets in their heads.

That shower would just have to wait.

CHAPTER 10

The rain had stopped, but the water was still beaded on the jacket John Alton had bought the day before. The rifle, bought at the same time, was appropriate for the game that was currently in season. Despite the small caliber, it felt heavy in his hand, contributing to the numbness spreading through his fingers. Not buying a strap that would allow him to sling it across his back had turned out to be a serious mistake.

The slope was steeper than it looked on Google and he could feel the sweat dripping down his sides despite the cold temperatures. The sun was up, though, making it easier to pick out a path through the trees.

His breath came out as a fog that was immediately dispersed by the wind. The rhythm of it continued to increase, but it wasn't just from the climb. It was from the rage that grew with every labored step. How could people be so fucking stupid? Were they partially strangled by their umbilical cords when they were born? Kicked in the head by horses—or in this case, camels—in childhood?

It was a minor miracle that the average human being could even figure out how to tie their own shoelaces. And he was forced to deal with them every day. At work. At the grocery store. When they pulled him over for speeding. It was endless.

When he finally came to the summit, he bent forward at the waist, trying to free himself from the pain of the stitch in his side. The very idea that the leader of ISIS would buy into that Spanish plane crash boggled his mind. And not just buying into it—now they were online claiming credit!

The government's story that they weren't releasing names until all the next of kin were notified was hilarious. He was supposed to believe that not a single person—mother, brother, child—had commented on the death of their family members? In a time when people would slit their own mothers' throats for five seconds on TV or a few Facebook views?

Please . . .

Alton continued north, finding the rocky outcropping he'd seen on satellite photos and walking along it. Terrified of heights, he stayed well back from the edge, going only far enough to bring into view a building situated in the valley below.

The Sunset Motel.

The scope he'd had installed on the rifle allowed him to examine the dilapidated property in detail. Weathered siding, a faded sign, and a diner with too much glare on the windows to see inside. There were a few vehicles in the lot, but no indication of human activity. Nothing but a Norman Rockwell–worthy portrait of the brain-dead rhythm of rural America life.

So, exactly what they wanted him to see.

There was no question in his mind that the FBI—or some other acronym—had snatched ISIS's original tech expert. And if that was the case, he calculated a ninety-nine percent chance that they'd cracked him and gained access to the terrorist group's Internet communications. And if, in turn, *that* was true, then they knew all about the Sunset Motel and the clandestine meeting that was to be held there that morning.

Again, he felt the rage pounding in his temples. If he hadn't insisted that they tell him why they were delaying the meeting, he'd be sleepwalking into a government trap right now. Instead of eating popcorn while watching the most powerful country in the world collapse, he'd be spending the rest of his short life getting waterboarded by some government stooge.

But he *had* insisted and now he was going to stand up there out of danger and watch these ISIS morons get what was coming to them. A room with a view in Gitmo.

He continued scanning the motel property for a few more minutes, but finally put the rifle down. It was hurting his shoulder and he wasn't going to see anything. Not until the ISIS guys arrived. And even then, there was a good chance that it would be a pretty boring show. The government was dumb, but they weren't *complete* idiots. They wouldn't charge in like the Keystone Kops. They'd more likely put tails on them and try to uncover their network. Most important, a shadowy criminal mastermind who went only by the name PowerStation.

He turned up the collar on his coat, keeping his eyes locked on the distant motel.

Five years of his life.

That's what he'd put into this thing. Seven days a week, from when he got up in the morning to when he went to bed at night. And not just studying every aspect of taking down the power grid. There was also the not-so-trivial matter of his survival after the attack. The details of how he would eventually escape when all that was left of America was wide-open spaces dotted with leathery, emaciated corpses.

All wasted.

Once again he found himself faced with the same problem that plagued every aspect of his life: being occasionally forced to count on the idiots who surrounded him. All he needed was a few marginally competent operatives. Ten or so men who knew one end of a gun from the other and could handle some basic explosives without blowing themselves up. Apparently that was too much to ask on a planet crammed with almost eight billion people.

Without that handful of critical players, his plan was transformed. Sure, the cyberattack he'd developed would shake the world's economies. And a few million Americans would die of heat, violence, hunger, or lack of medicine. But it wouldn't change the face of the planet. It wouldn't be the fundamental force that shaped the twenty-first century. He wouldn't join the likes of Julius Caesar, Genghis Khan, and Adolf Hitler as one of history's great men. Because at their foundation all great men were destroyers. To change the world order, you had to wipe away the old one. And to accomplish that, Caesar had had the Roman Legions. Khan had had his Mongol hordes. Hitler had had the SS and Luftwaffe. He, on the other hand, needed just ten fucking men. And they didn't need to be able to shoot an arrow from running horses or defeat half the world's armies. They just needed to be able to walk and chew gum at the same time.

But he didn't have them. One of the most pivotal moments in modern history would occur in less than twenty minutes at the Sunset Motel and no one would ever know about it. America would still take a hit like it hadn't seen since the Civil War, but it wouldn't be broken. He wouldn't alter the course of history.

Just as his rage began to fade into depression, the rain started again, filling the air with fine droplets that intermittently obscured the landscape below.

Fuck.

This was it. This was his chance. His moment. But he just couldn't do it himself.

Reluctantly, Alton reached for the burner phone in his pocket and dialed a number from memory. It was picked up on the first ring by a man with a heavy Middle Eastern accent.

"Is there a problem?"

"Hell yes, there's a problem, dumbass. You're driving into a trap."

"What are you talking about?"

"Do you know what the odds of dying in a commercial plane crash are? More than ten million to one. And now, suddenly, an airliner goes down in an inaccessible part of Spain with an ISIS operative on board. Pretty convenient, huh?"

"The press is showing footage of one of my people being discovered and firing shots," the man on the other end argued.

"It's faked, you moron! They provoked him and I'd bet everything I have that those overhead bins he shot were full of Kevlar. They wanted to question your man without you knowing he'd been caught. And now they're monitoring all your online communications and probably have a hundred guys in the woods around that motel waiting for you."

"You're ranting like some kind of insane conspiracy theorist," the man replied. "You agreed to meet with us and—"

"Yeah, but I didn't agree to spend the rest of my life with a car battery attached to my balls. And if that's not your idea of a good time, either, you should turn around right now."

There was a long pause before the man spoke again. "I have men there already."

"You've got to be kidding me . . . Where are they? In the diner?"

"Yes."

"How many?"

"Two."

Alton paced back and forth on the stone outcrop. "Well, they're screwed then."

"What do you mean?"

"If they leave, they're going to be tailed, dumbass."

"No one could fake a plane crash like that. This is paranoia. Or is it something more than that? Maybe it's you who is a government agent. Or maybe you can't do what you say you can. And now you're trying to escape. Well, let me assure you that isn't going to happen. We'll find you. And when we do, we'll make you wish with all your heart that you had been taken by your government."

Nobody could be this stupid. It just wasn't possible!

"You want me to prove that I'm not a government agent? No problem. You can't afford to have those two assholes in the diner captured alive. So tell them to shoot everyone in there with them. You assholes like doing stuff like that, right? And when they're done, there's a high school about ten miles up the road. Tell them to go shoot that up, too. And then have them blow their brains out. Think how happy Allah will be. He'll be a pig in shit watching all those American kids get blown away."

"Don't blaspheme."

"Fuck you," Alton said, and then disconnected the call.

CHAPTER 11

Rapp glanced down at his phone and then redirected his gaze to the narrow gap between window shade and sill. The sun was hidden behind a dense layer of clouds that continued to produce light, intermittent rain. His view of the target rooms was solid through the video feed from the cameras in Bebe's car and he had an unobstructed line of sight to the diner.

Currently, it contained five customers, one waitress, and an unknown number of kitchen staff who had entered through a rear entrance invisible from his position. Two of the customers looked local—a Caucasian couple who interacted with the waitress as though they knew her. The third was a heavyset African American woman in her fifties who had come out of one of the second-floor rooms.

The other two were more of a problem. Both were male, of Middle Eastern descent, and in their mid-thirties. One had arrived in a semitruck that he'd parked on the far side of the lot. The other had arrived in a late-model Dodge pickup. It looked right for the area, but he'd spent too much time screwing around getting it locked. Clearly not a vehicle he was familiar with.

Rapp focused a pair of compact binoculars

on the diner's front windows, but the streaking from the rain gave him a pretty hazy view. Forty minutes from the predetermined meeting time, all three of the target rooms were still empty and neither of the men in the diner had made any move to go to the office for keys.

He dialed a number and waited for the woman on the other end to pick up.

"Bebe. Anything strike you as unusual this morning?"

"You mean other than the fact that forty percent of the customers in a rural Virginia diner are Arab?"

"Are you up for taking a closer look?"

It was a question, not an order. While Kincaid was one of Scott's people, she was very much not a shooter. In fact, he wasn't certain she even owned a gun.

"Sure, Mitch. No problem."

"You have cash on you?"

"What do you mean?"

"Do you have cash in your purse or just a credit card?"

There was a brief pause while she checked. "I have sixty-three dollars and some change."

"Put a twenty in your pocket. If I give the word, you slap it down on the table and walk out."

"Got it. I'm on my way."

She appeared a moment later in clothes that looked like they'd been chosen to match the gray of the day. A formless coat, brownish slacks, and Hush Puppies beneath a black umbrella.

"Sit near the door," he ordered through the earpiece she disguised as a hearing aid.

Rapp watched her settle behind a table that gave her a solid view of the restaurant's interior. She exchanged a few words with the waitress pouring her coffee before pulling a tablet from her coat and pretending to read. A moment later, its camera was feeding to Rapp's phone.

She zoomed in on the Arab near the northwest corner for a moment and then adjusted the tablet to get a similar close-up of the one near the kitchen door.

Good vid? she texted.

He confirmed that it was and rewound the video to examine the two men more closely. Disappointingly, neither resembled Muhammad Nahas. And neither looked particularly techy. Rapp's gut told him that they were just muscle.

Advance team, he texted.

Agreed

Eyes open. Figure they'll go for keys and secure rooms just before the scheduled time. 31 min & counting

That time passed slowly with no updates from the rest of his team. The CIA had surveillance on the road leading to the motel and by now they should have picked up someone coming for a 10 a.m. meeting.

Eventually, the scheduled time for the rendezvous came and went. Most of the original customers in the restaurant had moved on, but they'd been replaced by an equal number of new ones. So three civilians, two likely terrorists, and Bebe.

Ten minutes overdue, Kincaid texted.

It wasn't just a reminder that something had gone wrong, but a reminder that she'd finished breakfast and was now on her third cup of coffee. Eventually the Arabs would take notice even of someone like her.

Rain could have slowed them down, Rapp responded. *We wait a few more minutes.*

You're the boss.

The tone of her text suggested that she shared his skepticism. Everything he knew about Muhammad Nahas indicated that he should have pulled in at 10 a.m. on the dot.

Rapp stared down at the streaming video of the terrorist near the northwest corner of the restaurant. He had done nothing but pick at his food and sip coffee for the last hour but now he'd forgotten both and was staring down at the phone next to him. His face went dead for a moment and then he looked toward his off-camera companion.

Rapp picked up his binoculars again, aiming the polarized lenses at the diner's windows. The man he'd been watching put some cash down next to his plate and went for the door. The one left behind began scanning the restaurant with an intensity that Rapp didn't like. But what he liked even less was that the tango outside didn't go for the office, instead striding purposefully toward the semi he'd arrived in.

Get out, Rapp texted.

Bebe did as instructed, but instead of going for her car, she followed the tango.

Rapp connected to her earpiece. "What the hell are you doing, Bebe? Get in your car and get out of here."

She gave no indication of having heard, holding a course that gave her a decent view of the driver's side of the semi as the tango opened the door. A moment later, she diverted toward her car and activated her microphone.

"Assault rifle, Mitch."

Rapp swore under his breath. They were blown. He had no idea how, but they were blown. He pulled the Glock from beneath his jacket and moved toward the door, hesitating as he reached for the knob. While Kincaid could surveil an ISIS operative from a few feet away, Rapp knew that he would be immediately spotted. The second he walked out that door, the shit was going to hit the fan.

"Mitch," Coleman said over his earpiece. "Should we be on our way to you?"

"Stand by," Rapp said, pulling his hood up and hiding his gun in his pocket before calmly opening the door. He glanced at the sky as though he was checking for rain and then began wandering casually toward the diner. The semi driver was still out of sight behind his vehicle and without the benefit of binoculars, Rapp couldn't make out the man still in the diner.

If they knew they'd been ID'd, they wouldn't be able to go back to where they came from. The chance of leading authorities to their network would be too high. And in the twisted mind of an Islamic extremist, that left only one option: go out in a blaze of glory. They'd murder everyone at this motel complex and then take their killing spree on the road. It wouldn't stop until they killed themselves or someone did it for them.

"Negative," Rapp said finally. "If I can't stop them here, they're likely going to be coming your way. Take them out before they get to town."

"Roger that."

Rapp followed the best trajectory available but his tactical position was still a fucking nightmare. He had an assault rifle–armed man behind him, a parking lot largely devoid of cover, and a bunch of civilians trapped in a building with a second shooter invisible to him. He forced himself to keep his stride casual. With a little luck, the tango inside would get greedy and wait for him to come through the door before he started shooting.

As usual, luck wasn't with him. A shot rang out and Rapp reacted immediately, pulling his Glock and firing three rounds into the top of the diner's expansive front window. The goal was twofold: First, he hoped to shatter the window to give him an unobstructed view inside. Unfortunately, the effort failed and instead he ended up with three relatively neat holes and some spiderwebbing that made the glass even more opaque. The second was to draw fire away from the civilians inside. For better or worse, that worked perfectly.

He sprinted to the right just as a burst of automatic fire rose up behind him. The hum of the rounds was clearly audible as they passed through the place he'd been standing a moment before. The tango's fire discipline was good, as was his aim. Rapp found himself with no choice but to go for the cover of a pickup parked in front of the motel. The terrorist inside the diner suddenly kicked the door open and let loose a couple of rounds from a pistol, using the brick jamb for cover.

He could shoot straight, too.

Rapp fired in his general direction from a full run, but there was no way to get particularly close. He just needed to buy the two seconds it was going to take him to get to the pickup.

The gun behind him sounded again, but this time only a single shot. Its owner was no longer satisfied with the spray-and-pray method. He was going to take his time.

The first round went wide, but the second

impacted Rapp's side right above his hip. He managed to keep his footing and jump, letting his momentum carry him over the side of the pickup as the pain signals started reaching his brain. He slammed headfirst into the back of the cab, knowing that this could only be a brief stop—the vehicle's metal skin was too thin to protect him.

He was in the process of using what was left of his momentum to flip over the other side when he realized the bed was stacked with bags of fertilizer, sand, and soil.

Finally, he'd caught a break.

While bullets tended to go through modern passenger vehicles like they weren't there, sand was another story. He shoved two bags behind him and lay out flat as the tango went back to full auto. Rapp could hear the ring of the rounds penetrating metal and then the dull thump as the bags absorbed the impacts.

He was in good shape from that angle, but it seemed certain that the terrorist in the diner was lining up on the exposed side of the truck. The bottom line was that fighting from the middle never worked out particularly well. He had to choose one of these assholes and fully commit. Unfortunately, it was going to have to be the one with the rifle. He had the superior firepower but lacked the cover of the diner.

Rapp lifted one the bags as he rose, aiming around the left side of it. His target was about twenty yards away, crouched on one knee with his rifle butt pressed firmly against his shoulder. The bag bucked, and based on the cloud of dirt rising around him, the rounds were now penetrating. The first two missed him, but the shooter was already calmly adjusting his aim. Rapp lined up as well as he could for a virtually impossible shot when he saw a flash of movement to his target's left.

Bebe Kincaid's minivan caught the terrorist dead between its headlights. The front grill caved in, snagging him on the radiator for a moment before he was sucked beneath the wheels. Rapp didn't take the time to watch the aftermath, instead throwing himself over the truck's side and landing shoulder-first on the wet concrete next to it.

By the time he got to his feet, the remaining tango had realized the situation was reversed—that it was his turn to engage on two fronts. He made the mistake of prioritizing the minivan and managed to get a couple of rounds through the windshield as Bebe ducked down behind the wheel.

Only the tango's arm and a small patch of his side were visible around the door frame. Rapp steadied his hand on the truck and squeezed off a careful shot. There was no way to know precisely where it landed, but it was unquestionably a hit. The tango jerked back and disappeared inside as Bebe just missed crashing through the northwestern edge of the diner.

Rapp came around the back of the truck and saw a flash in the windows. A gunshot—but not aimed at him. He began to sprint toward the building, gritting his teeth against the searing pain in his side.

When he made it to the door, the Arab was crawling on his stomach toward a terrified woman who had crammed herself into the back of a booth. The only other civilian visible was a man lying by the cash register with part of his face missing.

The tango had a wound in his back that had likely destroyed one of his lungs, but missed his heart. Enough to keep him from aiming accurately, but not enough to make him lose consciousness.

The Agency needed the man alive, but he'd lined up on the woman in the booth and was about to pull the trigger. Reluctantly, Rapp put a round into the back of his head.

The woman's screams followed Rapp into the kitchen, where the staff had escaped through the back door. It was still open and he could see them and the remaining customer a few hundred yards to the east, stumbling their way across a muddy field.

"Bebe," Rapp said into his radio as he began searching the drawers in the kitchen. "You all right?"

“I’m fine. You?”

“I’ll live,” he said, pulling up his shirt to examine the wound in his side.

It was only a graze, but probably three-eighths of an inch deep and bleeding badly. A dishrag and a roll of duct tape were the closest thing he could find to medical supplies, but they’d have to do.

“Mitch,” Scott Coleman said. “Give me a sitrep. The police scanners are lighting up. Are the tangos down?”

“They’re down,” Rapp said, stepping back out into the rain. “And one civilian.”

“Ambulance?” Coleman said.

“Hearse,” Rapp responded.

“What the hell happened?”

“Somehow, these assholes got tipped off. But unless I miss my guess, it wasn’t until just a few minutes ago.”

“What makes you think that?”

“Because if Nahas knew this was a setup he wouldn’t have sent an advance team to drink coffee for forty minutes and then shoot up a nearly empty diner. No, he sent these guys here still thinking this meeting was a go. Then, when he found out we were watching, he cut them loose.”

“And they decided to go down in a blaze of glory,” Coleman said.

Rapp pressed the dishrag a little tighter to his side as he passed through the open door and started for the tree line. What he didn't need was a run-in with the cops. "It wouldn't be the first time."

"If you're right, then it seems like Nahas would be close. He was on his way when he realized we were watching."

"Agreed," Rapp said. "We're looking for two or more Middle Eastern men somewhere within . . ." He paused. The blood loss was making it hard to do math in his head. "Hell, I don't know. Call it a hundred miles."

"We're on it," Coleman said. "Can you get to the road where we dropped you off? I can have a chopper inbound in five minutes."

"Yeah. I'll be there."

CHAPTER 12

Rapp leaned a little farther out the chopper's open door, feeling his harness tighten against the wound in his side. The speed of the aircraft drove the cold mist through the jeans he hadn't had time to change out of. His legs were pretty much numb, as were his face and hands. What he could still feel, though, was the warmth of the blood leaking from his side.

They were staying low, skimming the treetops next to a rural highway south of the motel. And while having branches nearly slapping the runners wasn't the safest way to fly, there wasn't much choice. Visibility was bad enough that if they rose even another twenty-five feet, the road below would be invisible.

He glanced back at Joe Maslick, who was sitting behind him with a HK417 rifle in his lap. Instead of the silent resolve that he normally exuded during operations, he was hunched and talking heatedly into his headset. Rapp slapped a hand into the side of his own earphones to no effect. He couldn't hear either Maslick or the person he was talking to.

"Fred," he said to the pilot. "Can you hear me? I'm having a problem with my comm."

Maslick suddenly stopped talking, his expression

making it clear there was nothing at all wrong with the equipment. He'd been deliberately cut from the channel.

"What?" Rapp shouted over the howl of the wind coming through the door.

In lieu of a response, Maslick pointed at the blood that had spread across pretty much Rapp's entire lower right side. Even his sock was starting to skew crimson.

"We gotta get you to a hospital," the former Delta operator said, looping him back in.

"I'm fine."

"You're not fine, man. You're gonna die."

Before he could respond, the pilot's voice came on. "We've got a vehicle ahead. Blue SUV."

"Same drill as before," Rapp said, and Maslick's jaw clenched visibly. He looked like he was about to say something, but then thought better of it.

"All right. We're coming in, Mitch. Hopefully, this'll go better than last time."

He was referring to a pickup they'd intercepted about ten minutes ago. A family of four dressed in their Sunday best, as it turned out. No idea, but the fucking weather made it impossible to see through windshields.

Fred Mason overflew the vehicle and then banked, flying sideways about thirty feet above the deck and matching its speed. Rapp had a perfect vantage point, but the glare was still a problem.

Mason's voice boomed over a speaker mounted to the bottom of the helicopter. "This is the police! Pull over immediately."

Rapp had a hand on his rifle, but wasn't quite ready to shoulder it in light of what had happened last time. One of the kids crying inconsolably in his sights had been about Anna's age.

The SUV slowed and eased to the muddy shoulder. This time a family on their way back from church didn't materialize. Instead two men with medium builds got out but didn't move from behind their open doors. The mist made it impossible to discern detail and for a moment Rapp thought they were African Americans with short hair. It took about a half a second for him to register that he was looking at dark ski masks.

"Back us up!" he shouted just as the men's weapons appeared over the tops of the SUV's window frames. Mason jerked the chopper to the side and Rapp slammed his rifle to his shoulder just as the flash of gunfire appeared below.

Despite the sound of rounds tearing through the aircraft's metal skin, Rapp didn't aim directly at the targets. Killing them was very much not the plan, so instead he concentrated his fire on the front grill and hood of their vehicle. If they decided to take off, they'd now be doing it on foot.

The tangos continued to track the chopper as it moved back over the forest. Instead of climbing to put distance between them and their attackers, Mason actually lost a few feet of altitude, creating an angle that forced them to shoot through the dense trees.

"Hold it here!" Rapp shouted into the comm. "I'm out."

The harness holding him in position was attached to the chopper at two points. On Rapp's right was a short static line with a carabiner clipped through a bolt. On the left was a much longer dynamic rope that snaked through a rappelling device at his waist.

Rapp disconnected the carabiner and jumped, letting the rope slide through the device at a speed that was just shy of a free fall. He didn't arrest until he was only about five feet from the ground. The combination of rope stretch and the helicopter rolling to the side took him to the ground.

The guns had gone silent by the time he disconnected and started running toward the road, knowing that Maslick wouldn't be far behind.

"I'll go west, you go east," Rapp said, inserting an earpiece and toggling his throat mike. "But take it easy. There's a good chance they're in the trees by now."

"Roger that," came the immediate reply.

Whoever these two men were, they had enough training to stay cool and shoot straight. And if that was the case, they were likely smart enough to not stay with their vehicle. They'd go for the cover of the trees, either in an effort to escape or for an opportunity to go on the offensive. In his experience with terrorists, the second option was by far the most likely.

He slowed his pace, scanning the woods for any sign of an ambush, but didn't find any. In less than two minutes he'd made enough progress to get a view of the road cut through the trees.

"I'm about twenty-five yards out with no contact," he said into his throat mike.

Maslick responded immediately. "I'm about fifty yards behind them and fifteen from the road. No contact. I should have eyes on their vehicle in another minute or so."

"Watch your ass, Mas. I doubt these guys are going to run. They don't have anywhere to go."

"Understood."

Rapp slid his finger off the trigger of his weapon and flexed his hand in an effort to get some feeling back into it. Fuck, he was cold. Colder than he could ever remember. And it wasn't just the weather—it was the trail of blood he was leaving across the forest floor. How much had he lost?

No time to worry about that now.

He continued toward the road, going from tree to tree in a careful zigzag pattern. Still, no resistance. Maybe martyrdom wasn't on today's menu. If the two men were Muhammad Nahas and his new tech guru, it was possible that they'd try to live to fight another day.

When Rapp reached a position where he could see the car, it was clear that he'd miscalculated. For some reason, the men were still there. They'd broken out all of the SUV's windows so they could shoot through them and taken cover on the other side.

"They're both still at the car," Rapp said over his comm.

"What?" Maslick said, understandably confused. "Repeat that."

"I've got eyes on both of them. They've taken cover on the south side of the road. You're in good position. Cross the road far enough away that they can't see you and flank. Take it slow, though. I don't understand what these assholes are doing but don't bet on them being stupid. Nahas doesn't work with stupid people."

"I'm on it."

"Fred, do we have backup inbound?"

"You have vehicles coming from both directions and another chopper's on its way. ETA on the helicopter is five minutes and the vehicles should be here in about ten."

"All right. There's nothing you can do for us here. I want you to check the road and make sure there's no civilian traffic bearing down on us."

"I'm out, then. Good luck."

Rapp crouched and scanned the SUV again.

Nothing. The two tangos were still wearing their masks despite the fact that it was a little late to worry about anonymity. Otherwise they were just standing there, aiming their rifles through the empty window frames and waiting. But for what?

"I'm across the street," Maslick said. "Heading back in their direction."

"Roger that."

Rapp sighted over his rifle, determining that he had a vaguely viable shot on one of them. Unfortunately, it was a head shot and that wasn't going to go a long way to accomplishing his mission of taking them alive.

Four more minutes passed before Maslick's voice came back on the comm. "I'm in position behind them. I've got a shot on both."

"Can you put them down without killing them?"

"I can try."

"Hold on. I'll get their attention," Rapp said.

He squeezed off a burst into the vehicle's driver side door and, as expected, they returned fire. Instead of assuming they were being flanked and spreading out, though, they moved to take cover in the vehicle.

Maslick got a shot off, throwing one of the men forward but not killing him. He managed to lift his wounded leg into the vehicle and slam the door shut as his friend turned and fired in Maslick's general direction.

Rapp didn't like it. They'd put themselves in a disastrous tactical position—particularly in light of the fact that they'd know backup was on its way. With a superior force coming down on them, their best bet was a running fight in the woods. It was obvious now how this was going to end.

"I've lost my angle," Maslick said. "Moving in."

"No!" Rapp shouted.

A moment later, the SUV went up in a column of fire that rose a good fifty feet in the air.

He dropped to the mud as flaming parts of the car—and of the men who had been inside—came raining down around him.

"Mas, you all right?"

"Not a scratch. You?"

Rapp didn't answer, instead struggling to his feet and walking out to where the fire was starting to melt the asphalt. The force of the first explosion was such that a secondary was unlikely. Still he was getting too close. The heat from the flames was like a drug, though. It penetrated him, pushing back the numbness that had now taken over almost his entire body. He stared into the flames, strangely mesmerized.

They hadn't wanted to be identified. That's why they'd kept the masks on. Their goal had been to tie Rapp up here and then kill themselves in a way that would preclude a conclusive ID. To provide Rapp with the illusion that he'd taken out

Muhammad Nahas and his technology expert, when in fact they had used the time to escape.

Maslick appeared from the trees but stayed well back from the burning vehicle. “What the fuck are you doing, Mitch? Get away from there!”

Rapp tried to take a step back, but his legs collapsed beneath him. A few seconds later, Maslick had him under the arms and was dragging him away from the fire.

“It wasn’t them,” Rapp said, his voice sounding oddly distant. “Tell our people that Nahas and his man are still out there.”

“Fred!” he heard Maslick say into his comm. “We need a medevac. Call ahead to the closest hospital and give them our ETA. Tell them we’ve got a gunshot wound with heavy blood loss. O-positive. Do it now!”

CHAPTER 13

The White House
Washington, DC
USA

Mitch Rapp gave a quick knock on the Oval Office door and then entered. Everyone standing in the conversation area turned toward him and all the faces were familiar: CIA director Irene Kennedy, who had recruited him as a kid; her counterpart at the FBI, Darren Phillips; James Templeton, the chairman of the Joint Chiefs; and a wild card he hadn't seen in years—TJ Burton, the head of FEMA. But it was Joshua Alexander who began striding toward him.

He had just entered the last month of his presidency and was looking very forward to that month ending. Word on the street was that the Secret Service worried he might climb the fence and make a run for it.

It would be a shame to see him go. He was reasonably stable, capable of listening instead of talking, and had a genuine love of country. Most important, though, he was a man who understood when it was time to look the other way and let things get done.

Unfortunately, his successor was cut from

very different cloth. But that was a problem for another day.

"Mitch," he said, taking Rapp's hand in a grip that wasn't quite as forceful as normal. "Sorry to drag you away from home like this. You all right?"

"It's not a problem, sir. I'm fine."

He lowered his voice. "Don't lie to me. I heard you lost a lot of blood."

"The bullet didn't hit anything important and the docs topped me up. They tell me I'm good as new."

He grinned. "It's been a long time since either one of us was as good as new. You know you're not much use to me dead, right?"

"Yes, sir."

Alexander finally released his hand and turned back to the others in the room. "I think we can dispense with formalities and get to work. Mitch, take the chair on the right. It's the most comfortable."

Rapp did and everyone settled in around him murmuring greetings and asking about his health.

All were old friends, but the attention made him uncomfortable. He liked being at the White House even less than he liked being in Langley. His goal had always been to live as anonymous a life as possible and die of old age. Unfortunately, the former had already slipped through his fingers and the latter was about as likely as him being nominated for sainthood.

"First," Alexander said, "I want to thank Mitch on the behalf of the American people for what he did."

Rapp was a bit taken aback. "For screwing up?"

"I don't think most people would consider taking out four terrorists on US soil screwing up, Mitch."

"First of all, it was one at best. Bebe gets full credit for the diner. I'd probably be dead if it weren't for her. And the other two committed suicide."

Alexander frowned and shook his head. "Can't you just be satisfied for one minute? Take the win, Mitch."

"No, sir. This was a disaster. Setting aside the dead civilian, we somehow got made at that motel and we still don't know how."

"These things can get messy," General Templeton said. "We all know that. But the immediate threat's been neutralized and that was the goal, right?"

Rapp glanced at Kennedy, who leaned back with a slightly pained expression. "I haven't had an opportunity to provide them with the latest intel, Mitch."

"What intel?" Alexander said.

"We're fairly certain that the men in that car weren't Nahas and his technology expert. Because they seemed so intent on hiding their identity in both life and death, we looked further into the matter."

"But we know from their Internet activity that Nahas and his man were scheduled to be at that meeting," the FBI director said.

Kennedy nodded. "We believe the men who committed suicide were a bodyguard and a driver. Our search turned up a place by the side of the road where they'd pulled off. We have an exact tire tread match and we have the footprints of two individuals going into the woods. One of the boot prints is in Nahas's size, which we know from his time working with US troops."

"Shit!" Alexander said. "Where are they now? Were we able to track them?"

"No," Rapp responded. "The mud by the side of the road made for good impressions but the surface is different in the trees. And the rain made dogs useless. Our best guess is that Nahas and his man went over the mountain and his people stayed behind to buy him time."

"Do you think they could have made it to safety? It's getting down below freezing at night—"

Rapp waved a hand, causing Alexander to fall silent. "Nahas is a son of a bitch, but he's a tough, well-trained son of a bitch. Getting through those mountains—even with a tech geek in tow—wouldn't be a big ask for him."

"And the person who calls himself Power-Station never made an appearance at all? He's still out there?"

"That's correct," Kennedy responded.

Alexander leaned back in his chair and let out a long breath. "Okay, what kind of threat are we talking about here? What can these people really accomplish?"

"We don't know exactly," Kennedy said. "PowerStation is clearly knowledgeable about our grid but how deep that knowledge really goes is still a mystery."

"Is it possible he's a foreign actor?"

"Possible, but we're betting against it. A foreign actor wouldn't need ISIS as a partner."

"Okay," Alexander said. "We've got someone—maybe even an American—who's figured out a way to attack our grid and he's looking for soldiers. That leads me to believe that he's going to sabotage some of our infrastructure. Maybe he's even come up with some kind of optimized plan—a way to do the maximum amount of damage with the minimum manpower. What's our exposure to something like that?"

"High," Kennedy responded. "Someone could take out the entire US grid by destroying as few as nine critical substations. And that wouldn't be difficult at all. The facilities I'm talking about are full of delicate, difficult-to-replace equipment and none have any security beyond chain link fences and a few security cameras. What would be difficult, though, is *keeping* the grid down. We have enough excess capacity to reroute around a pretty significant amount of damage."

"But based on his online statements, that's exactly what he says he can do. Is it plausible that he's telling the truth?"

"Plausible? Yes. Likely? No. It'd take a combination of an extremely sophisticated cyberattack and numerous physical attacks around the country. The kind of access someone would need into hundreds—maybe even thousands—of utilities would be pretty extraordinary. For comparison, we've spent hundreds of millions of dollars penetrating Russia's grid and while we could shut down a large portion of it, we couldn't keep it down for very long without a massive coordinated effort from spec ops teams on the ground."

Alexander considered that for a moment. "But they're out there, they're clearly smart, and we know from experience that ISIS doesn't lack commitment. What can we do to protect ourselves?"

"There's actually a bit of good news on that front," Kennedy said. "The Department of Energy has been working on a report on our power grid's vulnerabilities and ways we can mitigate those vulnerabilities. A draft was just released to Congress."

"I'm vaguely familiar with it," Alexander said. "Enough that I know the recommendations are pretty elaborate. Even in an ideal environment, we're talking about billions of dollars and years of effort, right? And let me just tell you that we don't have an ideal environment. There are a lot of politicians and power companies that have reason to push back against the kinds of changes the DOE wants to make."

"Yes, sir. But with a potential imminent threat, I think we can use the report as a guide to create some emergency actions. Basically, things that'll be relatively noncontroversial and easy to implement."

"Noncontroversial," Alexander said. "You can't paint a bathroom at the Agriculture Department without nearly triggering a civil war anymore. But let's see what we can do. I want initial recommendations on my desk ASAP. But please . . . Keep them simple and cheap, Irene. I don't have much weight to throw around anymore."

"I'll do my best, sir."

Alexander turned toward TJ Burton, the head of FEMA. He'd been doing everything possible to make himself invisible and looked a little startled when everyone suddenly focused on him.

"I think we should talk a little bit about what happens if something like this were to actually happen. There's no question that we've left the door open for way too long and I'm curious about how we'd respond. TJ?"

"I . . . I don't think I understand the question."

"Worst-case scenario," Rapp interjected. "Let's say these sons of bitches take out the entire grid and it stays out for a year. What do we do?"

Burton was unquestionably one of the most competent people in the US government. He'd lived and breathed disaster relief since the day he graduated from college and had gotten his hands dirty in more countries than anyone could count. He was the kind of guy who could coordinate the relief effort for an entire African nation while welding a structural support into a collapsing bridge.

"I think it'd be safe to say that a successful attack on our grid keeps me awake more than any other threat."

"Why?" Alexander asked.

"Because it comes from nowhere, it's nationwide, and it could potentially be long-lasting. Those aren't things I deal with. Think about storms. Those we can handle. You see them coming, you know roughly what they're going to do, and they blow through pretty quickly. So, to answer your question, I have no idea what I'd do. I really don't."

"Come on," Rapp said. "You literally vacation in foreign disaster areas and you're telling us you've got nothing? I don't believe it."

"Okay. Maybe I've thought about it from time to time. But it's just musing, you know? Something to pass the time when I'm mowing the lawn."

"And?" Alexander said.

Burton let out a long breath, trying to put order to years of random ideas before speaking. "Look . . . Okay . . . America's become super-efficient over the years. For instance, it used to be that virtually everyone in the country produced food. Now machines do most of the work. Only about two percent of our population is in the food production business. When those machines go down, what do you do? Beyond that, how do you move goods and people from one place to another with no fuel? And even if you had fuel, a lot of the roads would be blocked by people panicking and trying to get out of the cities. If it's cold, people start to freeze. If it's hot, they die of heatstroke. In a few days you'd start to lose backup power for communications, hospitals, and so on. The biggest and most immediate problem, though, would be water and sanitation. Most of the country's pipes would run dry between a few days and a few weeks. Now people are dying of thirst and the lack of functioning toilets spreads disease at a time when medical personnel are either working in the dark or abandoning their posts. And then there's the civil unrest. When people run out of basic necessities, they're going to go looking for them. The grocery stores will be empty so they'll go to warehouses. Then farms. And, eventually, other people's homes. Not to put too fine a point on it, but if the power really went out for a year, you'd be looking at casualties in the three hundred million range."

"That's the vast majority of the population," Alexander said.

"Right. Everyone's going to die and there's nothing I can do about it. FEMA would be completely paralyzed. My job is to move resources from unaffected areas to affected areas for a few days until everything is up and running again. That's not the scenario we're talking about here. The only way to win this game is not to play it."

People had described Burton as a genius and in Rapp's experience, it was a fair assessment. But, like most geniuses, he was a little unstable. Rapp had gotten an up-close look at that instability in Sudan. Or was it Chad? In any event, his process always followed the same path. First, freak out. Second, calm down. Third, fix the problem.

Time for a little tough love.

"You think I like getting my ass shot off by terrorists?" Rapp said, letting a little anger edge into his voice. "But I went to work for the CIA, so that's my problem. You went to work for FEMA, so this is your problem. Now quit whining and fix it."

Burton pulled back in his chair and then just sat there, wetting his lips with quick flicks of his tongue. "Okay. Right now—and I mean tomorrow—we need to start a public campaign encouraging people to start preparing. They need water, filters, radios . . . I can make a list. And these announcements have to be persuasive, but not so much so that we cause panic or even suspicion. That would lead to hoarding and everything would just get gridlocked."

"That's quite a balancing act," Alexander said. "Easier said than done."

"It gets worse," Burton said. "If this were to really happen, it's the end of democracy. All hands have to be on deck and you have to become a dictator. Anytime bickering breaks out in Washington, tens of thousands of Americans will die. Seriously, if some congressman withholds his support because he wants something in return, you need to have him shot."

"I imagine Mitch would be happy to take care of that," Alexander said.

There was some nervous laughter, but it didn't do much to break the tension.

"Then there's the question of what we tell people," Burton continued. "Do we just stay silent and let the rumor mill go crazy? Do we lie to people and tell them that the power will be back on soon in order to stave off panic? Do we tell the truth and watch the cities burn? Seriously, does anyone know? Because I don't."

No one spoke up, so he continued. "Obviously, the military would have to be deployed. Not only for civil unrest but to protect food and fuel infrastructure."

“That’s not easy, either,” General Templeton said. “Even setting aside the legal issues, we rely on the same grid everyone else does.”

“You might be able to stage out of Alaska and Hawaii,” Burton said. “They’re on different grids and probably wouldn’t be hit. Also, the navy has to be called back—nuclear craft in particular. They have reactors that could be used to power critical systems to the degree it’s possible.”

“What about help from other countries?” Alexander said. “Europe has significant capacity and China would probably pitch in as well because taking us off-line would bring their economy to its knees. And then there’s Mexico and Canada. They have less capacity but better proximity.”

“You can probably forget the Canadians because a lot of their grid is connected to ours and would go down along with it. The Mexicans wouldn’t be much help because of our shaky relationship and their limited resources. Certainly, the Europeans and Chinese would be willing but there’s some question of whether they’d be able. Both countries import a lot of food from the U.S. When that flow stops, they’re going to need their domestic production to feed their own citizens. And even if they were able to send full cargo ships with all the supplies we need, how would we offload them without power?”

“Or distribute it,” Rapp said.

"Exactly. And then there's the most unpredictable element. Personnel. They're going to be affected by this the same as everyone else and eventually they're going to walk away. You might have the best electrical engineer in the world, but when her family is in danger, she's going to prioritize them over work. And without people, the whole thing goes into a death spiral. Nothing is getting fixed because our manpower is abandoning us and our manpower is abandoning us because nothing is getting fixed."

"I disagree," Rapp said. "Manpower is actually one of the bright spots in this thing."

"Explain," Alexander said.

"In my experience, getting people to work in this kind of an environment isn't all that hard. First, you identify your critical talent. And I don't mean some congressman from Ohio with a third-rate law degree. With resources this limited, you have to prioritize pretty ruthlessly."

"And what's step two?" Alexander asked.

"You make them an offer they can't refuse."

"Which is?"

"That if they work twenty hours a day, seven days a week, their families get protection and food."

"And if they decided one day that they don't want to be your indentured servant?" Burton said, obviously a bit horrified. "Would you just throw their spouses and kids out in the street?"

"I've done it before," Rapp said. "The good news is that it only has to happen once before word gets around."

"All right," Alexander said, standing. "I've heard enough and I have to get on a helicopter in fifteen minutes. As much as I hate to say this, my sense is that Nahas has what he needs to carry out an attack on some level. Irene and Darren—find these psychopaths and send Mitch to deal with them. TJ and Jim, get your people together and figure out what we're going to do if things don't go our way. All hands on deck, right? If you have any problems or run into any roadblocks, contact me directly. I'm looking forward to my retirement and I'd rather not spend it in the dark."

CHAPTER 14

Southeastern Ohio
USA

"I just texted you the address," John Alton said. "Key's under the mat."

He disconnected the call and looked at his hand as he placed it back on the steering wheel. Shaking. With fear. With excitement. With anticipation. It was hard to believe that this thing was finally in motion. That it was really happening.

He couldn't get what had happened at the motel to stop playing out in his mind. The van's impact and the lifeless body being spit from beneath its wheels had been thrilling for sure—just like in the movies.

What hadn't been so thrilling was the man who had come out of the room on the first floor. The speed he'd run at. The fact that getting shot hadn't seemed to even faze him. But mostly the hazy image through the diner window of him executing a man crawling across the floor.

Alton had walked off that mountain telling himself that everything he'd worked for was gone. The government was too close. And that man was too dangerous.

He'd reminded himself that he was rich. That

he never had to work another day in his life. He could sail around the Mediterranean in a yacht full of five-thousand-dollar-a-night whores. Kick back in his Mexican villa with servants waiting on him hand and foot. Whatever he wanted. He just had to reach out and take it.

Power was a narcotic, though. Watching that man in the parking lot die and knowing it had happened because of a phone call he'd made was an incredible rush—a sensation that he had the ability to multiply a million times over. Not only did he possess the most devastating weapon in the history of the human race, but he had the ability to actually use it. Not like the nukes that had become little more than tedious theater or the bioweapons that no one had the guts to deploy. This was real.

He eased to a stop at a red light and looked at the people in the cars around him. What would happen to them? Each one would live out what was to come in their own way. The couple in the minivan next to him. Would either of them survive? Maybe, but the two children watching videos in back wouldn't.

If he were to pull up to this exact intersection one year from now, what would it look like? He tried to picture it. Empty parking lots. Shattered windows. A few cars abandoned by the side of the road. Maybe a few scavenging dogs or wild animals.

The rewards of this were infinite and after a number of sleepless nights going over every detail in his head, he had determined that the risks were acceptable. There seemed to be no plausible way that the government could know his identity or have tracked the men he was about to meet. It was safe.

It had to be.

Everything seemed completely normal as Alton pulled into the remote hunting camp. He parked in the driveway next to a late-model Ford Explorer and stepped out into the cold. The dilapidated log structure looked unoccupied but the presence of the other car suggested that wasn't the case. They were already inside. Waiting.

His breath came out as a light fog as he jogged onto the porch and tested the front door. It was unlocked and he went inside, squinting through the gloom. He wanted to remember every detail. The deer head on the wall. The cabinets and kitchen full of mismatched appliances. But mostly the two men standing near the back.

"You're sure you weren't followed?" Alton said.

"Of course not," the one on the right said. He had broad shoulders, a neatly trimmed beard, and dark eyes that seemed full of hate. Someone accustomed to being in charge. Of being feared and deferred to.

The man standing next to him was different—taller, but slightly puffy and wearing glasses. ISIS's second-string technology expert. Hopefully, he wouldn't be a complete idiot.

"Of course not," Alton mocked. "I wouldn't get too cocky after what happened in Virginia."

"What did happen there?"

It was a reasonable question. There had been very little in the media about the incident. The cops were playing it as a couple of rednecks getting in an argument and shooting each other. Not particularly unusual or interesting, especially when compared to the lead story of the day—the unraveling of that bullshit story about the plane crash in Spain.

"The government had people there waiting for you, just like I said. Your people only managed to kill one lousy person before they got taken out."

"You're sure they're dead?"

"Very," Alton said. "And all the people connected to those two men have been moved?"

"Don't tell me how to do my business."

"Someone needs to."

The man's eyes narrowed, but he managed to control his anger. "Enough of this. Can you do what you say?"

"Yes. Can you?"

"You personally witnessed the devotion of my people."

"Well, you're good at dying, I'll give you that.

The problem is that dying isn't a great way of getting things done, is it? Maybe that's why you spend your days riding around on camels and getting your asses kicked by the Jews."

"What do you know of my people?" the man said, sounding a little strangled as he reined in his rage.

Alton didn't bother to answer, instead retrieving a laptop from his courier bag and setting it on the table. Less than a minute later, it was booted up and he'd used his fingerprint to unlock it.

"My entire plan is here. All the information on the grid, all the companies I've been able to penetrate. Most important, though, it's got pictures and locations of critical infrastructure your people would need to destroy. Take a look. See if you're satisfied and tell me if you've got the resources to hold up your end. If so, this could be the beginning of a very productive relationship."

The techy-looking guy sat down behind the computer and began working through the information stored there. Alton retreated to a sofa against the wall. Just like he had in the Russian meeting. But without the eye candy.

"And what do you want in return for all this information?" the man staring down at him said.

"Simple. I want to be in charge. You guys haven't been able to pull off anything since Nine/Eleven and that, frankly, had all the sophistication of a sledgehammer. This plan has a scale and precision that you can't even come close to handling."

"No?"

"No. Now how many reliable followers do you have in the US?"

"Enough."

"See? This is the kind of shit that worries me. Don't tell me 'enough' when you don't even know what the job is. And don't tell me God will provide. If he was looking out for you, the Middle East wouldn't be such a shithole."

"And so now you're going to tell me about God?" he said.

"Let's cut through this crap, okay? If God wanted America destroyed, he'd do it himself. Do you really think the entity that created biology and black holes sits around worrying about your facial hair and whether or not you eat hot dogs? I'm doing this for me. And so are you. Now, I'm going to ask you one more time. How many people do you have?"

"Eleven."

"And I assume they can do things like drive, shoot, and follow simple written instructions?"

"Yes."

"Then this is indeed a match made in heaven. I have the brains and you have the brawn."

The man looked behind him and spoke to his companion, who was still staring into the glow of the laptop. "Is it really all there?"

"Yes," he responded, sounding a bit stunned. "I have access to everything. Even the passwords necessary to activate malware in individual power companies."

The ISIS leader seemed confused. "Are you saying that we have everything we need to carry out the attack ourselves?"

"I . . . I'd have to confirm a few more things, but I would say yes."

A predictable smile spread across his face as he returned his attention to Alton. "You seem very confident in your intelligence, but I wonder how smart it was to make yourself redundant?"

Alton frowned. "I'm not smart. I'm a fucking genius." He pointed to the man behind the laptop. "Tell him."

He looked a little sheepish, but wasn't willing to disagree. "Based on what I've seen, he is indeed a genius. What he's accomplished here is staggering."

"And you," Alton said, now aiming his wagging finger at the man hovering over him, "are a cartoon villain. You've got a problem, though."

The terrorist's smile persisted. "Do I? And what problem is that?"

"You can't kill me."

"Ah, because you left out some critical piece of information, yes? A fragment of code. A password." His gaze intensified. "I truly hope that's the case. Because you have no idea how much pleasure I'm going to have extracting that information from you."

Alton shook his head disappointedly and held up his arms to expose devices attached to each wrist. "You probably think these are watches, but they're actually heart rate monitors that upload data via a satellite connection."

"What data?"

"My heart rate, dumbass. They're *heart rate monitors.* Didn't we just cover this? The part that's important to you, though, is that they have alarms on them. If my heart rate goes too low—like if I was dead, for instance—a notification gets uploaded. And if it goes too high—like if I was being tortured—a similar notification gets uploaded."

"To what end?" he said, obviously starting to see his perceived advantage evaporate.

"I'm glad you asked. If that notification goes out, an . . ." His voice faded for a moment. ". . . *antidote* for want of a better word gets sent to pretty much every government agency in the country."

"Antidote? What do you mean?"

"Basically, all the information on that laptop, a detailed plan to route around all the damage, and the code necessary to bring all the power company computers back online."

The man turned to his tech guru. "Is this possible?"

"Very much so."

That turned out to be too much for the terrorist. He grabbed Alton by the front of the jacket, lifted him from the couch, and slammed him against a wall.

"Arrogant bastard!" he shouted, spraying Alton's glasses with spit.

"Careful, man. My heart rate's going up. You don't want to scare me, do you?"

The Arab just stood there with his fists tangled in the fabric of Alton's coat.

"You can either destroy the Great Satan or you can kill me. It can't be both, asshole."

His grip began to relax and Alton looked directly into his eyes. He thought he was such a badass—just like so many others Alton had crossed paths with over the years. The high school football players. The corporate CEOs and government muckety-mucks. Men whose unwavering confidence made them blind and stupid.

Alton slipped a hunting knife from his waistband and rammed it upward into the man's stomach. It sunk to the hilt, but the Arab was too dumb to understand what had happened. Too much the alpha male. He just stood there, his grip failing and his dark eyes losing their intensity.

Alton stepped to the side and the man collapsed, landing on his back and looking at the knife protruding from him. Surprise more than anything else registered on his face.

"Didn't see that coming, did you?" Alton said.

He felt exhilarated. Sure, he'd been ultimately responsible for the deaths at that motel, but this was a completely different sensation. He'd been fantasizing about killing another human being since he was a kid. At first those fantasies had revolved around the people who picked on him at school, but later they became less focused. People he glimpsed on the street. People he saw on TV. It was the act that fascinated him. Not the victim.

He glanced down at his wrist and confirmed that his heart rate was still well below the upper limit he'd set. When he looked up again, he saw the man behind the laptop staring at him. Frozen.

"What's your name?"

He didn't respond at first, clearly unsure what to do. It wasn't until the man on the floor went still that he finally spoke. "Feisal Ibrahim."

The young Arab looked a bit like a caged animal. And why not? America had pretty much eradicated ISIS and what was left of its leadership was bleeding out on the floor. What was left for him? A short life spent searching the sky for the drone that would kill him. Unless there was no one left to fly those drones.

"So, what do you think, Feisal? About me being in charge, I mean. Do you have a problem with that?"

He thought about it for a few seconds and then just shook his head.

CHAPTER 15

North of Frederick
Maryland
USA

A GPS coordinate had been provided in lieu of an address and Alton followed his phone's instruction to turn onto a nondescript, tree-lined road. The landscape around him was largely agricultural and he passed a number of farms before passing through the open whitewashed gate of one with no signage.

The slight queasiness he'd been feeling since he left home increased, causing trickles of sweat to run down his sides. The hour-and-a-half drive had given him plenty of time to think and he'd used it to scrutinize every potential mistake. Every complexity. Every risk.

And he'd come up with nothing—not a single plausible reason that he would be summoned to a secret meeting in rural Maryland. The ISIS man's body had been disposed of without incident and his technology henchman seemed to be following orders. Even if the government had uncovered his plan, why would they have him drive to his own demise? Seems like that was what the black helicopters were for.

He came around a corner and saw a group of agricultural buildings that looked very much like all the others in the area. The only difference was that these were surrounded by a tall chain link fence with a posted guard. And not the overweight twelve-dollar-an-hour variety. This one looked capable of twisting a man's head off like a bottle cap.

Alton rolled down his window and let the vehicle begin to coast, but he was just waved through. Instead of returning his foot to the gas, though, he gazed through the windshield at the main building. There were a few cars parked out front, gleaming dully under overcast skies. Toward the north end, he spotted Janice Crane's Audi. Its presence calmed him enough to accelerate again. Throwing bags over people's heads and tossing them in holes wasn't her part of the bureaucracy. He just needed to stay cool and on his toes. Whatever was happening here, it was going to be fine.

He took the closest empty spot to the door and got out. The wind went right through his suit jacket, but it wasn't enough to prompt him to move at much more than a shuffle. When he finally reached the front door, no one was there to greet him so he took hold of the knob and reluctantly twisted.

The reception area he entered was completely unremarkable and dominated by a single desk.

The smiling woman behind it held out a plastic badge emblazoned with his name.

"You're running a bit late, Mr. Alton. I suggest you hurry."

He did as he was told, speed-walking down a nondescript hallway until he was intercepted by a man in a military uniform. He didn't really know much about soldiers—just a bunch of low-class cannon fodder, as far as he was concerned—so he couldn't identify the branch or rank.

"If you could just follow me, please, sir."

The place was a lot bigger than it appeared from the outside and smelled vaguely of fresh paint and new carpet. He didn't see anything more threatening than some bad landscape paintings, but he had to admit that he didn't really know what to look for. His knowledge of clandestine government operations came entirely from Hollywood.

When they reached what seemed to be the back of the building, the soldier opened a door and motioned him inside. The room was about twenty-five feet square, furnished with little more than a conference table, chairs, and a water cooler. Janice Crane was sitting near the far end next to a black guy with an Afro. They were surrounded primarily by generic people in generic suits, with a few soldiers thrown in for good measure. These men were older than the one who had escorted him there and their uniforms were fancier. His attention shifted to a man standing against the back wall but he immediately averted his eyes.

Fuck.

He was the one from the motel. The one who had gotten shot and then executed the man in the diner. Alton focused on keeping his expression serene, but that got even harder when a woman to his left greeted him. He recognized her from the news. Irene Kennedy. The director of the CIA.

"Thank you for coming, Mr. Alton," she said politely. "Take any empty seat."

He hesitated for a moment, then chose the chair farthest from the man staring at him from the back wall.

"We've all gone over the report you did for Congress," Kennedy continued. "And it's extremely thorough. Congratulations on a job well done."

He nodded uncomfortably.

"In the long term, we hope to implement all your recommendations, but we'd like your thoughts on what we could do in the short term. Protocols that could be quickly and easily implemented to improve the security of our grid. Obviously, we're looking at half measures here, but something is better than nothing, wouldn't you agree?"

Again, he nodded, surprise starting to overshadow his discomfort. Holy mother of God. They'd called him here to help them. To ask him how to stop an attack that he himself was going to carry out. The urge to laugh was overwhelming but quickly faded when he thought a little deeper about his situation.

Janice Crane wasn't exactly Albert Einstein, but she did have a master's in physics and a fair amount of knowledge about the grid. The black guy next to her screamed tech wizard and didn't look like someone you could just bullshit. Any obvious lies or spin could bring suspicion down on him. Better to earn their trust by throwing them a few bones. Those bones would have to be chosen carefully, though.

"Uh, yeah," he said, realizing that he'd been silent for too long. "Obviously, most of my recommendations are out of the question if you're looking for cheap and cheerful. The biggest bang for your buck would be to create a set of standardized procedures to allow the individual companies to do a security survey of their own systems. Global password changes, firewall upgrades, scans for malware, that kind of thing. It's not too intrusive and I'd be . . ." His voice faded for a moment. He'd been about to say "Happy to help," but that would sound suspiciously agreeable to Crane. "Willing to extend my contract to help set that up if you want. The hard part would be persuading them to do it. Those companies don't like spending time and money on stuff like this."

"You let us worry about persuasion," Kennedy said. "Now, what about physical infrastructure? We infer from your report that in order to carry out a truly devastating attack, cyber wouldn't be enough. Some critical substations would also have to be destroyed."

Shit. She really had read his report.

"Yeah, but you asked for quick and easy and that's neither. I mean, sure, some substations are more important than others—if you picked just the right ones, you'd only have to take out nine to put the whole country in the dark. But as you add more attacks you have more choices. For instance, if someone had the capability to take out fifteen substations instead of nine, the number of permutations goes up to over a hundred."

The man from the motel finally broke his silence and everyone seemed content to defer to him. "I need the locations of the twenty most critical by the end of the day. By tomorrow, I want the top two hundred and fifty."

Two hundred and fifty? Fuck.

Alton wanted to say it was impossible, but Crane would know that was a lie and this asshole didn't look like someone who took no for an answer.

"Sure. Yeah. No problem."

When Alton fell silent instead of offering more, his boss spoke up. "And what about the manufacturing facilities that make transformers,

John? Wouldn't we want to take a look at protecting those?"

Bitch.

"Yeah, but most of them aren't in the US."

His idea was to attack some of the domestic capacity in maybe a third or fourth wave—if he still had the manpower—but now that plan was going down the toilet. He wondered idly if ISIS had assets in Europe. Maybe it would make sense to get them to attack the foreign factories.

"Why don't you send us a list of those, too, then," Kennedy said. "And go ahead and include foreign manufacturers."

These two bitches were really starting to chap his ass. All this planning and now he was going to have to make modifications on the fly. That kind of seat-of-the-pants crap just introduced more complexity into something that was already hopelessly complex . . .

CHAPTER 16

Fairfax Station
Virginia
USA

Sonya Voronova glanced at the Timex on her wrist.

7:32 a.m.

The neighborhood slowly gaining detail through her windshield was pretty much what she expected of a posh Washington suburb. The homes were overly large, with ample yards and historic flourishes designed to camouflage bland McMansion bones.

The one she was interested in was across the street and two houses up—a brick monstrosity with a grand glass entrance and newly black-topped driveway. Based on an earlier recon, the fenced backyard was dog-free and accessed by a single gate secured with a Master model M175DLH padlock.

A woman jogging through the semidarkness became visible on the opposite sidewalk, and Voronova studied her features for a moment. It was a habit she couldn't break. There had been eight other children trained with her in Russia and she assumed that at least a few of them were living similar lives somewhere in America. Her brain told her it was pointless, but her heart told her something different. If she could spot one—even just a brief glimpse—maybe some of the loneliness that plagued her would dissipate.

Or maybe not.

The bottom line was that she was alone in the world—a realization that had been driven home like never before in the time since her return to the United States. She'd pretty much given up sleeping in favor of her new obsession with the electrical grid. She'd read old newspaper articles on blackouts around the world, surfed endless websites on the subject of long-term failures, and become hooked on the TV show *Doomsday Preppers*.

And then it had happened. She'd been clicking through Web pages relating to grid vulnerabilities when she'd come across an article about a recent congressional hearing on that very subject. Thinking she might be able to download a preliminary report, she'd followed a link to a *Washington Post* article that included a photo of the hearing.

And there he was.

Of course, she'd immediately slammed her laptop shut. It didn't take long for her curiosity to get the better of her, though. The next day, she'd found herself at the public library, using an anonymous computer to dig deeper. And now she was sitting in a rented car, wearing a blond wig and a pair of prosthetic teeth that changed the shape of her face.

Another fifteen minutes passed with no change other than a slight increase in the frequency of dog walkers. Finally, at 8 a.m. on the dot, the garage door on the house she was watching started to rise. A Porsche sport-utility vehicle backed into the street and she focused on the man behind the wheel.

John Alton.

She'd known it would be him, but actually seeing his profile filled her with emotion. Fear? Check. Dread? Check. Excitement? Maybe. Was that the same as an overwhelming urge to throw up?

The Porsche sped away and she let another minute or so pass before glancing at the laptop in her passenger seat. A spinning icon dominated the center of the screen, but then disappeared and was replaced by a pulsing smiley face. The program had captured John Alton's garage door opener code and sent it to a companion app on the burner phone she'd bought.

Still, she just sat there. Motionless.

"Do it!" she said after a few more seconds of inaction. Her shaky voice filled the car but it wasn't sufficient to motivate her. Repeating the sentiment in Russian seemed to help. It sounded more official that way.

Finally, Voronova stepped from the vehicle and walked quickly to the back. In the trunk next to the bolt cutters she wouldn't be needing were a mop and cleaning supplies. Not sexy, but that was the point. Laborers tended to be invisible to people who lived in these kinds of neighborhoods.

She used her phone to open Alton's garage door and walked casually inside before closing it again. There was no evidence that he had an alarm system and there was no keypad near the unlocked door leading to the mudroom.

After stashing her cleaning supplies in a cabinet, she penetrated deeper into the house. The living room looked even less used than the granite, mahogany, and stainless steel kitchen. She peeked in the pantry and fridge, then conducted a quick sweep of the entire house. One of the bedrooms had been converted to an office and there was a MacBook Pro sitting on the desk. She turned it on and was faced with a login screen.

In all likelihood it wouldn't be 123456, so she connected her phone to one of the ports and started an app designed to clone the hard drive. While it ran, she went through what documents she could find, but there weren't many. Alton appeared to be a man who organized his life in electronic pulses and not dead trees.

With nothing else to do, she went to the master

bedroom for a more thorough search. Besides the office, it was the most lived-in place in the house but still there wasn't much of interest. An improbably tall stack of science-oriented magazines by the bedside, a modest amount of cash tucked away in his underwear drawer. A huge TV with an Xbox.

What stood out wasn't what the house contained, it was what it lacked: the equipment and supplies necessary for survival. Where were the guns and power backups? Where was the water and freeze-dried food? If he did this thing, it wasn't just going to be other people freezing their asses off in the dark. It was going to be him, too.

The drive cloning software was at seventy-nine percent when an unmistakable sound floated up from the first floor. The front door opening.

She dropped to her knees and crawled back into the office, snatching her phone from the laptop. Who was it? A real maid? Had Alton forgotten something and come back? Did he have an alarm system she didn't know about?

She slithered on her stomach back out onto the landing. Through the railing, she caught a glimpse of Alton looking carefully around the living room. His body language answered her question. She'd missed an alarm. But if that was the case, what kind? Had it been on the door? Were there motion detectors? Cameras?

After a moment of indecision, she crawled back to the master bedroom and pulled the stack of magazines off the nightstand, carefully arranging them on the floor as though they'd fallen. An earlier search beneath his bed had turned up a loose arrangement of the same kind of junk that migrated under everyone's bed. She dug some of it out as the footsteps downstairs went silent. Either he'd moved out of earshot or he was coming up the carpeted stairs.

Voronova slipped beneath the bed and surrounded herself with Alton's disused possessions. If the house had sensors on the doors, he might just chalk an alarm notification up to a malfunction. If it was motion detectors, the magazines might fool him. If it was cameras, she was screwed.

Another minute passed before he entered the room—just long enough for her to find and close her hand around something hard. She wasn't sure what it was, but it was the only thing that felt even remotely like a weapon. She forced herself to stay motionless as he knelt next to the bed, trying not to think about the fact that she was probably holding the handle of a feather duster.

There was a shuffling of papers as he gathered the magazines off the floor. The breath was trapped in her chest as she strained to hear his movements. Finally, muffled footsteps. Receding.

His gait had lost some of its earlier uncertainty.

And not a moment too soon. She was getting light-headed. The air flowed quietly from her lungs and she inhaled cautiously as his feet hit wood. A few seconds later, a door closed. She pushed a neatly folded sweatshirt away from her ear and once again strained to hear. After a few seconds, the sound of a well-tuned engine became audible and then faded away.

Voronova glanced at the glowing hand of her watch and then let the side of her face sink into the carpet. She'd stay put for an hour. If he got another notification, hopefully he'd assume it was another false alarm. And even if he didn't, his office was a good forty minutes away with traffic. She'd have plenty of time to retrieve her mop and get the hell out of there.

Right?

CHAPTER 17

West of Manassas
Virginia
USA

"It says beans," Anna reported. "That's about a hundred boxes of them at least! You must really like beans. They're gross."

"I like lamb," Rapp replied.

"I told you, my sheep are pets! You can't eat them! And Snowpuff loves you! That's why she follows you around and gets sad when you go on trips and stuff."

"Write it down," Rapp said, punching his code into a closet containing weapons. "We need a good inventory of what we've got and what we still need."

The safe room they were in was the most secure place in a house that he'd designed entirely around security. The fact that the structure was elegantly postmodern and decorated in the always popular price-is-no-object style was entirely the doing of the architects, designers, and women in his life. All he cared about was reinforced concrete walls, blast-proof glass, and self-sufficiency.

He had electrical generation from both solar and

wind, a subbasement full of Tesla batteries, and diesel generators fed by a massive underground tank. Water was courtesy of a well that would be virtually impossible to tamper with. Air in the safe room was filtered against all known toxic agents.

The remote mountaintop subdivision had initially been owned by his brother, who had eventually given all the lots away to people loyal to Rapp. So now he wasn't just surrounded by concrete and steel, but by shooters he trusted.

"Another box of beans," Anna said. Boredom was starting to overcome the disgust in her voice.

"You know the drill," Rapp said. "Mark it and move it."

"Why don't we go look at our presents under the tree and try to guess what they are instead."

"Why don't you just wait a few days until you can open them? Then you'll know for sure."

"But this is boring and we've been down here *forever*."

"It's been fifteen minutes."

She groaned dramatically and began pushing the box across the floor.

The problem he was in the process of correcting was that he'd recently modified the space to handle a biological attack by Sayid Halabi. But with the man's corpse now rotting in the Somali desert, some of the changes were counterproductive. Everything needed to be retooled with a long-term grid failure in mind.

A woman's voice drifted down to them. "Anna! Are you in there?"

The question came in Claudia Gould's native French but Anna's answer was in English. It had become a battle of wills between her and her mother.

"I'm helping Mitch!"

Claudia appeared in the steel threshold a moment later wearing formfitting jeans and a silk blouse that clung in just the right places. Her brown hair was pulled back in a ponytail, revealing flawless skin and dark, almond-shaped eyes. In many ways, she seemed the perfect opposite of Rapp. His face was lined from too many years under the Middle Eastern sun, his hair and beard existed at the very edge of control, and he owned a total of three pairs of nontactical pants. The relationship was working, though. And not just for him. Her takeover of logistics for Scott Coleman's company had gone even better than expected. Coleman could now focus entirely on operations and his profits were up thirty percent.

"You promised you'd get the barn ready," Claudia said, sticking to French. "The meeting is in two hours and there are animals everywhere."

"But Mitch needs me!"

"He can manage on his own. Now go."

"You're always bossing me around!" she said, displaying a temper that would soon be hard to deal with.

He watched her stomp off, and felt the now-familiar twinge of fear when he thought about how reliant he was on the two of them. He'd finally managed to fill the emptiness of his life, but at the price of constant worry. As ulcer-inducing as it was, though, it was an improvement. And not a small one, either.

"Is all this rearranging really necessary, Mitch? I think the only thing we're not prepared for is an alien invasion."

He shook his head. "I've got a roof mount for the minigun. We can handle aliens."

She smiled and took a seat on a box. "Well, I never have to worry about being unprepared, that's for certain."

"No, you definitely aren't going to have anything to worry about."

She picked up on his tone and her smile faded. "What does that mean?"

"It means you and Anna are going to your house in Cape Town. I got you first-class tickets for after Christmas."

"Why? Wait. Don't tell me. Because there's a threat to America, right? There's *always* a threat, Mitch. We didn't leave when Sayid Halabi was trying to wipe out half the world's population with a coronavirus. Why would we leave now?"

When Rapp's wife died, his life had transformed into a simple one of barking orders and having those orders followed to the letter. He had to constantly remind himself that it was different at home. Explanations and compromise were how things got done.

"Because this is different, Claudia. That threat wasn't specific to the US and you were running logistics for our entire operation."

"Look, I understand the ramifications of a countrywide grid failure, but if this house is built for anything, it's built for that."

"Maybe. But why would I put you and Anna through something like that for no reason? You could be holed up here for the better part of a year. And when you're finally able to leave, there won't be much of America left. You have a house in South Africa and they aren't all that heavily linked to the US politically or economically. They'll still take a big hit—the whole world will—but it'll be less than a lot of other places."

"What if you need my help?"

"Then I'm better off with you there. What can you do for me from Virginia? No Internet. No way to move around. Communications down nationwide. You'd actually have *more* capabilities from Cape Town."

She didn't respond, instead staring straight ahead. Beneath her warmth and humor was a core of calculation. It was what made her so good at her job. And it was what would eventually force her to admit that he was right.

• • •

Weightless flakes of snow swirled around Rapp as he walked down the empty street. The barn that was his destination served the entire subdivision and his initial plan had been to turn it into a gym. Unfortunately, by the time he was ready to start work, the space was overrun by Anna's collection of farm animals. She had Scott Coleman wrapped around her little finger and the herd seemed to grow under the cover of darkness or when Rapp was out of the country.

He'd been about to put a stop to it but was now reconsidering. While an elaborate gym would be a nice thing to have, livestock had an undeniable upside. While he wasn't as opposed to rehydrated beans as Anna, he also wasn't opposed to lamb chops and chicken wings.

When he entered the barn, the space was in surprisingly good shape. It had been largely cleared of animals and a bunch of folding chairs had been set up. They were occupied by his neighbors—mostly former military, FBI, and CIA. Some were getting a little long in the tooth, but not one had ever let him down when he needed them.

"Thanks for coming," Rapp said, taking a position in front of the group. "I know it's cold so I'm going to make this as quick as I can."

Anna was at the back of the barn with her shoulder in the last sheep's side. It seemed reluctant to go out into the wind, but she finally persuaded it. When the door closed behind her, Rapp continued.

"First of all, nothing I say here gets repeated outside these walls, understood?"

There were general nods, but none were really necessary. Every one of them had proven their ability to keep their mouth shut years ago.

"Some of you might have already heard this, but there's a credible threat to the electrical grid. We've picked up chatter from a terrorist group that may be capable of taking down the entire country and, worse, keep it down."

Mike Nash's wife was the first to speak. "When you say 'keep it down' what kind of time frame are you talking about?"

"As much as a year."

That got some quiet murmurs as everyone looked at each other.

"We're doing what we can to track down the people involved and harden the grid, but both are easier said than done. So, while we can hope for the best, we need to plan for the worst."

That got a few more nods, but expressions weren't exactly confident. A year was a long time and the ramifications of an attack like this weren't easy to wrap your mind around.

"What are you suggesting we do?" Maggie Nash said, speaking up again. "I mean, we've got four kids."

"Well, we're already set up pretty well here. Everyone has separate power generation and storage, well water, and weapons. But that's just a start. First, you're going to want to recalibrate your investments—move them around the world and focus them on gold, businesses that don't operate in the US, and maybe even companies that are in the disaster relief business. For those of you who can, I'd suggest an extended foreign trip. If that's not viable, then you're going to have to lay in a significant amount of food." He pointed to the front row. "Use Claudia as a resource. You're going to have to order things from various places, use multiple shipping methods, and have it sent to different addresses. If you go to a physical store, pay cash. Because if this happens, people are going to get desperate fast. You don't want someone at Sam's Club or UPS or Cabela's remembering you."

"What about our families?" Skip McMahon said. He was a retired FBI agent with family spread across the United States.

"Again, nothing I'm saying can leave these walls. If you want to bring your family here, you need to make a plan as to how to accomplish that. Keep in mind that the first few days won't be that bad. Everyone's lived through blackouts and they're going to equate what's happening with that. Again, Claudia will be happy to help. But it's not going to be easy. Communications are going to be one of the first things to go down and driving long distances is going to be a problem for a number of reasons—particularly if you have to go through or get out of cities."

McMahon nodded, staring at the ground and thinking the same thing everyone else was. That his life didn't exist just on top of that mountain. He had friends he'd known for years. An extended family spread throughout the country. All of whom would be trapped in the dark.

"If this happens, we're going to have to treat this subdivision as a fortress. Blackout protocols will go into effect immediately. Any visible light is going to stand out and after about a week or so people are going to want to know what's generating it. I know we all have weapons, but the last thing we want to do is put ourselves in a position that we have to use them." Rapp paused for a moment and looked out over the worried faces of his neighbors. "There's no way to sugarcoat this. In a scenario like this, a lot of people aren't going to make it. And some of those people are going to be close to us."

CHAPTER 18

Near Luray
Virginia
USA

It was just after 10 p.m. and John Alton had been driving a mix of freeways, rural highways, and residential neighborhoods for hours. He'd seen nothing, but that didn't prove much. The government no longer communicated over open radio frequencies and they sure as hell didn't tail people in late-model sedans. This was the era of satellites, GPS trackers, and secure cell phones.

His nerves were stretched to the breaking point, but there was really no reason for it. Why would the CIA or any other government agency be watching him? He'd just spent six hours responding to every question Irene Kennedy had about the grid. And while he hadn't always answered fully, he'd answered truthfully. There was absolutely no reason for anyone to suspect him. In fact, the opposite was true. To anyone paying attention, he'd look like the poster child for grid security.

So, he was safe. That was the good news. The bad news was that his meticulously planned timetable was fucked. That CIA bitch had an almost supernatural ability to ask the right questions. He'd been forced to provide her with enough actionable information that she could actually throw a wrench into his machine. Time, which had been on his side only a few days ago, was now his mortal enemy. Not only had they already started physically securing America's critical power infrastructure; they were talking about doing a deep dive into major power company mainframes. How long would it be before they uncovered the malware he'd put on those servers? The list of people with sufficient access and expertise to do something like this was pretty short. And he was at the top of it.

Alton turned onto a narrow street that climbed steeply to the north, taking him into clouds that were spitting a mix of rain and snow. The outside temperature was hanging in at thirty-three degrees—a number that darkened his mood even further.

Most people believed that a power failure during winter would be a worst-case scenario. That was just their gut talking, though. Millions of years after descending from the trees, his species's fear of cold and darkness persisted.

In truth, an attack on the grid would be far more effective during the hottest part of summer. That's when air conditioners were pushing the grid to its limit. That's when fires from overloaded transformers and sagging power lines would run out of control. And while it was possible to wear more clothes to combat frigid temperatures, there was very little that could be done in the face of unbearable heat.

Even more infuriating to him was winter's dampening effect on civil unrest. During the summer, nighttime streets would be filled with angry, frightened, and hungry people too hot to sleep. The freezing rain currently splattering his windshield would keep all but the most desperate people huddled inside.

Of course, as the darkness stretched into weeks and months, it wouldn't matter. But instead of dying in an explosion of fire and violence, America would just fade away in a rising tide of starvation, thirst, and disease. Boring, but he didn't really have much choice at this point. He couldn't give the government time to put defensive measures in place and, even more important, he couldn't give them time to discover his involvement.

The unpaved road he was looking for appeared in the haze of his headlights and he turned onto it. After another hundred yards, he spotted the agreed-upon pullout and coasted to a stop. A moment later, the SUV's doors opened and three men got in.

It was two more than he'd initially planned on, but again he hadn't had much of a choice. Irene Kennedy was hard to get a bead on. She worked really hard to exude bland competence, but there was more going on behind those eyes than she let on. In the unlikely event that he'd made a mistake at any time over the five years he'd spent planning this thing, she was going to find it. And if that happened, it wouldn't hurt to have a little muscle on his side.

"Do any of you have communications devices?" he asked as he pulled back out onto the road. The man in the passenger seat was Feisal Ibrahim, the tech expert he'd met before. The one who had helped him dispose of his former boss's body.

"You told us not to carry any."

"So, no phones. No smart watches. No radios. Nothing that has an electrical charge or battery."

"I said no."

Alton made a U-turn and glanced in the rearview mirror at the shadowy faces behind him. As expected, they looked dangerous. Which was a good thing as long as they could be controlled. Or gotten rid of, if it became necessary. In the end, they represented yet another unpredictable element in a plan that a few weeks ago had been a Swiss watch.

"Why are we here?" Ibrahim said.

"Because you fucked everything up so bad that I can't fix it alone."

"Meaning what?"

"First, we have to move the timetable forward."

"I thought you said that summer would be—"

"That was before we had Homeland Security

breathing down our necks. In fact, I just had a meeting with the bastard who killed your people at the Sunset Motel."

"What?"

"That's right. They called me in to talk to them about the grid."

"But they don't suspect you," the man said, his voice turning sharp enough that the men in back perked up.

"Not yet. But it's only a matter of time. So, we need to get this thing done now. And that isn't just a matter of blowing up a few random substations and tapping a few commands into a keyboard. In order for it to have full impact, the attack has to be managed over the long term. The government's going to do everything they can to get the power back online and I can block those efforts. But not if I'm dead. Do you understand?"

"That you be protected at all cost?" Ibrahim said with a hint of unhidden distaste. "Yes, I understand."

In truth, the need to manage this thing after the initial attack was almost nonexistent. But Alton needed these assholes motivated in case the man from the motel showed up on his doorstop. While it might be true that they wanted nothing more than to die for Allah, his plans were different.

"I knew you were a smart guy," Alton said. "We're in the homestretch, Feisal. This is it. You are on the verge of doing something no one's ever come even close to—destroying America. If you follow my orders to the letter, this is going to happen. Do you understand?"

"Yes."

Alton thumbed at the men in the back seat.

"Do they speak English?"

"Only a little."

"Then tell them what we just talked about."

Ibrahim turned in his seat and started speaking to his men in Arabic. Alton hated not understanding what they said but, once again, there was nothing he could do about it. He was starting to feel like a man floating in the ocean getting pummeled by waves. It was an uncomfortable position for someone used to things being the other way around. His nature was to be the wave, not the man.

When Ibrahim finished talking, Alton reached between the seats and retrieved three hoods. Really just black pillowcases he'd bought from Amazon, but functional nonetheless.

"Put these on."

"Why?"

"Because I don't want you to know where we're going. If I have to send you out on a mission and you get caught, I don't want you leading the government back to our base of operations."

Ibrahim stared down at the dark cloth for a moment and then put it on, ordering his men to do the same.

• • •

After three hours of driving at random, Alton finally pulled onto the mud and gravel road that had always been his destination. The men in the car with him were still reclined and wearing their hoods, making it impossible for them to pinpoint their location or even be certain as to what state they were in.

"Don't move," he ordered as he pulled up to a dilapidated gate and stepped out. "I'll be right back."

The cold penetrated his sweatshirt like it wasn't there, but he ignored it. The time had finally come. The planning, the worry, the hesitation . . . It was all over. This was really happening.

Numbness was already taking hold in his fingers as he slid a key into a rusted lock and released the gate. Once the SUV was through, he relocked it and continued on, leaving nothing but a faint set of tire tracks.

When they reached the clearing five minutes later, the darkness was profound. Alton's headlights swept over the burned ruins of a farmhouse before revealing the vague outline of a barn seventy-five yards to the northeast. Its weathered doors opened at the touch of a remote and he pulled in.

The cavernous space was strewn with rusting agricultural equipment and dominated by an old military truck that looked like it had been abandoned there for decades. He pulled in behind it and shut off his engine. The lights would stay on for another minute or so, which would be just enough.

"Everyone out. But keep the hoods on."

He had them link arms before leading them out into the rain. A penlight kept him on course, but it still took longer than expected to reach the burned house and pick through its blackened remains.

He'd bought the property four years ago, using a series of shell corporations and foreign partnerships to hide his identity. The remoteness of the hundred-acre lot had been the thing that first attracted him, but it was the house that sealed the deal. Or, to be more precise, the extensive Cold War bomb shelter that had been built beneath it.

After reducing the building to cinders with a carefully orchestrated electrical fire, he'd called in several out-of-town contractors to reinforce the shelter's walls and rough in modern plumbing and wiring. The pretense was that he planned on rebuilding a new house on top of it and would eventually use the shelter as a basement.

At the same time, he'd had an apartment built above the barn—a modest weekend getaway spot until he could get the main house rebuilt. Nothing that would stick in the feeble minds of the construction people who'd participated.

The rest of the work had been substantial, but he'd done it himself. The shelter now boasted off-grid power, state-of-the-art communications equipment, and enough food and booze to last two full years without rationing. Not that he expected to need it. He'd spent months devising a plan to get him across the border to his mansion in Mexico after the show was over. Specialized vehicles, fuel caches, alternate routes . . . It'd be fun. Like Mad Max, except without the weirdos with Mohawks. They'd all be dead.

Despite being the one who'd installed it, finding the bunker's entrance took Alton another couple of minutes. Finally, he located the hidden latch that freed a collapsed wall designed to be light enough to lift. Beneath it was the original steel hatch.

Once the hooded men were down the ladder, he resealed the hatch and turned on the lights.

"You can take them off now."

They complied and he spread his arms wide. "Welcome home."

The narrow passage was made of concrete, but painted white over a floor covered with plush carpet. The shelter was laid out roughly in the shape of a capital *I* and he pointed to the southern end.

"Storage on that side. Mostly food, some emergency equipment, and batteries. Water comes in from a well."

"Weapons?" Ibrahim asked.

Alton nodded. "An assault rifle and pistol, among other things. Plenty of ammo. But we won't need it. More important for you is that I put some mattresses and blankets back there. With a little TLC, it should make a pretty decent barracks. Only one bathroom, though. We'll have to make do."

He pointed to the other end of the space. "My living quarters and the command center are over there. And that's it. Not particularly complicated."

One of the men spoke in Arabic and Ibrahim translated. "They would like to examine the weapons."

Of course they would.

Alton shrugged. "Whatever."

"And I would like to see your command center."

Alton motioned for the man to follow as he started along the corridor. They passed through a steel door at the far end that opened onto a room about ten feet square. Along one wall was a desk arranged with computer and communications equipment. Above it hung numerous monitors and when Alton hit the main power switch, everything came to life.

He took a seat in a high-backed leather chair and spun it toward Ibrahim as national newsfeeds appeared on the monitors.

"I need the exact locations of your other nine men as well as detailed information on their backgrounds and training."

"Of course."

Alton tapped a few commands into his computer and the newsfeeds were replaced with maps of the United States, each covered with hundreds of red dots in various sizes.

"These are all the critical physical targets. With only nine guys, they're going to have to work individually. Basically, knock one out and move on to another until someone puts a bullet in them. Once you give me their information, I'll work out an attack protocol for each of them."

"Understood."

"Then don't just stand there. Get on it."

Ibrahim disappeared through the door, leaving Alton to contemplate the maps around him. Nine men. And now a good half of them would likely have to be immediately sacrificed. While it would be easy to have them avoid the sites he'd told the government about, it'd be too obvious. That suspicious bitch Irene Kennedy would figure out he was behind it in about two seconds.

Not that there would be much she could do with the information. But it didn't pay to take chances. The last thing he needed was that freak from the motel showing up on his doorstep.

CHAPTER 19

Outside of Asheville
North Carolina
USA

The mountains surrounding Rapp reminded him of home. The only difference was that instead of lying on his sofa by the fireplace, he was sitting on the frozen ground getting snowed on. Not the best Christmas morning he'd ever had. Though, sadly, also not the worst.

His winter camo jumpsuit was made from Gore-Tex with a synthetic down underlayer that maintained his body heat reasonably well. Snow tended to collect on the hood, shoulders, and thighs, but it added to both the insulation and camouflage, so he left it alone.

It was times like these that he felt the years he'd spent in this business. When he was fighting in the heat of the Middle East, his body didn't function that much differently than it had fifteen years ago. But the cold and boredom of this kind of operation made him remember every wound, every aging joint, and every regret. Dead friends and enemies seemed to hover just out of sight in the woods, waiting for him to join them. And one way or another, it wouldn't be long.

He blinked hard, clearing the ice from his eyelashes and shifting his gaze right. About fifteen yards away, snow hung from the chain link fence surrounding an electrical substation that had been deemed the most strategic in America. Why something that important would be perched on the side of a mountain in North Carolina was beyond him, but that wasn't surprising. His knowledge of electricity was limited to keeping his solar panels running and changing lightbulbs.

Scott Coleman's men were spread out across the country guarding other critical points on the grid. Between them, local law enforcement, and various private contractors, they'd already managed to secure forty-three sites. Over the next week, that number would rise to ninety. And by the end of the month, they'd have a sustainable program in place to cover more than three hundred.

He turned his attention back to the forest, scanning the trees through a snowstorm predicted to reach full force around 3 a.m. The clouds were low and dense enough to reflect the distant glow of Asheville, making night vision gear unnecessary. So, while he didn't have much to look at, at least he didn't have to do it through fogged lenses.

Rapp closed his eyes and let his ears take over, listening to the light wind and the occasional muffled thump of snow dumping from laden branches—trying in vain to pick out something that suggested another human presence.

He let himself drift, devising a plan to trade Scott Coleman for the sunny substation he was watching outside of Dallas. It would serve him right for suggesting Anna ask Santa for a llama.

Rapp was snapped from his stupor by something that sounded like nylon rubbing a tree branch. Too vague to prompt him to open his eyes, but well defined enough for him to turn his head to hear better. Probably another ten seconds passed before the muffled crack of a branch reached him. Still a ways off. He continued to focus on his sense of hearing, not opening his eyes until he heard a crunching of snow that had the unmistakable rhythm of bipedal motion.

He opened his eyes, slowly sweeping them through his full field of vision. Nothing but trees and falling snow.

Another quiet crunch sounded to his left, but the angle was such that Rapp's hood blocked his view. Unwilling to move, he had no choice but to wait.

A couple more minutes passed before an outline appeared in his peripheral vision. A man wearing a poncho that covered a sizable backpack. He had a rifle slung over one shoulder, but visibility wasn't good enough to pick out the model. What Rapp could see, though, was the large silencer attached to the barrel.

It was a critical piece of information that made it possible to predict the man's trajectory as he disappeared behind a dense section of trees. According to the information he'd been given, the substation could be taken off-line in two ways. The first and most obvious was explosives. That method wouldn't take a lot of expertise on the attacker's part, but it would force him to pass through the padlocked gate in order to set the charges.

The second method relied only on a rifle. It would require more detailed knowledge of the substation's design but would attract a lot less attention. The optimal vantage point for that kind of an attack would be a patch of high ground to the east of the gate. For obvious reasons, Rapp had positioned himself right between those two tactically critical locations.

He tipped slowly to the right and began slipping along the snowy ground on an intercept course. It would have been a hell of a lot easier to just charge and get off a quick head shot, but that plan had problems. First, he might blow the brains out of some local using the cover of the storm to do a little poaching. Second, people with bullets in their skulls tended to be hard to interrogate.

When he'd arrived at the substation two days ago, Rapp hadn't just reconned the spot he was slithering toward, he'd modified it. Thanks to him, there was now an extremely obvious place for a sniper to set up—a log at just the right height to use as a gun rest with a clear view to the substation's critical equipment. He'd even dug in a comfortable place to kneel.

More important was the fact that he'd excavated an indention beneath the log about six feet long by a foot deep. The side facing the substation was still open, but he'd packed a thin layer of snow on the other side to hide it from anyone settling into the obvious shooting position.

Rapp made it to the edge of the clearing, slipping through a shallow ditch and rolling under the gap beneath the log. Now it was just a matter of waiting and hoping to hell he'd made his trap too inviting to pass up.

The man took his sweet time, but the sound of approaching footsteps finally became audible again. Another thirty seconds passed before Rapp heard him kneel to remove his poncho and pack. The quiet rustling continued for maybe another minute before the barrel of a rifle extended out over the log.

The idea was to give himself as much of an advantage as possible. ISIS's remaining core fanatics were tough, disciplined, and well trained. Further, the stitches in his side weren't going to hold up to rolling around in the snow and throwing punches through insulated gloves.

So quick and easy was the order of the day.

He shoved a hand through the snow and grabbed hold of the man's legs, using the log as leverage to yank him beneath it. For once, everything worked exactly as envisioned. The gun barrel went straight up and a single silenced shot pierced the cloud layer. Rapp continued to pull, wedging the man's torso between the ground and the fallen tree. His hands were still free and he still had hold of the rifle, but it was too unwieldy to be of much use in a close-quarters fight. He didn't even have enough range of motion to use it as a club.

Rapp, on the other hand, had chosen a more agile weapon. He threw himself over the log and swung the butt of his Glock down on the man's forehead. It should have knocked him cold, but his thick wool hat absorbed a surprising amount of the impact. Rapp was lining up for another blow when his opponent shoved against the log hard enough to slide out from beneath it. He rolled onto his stomach and managed to get to his knees but was too dazed to stand on the slippery surface.

Rapp leapt onto the man's back, snaking an arm around his neck and applying enough pressure to cut off the blood flow to his brain.

He thrashed impressively, but there was no way to escape. His strength was just starting to fade when everything went black. The change was so abrupt and the darkness so deep that Rapp thought for a moment someone had hit him from behind—that he was losing consciousness.

But he could still feel the cold and the strength in his arms. He could still hear the crunch of the snow beneath them and the man slowly losing his ability to fight. Rapp turned his head and saw that the distant glow of Ashville had disappeared. But not just that. *Everything* had disappeared.

The man beneath him went still for a moment and then started to convulse. At first Rapp thought he might be having a seizure. But that wasn't the case.

He was laughing.

CHAPTER 20

Northern Virginia
USA

John Alton turned off his Porsche and killed the headlights. He'd chosen this place after endless hours exploring the less traveled roads that sprawled around Washington, DC. The lonely hillside was accessible only by a dirt service road and provided an unobstructed view of the metro area. Ten yards to his left, a series of transmission lines hung too close to a stand of trees, carrying the current that kept America's seat of power alive.

After discovering this place almost two years ago, he'd bought a comfortable beach chair, a fancy cooler, and a twelve-hundred-dollar bottle of Krug champagne. The plan had been for a sweltering night under the stars. Flip-flops, a pair of Bermuda shorts, and a fountain of icy champagne flowing into his glass. He'd even bought a special machete designed to cut the top off the bottle. Why? Why not? It wasn't every day you collapsed the world order.

Infuriatingly, the reality that had been forced on him was very different. Instead of ninety degrees and a sky full of stars, he had thirty-five degrees and rain. And the carpet of twinkling lights that should have been spread out in front of him was more of a muted glow with no obvious source.

Despite being huddled in his vehicle instead of sprawled in a lounger, the sense of power remained. As did the reality of what he was about to do. Of what he was about to accomplish. The Nazis and Japanese had attacked ships in American waters. The Soviets had blustered ineffectually about nuclear annihilation. The Muslims had knocked down a few buildings. But in the end, it would be him.

No more backyard barbecues and debates about who would get more balls across lines and into nets. No more women who thought their kids were geniuses because they'd learned not to shit in their pants. No more people filling the streets to protest whatever idiocy the media was flogging that week. No more politicians sitting in safe, warm offices telling lies and getting their asses kissed. America was about to come face-to-face with reality. Something they'd lost touch with seventy-five years ago.

He stared through the rain-spotted windshield, studying the haze of light to the east. The sense of excitement and anticipation didn't flow just from the sensation of absolute power. Uncertainty also played a part. With an act this grand, what would be the unintended consequences? How great would the impact on the rest of the world be? Could the Chinese feed themselves without US food imports and the ability to sell cheap crap to the American people? Would countries like Russia, North Korea, and Iran become aggressive in a world undefended by American might? Would the alliances of Western Europe crumble?

And what about closer to home? Why wouldn't a foreign power in search of resources move into a defenseless and increasingly uninhabited United States? He grinned at the thought of Mexican tanks rolling across Texas while the last few surviving hicks cowered and begged.

Por favor, señor! I will give you my daughter for a can of refried beans!

He grinned at the image and checked his watch for what must have been the hundredth time that day. Only a few minutes more. The malware he'd uploaded to America's power companies was set to execute at 3 a.m. Zero Hour.

The rain stopped and he stepped out into the cold, enjoying the last glimpse of an America that would likely never exist again. A moment later, he heard a hum starting in the transmission lines above. No need to look at his watch again. Ever.

It had begun.

Across the entire grid, his malware was rerouting power, overloading systems, deactivating circuit breakers, and overriding fail-safes. False data would be flooding operators throughout the country, hiding real damage, reporting phantom attacks, and even tricking them into using what control they had left to make the situation worse.

He turned and squinted through the semi-darkness at the power lines beginning to dip toward the trees beneath them. As the load rose above the level they were capable of handling, the heat caused them to expand. In the dead of summer, the effect would be complete devastation. Wires would sag, touching tinder-dry foliage that hadn't been properly maintained and igniting thousands of fires just when the country lost its capacity to fight them.

The fact that much of the East Coast was blanketed by a winter storm would significantly mitigate the damage in the region but would do nothing to protect the South and West. There, the flames would already be spreading.

He watched, fascinated, as the lines continued to sag, finally coming into contact with the upper branches of a tree. Sparks showered the wet ground but, disappointingly, flames struggled to take hold.

The expansive glow coming from the east began to falter and finally went completely dark. The vast majority of people were asleep at this hour, completely unaware of what was happening. Blissfully ignorant that they would awake to a world transformed.

Merry Christmas, America.

CHAPTER 21

Southwest of Wytheville
Virginia
USA

The pickup's headlights washed over yet another vehicle that had slid from the road but there wasn't anyone inside. Despite sunrise still being an hour away, the temperature had already climbed to just above freezing. The mix of snow and ice that covered everything was getting wet, turning the asphalt into a skating rink.

Rapp had prepared for that—and pretty much every—eventuality. The oversized tires he was riding on were studded and he had a fifty-gallon auxiliary tank in the bed along with enough food and survival gear to last a couple of weeks.

He accelerated to just under forty miles an hour, listening to the hum of the wipers as they struggled to keep his windshield clear. The last radio station he could find had died a few minutes ago and he hit the scanner again. After running through the dial a few times, it stopped on the static-ridden voice of a man speculating about the scope of the blackout. With the normal sources of information down, there wasn't much else he could do.

Rapp's phone was in a mount on the dash and he reached out to try Irene Kennedy again. There was no cell signal, but the phone had the ability to connect to dedicated Homeland Security satellites. It dialed, but immediately returned the now-familiar message that the system was overloaded. Try again later.

The Agency would be working to disconnect all noncritical personnel, but that would take a while. Preparations for this scenario were still very much in the planning stages. As far as he knew, the government hadn't gotten much further than fighting over the wording of the public service announcements that were supposed to have been urging people to stock up on a few emergency supplies.

Whoever this PowerStation was, he'd once again proved that he wasn't stupid. After what had happened at the motel, he'd known the government was onto him. Pulling the trigger now destroyed many of the investigative tools authorities could bring to bear and would force the government to divert resources to disaster relief.

Whether those relief efforts would make any difference remained to be seen. Outside the arc of his headlights existed a level of darkness that Rapp had experienced many times before. In Yemen. In Somalia. In the Iraqi desert. But never in America. If the rest of the country was like this and the damage was anywhere close to what the eggheads had outlined as a worst-case scenario . . . Then what?

The timer on his phone sounded an alarm and he eased carefully to the side of the road. The sleet was being whipped around by the wind with enough force that he had to squint as he walked around and opened the truck's gate. He grabbed hold of a rolled tarp secured with duct tape and immediately felt it begin to squirm.

"No!" came Rashad Asfour's muffled voice as Rapp dragged him to the ground. He'd learned the man's name during their last little chat, as well as a number of other interesting tidbits. Muhammad Nahas was dead but Asfour didn't know how or why. All he knew was that his communications were now coming from someone called Ibrahim. After that last revelation, he'd clammed up.

"Stop!" the man managed to get out as Rapp dragged him, naked inside the tarp, toward the pickup's cab.

The terrorist was in the process of learning something that Rapp had experienced a number of times in both training and the real world. It wasn't the cold that got you. It was the warmth. Freezing to death wasn't as bad as most people imagined. But thawing out sucked. At first, there was enough pain that you actually wanted to go back out in the cold. But then the heat began sinking into you—first your chest but then working its way outward. After a while it started feeling like a combination of your first love and Christmas morning. That sensation became your entire universe. Giving it up or, far worse, repeating the freeze/thaw process became unthinkable.

Rapp opened the back door and wrestled the man into it, trying not to strain his still injured side. It took longer than planned, but finally Asfour was lying across the rear seats. He writhed in despair as Rapp pulled the tarp back from his face and then slammed the door behind him. Less than a minute later, they were back on the road.

"How are you doing, Rashad? Can I turn the heat up a little for you?"

They drove in silence while the man pushed through the initial pain to become intoxicated by the miracle that was electric heat. Finally, Rapp spoke.

"How many more people like you are out there?"

There was a pause long enough for Rapp to wonder if the man was unconscious or even dead, but finally a feeble voice rose above the ambient noise.

"I don't know. Why would they tell me?"

It was likely the truth. Compartmentalization was as critical to ISIS as it was the CIA. The question had been intended as a softball to get the man talking.

"Then tell me about PowerStation."

"What?" he said, the confusion in his voice sounding genuine. "You stopped me . . . You stopped me from destroying the power station."

Again, his response was completely credible. Asfour was obviously a foot soldier—a man you sent to die, not one you told your plans to. But there was something he had that Rapp wanted. No hurry, though. It would take at least another seven hours to get to Langley.

He connected his phone to the truck's Bluetooth and selected a classic country mix. "You like Patsy Cline?" he asked as the strains of "I Fall to Pieces" filled the cab.

No answer.

"I'll take that as a yes."

They drove like that for another twenty minutes. Johnny Cash had just started lamenting his time in Folsom Prison when an incoming call muted him. Rapp shot a hand out and picked up. "Yeah. Go ahead, can you hear me?"

"Mitch?" Claudia's voice. "You're cutting out. Can you—"

"Hang on." He put in an earpiece and connected it. "Is that better?"

"Yes, I can hear you now. Are you all right?"

"Fine. You?"

"Yes, but it doesn't look like we're going to make it to Cape Town."

Rapp swore under his breath. She and Anna

were booked on a flight going out in a couple of days.

"Tell me where you are, Mitch. We're having a lot of problems with communications and I'm probably going to lose you."

"On the road somewhere around Wytheville, Virginia, on my way to Langley."

"Don't go to Langley," she said. "Irene and her team are relocating to the Seneca bunker."

He let out a long breath, but didn't immediately respond. The government had various doomsday bunkers around the country—some dating back to the Cold War. The Seneca facility was the newest and largest, built to replace Mount Weather.

"It's that bad?" Rapp said finally.

"I'm afraid so. Hold on. Let me see if I can . . ." Her voice faded for a moment. "There. On your phone's screen. Can you see it? It's a view of America from a NASA satellite."

An overhead of the country came up and he cocked his head to take it in. Most of the East was dark, but that wasn't surprising considering the cloud cover. The rest of the country looked a little better with widely scattered pockets of light.

"Could be worse," Rapp said. "Seems like there's enough power still on to work with. FEMA and the military can—"

"That's not power," Claudia interrupted. "Those are fires started by overloaded transformers and transmission lines."

Rapp nodded in the darkness of the cab. "What about the other infrastructure we were watching?"

"Our people stopped two attacks, but both saboteurs were killed. Beyond that, we don't know."

"What *do* you know?"

"That on top of whatever physical attacks were carried out, there was a massive cyberattack. Power companies—even minor ones—are either locked out of their systems or can't trust them. Because of that, we have no idea what infrastructure's been damaged and what infrastructure is still intact. It's possible that the entire US grid will have to be physically inspected."

"How long will that take?"

"Under ideal circumstances, a year. Under these circumstances maybe never. There isn't—"

The line went dead. Rapp waited for a few minutes to see if she could reconnect, but it didn't look like it was going to happen.

"We won."

Rashad Asfour's voice had gained a bit of strength. Whether that was because of what he'd gleaned from Rapp's side of the conversation or the pickup's heater was up for debate. Probably a little of both.

"Did you say something?" Rapp said, glancing in the rearview mirror.

"Sayid Halabi's dream has finally come true. Your people will die of cold and starvation.

Violence and terror. America's reign is over. And from its ashes a new caliphate will rise."

"Very poetic," Rapp said, seeing a potential path to getting what he wanted. Not the normal path, but this business was all about flexibility.

"You're right, Rashad. You *have* won. The power's out all across the country and there are fires burning everywhere. With no electricity, I don't see how we're going to put them out. And even if we could, more are going to start. The cities aren't in flames yet, but they will be. My people aren't used to using fire for heat and light and they'll have accidents. The people who stay in the cities will burn. The people who escape them will freeze."

"Why are you saying this?" Rashad said, understandably confused by Rapp's sudden resignation.

"Because it's the truth. And because I can still survive this."

"I don't understand."

Rapp opened the console next to him and pulled out the phone he'd found in Asfour's backpack.

"Let's make a deal," he said, holding up the device. "You give me your password and I'll let you die a martyr."

"No."

"Come on, Rashad. Allah's not going to care. You've done his bidding like no one before you. You've accomplished what Osama bin Laden and

Sayid Halabi never even got close to. America's done. We're in the dark and on fire. There's nothing on this phone that can save us. We both know that. But the government doesn't. And that means I can trade it to them for a place in one of their bunkers."

"No," he repeated.

There was a finality to his tone that Rapp recognized well. Asfour wasn't broken. Not yet.

He pulled to the side of the dark road and dragged the thrashing terrorist onto the wet asphalt again. Gravity fought against Rapp as he wrestled the man back into the bed of the truck, but when he finally slammed the gate closed, all his stitches were still intact. He leaned over the side, looking into Asfour's terrified eyes before covering his face again with the tarp.

"We'll talk again in an hour or so."

CHAPTER 22

Washington, DC
USA

Sonya Voronova awoke to silence.

The fan she used for white noise wasn't running and the comforting red numbers of her alarm clock had disappeared. She rolled over, looking toward the glass doors to the left of her bed. Despite opening onto a high-walled private courtyard, they usually filtered a significant amount of city light. Tonight, though, there was nothing but darkness.

She felt around for the phone charging on her nightstand, taking a few moments to locate it. Her mind didn't normally come fully online until after three cups of coffee, but at that moment she felt uncomfortably awake.

The clock on her cell said 5:12 a.m. More striking was that it had no Wi-Fi connection, no data, and only one bar. She slid out of bed and used the screen's glow to find her robe. The modest below-street-level flat was cheap to heat so she kept the thermostat set around seventy degrees. It felt noticeably colder than that now, suggesting the power had been out for at least a couple of hours.

No, no, no, no . . .

She sat at a small writing desk and began fiddling with one of the radios that she'd gotten off Amazon. It was quite a piece of survivalist gear for $39.56. Metal exterior, built-in flashlight, waterproof to ten feet. Power could come from batteries, solar, or a hand crank, and all critical bands were covered. The drawback was that all that complexity made it hard to figure out how to turn it on.

Finally, she stumbled on the right button and was rewarded with the crackle of static. She turned the dial until the hiss was driven back by an official-sounding voice.

With every word, she felt a little more of her strength drain away. Power was out all across the DC area, with reports of similar outages throughout the country and parts of Canada. The announcer recommended that people stay in their homes and travel only if absolutely necessary. He went on to provide some laughably banal advice about layering clothing and the use of woodstoves. Mostly, though, he just told his listeners to stand by. Government authorities and power companies were working on the problem.

He'd done it. And not only that, the creepy little psycho had done it on Christmas morning.

Voronova slipped on a pair of clogs and stepped into her courtyard. The space was no more than thirty feet square with high, windowless walls that were actually the backs of other houses. It was one of the main reasons she'd bought the place—a private and secure oasis in the middle of America's capital. Sure, it would have been nice to get a little more sun, but when one was a Russian mole, natural light got pushed down the priority list.

The cold helped hold back her nausea and clear her mind. But to what end? She'd bought a couple of radios and done a few Sam's Club runs since finding out about John Alton, but that was it. Procrastination, uncertainty, and a maxed-out credit card had prevented her from buying the solar panels, rainwater collectors, and composting toilet currently cluttering her Amazon cart.

The irony du jour was that a youth filled with survival training was turning out to be completely useless. Her expertise was disappearing into the mass of humanity that shared the planet with her. Traveling on bogus documents or no documents at all? Piece of cake. Avoiding being tracked by the ever-increasing number of Internet snoops? No problem. Keeping her face obscured from security cameras? Second nature. She'd even been instructed in the fine art of killing silently and disposing of bodies. Though that last one was probably more theoretical than practical. When she found a spider in her house, she tended to capture it and set it free on the front porch.

So now there she was. Standing in the rain with a kitchen stacked with a maybe a month's worth of canned food, dried beans, and chocolate pudding. Oh, and a good three months' worth of toilet paper. That'd be helpful. Because if there was anything starving people were known for, it was their prodigious bowel movements.

She went back inside, heading straight for her gas fireplace. The pilot was still burning and she activated the battery-operated thermostat. A moment later, the living area was bathed in flickering light and she could feel the warmth on her face. For the moment at least. She'd never been able to find reliable information on what would happen to the natural gas supply in a long-term blackout.

Might as well enjoy it while it lasted.

She finally stepped back and turned a full revolution in the tiny room, trying to realistically assess her situation. The front door was metal and the window next to it was protected by bars—widely spaced, but sufficient to stop anyone over four years old. The only other ingress point was her courtyard and the only access would be from the roofs of adjacent houses. Very few people were aware of the existence of her little alcove and it was hard to picture any of them climbing down into it.

She kept a compact Beretta Px4 and a box of spare rounds in her nightstand, but after those bullets were expended, she'd be down to fighting with kitchen knives. Not ideal.

Voronova dug through one of her kitchen cabinets, coming up with a roll of black drawer liner, a staple gun, and some duct tape. She dropped the items at the base of the living room window, looking at her reflection in the glass for what might be the last time. Despite her front porch being a protected hollow at the bottom of a set of steps, the light still made its way to the street. If this was John Alton's blackout, she had to make her home look abandoned—unworthy of the considerable effort it would take to break in.

She reached for the drawer liner but couldn't quite bring herself to pick it up. Her adult life had always been one of isolation—either self-imposed or imposed on her. The glass in front of her sometimes felt like her only connection to the world. Cutting that last link was harder than she imagined. So, instead, she just stood there, trying futilely to see past her reflection and into the darkness. The darkness that she'd had a hand in creating.

Americans were incredibly pampered. Few had ever experienced anything that could be described as real hardship. They had no inkling of what it was like to have to fight for their own survival and the survival of their families. To know that death, and not embarrassment or financial difficulty or loss of social status, was the price of failure.

She should have done something. She should have stopped this. But how? Even if she weren't being watched by her Russian masters, what could she have done? Called 911? How would that go?

Hi, I know a guy who wants to take down the US power grid. Evidence? Of course! I have half of a heavily encrypted hard drive that I got through breaking and entering.

Or maybe the FBI would have been a better idea. She could have marched down to the J. Edgar Hoover Building and announced that she was a Russian sleeper agent with important information about an imminent terrorist attack. They'd have probably tossed her out of the building, but what if they'd actually taken her seriously? What if she'd managed to convince them of her identity? She saw the outcomes as binary:

A: Spend the rest of her life being tortured in an undisclosed CIA dungeon.

B: Get traded for an American agent being held by the Kremlin, then spend the rest of her life being tortured in an SVR dungeon.

And since neither of those outcomes sounded all that appealing, she was instead going to barricade herself in her little apartment and slowly starve.

A terrifying end but, in a way, she was glad for her procrastination and lack of available credit. If she'd managed to fill her flat with survival gear, what then? Sit around comfortably while the people she'd condemned died?

No. This was better. It was what she deserved.

CHAPTER 23

Near Seneca Rocks
West Virginia
USA

Dawn had broken a few hours ago, but it was hard to tell. The clouds clinging to the mountains were battleship gray and thick enough to keep everything murky. If Rapp's GPS hadn't still been functioning, he would have missed his turn off the empty rural highway.

No-trespassing signs were plentiful on the narrow gravel road, but they weren't fancy—basically the same beat-up plaques that everyone bought to warn off wayward hunters and partying teens. He wound through a heavily treed canyon for a good five miles before spotting a rusty chain link gate cutting across it. No guard was in evidence, but there was a late-model Toyota Highlander blocking the road about fifty yards in front. It looked to be crammed to the headliner with personal effects.

As he approached, a man in dark slacks and a rain jacket got out, waving his arms in the air. He was pale, middle-aged, and had a really nice haircut. Something about him looked familiar, but it took Rapp a few seconds to put a name to the face.

"Thank God," the man said, putting his hands on the pickup's sill as it drifted to a stop. "I've been out here for hours. The app on my phone won't open the gate. It says it's been deactivated. I'm Senator Davis Graves. I need to drive in with you."

As part of his pre-op briefing, Rapp had suffered through a seemingly endless video of a recent congressional hearing on the electrical grid's vulnerabilities. The asshole leaning his wet head through the window was the same one who had insisted the DOE was exaggerating the threat.

Un-fucking-believable.

Rapp was accustomed to bad behavior in politicians, but this had to be top five in his career. Graves had fought tooth-and-nail to prevent the government from laying in additional security. And now that America was suffering the consequences of his actions, he thought he should be first in line for protection. Based on the time it would have taken him to pack that much shit into his vehicle and drive there, he must have started ten minutes after the lights went out.

On the positive side, though, the gate wasn't opening for him. Had his access been purposely revoked? Had Alexander actually managed to wrap his mind around the seriousness of this situation and what it was going to take to control it?

Nah. It was probably just a software glitch. But at least it was an entertaining one.

"Do you know anything about electrical engineering, Davis?"

"What? No, I—"

"Can you put out forest fires?"

"Are you an idiot? I just said I'm a US senator. And I'm telling you—"

"No, I'm telling *you,*" Rapp said, the tone of his voice silencing the man. "If you're a politician, go home and help your constituents. That's what they elected you for."

"Don't you dare talk to me like that," the man said, looking at Rapp like he was something that had just crawled from under a rock. "I *paid for* this place. I've been a member of this country's government for almost twenty . . ."

Rapp tuned him out. The opportunity to punch a politician didn't come up every day, but if there was any appropriate moment, this was it. The shit had officially hit the fan and no one seemed to be looking.

He swung his left fist out and caught Graves full in the mouth. There wasn't enough leverage available to knock out any teeth, but plenty to send the man stumbling backward. When he hit the icy mud at the edge of the gravel, he fell backward and slid a good ten feet down the slope.

Rapp gunned the truck around the man's Highlander and used his phone to open the gate. In the rearview mirror he saw Graves struggle back to the road and start running. It looked like the first time in a while and there was no way he was going to make it. The gate was already sliding back into place.

As he drove, Rapp wondered idly what would happen to the man. It was fun to think Graves would run out of gas on the way back to DC and freeze to death but it was unlikely. Parasites had an incredible ability to survive. He'd figure out a way to convince someone to help him, use that person up, and then move on to another. It was the way of the world . . .

After three more miles he came to another gate. This one looked significantly sturdier and was being tended to by a soldier armed with an M4. Rapp pulled up and passed him an ID card through the open window. Another soldier appeared from a hut near the trees and used a rolling mirror to check the pickup's underside.

Not finding any contraband or explosives hidden in the chassis, he turned his attention to the truck's bed. A moment later, he came alongside his companion for a brief, but urgent, whispered conversation.

"Sir, there seems to be a man wrapped in a tarp back there."

"Yeah," Rapp agreed.

"Uh, entry is strictly controlled. Authorized personnel only. That's you—and according to my orders—only you."

Rapp nodded and stepped out of the truck. He

leaned over the side and pulled the tarp back from Rashad Asfour's face.

"How you doing back here?"

The man had turned a vague shade of blue over the last hour despite the fact that temperatures had risen to almost forty degrees. He tried to respond but his words were unintelligible.

"Here's the situation," Rapp said. "This mountain is full of medical personnel and professional interrogators. And they aren't going to make the deal I did with you. I believe that you don't know anything, but they won't. They're going to want more than your phone's password and they're going to be a lot more scientific about it than me. They're going to shove a thermometer up your ass and chain you to a tree. Then, when you're just about dead, they're gonna bring you inside and put you in a nice warm bed. And they're going to keep doing it until you die of old age. No one deserves to live like that, Rashad. Not even you. Now this is your last chance. Tell me what I want to know and we'll finish this."

The man stared up at him, though one of his eyeballs was covered in a thin film of frost. After a few seconds, his mouth began to move. Rapp leaned in close and entered the string of letters and numbers as Asfour said them. It worked. He was in.

He pulled his Glock and pressed the barrel against the man's chest. "A deal's a deal."

Both soldiers jumped back at the sound of the shot, reaching for their weapons, but uncertain whether they had the authority to do any more. Rapp climbed back into his pickup and pointed at the gate.

“Open it.”

CHAPTER 24

The chaos inside the bunker's entrance was just below that of full-fledged combat. The space was massive—probably fifty feet high by two hundred and fifty wide. Rapp couldn't see as far as the back. People were running in every direction, dodging trucks, forklifts, and occasional bicycles. The dull buzz of countless voices combined with the stench of sweat to give the air a strange weight.

He waded in, making it about twenty feet before he saw a woman angling toward him from the right.

"Mr. Rapp," she called when she got close enough for him to hear. "I'm Amy Case. Sorry to be late. I assumed you'd pull into the indoor parking area."

"I have something in the back that needs to stay cold."

She gave him a quizzical look but had clearly been trained not to ask questions. Instead, she held out a yellow badge that he hung around his neck.

"That gives you full access," she said. "It'll open any door in the place, but be careful how you use it. One wrong turn and you'll be lost for a week."

"Got it."

He followed her for a good ten minutes before they entered a significantly less crowded passageway that terminated in a heavy steel door. Her card opened it and they passed into something that looked like an oversized NASA mission control room. People wearing headsets were lined up at desks and a huge screen depicting the United States dominated the wall in front of them. He paused to examine the pulsing lights on it, but his guide grabbed him by the arm and kept him moving. They crossed unnoticed, finally stopping in front of a more nondescript door at the back. This time she pointed to his badge. "This is as far as I can go."

After a respectful nod, she started back the way she'd come, leaving him to tap his badge against a pad next to the door. The room he entered had a similar monitor hanging on the far wall, this one spanning probably fifteen feet by ten. At the center of the room was an oval table so large that the people around it had to have microphones to be heard. The resemblance to the war room from the movie *Dr. Strangelove* was obvious enough that Rapp wondered if some smart-ass architect had done it intentionally.

The president was sitting quietly while the secretary of the interior made full use of the microphone in front of him. Rapp couldn't find Irene Kennedy in any of the chairs, but finally spotted her standing against the wall with the directors of the FBI and NSA.

". . . we're still in the process of evaluating the fires based on satellite imagery and weather forecasts. What I can say without further analysis is that there are too many and they're too spread out to fight in a conventional way, even if we were at full capacity. We're going to have to prioritize the ones threatening large population centers and let a lot of the others just burn. Calls for evacuations are already under way, but communications are spotty and the logistics are a nightmare. As they start moving out, people are going to find gas stations out of commission and their cars are going to block the roads when they run out of fuel. And then there's the matter of not having anywhere to send them. We don't have the capacity to set up refugee camps—"

"TJ?" the president interrupted, sounding exhausted. "What about that? What can you do for these displaced people?"

The head of FEMA leaned hesitantly into his mike. "Not much, sir. It's too many people in too many places. State and city systems are spooling up and we'll have to rely on them to a large extent. The problem is that over the next few days their resources are going to start to run out. After that—"

"We're not worrying about next week," the president said. "We're worrying about right now.

You've told me in the past that the water supply is your number one concern in a scenario like this. What can we do to keep it online?"

Burton swallowed. "This is one of our better emergency scenarios in the short term—a lot of the agencies actually do drills to train for potential disasters. Also, a lot have fairly robust backup power systems. They won't last though. The problems will come in waves, depending on the individual situation and design of the delivery system. We're prioritizing aid based on that and based on whether we realistically think we can help. With the exception of the fires, this is absolutely the most critical piece right now. Without drinking water, everyone dies in a few days. And without water for sanitation, disease is going to run rampant, which would be—"

"What about food?" the president said before Burton could fall down another rabbit hole.

"Less crucial in the short term. Cities tend to carry about a three-day supply and in winter spoilage won't be as bad. We have to take control of food production, distribution, and storage, though. Security will also become an issue pretty quickly. When the grocery stores go empty, it won't take long for people to start looting the entire supply chain."

"How long can people survive without eating?" someone asked.

"A month. Maybe a little more. By then, we

need to have food production back online and a way to distribute that food. But it has to be completely government controlled. The free market ceases to exist when banks do because no one has money. In fact, pretty much everything has to be government controlled. For instance, after initial evacuations, I can't think of a single reason anyone should be out at night in the middle of the winter. If they are, I can pretty much guarantee you they're up to no good."

Everyone looked to the president, who considered the issue silently for a few moments before speaking. "I understand the need for a curfew, but my question is can we enforce it?"

General Templeton shook his head. "Not at this time, sir."

"I'm hesitant to make decrees that we can't enforce. It'll undermine the authority of the government and potentially add to the panic. So, let's put that on the back burner for now." He paused for a moment. "While we're on the subject of the military, General, what's your status?"

"Obviously, our power is down, too, sir. We can deploy mobile medical facilities and we're recalling all feasible nuclear vessels. They can provide at least some power to coastal areas and particularly the docks that we're going to need to unload critical supplies. Obviously, we have a lot of troops stationed in foreign countries and we're going to have to consider whether to bring them back. Right now, we don't have the capacity to absorb them, but we might in the future."

"Okay," Alexander said, obviously fighting to stay outwardly calm. "How long do we have before this thing turns south hard? TJ?"

"Assuming we can keep the water on, about a week. That's when a significant number of people will start getting hungry. Most Americans have no experience with that. They won't be dying, but they'll think they are. At that point, we'll need the military to maintain order, particularly in the warmer areas of the country where the weather will be more conducive to civil unrest."

"Then we need to get the power on before that." He turned to Janice Crane, the Department of Energy's representative at the meeting. "Where do we stand?"

She looked a little stunned and there was a good five seconds of silence before she spoke. "The scope of this attack was . . . incredible. We don't even know what we're dealing with yet. Power company computer systems were lying to them and now they're locking down. We know that the infrastructure damage is massive, but it's unlikely that I'll be able to be any more specific than that without a physical inspection. That's hundreds of thousands of miles of lines and tens of thousands of substations—much of it difficult to access and some of it completely cut off by fires. Once that evaluation is done, then we're going to have to come up with a repair plan and execute it."

"What are we talking about time-wise?"

"If everything goes right, maybe two months."

"You're telling me the power is going to be out for two months? That's not acceptable, Janice."

"No, sir. Two months to complete the initial inspection."

The room fell into a deep silence. After a desperate-looking sip of water she continued. "During that time, we hope to bring back power selectively. Essentially, islands around power plants. Also, renewables remain online, though obviously they're intermittent. There's potential for moving people to camps around those areas."

"The problem with that is what can you really do with the power?" TJ Burton interjected. "Heat in cold areas and maybe some light? But what people need is food, water, sanitation, and shelter. Those things tend not to be in the same place as power plants. It's the same problem we have with the navy's ships. Unless we have some really long extension cords, we can't get the power to the critical industries that keep the country alive."

"I'm doing the best I can," Crane snapped.

"Relax, Janice, he's not blaming you," Alexander said, and then turned to the secretary of state. "I hate to say it, but what about foreign aid?"

"The European Union is one hundred percent behind us, sir. The problem is that the question is capacity not willingness. The US is the largest food exporter in the world and that spigot is about to be shut off. Their first order of business is assessing how they're going to feed their own people. Not ours."

"And even if they can ship us the food and other supplies we need," Burton said, "we still have to figure out a way to unload and transport it."

"What about closer to home?" Alexander said.

"With the exception of part of Canada, which is interconnected to our grid, the attack doesn't seem to have extended past the continental US in any meaningful way. So, we have Hawaii and Alaska as well as the territories. Latin America has pretty limited capacity and the collapse of our trade with them is going to hit hard."

When the conversation turned to the worldwide depression that would inevitably follow the complete collapse of the world's largest economy, Rapp made his way toward Irene Kennedy and the men she was speaking to.

"Looks like we screwed up, bad," he said when he got within earshot. "What now?"

"We were just talking about that," the FBI director said.

"And what did you come up with?"

"That we're the only people who can fix this."

"I'm not an electrician, Darren"

"In a way, that's the point," Kennedy said. "It wouldn't matter if you were. Evaluating the physical damage to the grid, repairing it, and bypassing the frozen computers of thousands of individual utility companies is going to take six months if everything goes our way. It can't take that long, Mitch. The majority of our population will be dead and America will have ceased to exist."

"I assume you have a plan?"

"There's only one person in the world who can answer the questions we need answered—what lines are down, what substations have been damaged, and how to access utility company computers."

"PowerStation," Rapp said.

She nodded. "With the information he or she has, we could get at least intermittent power to our major population centers and other critical infrastructure."

Rapp dug Rashad Asfour's phone from his pocket and handed it to the NSA director.

"What's this?"

"Call it a Christmas present. I took it from the man who tried to hit the substation in North Carolina," he said, turning to leave. "I doubt there's much on it, but it'll give the three of you somewhere to start."

"Where are you going?" Kennedy asked.

"Home. I don't know shit about the grid or disaster relief and I'm not taking a bunk from someone who does. You know where to find me. Get me a name and a location on this asshole and I'll take care of the rest."

CHAPTER 25

West of Manassas
Virginia
USA

Rapp felt around on the floor next to the sofa, finally finding the beer he was searching for. Drinking it proved to be problematic, though. His refrigerator was wildly energy efficient but, still, opening it for no good reason seemed like a waste of hard-won electricity. Unfortunately, his back porch lacked the kind of cooling precision he was used to.

He slid the bottle across the wood floor, getting it to within a foot of the fireplace that had raised the temperature in his den to a decadent seventy-three degrees. The rest of the house was being kept twenty-five degrees cooler. With the dense cloud cover, his solar panels weren't worth much, so he was relying entirely on wind. No reason to drain his batteries or cause his generators to kick on. They were only a few days into a situation that could stretch out for a very long time. In fact, if Kennedy and her brain trust didn't come through, it could be permanent.

Confident that his Sam Adams was on its way to being fully liquid again, he turned his attention back to the television. It was tuned to a French news report focused on the recent drops in the world's stock markets. Most were down more than twenty-five percent, but there was a lot of confusion because the US markets were completely off-line. The economist being interviewed actually looked a little panicked. Probably not a good sign.

The clock on at the edge of the television said 22:57 and he turned it off in favor of the radio. Over the last few days of inactivity, he'd stumbled upon an amateur radio show that was a hell of a lot more entertaining and informative than the mainstream media reports or government public service announcements. And, apparently he wasn't the only one who thought so. A number of commercial stations that were still operational had taken to rebroadcasting it live. So, while the normal outlets extolled the virtues of warm hats and standing by, this guy would tell you the best way to cook grasshoppers or wipe your ass when you ran out of toilet paper.

A recycled segment on treating contaminated water was just winding down and Rapp half-listened to it as he rolled off the sofa to retrieve his beer. Apparently, the guy had been doing survivalist podcasts for years, but their appeal had been limited to the fringe. Now he was headed for rock star status.

When the clock hit the top of the hour, the

prerecorded program faded and was replaced by a familiar southern drawl.

"Good evening, America! This is your host Jed-The-Survivalist-Who-Doesn't-Seem-Quite-As-Crazy-As-He-Did-Last-Week-Jones. I hope you're staying warm and safe out there. I've got Claire radioing in from Los Angeles and I'm not sure how long the connection is going to last, so let's kick off the show with her. Claire, you there? What's going on in the City of Angels?"

"Hi, Jed. The local authorities are reporting that they're getting control of the fire on the south side of the city."

"Are they telling the truth or is this just more government bullshit?"

"It's hard to say. The smoke is still really bad where I am. They're calling for rain tonight, thank God. So, we're keeping our fingers crossed."

"What about aid stations. Do you have a list?"

"I do, but it's a moving target. Most of these locations were good as of an hour ago."

She started going through them but was abruptly cut off after about thirty seconds. These kinds of radio connections were tricky—dependent to some extent on atmospheric conditions.

"We've lost her. Hopefully, I'll get her back before the show's over, but the aid station thing makes me think I should talk a little more

about food. I know some of you are hungry out there, but you've got to conserve. Don't trust the government when they say they're going to get this under control. A little food every day—particularly protein—will double or triple the time you can survive over just eating everything you've got during the next week and counting on your Safeway getting restocked. Hell, look on the bright side. If you're like me and just about everyone else, losing a little weight isn't going to be the worst thing in the world. My wife says my abs are getting— Hold on. I think we've got someone on the line. Let me patch them through.

"Yeah. Go ahead. Who and where are you?"

"Tom. I'm in Alabama."

"What's going on down there?"

"I just wanted to say that those people in LA had it coming. They—"

"Fuck off!" Jed said, shutting the man down. "Do I really have to go through this again? The shit has officially hit the fan and we are all Americans. There are no more Democrats and Republicans. No more rednecks and snowflakes. We've got to work together. Us knuckle draggers might be able to kill and gut a deer, but those little nerdy guys might be able to set you up with solar panels or keep you alive if you eat some bad barbecue. United we stand, assholes. Divided we're screwed."

Rapp heard the door behind him open followed

by Anna's padded footfalls. A moment later she took a position in front of him wearing the fleece onesie her mother had wrapped her in.

"Why do you listen to that guy? I could hear him all the way down the hallway. He's so *rude!*"

"Never confuse delivery with content," he said, muting the feed.

"I don't even know what that means," she said, flopping on top of him.

Not long ago, he'd have gone stiff the moment she landed on him, but his comfort level was improving. The truth was that he was actually starting to like having her around. And it scared the shit out of him.

"It means that when someone's smart and knows what they're talking about, you shouldn't worry so much about whether you like them or not."

She nodded thoughtfully. "Mom wants to know if you're stirring the beef burgy-on like she told you."

He let his head loll to the left and contemplated the iron pot hanging over the fire.

"Yes?"

"You're such a liar! And you're not even good at it. I can always tell."

She rolled off him and used a potholder to take the lid off. "When is it going to be time for me to go back to school?"

"It's Christmas break," he said as she used a wooden spoon to stir.

"Yeah, but Mom says we won't go to school when there's no lights. And we're supposed to go back in a few days. And if we don't I'm going to miss Tina and my other friends. Plus, I need school. I want to be a vet-a-narian and it's super hard."

"Yeah, I think you actually have to be able to pronounce it."

"Shut up!"

"It won't be long," he said, demonstrating that he was better at lying than she thought.

"Do you think Tina's all right? She doesn't live in a big fort like us. She just has, like, a regular house."

"Yeah. I'm sure she is."

That second lie was a little harder for him to get out. One day would she hold it against him? Because most likely Tina wasn't going to be okay. And to make things even worse, it was his fault. It was his job to make sure things like this didn't happen.

His satphone started to ring and he pulled it from the pocket of his sweatpants. "Why don't you go tell your mom that I've been taking good care of the stew?"

"Because it's not true."

"What if I were to let you plug in some of those presents you got?" he said, looking down at the screen and seeing that the call was from Irene Kennedy.

Anna's eyes narrowed suspiciously. "How long?"

"A few hours?"

She nodded thoughtfully and went for the door.

"Close it, you're letting the heat out!" he called after her and then picked up. "How are things going?"

"Badly," she said, sounding exhausted. "We just got a report of someone shooting into a crowd of protesters in Phoenix. At least five casualties and rumors are circulating that the National Guard was responsible."

"Were they?"

"We don't know. That kind of information is hard to come by in the current environment. Either way, violence has been on the uptick. So far, it's been opportunistic and probably carried out by people already predisposed to it. But that won't last. Pretty soon, we're going to have suburban mothers gunning people down for a can of food to feed their kids."

"What's TJ saying?"

"You don't want to know," she said. "You really don't."

"Then we need to fix this, Irene. It's our mess and we need to clean it up. What about the phone I gave you? Was there anything on it we can use?"

"Basically, what we expected. A list of targets with very detailed information on how to hit each of them most effectively. We've confirmed the identity of the body you left in the parking area as Rashad Asfour and we're trying to track his known associates, but, again, it's not easy in this environment. The chance that it will lead us to PowerStation is low."

"What about his ISIS buddies? Are they still active?"

"Yes, but they're moving to less obvious targets. And there are just too many of those for us to cover."

"They'll just keep going until they're all dead. If you need more manpower, I can go back out with Scott's guys."

"The damage is so extensive that losing a few more minor substations isn't going to make any difference. And even if we were able to catch one of them, it's unlikely that they would know any more than Asfour did. Thank you, but I'd rather have you rested and ready to go if I need you."

"*If* you need me. I'm not sure I like the sound of that."

"We're drilling down on the people who have the necessary knowledge of our grid to do something like this, but with most computer networks down, it's a slow process. And even if we do come up with a name, it's only a start. Phones largely don't work and a lot of people are leaving their primary homes to help relatives. Someone suddenly disappearing from the radar isn't necessarily an indicator of guilt anymore."

"So, you're looking for an individual. Not a government."

"The more we analyze what's happened, the more we think PowerStation is unaffiliated," she said before her voice trailed off.

"I hear a 'but' hanging at the end of that sentence."

"Do you remember the transcript of the ISIS chat room discussions?"

"You're talking about the one where he mentioned the Russians? It sounded like he'd approached them but couldn't get traction."

"And if that's the case, the Russians might know who he is."

"Thin," Rapp said.

"Agreed. But desperate times call for desperate measures. We're putting our case together and then we're going present it to the Russian president. Alexander would like you to attend that meeting."

"Why?"

"Because he wants it to be crystal clear that we expect full cooperation from Russia. And that anything less than that is unacceptable."

CHAPTER 26

Washington, DC
USA

Electric *can openers!*

Perhaps the culmination of ten thousand years of human stupidity. And she'd fallen for it hook, line, and sinker. Thank God for the brilliant nut who'd started a survival radio show that she now listened to obsessively. If it wasn't for Jed Jones, she'd have opened her can of peas with a butcher knife instead of a spoon. He was probably the reason she still possessed all her fingers.

Voronova squinted as she turned into the sun, avoiding a glittering patch of ice on the sidewalk in front of her. Just before dawn, she'd climbed a drainpipe onto her neighbor's roof and then down the other side to the street. The government had finally imposed an official curfew from dusk until dawn, but that wasn't why she'd been reluctant to go out after dark. The opposite, really. Based on what sound filtered down to her basement flat and what she could piece together from radio reports, the curfew was yet another complete fail.

Of course, there was the lack of enforcement manpower, but that wasn't the worst of it. No, the main problem was that as the nationwide blackout moved into its second week, many people *wanted* to get caught. They figured they'd be thrown into a detention center where they'd be fed, protected, and provided medical care. And she could sympathize one hundred percent, despite being in a far better position than most Americans.

For now, the natural gas was still flowing. Her gas fireplace was keeping her comfortable and providing enough light to pass the endless hours of solitude reading. Also, the water in DC was still on while there were reports of it starting to falter in other major cities. And, of course, she'd had an opportunity to lay in some food before the lights went out.

Likely nowhere near enough, though. And, in light of that, she'd cut her food consumption to twelve hundred calories per day. Based on her calculations, that would get her through two months. According to Jed, she could cut back even further and survive for more than double that. A full-on starvation diet was something she'd have to ease into, though. If things were looking as bad in two weeks as they were now, she'd pull the trigger. Six hundred calories per day.

Today, though, the nagging hunger she was trying to become accustomed to was gone. She'd doubled her rations for this expedition and, in addition to returning some of her strength, it had significantly improved her mood. It was just the carbohydrates talking, though. Outside of her sugar buzz, hope was hard to come by. Government-controlled radio—TV, the cellular network, and the Internet had died days ago—kept repeating the same nonsense about staying calm, staying warm, and standing by. They weren't even calling out the locations of aid stations anymore because they found they were being immediately overrun.

Three men appeared on the sidewalk in front of her and she forced herself to maintain a relaxed gait as her hand moved closer to the Beretta hidden beneath her jacket. They didn't look particularly threatening—probably a father in his early fifties and two sons in their twenties. But it would be stupid to take chances. Desperation did things to people. Even fundamentally good ones. It was the reason she'd worked so hard to make herself as unappealing a target as possible. A ten-year-old coat, jeans, and a pair of waterproof boots splashed with mud. No backpack or bag that might contain something useful. No fancy technical clothing that might fit a sister or wife.

She held her breath as they passed, but none so much as looked at her. Still, she didn't let her hand drop to her side until their footsteps had completely faded.

Voronova turned off the residential street in favor of one of DC's critical thoroughfares.

Or at least what used to be one of its critical thoroughfares. Now it was utterly impassible, clogged with cars abandoned by people who had run out of gas trying to flee the city. She couldn't help but stop and gaze out over it all. Another reminder of how delicate the threads holding together modern society were.

Having said that, it might also have been part of the government's haphazard plan. She suspected that they wanted to keep people corralled and because of that they'd done virtually nothing to keep roads clear. Now, if you were going to get out, it would have to be on foot. Maybe a motorcycle, but you'd need gas for that and would risk the possibility of being attacked by someone who wanted out of the city just as much as you did.

Eight days. That's all it had taken. What would happen in ten? Twenty? God forbid one hundred?

It was that precise question that had forced her from her improvised basement stronghold. For the first few days, she'd told herself that there was nothing to be done. That it was too late. But it was just her cowardice talking. That geeky little asshole John Alton was out there somewhere and he had a laptop that outlined everything he'd done in gory detail. She'd seen it with her own eyes.

There was no way that information wouldn't be helpful to the people trying to fix this thing. And even if it wasn't, at least he could be slapped in chains and thrown in a hole somewhere for what he had done.

She pulled the collar of her jacket closed against the cold as she began weaving through the cars. At least the FBI's headquarters wasn't far from where she lived. Getting there probably wouldn't be too bad. It was what she was going to do when she got there that she wasn't so sure about.

The conspiracy theorists were all over the airwaves going full guns against the government. They said it was all a plot to get rid of democracy and replace it with a dictatorship. That the suicide of this year's lead presidential candidate had been faked by the Deep State, that lizard people had taken over Congress, and so on.

The first thing she'd have to do is establish that she wasn't one of them. And after that she'd have to hit them with the Russian mole thing. On her side, she actually did speak the language and had a few classified tidbits bouncing around in her head. Unfortunately, *few* and *tidbits* were the operative words here. She wasn't an active agent and sleepers just didn't need to know that much until they were called upon.

It didn't matter, though. She was going to make this happen. She was going to make it right. She had to.

• • •

The yelling became audible when Voronova was a little more than five blocks from the J. Edgar Hoover Building. She tried to detour around it, but no matter what she did, the infuriated shouts of what sounded like hundreds of people followed.

One of the reasons she'd left at the crack of dawn was to avoid this. A high-pressure system had moved in overnight, bringing blue skies and still air that would coax people into the streets. But it was barely eight fifteen in the morning and still well below freezing. Who rioted in that? Why not wait until afternoon, when it was supposed to climb into the forties?

With no better option, she set herself on the shortest route to the FBI's headquarters and crossed her fingers.

What she found when she arrived was well beyond anything her imagination could have devised. It wasn't an informal gathering of a hundred scared, frustrated people in danger of losing hope. It was a near riot consisting of what must have been a thousand people, all targeting their rage directly at the FBI. Her pace slowed and she finally came to a halt in the middle of the road. The building appeared to be completely surrounded. Barricades had been erected and men in riot gear stood just behind them, absorbing the screamed insults and occasional projectile thrown by the crowd. Some protesters had crafted handmade signs talking about freedom, America, and the Constitution. A good half were armed—many with assault rifles. A bottle glinted in the sun as it arced through the air and shattered against a Plexiglas shield.

She'd never had any illusion that she was the only person listening to the conspiracy theorists on the radio, but she'd never dreamed that their influence could spread so quickly. Or so powerfully.

Eight days. That number kept swirling around in her head. The time it took to get something from a particularly slow mail order catalog. Or to secure a dentist's appointment. Or to abandon her latest New Year's resolution.

She took a hesitant step forward, but then stopped again. Even if she had an official SVR badge and a letter of introduction signed by Boris Utkin himself, it wouldn't matter. The chance of her fighting her way to the barricades were pretty much zero. And the chance of her then embarking on a detailed explanation of her identity and suspicions was even less.

She would have laughed if she weren't about to break into tears. The FBI was desperate for information and she was standing outside their headquarters with just the intel they needed. But there was no way to get it to them.

And that begged the question, what now?

She couldn't climb the drainpipe to get back into her courtyard until it was too dark to be seen. Another nine hours at least. What about a pay phone? Were those even a thing anymore? And if they were, was 911 still operational? The FBI undoubtedly had a phone number, but how would she find it? She hadn't laid eyes on a phone book in years.

This time, she actually did manage a laugh. A strained and bitter outburst that made her feel even worse. She'd been a sci-fi fan her whole life and one of her favorite themes was the machines taking over. The Matrix. The Terminator. What she hadn't realized until that moment was that they'd already succeeded. Millions of people were going to die. Why? Because without 4G, she couldn't look up a phone number.

CHAPTER 27

Near Seneca Rocks
West Virginia
USA

Rapp pulled through the blast doors and stopped in front of the Marine who seemed to be in charge of the cavernous parking area. The power outage was in its eleventh day now and the space was wedged to capacity with civilian and military vehicles. She motioned for him to roll down his window.

"We're fitting them in like puzzle pieces, sir. If you don't mind, I'll take it from here. When you want it back, we'll need a few minutes' notice and a license number."

He nodded and stepped out. "And while you're at it, why don't you gas it up for me?"

It was intended as a joke and she started to grin, but it faded when she saw the color of the badge hanging around his neck. "I'll take care of it personally, sir."

He handed her the keys and watched her drive away. A pleasant surprise. He was having to pull diesel intended for his backup generators to fuel his pickup. Claudia's Tesla was currently sidelined, but the sun was out so he was hoping to get the battery charged over the next couple of days. Until then, if the government wanted to help him out, he wasn't going to argue.

The elevator on the north side of the parking area took him down a few hundred more feet to the main bunker. The quiet hum of the electric motor was the only sound as he descended, making the turmoil when the doors opened that much more disorienting. In the time since his last visit, the already considerable level of activity had multiplied by at least a factor of three. The smell of hundreds of unwashed bodies was familiar but overwhelming as he stepped out and dodged a hydraulic lift carrying pallets of MREs. From what little he could see through the crush of people, the walls were now lined with cots, most unmade and piled with their occupants' personal possessions. A significant number of civilians had been added to the mix, including children. Some of the kids were being herded in groups, but others were free range, wandering around and trying not to get stepped on or run over.

There was no one there to meet him, which wasn't surprising given the situation, so he just headed in the direction he'd gone last time. It was a little like trying to fight your way to the stage of a rock concert, but he managed to make steady progress.

He spotted a boy a little older than Anna sitting on a stack of boxes, calmly taking it all in. He looked like he had a good head on his shoulders and clearly wasn't busy, so Rapp angled toward him.

"Hey, kid. I don't suppose you know what the director of the CIA looks like."

He pondered the question for a moment and then just shook his head.

"How about the president?"

That got a nod.

"You know where he is?"

The boy pointed and Rapp set off in the direction he indicated. After about another twenty-five yards, he heard someone call his name from behind. It wasn't another anonymous escort, though. When he turned, he saw people scurrying to get out of Joshua Alexander's way.

Instead of his customary dark suit, he was wearing a pair of jeans, running shoes, and a Crimson Tide sweatshirt. His normally perfect hair was a little wild, framing a gaunt face and eyes that had seen more than they wanted to in the past week. It was an expression that Rapp was familiar with from decades in combat zones. The man was barely holding himself together.

"Thanks for coming, Mitch."

"Not a problem, sir. Are you all right?"

The president let out a short laugh and put a hand on Rapp's back, prompting him forward again. "A few more weeks," he said. "That's all I had. Then I was going to hand the keys to the next administration and disappear."

A group of kids ran across their path, forcing them to stop for a moment.

"Electrical engineers?" Rapp said, watching them disappear into the bodies around them.

"I took your advice. They might not be electrical engineers, but there's a good chance their parents are. And I've told them that their kids are safe here as long as they keep working their asses off eighteen hours a day."

"What about the politicians?"

"I sent them home to their districts with protection and the promise of supplies for them and their families."

"And how's that working out?"

"Depends on your perspective. I've made it clear that when I say jump, the only acceptable response from them is to ask how high. If I get any other response, they're going to find themselves on their own."

They finally reached the back wall and the president ushered him through a nondescript door. What they entered wasn't the grand replica of the Oval Office Rapp had expected, though. More like a repurposed storage room furnished with a modest desk, a few chairs, and a television propped on a stack of boxes.

Alexander dropped into the chair behind the desk, obviously registering Rapp's surprise. "My office was a waste of space. It's full of bunks now."

Rapp nodded. "You said things were working out depending on how you look at it. The way I look at it, you're getting things under control."

"I'm becoming a dictator."

"You're becoming the military commander this country needs."

He smiled enigmatically. "Did you hear that the riots in Phoenix have quieted down?"

The civil unrest plaguing that city had been growing and becoming increasingly organized. With no phones or social media, the rioters had begun communicating through graffiti. The day before, there had been an incident that left hundreds injured and generated enough property damage to leave a few hundred more homeless.

"I didn't," Rapp admitted. In fact, he'd spent the last day and a half crawling around under Scott Coleman's house trying to figure out why his batteries were draining.

"Do you want to know how I did it?"

"The military?"

Alexander shook his head. "I cut off their water. Kind of ironic, isn't it? TJ's been killing himself to keep their water on and then I shut it off. And I made it clear that they were going to go home or they were going to die of thirst."

Rapp took a chair. "They didn't have any demands, sir. And if they did, you don't have the ability to meet them or you would have already. They were just wasting energy, injuring themselves and others, and sucking up critical resources. Your solution beats the hell out of any alternative I can think of."

"I wonder if that's how the American people will see it when this is all over."

"Whether they see it that way or not doesn't matter. That's the way it is."

"Still, I might need you and Irene to set me up with a little plastic surgery and a new life. You're good at that, right?"

Rapp grinned. "We're great at that. What did you have in mind?"

"Maybe a little commercial fishing boat in Panama. I've always liked the ocean."

"We'll see what we can do. Now I have to ask, sir. Why am I here? Not to talk about fishing."

"No. Not to talk about fishing," he said, sounding a little distant. "Irene finished building her case against the Russians and sent it to them. We have a conference call with President Utkin and the head of the SVR in . . ." He looked at his watch. "Ten minutes."

Rapp nodded. "Are you sure about this, sir? If I'm in that meeting, you're sending a pretty strong message. I'm not exactly a political advisor. I only do one thing and Utkin knows better than most what it is."

Alexander's face seemed to lose all expression. "I'm sure. And I want you to understand that I'm serious, too. If he decides to play games, I'm not denouncing him at the UN or suing him in the World Court. I'm sending you."

The communications room they entered was a little better put together than the president's improvised office—lots of glass and stainless steel with windows frosted opaque. The ubiquitous monitors hung on the walls, with most running what looked like live webcam feeds of Moscow. Rapp focused for a moment on the hazy lights of Red Square before walking over to Irene Kennedy at the far end of a conference table.

"How's Tommy?" he asked, referring to her teenaged son. "The offer still stands. We'd be happy to take him."

"Thank you," she said as they exchanged their customary kiss on the cheek. "But the president has promised he'll provide for him as long as I remain useful."

"Don't break my balls, Irene," Alexander said. "I'm about at my limit."

And he looked the part. He hadn't bothered to change into a suit or even comb his hair, and his resigned desperation now seemed to hide a little fear. All indications were that this was going to be an interesting meeting.

"Let's do it," Alexander said simply.

Kennedy nodded and tapped a few commands into the laptop in front of her. A moment later, one of the monitors faded to black and the image of Moscow was replaced by the words STAND BY. About thirty seconds passed before the office of the Russian president appeared on screen. The difference was striking. Utkin and Kedrov were both perfectly groomed, wearing tailored suits, and surrounded by the over-the-top opulence left over from the czars.

"We've reviewed your communiqué in detail," Utkin said by way of greeting. "And while I sympathize with your present situation, I won't tolerate these kinds of dangerous and unfounded accusations."

"Good to see you, too," Alexander said.

Utkin didn't seem to hear, instead focusing on Rapp. "What's he doing in this meeting? Is this some kind of attempt to intimidate me?"

The fear that had been hinted at in Alexander's expression only a few moments before had completely disappeared. The consummate politician, his face projected only icy resolve.

"Let's cut the bullshit, Boris. Shortly after we intercepted chatter about you being approached by someone with plans to take out our grid, you and the people close to you started shifting your money around. Now your investments seem to be positioned in a way designed to specifically protect you from a serious economic crisis."

"I can't help feeling that the stress of your position is unbalancing you, Joshua. And I'm surprised that Dr. Kennedy wasn't able to reason with you before you sent this file full of nonsense. Your entire case against us is based on an anonymous comment on the Internet that doesn't even contain a direct indication of Russian involvement."

"I don't need—"

Utkin kept talking, cutting Alexander off. "And the financial transactions you call evidence? *Why wouldn't* I make these changes? The European Union is beginning to shatter. The Middle East is increasingly unstable. The US seems committed to its own destruction and will soon have a new president elected under highly irregular circumstances. China's entire economy is floating on unsustainable, hidden debt . . ." His voice faded for a moment. "It was frankly irresponsible of me not to make these investment adjustments sooner."

Alexander took in a deep breath and let it out slowly before speaking again. "If someone came to you with information about our power grid and you turned them down, fine. But now things have changed. We've been attacked, we're aware of your involvement, and I expect you to come clean."

A translator suddenly appeared in the frame and whispered something in Utkin's ear. The definition of "come clean," Rapp assumed. While the Russian president's English was strong, it wasn't perfect.

"We have nothing to *come clean* about," he responded. "Now let's put this idiocy aside before things go too far. You're not in a position to make enemies."

Alexander leaned forward and put his elbows on the conference table. "Russia's managed to inflict a lot of damage on the world without much in the way of resources. I'll give you that. But keep in mind that my cyberwarfare budget is more than you spend on your entire navy."

"Is that a threat?"

They stared at each other for a few seconds and it was Alexander who looked away first. But not in a gesture of submission. He glanced over at Kennedy and gave her a barely perceptible nod. In response, she tapped a few more commands into her laptop. A moment later all the monitors in the room went dead.

Or at least that's what Rapp thought at first. After a few seconds, he realized that car headlights were still visible on the webcam feeds. No streetlights, though. No lit signs or glowing windows. Moscow had gone dark.

Alexander leaned back in his chair, staring not at the monitors but at an empty section of frosted glass. The next three minutes of silence in the room seemed like an hour, but then the STAND BY screen came back up on the main monitor. A few more seconds passed before Utkin's enraged face appeared.

"This is an act of war!" he shouted. "You can't—"

"I can," Alexander said. "And this isn't the end of it, Boris. I have five switches. That was just the first of them. I also have more than thirty of our top operators in Russia waiting for my signal to go after your physical power infrastructure. And I can have Mitch in Moscow by this time tomorrow. But his target will be different."

"You haven't shut down our nuclear arsenal," he said, sounding a bit strangled. "It's connected to its own power supply."

"So is ours," Alexander said calmly. "Go ahead and launch. Then we'll do the same. Because I've got nothing to lose. But let me be perfectly clear. If my people are going to starve to death in the cold or go up in a bunch of mushroom clouds, you are too."

Pavel Kedrov, who had been standing dutifully by his boss's desk for the entire exchange, was looking increasingly alarmed. Rapp had met him on a number of occasions and while he was a typical Russian son of a bitch, he wasn't stupid or suicidal.

"Excuse me, President Utkin. Can I interject? I haven't had time to brief you, but I received some intelligence just before I walked into this meeting. It might shed some light on the matter."

"What luck," Alexander said wearily. "Let's hear it."

Utkin seemed a little confused, but that didn't stop his man from continuing. Apparently, a nuclear exchange didn't fit in with Kedrov's weekend plans.

"I spoke with our embassy in Washington to ask if they had any information that might be related to this. One of our more junior people said he sent someone to talk to an American man who claimed he had information on vulnerabilities in the US power grid. However, our agent didn't find the man credible and that was the end of our communications with him. In the end, the exchange wasn't given enough importance to merit a report to my office."

"What's his name?" Alexander said, clearly uninterested in playing the normal games.

"To be clear, he may have had nothing at all to do with this. It could just be a coincidence. As I said, he—"

"What's his name?"

"I don't know. He didn't provide it and we had no reason to ask. He—"

"Irene," Alexander said, pointing to her laptop.

"Wait! I can give you the name and address of the agent who was sent to meet him. At a minimum, she would have a physical description."

Alexander glanced at Rapp, who just nodded.

CHAPTER 28

Near Luray
Virginia
USA

We have confirmation from three separate sources that the water has been intentionally cut off in parts of Phoenix. I think it's time to start believing it's true . . .

John Alton leaned back in his chair, listening to the informal news report and reveling in the sensation of sitting at the helm of a warship. The voice reverberating from his computer's speakers belonged to some redneck named Jed who was on his way to becoming the most famous man in America. He sounded like he'd barely graduated from second grade, but his growing influence was undeniable. As was the fact that he was probably the most reliable source of information currently on the US airwaves.

. . . and I don't know how to feel about it. I really don't. I'm as anti-government as they come, but what were those riots supposed to accomplish? To force the military to get involved? They have bigger fish to fry and why would we want to put them in that position? Those soldiers don't just drop from the sky. They're our brothers and

sisters and kids and parents. They're the people who've protected us and democracy since the early days of this country.

He went silent and the dead air stretched out long enough that Alton thought for a moment that he'd lost the feed.

I was awake all last night thinking about what I'm doing in front of this microphone. I've been telling you about capturing rainwater and how not to chop your foot off cutting firewood, but I'm not sure it matters. The government says you should stay quiet and in your homes, but that's about all they're saying. And about all they're doing. I can tell you from twenty years of prepping that the government can't handle this scenario. That's why they're not giving you any information. That's why they're not telling you that if they can't get the power back on, you're screwed. So, maybe I'm wrong. Maybe you should *be rioting. Go out in a blaze of glory instead of starving in a dark room and ending up with your body frozen to the floor.*

Another silence, this one not quite as long.

My wife just walked in and is giving me the shut-the-hell-up hand signal. You guys out there know the one. And she's right. I'm just talking shit. Don't listen to me. I'm going to play some music. Something upbeat . . .

Alton shut off the feed and then leaned back again. A little more than a week. That's all it had taken for America to crumble. And it was a process that would do nothing but accelerate. The battle for survival would soon start in earnest. The weak would die off and only the most brutal and ruthless would be left.

He heard footsteps and spun his chair toward them. Through the open door, he could see Feisal Ibrahim making his way along the dim corridor. His companions—the two ISIS soldiers—weren't in view but they were back there somewhere. Sequestered in the shadows. Breathing his air. Eating his food. Shitting in his toilet.

He'd packed away enough food for two years, but with four of them, the supply was cut to around six months. Just as bad, they creeped him out. Staring at him all the time. Talking among themselves in Arabic. They understood the heart rate monitors he wore and that everything would unravel if he died. Was that the only thing keeping them from killing him? The answer was almost certainly yes. And that was something that would have to be dealt with. Sooner rather than later, probably.

In fact, he was starting to think he'd made a mistake bringing them there. That he'd panicked when he'd started feeling the government breathing down his neck. Correcting that mistake wouldn't be all that complicated, though. There were various cleaning products available that could be used as poisons, but it was unlikely they'd be necessary. These men *wanted* to die. In all likelihood, he'd be able to just send them out into the world with a bullshit list of substation targets and let them get their wish.

But for now, they were keeping their distance and the bunker was holding up. Power generation was poor, but that was to be expected. He had solar panels strewn all over the property, but he'd been forced to prioritize camouflage over optimal placement. Combined with the intermittent cloud cover over the past week, he was paying the price.

In the end, though, it didn't matter. The bunker's position underground kept it at a reasonable temperature. The water pump was driven by a bicycle—a conscious decision designed to force him to exercise. A few LEDs were sufficient for lighting. Computers and communications—the biggest power draws—weren't really even necessary anymore. Once set into motion, his plan generated its own gravity and momentum. The monitoring of it was really just entertainment at this point.

"Is there any news?" Ibrahim asked, stopping in the threshold.

"No," Alton replied. He waved a hand back toward the equipment on his desk. "Based on what I'm seeing, none of your people have carried out a successful attack in more than seventy-two hours."

"I imagine it is getting hard to travel. That would slow them."

"Yeah. Or they may all be dead."

"We could try to contact them."

"All risk, no reward, Feisal. They have their orders and detailed instructions on how to carry them out. You told me they're reliable and I'm taking you at your word. Besides. It's done. It worked. Everything they're doing now is just gravy."

"How many American casualties?" the Arab asked.

"Believe me, that's not something the government is talking about. For sure in the tens of thousands. Keep in mind, though, that we're still in the culling-of-the-herd phase. Old people, cripples, people with existing medical conditions. But the worm's about to turn and the mortality rate will start to follow a geometric progression. Every day, twice as many strong, healthy people will die as the day before. One today. Two tomorrow. Then four, eight, sixteen . . . It's kind of a fascinating quirk of math. If it works out that way—and it won't be far off—do you know how many people will be dying every day a month from now? Millions. Congratulations, Feisal. By backing me up, you've helped do what no one's ever gotten even close to. You've defeated the United States of America. And not quickly and painlessly. This isn't some massive nuclear strike that lets everyone off the hook by killing them over the course of a few seconds. Try to imagine what's happening out there. What's *going* to happen. The violence. The desperation. I bet you ten worthless US dollars that people will turn cannibal before all this is over. When those nacho-inhaling fat asses get hungry for real, it'll be Fido first. And then they'll be throwing the local Little League team on the grill. Like the Donner Party. Tastes like chicken, right?"

The vague disgust in the Arab's expression surprised Alton, but then he remembered all the Muslim food phobias. It was one of their problems, really. All that austerity. Take away pork, booze, and casual sex, and you produced a lot of angry young men.

"When will—" Ibrahim started, but then fell silent when a ringtone began emanating from the speakers behind Alton. After his voice mail message, Janice Crane came on. It must have been the twentieth time, but it still brought a smile to his face.

"Hi, John. You haven't responded to any of my messages and I hope you're okay. Obviously, we could really use your help. And we'll make it worth your while, of course. Not only with money, but with shelter, food, medical attention . . . Whatever you need. Call me as soon as you can. Your phone's been added to the system as critical, so you'll be able to get on any remaining networks

with no problem. Anyway, again, I hope you're okay."

She hung up and Alton's grin widened. How fun would it be to pick up? Maybe even go in and fix a few things. Get a close-up view of the government's desperation while making himself a hero. Of course, there was no way. Too risky. But a kick in the ass to fantasize about.

"Why is your phone still turned on?" Ibrahim said, sounding a little alarmed.

"So I can get calls just like that one. Listening to the radio and looking at computer readouts is great. But hearing them beg . . . That's just priceless."

"What if they track you here?"

"Impossible. I've forgotten more about their communications systems than they'll ever know. Relax, Feisal. Allah's happy. Life is good. And the show's just starting."

Alton didn't realize he'd dozed off until the speakers around him sounded again. At first, he thought it was that idiot Janice Crane refusing to give up, but then he registered the different tone.

The perimeter alarm.

He'd shut down much of the exterior surveillance equipment to save power but now brought them back online. Various feeds from hidden exterior cameras appeared on his monitors and the hiss of wind in microphones filled the room.

The sun was approaching the cloud-covered western horizon, throwing long, poorly defined shadows over the landscape. Alton switched between cameras, but already knew that this wasn't another deer herd or feral dog. The mikes were enough to tell him that.

"Mr. Alton!"

He used a sound processor to filter out the wind and then zoomed a camera hidden in the burned-out house above him. The approaching figure was only an outline at first, but soon gathered detail. Brown work pants, heavy canvas jacket, baseball cap. His dilapidated pickup was just barely visible near the tree line.

"You put way too much steel into that old bomb shelter, Mr. Alton. And I saw the plumbing and electrical you were roughing in. I'm not stupid. That ain't no normal basement like you said."

The man finally got close enough for Alton to place him. He was the one who had done the structural reinforcements to the shelter. And what he was saying was exactly right. They'd been purposefully overbuilt to survive the collapse of the house when it burned.

Alton watched as he began picking through the ruins above the shelter, trying to find the entrance.

"Come on, Mr. Alton. I haven't told nobody." He motioned back in the direction of his pickup. "I have my wife and my son with me, but that's it. They're the only ones I said anything to. I know you can't afford to have a bunch of people up here. But we just need a little help. You know? Just a little."

CHAPTER 29

Washington, DC
USA

Fred Mason banked the chopper left and began to descend. "We're coming into position, Mitch. Thirty seconds."

Rapp slid the side door open and felt a blast of frozen air. He'd left his tactical clothing in the closet, opting for a pair of jeans, a Carhartt parka, and stocking cap. Not ideal, but they were casual enough to let him blend in during the day and dark enough in color to let him blend into the night. Keeping his sweater from getting caught in his rappelling gear, though, was proving to be a challenge.

The darkness that blanketed the nation's capital was broken only by the glow of a few isolated fires, likely started by people trying to stay warm. It was an increasingly common story and one that had played out two days ago in the neighborhood below him. Six city blocks had burned to the ground before being put out by an overtaxed and undersupplied fire department. A few sections were still smoldering beneath the light rain, but they'd been deemed safe enough for the fire suppression teams to move on. A perfect insertion site.

"All right, Mitch," he heard over his earpiece. "This is as good as it gets. Go!"

Rapp threw himself from the chopper's door, sliding down the rope as the rotors enveloped him in a swirl of ash and embers. By the time he hit the ground, his right boot was on fire, but it was easily smothered by a gloved hand.

"I'm clear, Fred."

"Good hunting."

Rapp covered his mouth and nose against the debris in the air and listened to the sound of the aircraft fade. The hope was that no one would notice that it had paused over the abandoned site or that a lone human figure had been briefly suspended beneath. Technically, the city was under a curfew but, without enforcement resources, it didn't mean much. The cold rain was more effective than troops, but that effectiveness was starting to wane as the situation got more dire.

Rapp began picking his way east through the rubble, pausing for a moment when he heard gunfire, but then determining that it was a long way off. When he reached the sidewalk, he put his head down and thrust his hands in his pockets. There was barely enough light to keep him on track, so it was unlikely anyone would spot him. And if they did, he'd just look like another desperate citizen trying to figure out how to get by.

He had a functioning phone in his pocket, but didn't pull it out to use the GPS. The light from even that tiny screen had the potential to draw unwanted attention. Instead, he'd memorized the route to Sonya Voronova's basement apartment and would be navigating by that mental map.

There was no guarantee she would still be there, of course. With the advantage of advance warning, she might have fled the city weeks ago. There was also no guarantee that she even existed. It could be that Boris Utkin didn't like the idea of Rapp slipping into Russia to put a bullet in his head and was leading him into a Spetsnaz ambush. Not that there was much he could do about it at this point. Ironically, it's why he'd ordered Scott Coleman to stay home. Rapp figured that if he got taken out, he could at least bleed to death knowing that the former SEAL wouldn't stop until he saw Utkin do the same.

Washington had the feeling of a war zone between bombing runs, but it was apparently in better shape than most of America's other cities. President Alexander was trying not to play favorites, but there was no way he couldn't tilt the playing field in DC's direction. A number of critical government agencies were still functioning there, and the president-elect had taken refuge in the White House in anticipation of the impending transfer of power.

Whether that would actually happen, though,

was far from certain. As was whether it even mattered. The government and power companies were still in the preliminary stages of trying to figure out what had happened. The logistics of inspecting the damage that would have been complex under ideal circumstances were being further hampered by a lack of personnel, raging forest fires, and access roads turned to mud and ice.

According to Janice Crane, the best-case scenario was that they could start getting a few small power networks online in a few months. The worst-case scenario was that everything descended into chaos before repair efforts even got off the ground. If that happened, the lights that finally came on would cast their glow over a very different country.

CHAPTER 30

Sonya Voronova peeled the tape back from the edge of her window and peeked out, scanning the night for the source of the shouts she'd heard. The forecast was for mostly sunny skies by morning and there was already enough starlight to make out vague shapes. Unfortunately, the sight line up her stairs was pretty limited and largely dominated by her car parked at the curb. Getting that optimal spot right in front of her flat was a rare event that usually gave her a pathetic sense of victory. Now all it gave her was an unobstructed view of her shattered windows and crowbarred gas tank filler.

Her Realtor had called the neighborhood up and coming, which was just a euphemism for fringe. It was all she could afford in the city, though, so she'd closed her eyes and jumped. And it hadn't been so bad. Sure, you had to be careful coming home late at night and owning a nice car wouldn't have been a good idea, but otherwise things had gone pretty well.

Until now.

More and more, the nighttime streets were controlled by groups of young men looking for whatever they could find. And it didn't seem like the government had any interest in stopping them.

There hadn't been so much as a hint of a patrol in days. The military was probably too busy making sure the wealthy residents of Chevy Chase didn't suffer a delay in their garbage pickup.

She spotted them a few minutes later. Five, maybe six, walking up the middle of the street in a tight, animated group. They seemed to be unaffected by the cold and all looked well fed—likely at the expense of others. The one in the lead broke off and entered the open door of a brick house across the street while the others waited. He reappeared less than a minute later after having discovered what she already knew—it had been ransacked two nights ago.

Voronova rubbed the tape back in place and walked to her fireplace, turning the flame on low and holding her hands up to it. They still felt stiff from her excursion into the outside world two days before. It had taken a while, but she'd finally managed to find an operating pay phone. Not that it had done her any good. The lines had all been jammed.

Unwilling to give up so easily, she'd gone back to the J. Edgar Hoover Building and tried to fight her way to the barriers. It had been a worthy effort but, in the end, all she had to show for it was a black eye.

So, with the complete failure of Plan A, Plan B, Plan A again, and Plan C, it was time to dive headlong into Plan D.

She'd spent the last few hours putting together everything she could remember about her Russian past. Her recruitment, where and how she'd been she'd been trained, the parameters of her mission. Whatever she could use to convince people that she was who she said she was. Now it was time to blast that, along with everything she knew about John Alton, out over her wimpy little ham radio. Hopefully someone in the government would hear her before the Russian embassy sent an errand boy to put a bullet in her head.

A loud, metallic clang resonated through her apartment and she leapt to her feet. The unmistakable sound of a fist on her door. She stood frozen as it came again, this time louder. The source was almost certainly a member of the gang she'd seen outside earlier. So far, the young men roaming the neighborhood seemed satisfied with stripping cars and breaking into unoccupied homes. Had things gotten desperate enough that that was changing?

The next sound wasn't a fist, but probably a foot. They were trying to kick in the door.

Her mouth had gone dry but she finally managed to get it working. "Go away!"

The kicking stopped and was replaced with a male voice. "Oh, come on, baby. Wouldn't you like some company in there?"

Laughter.

"No. Go away! I'm warning you, I have a gun!"

"Fuck your gun."

More laughter, but it was followed by retreating footsteps. Her racing heart began to slow. They were leaving. She was going to be okay. For now.

A moment later, something hit the window, shattering the glass and ripping down the thick material taped over it. She recognized one of the bricks used to elevate the flower pot on her porch as it sailed across the room and crashed into her kitchen island.

She dove for the fireplace control to turn off the flames illuminating the room and, more important, the food she'd piled on the counters. Her hand hit the edge of the plastic thermostat hard enough that it separated from the wall and was left hanging by wires. Despite her jabbing desperately at the button on the front, it wouldn't respond.

"Oh, shit, man! Come back! And bring the flashlight!"

She ran through the gloom toward the hall, as a powerful beam began wandering over her meager supplies. Excited shouts followed her as she slipped into the bedroom.

"Go away!" she shouted again, retrieving her Beretta. "I told you! I have a gun!"

"So do we, bitch!"

The light beam disappeared and the hammering on the door started again, but this time it wasn't flesh or shoe leather. It was some kind of tool.

During her time in Russia she'd been taught countless ways to kill but it had never seemed real, even at the height of her training. More like an academic exercise. Like watching flight attendants tell you what to do if your plane crashed.

She aimed around the jamb but couldn't immediately conjure the resolve to pull the trigger. Finally, she managed to squeeze off a round in the general direction of the rug in front of the threshold. The noise was deafening. Terrifying. Anyone in their right mind would run.

Unfortunately, no one in America—especially these men—was even remotely in their right mind. Instead of scaring them off, the gunshot whipped them into a frenzy. Voronova dropped to the floor and covered her head as they started returning fire through her shattered window. Flashes lit up the shadowy interior of the apartment as bullets crashed into kitchen cabinets, walls, and furniture. And somewhere beneath the sound of shattering wood and crumbling drywall was the low drone of inevitability. Her life as she knew it was over. No, that was too optimistic. Strike the "as she knew it" part. Her life was over. She might survive out in the world for a week. Maybe two. But after that, she'd be buried in America's collapse just like everyone else. Starvation. Cold. Violence. Take your pick. But it would be one of them.

She undressed quickly, replacing her sweats with a change of tactical clothing folded near the door leading to the courtyard. By the time she'd outfitted herself in cargo pants, boots, and down jacket, they'd started in on the door again. She snaked the gun around the jamb and let loose an unaimed round, but this time got no reaction at all. They just kept hammering on her door.

There was a six-pack of chocolate pudding on her desk and she used a finger to scoop the contents of all six into her mouth then slipped on a backpack prepared for just this kind of disaster. At the front of the flat, it sounded like the door was starting to give way. It wouldn't be long before they would be inside. And then it would be too late.

Starlight and memory provided enough illumination to get her across her courtyard to the drainpipe she'd climbed days before. It had connectors holding it to the wall every few feet, making the ascent fairly easy for anyone who took their time and wasn't wearing a fifty-pound pack. No longer her situation, unfortunately.

She was barely a couple feet off the ground when the sound of the door failing reached her. The men didn't show any caution at all, pounding across her floor amid excited, unintelligible shouts. Over them, she could hear her least favorite instructor's voice.

Move that sweet little ass of yours, Voronova!

The metal connectors cut her hands as she climbed, making an effort to put her backpack between her and anyone coming into the courtyard. Would it be enough to absorb the impact of small arms fire? She had no idea. But it would be better than nothing.

The sound of shattering glass became audible as the door that led from the bedroom was thrown open. Then running footsteps on flagstone accompanied by a stream of shouted taunts and insults.

She was still only about six feet up the pipe. Well within the reach of pretty much anyone.

Voronova looked back and was shocked to see fate finally cut her a little slack. The flagstones that made up her shadowy courtyard took forever to thaw and the man running across them found that out the same way she had. His feet went out from under him and he went down hard, cracking the back of his head on the unforgiving rock. Finding himself unable to stand, he instead rolled on his stomach and tried to push himself to his knees.

She continued to climb as a second man appeared in the shattered doorway. He was smarter, keeping a more cautious pace as he crossed the slick surface and leapt for her. His hand brushed her boot and then fell away. He managed to stay upright when he landed and immediately started coming after her. The darkness and his unfamiliarity with the drainpipe attachments worked against him, though.

She got a hand on the edge of the roof and used it to swing herself up onto it. A quick look around suggested there was nothing particularly weighty to throw down at the man pursuing her. The use of her gun was an obvious option but her ammunition was limited. So, instead, she just raked a thick layer of frozen leaves off the edge.

It landed right on top of his head and turned out to be enough. Whether it was the weight or just the surprise, he lost his grip and he fell five feet to the ground.

Temporarily out of danger, she found herself pausing to examine the place that had been the only real home she'd ever had. But not anymore. Now it was theirs.

CHAPTER 31

A single shot sounded, muffled in a way that suggested it emanated from inside one of the houses ahead. A few seconds later, the response came—this time multiple guns, undisciplined and outside. Probably pistols.

As a practical matter, Washington, DC, was no longer the seat of government, but its institutions were still critical to the functioning of the country. As such, the intel on the city was still pretty solid. Rapp could easily use his phone to pull up a feed of everything happening in the area—from demonstrations to functioning aid stations to fires. But it didn't seem worth the trouble. What he'd heard wasn't coming from trained government operatives or military. More likely just a skirmish between the gangs that were reportedly taking over the city's residential areas. Unfortunately, it sounded like it was coming right from where he was headed.

The intermittent gaps in the cloud cover had widened, providing enough starlight for him to make out the sidewalk beneath his feet. Not enough to safely run, but enough to sustain a moderate jog.

A few more shots rang out as he cut left, skirting a vacant lot and then turning onto the street that was his objective. There was a flickering glow that looked like it came from a fire about two hundred and fifty yards ahead, dim, but obvious in the dead city. Based on the map in his head, he registered that if it wasn't coming from Sonya Voronova's apartment, it couldn't be more than a door or two away.

Gleeful shouts were discernible, as was movement in the shuddering gloom. He retrieved his Glock and screwed a silencer to the end. With a little luck, this wouldn't have anything to do with his target and he'd be able to stick to the shadows until these idiots moved on.

Staying on the opposite side of the road, he slowed enough to allow him to take in the scene. A man carrying a box ran up from a below-ground apartment, tripping on the top step and losing his grip on the container. He stared at the contents strewn across the ground for a moment before heading back down, nearly knocking over another man in the process.

It was something Rapp had seen more times than he could count. A group of looters had found a fat target and were still in the ecstatic frenzy phase. In a few minutes they'd start to realize that there was no realistic way to transport the stuff they were stealing and that they had no use for about half of it. Shortly thereafter, they'd start to fight among themselves. No matter where you were in the world, it played out exactly the same way. Like it was a law of nature or something.

Rapp stopped next to a tree and went completely still as the men continued to haul things up the stairs. There was also activity in a few of the windows around him, but he didn't pay much attention. Just people wanting to know what was happening and whether there was potential for them to get dragged into it.

Unfortunately, the architecture in this area was pretty monotonous and the illumination wasn't sufficient to differentiate one below-ground flat from another. He was going to have to get closer.

Waiting until all the men were inside, he jogged across the street and jumped an iron fence to access the small front garden. It took a few seconds to find the number on the building but when he did he swore under his breath. Five twenty-three.

A man carrying an armload of dried beans ran up the steps and dropped them alongside the rest of the booty. When he turned, he spotted Rapp standing at the far edge of the garden.

"Get the fuck out of here," he said, pointing a menacing finger. "This is our shit and you don't even get to look at it."

"The woman who was living in that apartment. Where is she?"

"Woman?" the young man said incredulously. "Who the fuck do you think you are asking me questions?"

Rapp aimed his Glock at the man's chest. "Don't make me repeat myself."

A condescending smile, barely visible in the flickering light, crossed the man's lips. "You think that makes you a tough guy? Everybody's got a gun."

"But not everybody's got one with a silencer, dumbass."

Rapp fired a single round and the man crumpled to the ground just as one of his companions hit the lower steps. He hadn't heard the shot and was looking down at the box in his hands, not paying attention to what was going on around him until he tripped over the body.

Rapp watched him fall forward, bouncing off the box and landing face-first on the brick walkway. Finally noticing his dead companion, he went for the gun in his waistband but then froze when he found a silencer pressed to his forehead.

"Where's the woman who lived in this apartment?"

"What?" he said, sounding genuinely confused.

"It's a simple question."

"She . . . She's gone, man!"

"Gone because she ran or gone because she's dead?"

Another man came up the stairs and Rapp reoriented his weapon, firing a round through the duffle he was bear-hugging and sending him toppling backward through the open door.

The man on the ground took the opportunity to go for his gun again, but was thwarted when the butt of a Glock slammed into the bridge of his nose.

"You haven't answered my question," Rapp reminded him.

"She ran!" he said, starting to choke on the blood running down the back of his throat. "She went out the back."

"There is no back," Rapp said, pushing the end of his silencer to the man's forehead again. "Just a courtyard surrounded by walls."

"She climbed the drainpipe and went over the roof."

Rapp pulled the trigger before descending the stairs and stepping over the body in the threshold. Muted flames in the gas fireplace accounted for the unsteady light and illuminated a small, simply decorated space.

Voices were audible near the back and a moment later a man carrying a suitcase appeared in the hallway. Like his comrade from earlier, he wasn't paying much attention and completely missed Rapp standing in the kitchen with a carving knife.

The CIA man stayed in the shadows next to the refrigerator, only reaching out when the man came even with him. He ran the knife across his throat, opening a deep gash that immediately began pulsing blood. Messy, but he'd only brought a few extra magazines and his day looked like it was going to be longer than planned.

The man took another two steps, seemingly unaware of what had happened, and then dropped.

Rapp continued down the hallway, finding only a single bathroom and bedroom. In the latter he spotted a lone man with a penlight in his mouth, going through a chest of drawers.

He glanced back, squinting into the narrow beam of light for a moment before realizing that the man in the doorway wasn't one of his. He'd left his gun on a desk to his right and went for it, but Rapp shot him in the stomach before his hand could close around it.

He went down, writhing and groaning in pain as Rapp picked up his penlight and swept it across the room. They'd torn through her closet and most of the drawers had been dumped, but there wasn't much more than clothes. The door at the back was open to the courtyard he'd been briefed on and he glanced out into it.

No Sonya Voronova.

Rapp returned to a small desk that contained a microphone and what was left of a rudimentary amateur radio setup. On the floor next to it, he found a notebook with a feminine scrawl covering the first few pages. It made for interesting reading. Essentially, Voronova's life story—from her early life in a Romanian orphanage to her infiltration into the United States. Toward the end he found the names of personnel at the Russian embassy and the admonition to "speak some Russian." He ripped out the pages and stuffed them in his pocket.

"You shot me," the man on the ground moaned. "You gotta take me to the hospital! I'm bleeding bad."

Rapp ignored him and walked out into the courtyard. The drainpipe was an easy climb and he quickly found himself on the roof of the neighboring house. It was scattered with partially frozen leaves, making it easy to follow Voronova's footprints to where she'd climbed down to the street. Her current location was anyone's guess.

He pulled out his phone and dialed.

"Do you have her?" Irene Kennedy said by way of greeting.

"I was too late."

"Is she dead?"

"Probably not, but she's gone. What I did find, though, is a bunch of notes about her life and how she's a Russian agent. It looks like something designed to build her credibility."

"I don't understand."

"They were sitting next to an amateur radio setup. If I had to guess, I'd say she knows something but hasn't been able to find anyone to listen."

"We'll check to see if there's any record of her broadcasting. The military's monitoring radio frequencies in Washington. It's possible they heard something but dismissed it. There's a lot of chatter out there."

Rapp looked up at a half-moon revealed in a break in the clouds. "What I haven't found yet is her cell phone. It's possible that she's got it with her. Is there any way we can track it?"

"Hold on, let me loop in Marcus."

The CIA's tech guru came on a moment later. "Mitch! Did you find her?"

"No," Kennedy answered for him. "But he thinks she might have her phone on her. Is there anything we can do with that?"

"I authorized her on the network right after we found out about her. But we haven't been able to get anything. It's turned off."

"Can you turn it on remotely?"

"No, but I bet I know someone who can."

"The Russians," Kennedy said.

"Yeah. They're pretty obsessive about keeping tabs on their people."

"Then call them," Rapp said. "And remind that piece of shit Boris Utkin that if I don't find her, I'm flying to Russia and finding *him*."

CHAPTER 32

Near Luray
Virginia
USA

John Alton stared through stinging eyes at the computer monitor. He was exhausted but the man on-screen didn't seem to be. He continued to dig through the rubble of the house above and had now been joined by his wife and young son. Together they were doing an inefficient but energetic search for the bunker entrance. Desperation was the ultimate motivator.

His name was Burt Simmons, but it pissed Alton off that he remembered it. He had brought America to its knees. The government was using water as a weapon against its own citizens. Reliable reports were coming in about the lights flickering in Moscow and speculating that it was part of a US retaliation. He had unquestionably joined the ranks of history's greatest men and now he was being threatened by a construction worker, his fat-ass wife, and their retarded-looking-son. Genghis Khan and Caesar hadn't had to deal with people named Burt.

Alton had legal residency in Mexico and a house there owned by a maze of offshore corporations that also held millions in investments designed to do well in an economic collapse. Beneath the basement floor was a stash of gold, pesos, and euros. Ocean view, palm trees for shade, and servants who worked for peanuts. The good life by any standard.

He chewed his lower lip for a moment, thinking about basking in the warm sun with a margarita in his hand and a señorita's face in his lap. Maybe he should have triggered this thing from the comfort of his Saltillo tile veranda. Maybe the romance of sitting in his bunker command center right under the noses of the authorities had overpowered his logic.

There wasn't much he could do about that now, though. Crossing into Mexico was exactly the clusterfuck that he'd predicted. The Mexican government wasn't any more sympathetic to American refugees than the US government had been to Latin American ones. All official crossing points were completely jammed and there were credible reports of particularly desperate Americans trying to make it to Mexico illegally. A number had already died in the desert and, ironically, others had been stopped by the US-built wall—now guarded by gleeful Mexican vigilantes.

He had no choice but to wait until everything died down. Literally. Within the next year or so, the majority of Americans would be worm food. At that point, it would be easy for a well-equipped Mexican visa holder to drive through the empty middle of the country and cross the border. Then it'd be nothing but coconuts and paddleboard.

And now all that was being jeopardized in the most asinine way imaginable.

Simmons tossed aside a charred two-by-four and then stood, looking at the sun rising into a clearing sky. They'd been at it all night and had nothing to show for it. By now, even this idiot had to be wondering if he was wasting his time and precious energy by digging for one of the thousands of half-built and unsupplied bunkers scattered across the United States—victims of procrastination, lack of funds, and wandering attention.

The man seemed to read his mind, turning and picking his way through the rubble on course for his truck. A surprisingly powerful sense of relief washed over Alton as Simmons climbed in and a cloud of exhaust billowed from the tailpipe. And again he felt his anger rise at the fact that this cretin could have that effect on him.

"Good-bye, asshole . . ."

On-screen, the pickup started to move, but instead of collecting his family and heading back to the main road, Simmons drove it to within a few feet of the ruined house.

"I got a winch, Mr. Alton!" he shouted as he

stepped out of the cab. "And if that don't work, I got a friend with a backhoe. If I tell enough people about this, I figure we'll be able to scrounge up enough gas to get it up here!"

He began playing out cable from the unit on his bumper as Alton swore quietly.

"They're still here," a voice behind him said.

Alton jerked at the sudden sound and spun in his chair. Feisal Ibrahim was standing in the doorway looking down at him. The two men flanking him did the same, but through dead eyes.

"It's only a matter of time before they find the entrance," Ibrahim elaborated. "And if they don't, they'll get help. At that point, the situation will no longer be controllable."

As much as Alton hated to admit it, the sneaky Arab bastard was right. Suddenly, bringing the three of them there didn't feel like as big a mistake as it had earlier. What if he'd been alone? What would he have done? Go out there and help them? If he did that, there would be no end to it. Every time they ran out of supplies, they'd be back demanding more and threatening to tell their friends if he refused. Maybe he could have lured them down into the bunker and killed them, but that would be a messy and unpredictable business. Three wary people—even if one was a woman and another a child—would have been hard to deal with.

"No shooting," Alton said. "Someone could hear."

The men behind Ibrahim nodded and disappeared back down the corridor.

Alton focused on the screen again, watching Simmons wrap a hook around a fallen wall and start back toward the truck. His wife and kid had returned to the cab and she handed him the winch's controller through the window.

"Last chance, Mr. Alton!" he shouted.

When he got no response, he pressed the button and began dragging the wall through the debris.

Alton just leaned back in his chair, fascinated to see what would happen next. The anticipation was strangely powerful. Not as powerful as it had been before he'd knifed Muhammad Nahas or turned America's lights out, but surprisingly close. Ordering death, it turned out, was almost as exhilarating as bringing it about personally. And a hell of a lot easier.

The wall was halfway to the truck when the hidden hatch began to open. Simmons redirected his attention to the sudden movement, a smug smile spreading across his lips. A man like him would be unlikely to feel physically threatened by someone like Alton. In his tiny little mind, he was now in charge.

Predictably, his smile faded when an Arab leapt from the hole, aiming an assault rifle and barking orders in broken English. The second ISIS man appeared a moment later, running toward Simmons with a pistol while his companion provided cover.

Overall, it was a surprisingly professional operation with none of the *Allahu akbar* crap that Alton had been expecting. After barely five seconds, Simmons was facedown on the ground, begging for mercy. The Arab with the rifle used the butt to smash the passenger-side window of the truck and a moment later, the whole family was lying in a neat row on the ground. Simmons continued babbling, but then went silent when the rifle butt connected with the back of his head.

The woman screamed and made it to all fours before the man behind her dropped his pistol and drove a hunting knife into the back of her neck. Their son, on the other hand, had the quickness of youth on his side. He bolted, but found his escape thwarted by short legs. And a delicate neck, apparently. The man who chased him down twisted it a good hundred and eighty degrees, leaving him chest down and faceup in the mud.

Then it was over.

Alton could feel his heart pounding and double-checked the monitor on his wrist to make sure it was below the threshold he'd set.

"Oh, shit!" he said when he confirmed he was nowhere near triggering the release of the antidote he'd created. "That was harsh!"

He could hear Ibrahim breathing behind him but he remained silent.

"Tell your men to get the bodies in the ground," Alton ordered. "And to hide the truck in the woods. Oh. And tell them nice job."

CHAPTER 33

Washington, DC
USA

After the miserable failures of Plan A twice, Plan B, Plan C, and now Plan D, Sonya Voronova was on to Plan E. Its chance of success was pretty dismal, but it narrowly beat Plan F. Drowning herself in the Potomac.

The sun was still low on the horizon, filtering through a cloud layer in the process of breaking up. The neighborhood surrounding her was more than a little sketchy, made up of dilapidated brick houses, empty lots strewn with garbage, and the occasional boarded-up building. Cars lined the street, but pretty much all looked like the one she'd left outside her own house. Broken windows, missing radios, and jimmied gas filler covers.

Her timing had been good, though. The dangerous people who prowled the night tended to evaporate in the light of dawn.

She stopped to adjust the backpack that, only seven miles into a thirty-two-mile hike, was already cutting into her shoulders and hips. But worse, she was starving. The wolfed-down six-pack of pudding had burned off a lot faster than anticipated.

She started walking again, picking up her pace in an effort to forget her empty stomach. When the food in her pack was depleted, she was done. Best to keep her grubby paws off it until she started to get shaky.

The goal was to be across the bridge to Alexandria before anyone woke up. Whether the suburbs would be safer, though, was hard to say. America was completely different than it had been even a few days ago. People were becoming desperate. Based on the last radio reports she'd listened to, cold and fear still dominated, keeping most people huddled in their homes. For how much longer, though? How much longer would everyone be content to sit in their homes and slowly waste away? At what point would they take to the streets?

Her gut said it wouldn't be long. Maybe even today. And when that moment arrived, she'd be as likely to be murdered and robbed by a kindergarten teacher as a gang member.

If everything went right—a laughable concept in itself—she'd make it to John Alton's house forty minutes before sunset. After that, she wasn't sure. Would he still be there to confront? If so, what would she do? What would he do?

More likely, she'd find an abandoned house. And if that was the case, what then? Would she hole up there and try to survive on what was left in his cupboard? If she remembered right, that consisted of a few cans of chili, some dried pasta, and a surprisingly elaborate assortment of Hostess products. All of which had probably been looted by his hoity-toity Fairfax Station neighbors days ago.

At that point, Plan F would be in play. But walking all the way back to the Potomac to carry it out seemed like a lot of trouble. If the water was still on, maybe she could just stick her head in his bathtub. If not, she'd have to track down a convenient mud puddle.

Voronova passed a narrow alley and spotted a leg sticking out from a pile of garbage overflowing a dumpster. She tried to keep moving but felt her pace slow. A quick look around suggested that there was no one watching and it would only take a few seconds to check on the person. But to what end? What was she going to do? Call 911?

In the end, logic didn't matter. She diverted into the alley and approached the leg with caution. By the time she got to within fifteen feet, it was clear that its owner was dead. But from what?

The fact that it was completely irrelevant and that she was probably going to end up in a similar condition soon didn't matter for some reason. Something kept propelling her forward. Sympathy? Guilt? Morbid curiosity? Whatever it was, the pull was irresistible.

She used a gloved hand to brush away the

debris and found that the body had been wrapped in a hand-sewn quilt. When she pulled back its edge, she found a woman who looked to be in her late seventies. Her eyes were closed and her hair and makeup perfect. Not murder. Or even an accident, probably. She'd likely just died and her family hadn't known what else to do with her.

Voronova felt the warmth of tears on her cheeks as she carefully replaced the blanket. Who she was crying for, though, was hard to know for certain. Nothing was certain anymore. Other than that she had to keep moving.

The purely residential neighborhood eventually gave way to a section of the city with commercial space on street level and residential above. Most of the store windows had been shattered, leaving shards of glass and dangling Christmas decorations. Voronova hurried past, staying as far from the dark interiors as she could.

In the end, though, the threat appeared from the sun-dappled sidewalk, not the shadows. Three young men in hooded jackets and baggy jeans came around the corner about twenty-five yards ahead. Their eyes immediately locked on her and none seemed surprised at seeing a lone woman strolling through their territory. That prompted her to glance back over the top of her pack. Two similar men were coming up from behind.

The sight of them was enough to break her from

the fog she'd been in since finding the woman in the alley. It looked like she'd just run out of road. Even if they didn't kill her outright, there was no question that they'd take her backpack, which was pretty much the same thing. It contained all the food she had left, a sleeping bag, dry clothes, and medical supplies. The one important item it didn't contain was the Beretta. That was beneath her jacket.

The likelihood of finding John Alton and putting all this right was microscopically small. She admitted that. But it would be even smaller if she was dead or wandering around the streets in her underwear. Surprisingly, the training she thought was long forgotten came back to her on a river of adrenaline. Right now, she had the element of surprise. And she assumed she could still shoot straight enough to hit something a few feet away. But at a human being? That was very different than the paper targets she'd been so mediocre at punching holes in when she was a kid.

"What you carrying in there?" one of the men called when he and his posse were still a good twenty feet away.

How was it possible that her luck kept getting worse? There had to be a bottom somewhere. When would she reach it?

To her left, there was an indented store entrance with a still-intact door. She backed into it, protecting her flank while still giving her a view of all five approaching men. She moved a hand inside her jacket in a gesture that they wouldn't be able to misinterpret. None seemed to care, though. They just kept walking toward her.

"Nothing you'd be interested in," she answered finally.

The three men to her left were within ten feet and the ones to the right were just breaking the twenty-foot mark. All were likely armed, but their long down jackets were zipped against the cold. Apparently, they weren't feeling particularly threatened by the pale, skinny girl cowering in an alcove. And she needed to take advantage of that. While she still could.

But her hand wouldn't move.

They collected in front of her, some folding their arms across their chests, others with hands in their pockets. All staring at the crazy woman hiking through the wasteland. *Their* wasteland.

A shout floated down from above. "Leave her alone!"

The man—more of a teenager, really—who appeared to be in charge yelled back. "Shut up, you old fool!"

"Seriously," Voronova said. "It's a little backpack with barely enough to get me into Virginia."

"What are you gonna do in Virginia?"

"Try to get the lights back on," she said

honestly. Why not continue to play the crazy woman? Maybe they'd feel sorry for her and let her go.

"It's not that far," the young man said. "You can make it without the pack." He indicated with his head. "And the jacket."

A cruel smile spread across one of his companions' faces. "I don't think she's gonna need them pants, neither."

Instead of causing panic, their words had a strange calming effect on Voronova. This wasn't a scenario where she could rationalize some compromise. Where she could give up her pack in return for safe passage. Over the course of the next five minutes she was going to either live by the sword or die by it.

Her hand finally closed around the weapon beneath her jacket and a cold finger slipped through the trigger guard. She was about to warn them off one last time when the sound of her phone powering up became audible from her pack. She had no idea how it had suddenly been switched on, but it was hard to miss the fact that the tinny music had temporarily distracted the men in front of her. In all likelihood, none had heard that once-ubiquitous sound in more than a week.

She pulled the pistol and fired point blank at the man in front of her. He jerked back but didn't fall. Her conscious goal had been to hit him center of mass but her subconscious had pulled her hand right, causing the bullet to hit him in the shoulder.

Shit.

The other young men seemed suspended in time for a moment, but then all began reaching for their waistbands. She took a step forward, firing three more rounds at head level. They went harmlessly past them, but the proximity to their ears and eyes took its intended toll. All stumbled backward, clearing a path wide enough for her to run.

When she did, though, she saw two similar men coming in her direction from an alley across the street. A quick look to the right revealed another angling in from that direction.

Backup? To mug, rape, and murder a lone woman? What a bunch of wimps.

Unfortunately, one of those wimps must have gotten his gun out because a shot sounded behind her. She tensed, but there was no impact. Maybe he'd been partially blinded by powder burns from her Beretta. Or maybe he just couldn't shoot. But counting on her luck to hold wasn't much of a strategy. Particularly when more shots followed. Eventually one would find its target. Or worse, they'd just chase her down. That wasn't likely to end well. She needed to get off the street.

One of the dark stores that she'd been avoiding came up on her right and she leapt through the broken window. All the shelves were empty and many were overturned, lying alongside products not worth looting. She stumbled through it all, taking cover behind a counter. Bullets struck the shelves and walls around her but none got particularly close. The gloom was deep enough that someone outside wouldn't be able to differentiate her from all the other useless junk.

She spotted a door hanging open on bent hinges at the back of the building and ran crouched through the barrage toward it. After lunging through and kicking it closed, she activated a light attached to one of her backpack straps. The room she found herself in was pretty good-sized, virtually empty and completely devoid of doors and windows that would allow her to escape. Apparently, her instructors had a point about her combat skills.

Maybe the men out front would just give up. One had a bullet in his shoulder and a few others would have to be half-deaf. Ammo was probably getting hard to come by, too. They had to be making the calculation that one backpack wasn't worth it.

The guns eventually went silent, which seemed like a good sign. The voice that rose up in their place, though, was definitely not.

"Kill that bitch!"

Voronova desperately tried to find something to barricade the door, but the only thing with any heft to it was a wooden shelf that seemed to be screwed to the wall. She knelt next to an old rope attached to one of its legs, thinking that she could use it to tie off the door's handle. It wouldn't hold for long, but it would provide a little time to think.

She began untying it but then stopped to examine the way it wound around a pipe and then became trapped between the wall and the back of the shelf. Rising to her feet, again, she studied it for a few seconds before turning her attention to the floor. Sure enough, there were four long scratch marks that corresponded to the shelf's legs.

Clever.

She went back to the door and saw two men coming in through the broken window. Their movements were hesitant, suggesting that they were taking her more seriously than they had before. She fired a single round in their general direction to reinforce that change in attitude. Both dove to the ground, shouting in rage and pain when they landed in the broken glass. That'd buy her a little more time. The question was, would it be enough?

She grabbed a piece of steel from a broken display case and went back to the shelf. As expected, she couldn't find any sign of the screws attaching it to the wall. More evidence to support the theory that it hid an entrance to a second-floor apartment. The owners of the shop had tied that rope to the leg, looped it around the pipe, and run it beneath the door that she really, really hoped wasn't just a figment of her imagination. Then they'd used the rope to pull the shelf into place and screwed it in from the back.

She jammed the piece of steel between the shelf and the wall and began prying as shouts filtered from the main part of the store. It took some effort, but she finally managed to free the unit and shove it out of the way.

The door was right where she'd thought. Locked, of course, but a little more work prying took care of that. She opened it cautiously, sweeping her pistol from left to right as she examined a set of stairs that disappeared into the darkness.

Detecting no signs of life, Voronova slipped inside, closed the door, and threaded the rope into the same position it had been in before. A few hard pulls scooted the shelf back in place but there were no tools to reattach it. The men coming after her didn't appear to be geniuses, but even they'd figure out where she'd gone pretty quickly. Hopefully, the delay would give her time to find another exit.

She ran up the steps and tried the knob on the door that she found at the top. Not surprisingly, it too was locked. A little more work with the piece of steel in her hand was rewarded with the sound of splintering wood and a two-inch gap. She stepped to the side, putting her back against the wall and holding her gun to her chest. A gentle nudge with her foot swung the door inward.

The business end of a baseball bat appeared a moment later, slamming into the jamb a few inches from her face. She went low, centering herself in front of the door and aiming the Berretta up at a middle-aged Asian man. Surprise overcame the fear in his expression as she entered and kicked the door closed behind her.

She pointed to an armoire against the far wall. "Help me."

The canned goods it contained made it heavy as hell, but they managed to scoot it into position in front of the door.

"Do you have more screws?"

He nodded and went to the kitchen for them and a power driver that, thank God, still had a charged battery. A few minutes later, they had the armoire firmly attached to the floor and wall.

She backed away, studying their handiwork for a moment before turning her attention to the man who had helped her. "I'm sorry" was all she could think to say before going to the window and peeking around the shade.

The climb down to the fire escape was easily doable, but it wouldn't help. There were already two men waiting for her in the alley. Neither had made a move to try to climb up—the ladder was probably fifteen feet above ground level and looked like it was locked in place.

When Voronova turned back around, she saw a woman and a girl of around six standing in the hallway at the edge of the kitchen.

"I'm sorry," she said again.

The phone in her backpack started ringing, filling the room with the disorienting sound of Blondie's "Call Me." She'd forgotten about it powering up earlier and now dropped her pack in order to retrieve it.

"Hello?" she said. "Hello? Is anyone there?"

The Russian that she was expecting didn't materialize. Instead, the male voice spoke with a neutral American accent.

"Sonya Voronova?"

"Yes. Yes, that's me."

"Do you know who shut the lights off?"

"Yes. I know who he is, where he lives, and even more than that."

A muffled crash reached her. The toppling of the shelf protecting the entrance to the stairs. A moment later, someone started shooting, probably spraying the staircase that led to the apartment.

"Is that gunfire?" the man asked calmly.

"Yes. I'm trapped in an apartment above a store and people are coming after me. I'll be lucky to survive another twenty minutes. And if I die, the name you want dies with me."

An irritated sigh came over the phone and then it went dead.

CHAPTER 34

Voronova dragged a box containing canned tomatoes across the living room floor and into the bathroom. The family living in the apartment had wisely transferred much of the store's inventory there after the lights had gone out and, while it wasn't necessarily survival specific, it would do the job.

She fit the box in among similar containers stacked in front of the bathtub. Once satisfied with the placement, she leaned over the tub and looked at the terrified woman and child inside.

"Stay in here. Do you understand? It'll protect you until help gets here."

Neither spoke much English, but that didn't seem to be much of a barrier to understanding. It turned out the international language wasn't love—it was fear.

When Voronova returned to the main living area, the men who'd attacked her were now turning their attention to the door. So far, it and the armoire reinforcing it were holding, but that wouldn't last forever. The temptation to fire a few rounds through the wall was hard to resist, but she remembered what happened last time she'd given in to that particular temptation.

The man of the house was standing in the

middle of the living room, staring at the piece of furniture that they were relying on for survival. Finally, his gaze wandered to her.

"You understand English, right?" she said, suddenly realizing that she wasn't entirely sure. Everything she'd said so far had been reinforced by a fair amount of desperate body language.

"Yes," he responded through a thick accent.

"Go into the bathroom with your family. You'll be safe there, okay? Help is—" She fell silent when someone on the other side of the door started shouting excitedly. Shoving the man toward the back of the apartment, she examined the blockaded entrance as more excited voices joined the chorus. Had someone showed up with a chain saw? An explosive? She remained frozen for a few more seconds before her training started to kick back in.

A diversion.

She spun just as a man's outline appeared through the shade. He'd managed to climb the fire escape and now swung his pistol into the window glass. The maneuver wasn't very well thought out, and he cut himself badly. Instead of risking another injury tearing down the shade and searching for a viable target, he just fired blindly. The rounds landed in the kitchen, penetrating cabinets and shattering the dishes inside.

This time Voronova's subconscious cooperated. She aimed carefully and squeezed the trigger like she'd been taught, hitting him in the chest and driving him back over the fire escape's railing. She ran to the window and slammed her back against the wall next to it, peeking down at his broken body lying in the alley. One of his friends crouched over it and then shouted something. Another shout, this one muffled, followed a couple seconds later. Without cell phones, it was the only way to relay a message to the people outside the door.

Predictably, all hell broke loose a moment later.

She dropped to the floor and put her hands over her head as bullets penetrated the walls. The air turned hazy with shattered plaster and feathers from the sofa while she lay there and tried not to throw up. After everything she'd done to the family that lived there, she drew the line at barfing on their carpet.

After a few seconds the shooting died down and something became audible behind it. A deep, rhythmic thumping. Chopper blades. Then more shooting, but this time outside in the street. Footsteps running back down the stairs. Familiar shouts, angry at first, then desperate. Finally, silence.

Her hands slid from the back of her head and she peeled her cheek off the floor. Through the dust she could that see that the armoire was still in place and the fire escape was empty. A moment later the eerie quiet was broken by a knock on the door. Not the enraged pounding that she'd come to expect. Just a knock. Like someone coming by to borrow some sugar.

She didn't move.

"Open the door, Sonya."

The voice was muted but clearly belonged to the man who had called her earlier. She hesitated for a few seconds before crawling forward. The electric driver was still on the floor and she used it to remove the screws securing the armoire. It was still impossible for her to move due to the weight, so she began dumping its contents onto the floor. Once empty, a shoulder and all that was left of her strength slid it out of the way.

The door swung open on its own, revealing the owner of the voice. He was about six feet tall, broad shouldered, wearing jeans and a leather jacket. His hair was hidden by a black stocking cap that traced a line over dark eyes. A pistol fitted with a silencer hung from one hand.

He motioned for her to follow and started back down the stairs. Scooping up her backpack and shouting "I'm sorry" one more time for good measure, she hurried to catch up. The bodies strewn across the steps and landing below made it a bit awkward, though. The bile rose in her throat as she came upon a man with half his head missing, but she held it together and stepped over him. While she might not be some superhuman Spetsnaz operator, she still had her dignity. In fact, it was about all she had.

When they exited back through the broken storefront window, a helicopter hovering overhead started to descend. She turned her face away from the gale it created and saw a man standing against a wall about ten feet away. He was wearing black fatigues, with a balaclava covering most of his face and a compact assault rifle in his hands. As he fell in behind her, they locked eyes for a moment. His were deep blue and unexpectedly beautiful.

They were still twenty feet from the chopper when a man wearing a red bandana on his head appeared from a side street. She ducked when he started shooting, but the man who had saved her barely seemed to notice. He just kept walking and pointed with an index finger instead of the weapon in his hand.

"Scott."

The crack of a single shot was barely audible over the rotor noise and she saw the bandana jerk back. A moment later, its wearer slid down the wall behind him, leaving the brick streaked with blood.

CHAPTER 35

Near Luray
Virginia
USA

Alton slid a charging wire beneath his shirt and connected it to one of the heart rate monitor straps around his chest. Both were still working fine, but he'd really designed them to only be worn during his initial meeting with Muhammad Nahas. In theory, that was the only time he was to be face-to-face with the Arabs. Now, though, his skin was getting increasingly irritated and he was spending more time than he wanted connected to batteries in his control center. He had no illusions, though. Without them, he'd end up just like that construction worker and his family. Probably worse.

According to his charging app, he had a solid hour before the units were topped up, so he flipped on the radio. The Eagles' "Hotel California" began playing over the speakers and he glanced at his watch, careful not to detach a second cable connected to it. Five more minutes before Jed's live evening show. Maybe he'd have some good news. That Chicago had burned to the ground and its surviving inhabitants were now freezing to death in the ashes. That the military was opening fire on protesters in Dallas. That the failing water system in Detroit had finally given up the ghost. Whatever. He just needed a little something to break him free of the malaise that had taken hold of him after the Burt Simmons incident.

"Hotel California" gave way to some moronic country tune about pickup trucks and beer, further darkening his mood. Mercifully, it faded out after less than a minute.

"Okay, for better or worse, I'm back. And the first thing I need to do is apologize for my freak-out earlier. That was pathetic and not helpful."

He sounded like a completely different man. The energy and hope he normally exuded had been replaced by anger and frustration. Apparently, he'd finally taken a realistic look at what was happening and perhaps even caught a glimpse of his own irrelevance. It wasn't a Canadian invasion of Montana, but it was enough to put a smile on Alton's face.

"I've been doing a lot of thinking. But I'm not sure what conclusions I've come to. None good. That I can tell you. The power went out ten days ago and I don't have any reliable reports of the government having fixed anything. As far as I can tell, basically the lights are on in a few military outposts, a couple of ports, and some off-grid hippie communes. That's it. If you want

to know where we're headed, you don't have to look any further than New Orleans. Their water's completely out and the place is in the process of melting down. Based on the reports I'm getting from people on the ground, the military's in full retreat. They don't have the manpower, they don't have a supply chain, and, even worse, they don't seem to have a plan. In a week, I'm not sure there's going to be a New Orleans. And in two, I'm not sure there's going to be a New York or LA or Chicago . . . Well, you get my point."

He paused and Alton's smiled broadened. This was exactly what he needed. He was feeling better already.

"I don't think this is temporary anymore. I think the power's going to be out for months. Maybe longer. So, a lot of the advice I've been giving you is bullshit. I'm sorry for that. I truly am. And I wish I had some new speeches to make or relevant podcasts that I could dig up. But I don't. The government's basically telling you to stay in the cities and that makes sense if they can provide food, water, and security. But what if they can't? The answer is that I don't know. If you're one of the hundreds of millions of people living in a city, do you try to get out? You need to think about that. Three months down the road, if the power's still out, will you still be alive? And if you do try to get out of the city, are you capable of it? And if you're capable of it, where are you

going to go? Because you don't want to end up standing in the middle of a rural highway getting snowed on. That's not an improvement. So where am I going with this? Simple. I want someone in the government who's smart enough to find his ass with both hands to contact me. And let me tell you who that person is. TJ Burton from FEMA. Everyone says he's a solid guy who gives a shit. Do you hear me, TJ? People are saying I have the biggest audience in the country right now. So why don't you cowboy up and come on my show? Tell the people who pay your salary what the hell's going on and what you're doing about it. They deserve to know and droning on about how they should stay calm and stay put isn't cutting it anymore. And let's be clear here. We all know people from the government are listening. So, if you don't *come on, everybody out there is going to know you got nothin'. That we're on our own to survive."* He paused dramatically. *"Okay. The gauntlet's been thrown. Let's see what happens . . ."*

More unbearable country music came on and Alton lowered the volume. Maybe he'd get into the snack cakes tonight. As a reward. It had taken less than two weeks to break the infamous Jed Jones. And where Jed Jones went, so went America.

After another fifteen minutes of boring battery charging, images of the two Arab enforcers appeared on his monitor. One had a shovel over his shoulder and the other was carrying an assault rifle. They'd been gone for quite a while, but that wasn't surprising. The ground was largely frozen, making the burial of the Simmons family problematic. And camouflaging their truck would have been an even bigger job.

He watched them open the hatch and then turned off his monitor when they started down the ladder. A rather energetic discussion in Arabic echoed through the tight space, followed by footsteps coming his way.

"Is it done?" Alton said, when the three Arabs entered his control room behind him. He wasn't able to turn because of the cables and instead looked at them in the reflection of his dark computer screen.

"They won't be found," Ibrahim responded, sounding a bit subdued. In contrast, the men with him had taken on noticeably aggressive postures and were still in possession of their weapons. They wouldn't make a move, though. They wouldn't dare.

"Good."

"My men want to know what we're doing here. If that man was able to find you, others can, too."

"Then we'll deal with them."

"I'm not so sure. This was one family. A woman and a small child. Are we sure he was telling the truth when he said he hadn't spoken to anyone about this place? Are we sure no one will miss them?"

Alton finally unplugged from his power source and spun in the chair to face them. There was no question he was between a rock and a hard spot. While he wanted rid of these Arabs in the worst way, they'd proven useful. Ibrahim was right. They might have more problems. And if so, he didn't want to be trying to handle them on his own.

"We'll deal with it," Alton repeated.

"Based on your monitoring of the situation, you've concluded that our people are all either dead or captured. That means that they can't destroy any of the remaining critical targets. These men can."

"Really? The most important target still standing is in Ohio. How do they plan to get there?"

"Both are very well trained and extremely motivated."

Alton shook his head incredulously. "You're one hundred percent dedicated to snatching defeat from the jaws of victory, aren't you? America is cratering. And this is just the beginning. In a week or two, we're going to reach the tipping point and three hundred and fifty million people are going to go completely insane. They're going to be starving, freezing, and dying of thirst. At that point, they're going to do anything—and I mean anything—to survive. Burning their cities, killing their best friends, attacking government installations . . . And all you have to do is sit here and not fuck it up. The most important thing you and your people can do is stay here and make sure I'm safe."

"To what end? If you've already been so successful, why is your continued safety so important?"

Alton held his arms up, displaying the heart rate monitors on his wrists. "Do we need to go through this again? If I get killed, the government gets a full report of everything I did and how I did it. With that, they could have half the country back up and running in a week. Basically, all you'll have accomplished is to create a really annoying blackout that two years from now no one will remember."

Ibrahim nodded thoughtfully. "So, we're your hostages. Our role is to protect you from any and all threats. Because your safety is all that matters to you."

"*Hostage* is an ugly word, but I think that's a pretty accurate assessment of your situation. And it's a fair trade. Hell, it may be the best trade in history. I've given you everything you ever wanted. And in return, all I ask is that you protect me for a while. In a year or so, when I'm safely across the Mexican border, you can run off and martyr yourselves in any way you want. But for now, you're going to just have to sit here and take the win. How hard is that? What? God isn't going to be impressed by you wiping out America because you didn't die in the first few days of the operation? Is he going to hold back some of your virgins or something?"

Ibrahim nodded, and spoke in Arabic to his men, undoubtedly explaining the unbelievably simple situation they found themselves in. Inexplicably, instead of comprehending that they were in the catbird seat, their expressions darkened further. What a bunch of complete tools. No wonder they still lived in tents and considered camels high-tech transportation.

CHAPTER 36

West of Manassas
Virginia
USA

Sonya Voronova came out of the bathroom wrapped in a towel, pausing once again to take in her surroundings. The bedroom was large and elegant, with massive log beams and floor-to-ceiling windows that were now blacked out. The sensation of warmth penetrating the bare soles of her feet suggested that the heat was still on, but not turned up very high. Clothes had been laid out on an impeccably styled bed that looked like it had never been slept in.

The jeans were almost exactly her size and the gorgeous cashmere sweater felt like a cloud, but smelled like another woman. Another woman with serious cash to throw around on her wardrobe.

The suede boots were a tad tight, but looked great with the sweater. Once dressed, though, it was hard to know what to do next. She'd expected to be thrown in a hole somewhere but instead the blue-eyed man had brought her here. After giving him John Alton's name, she'd half-expected him to kill her. Instead, he'd brought her a glorious peanut butter and jelly sandwich, installed her in this room, and left.

She'd sat upright on the bed for about an hour but no one ever came. Showering and getting dressed had taken her mind off both her looming fate and the man she'd killed, but now there she was again. Standing this time, but still surrounded by an empty house.

"Screw it," she said finally, and exited the bedroom into a dim hallway. It led to a truly grand entryway and then a kitchen and living room divided by a massive stone fireplace. There was a bunch of wood piled in it, so she figured she'd take advantage. A little crumpled newspaper and a lighter she scrounged from the kitchen were all it took.

The light danced disorientingly around the room, playing off a set of even larger blackout shades covering windows that looked like they belonged in a cathedral. The warmth was nice, though. She considered sitting directly on the hearth but then rejected the idea out of concern that a spark might jump onto her borrowed sweater.

Instead, she removed the boots, pulled up a chair, and propped her feet in front of the fire. A drink was all that was missing. A very large, very strong drink.

After she had spent fifteen minutes of staring into the flames, her fear, guilt, and uncertainty started to give way to a powerful sense of loneliness. Why? She had no idea. She'd lived alone since moving to the United States. Maybe it was the size of the place. Or the unfamiliarity. Or the fact that she really *was* utterly alone in the world. Even the superficial relationships she'd had with handlers, consulting clients, and local shopkeepers were now stripped away. It could be argued that her closest relationship in the world was with a blue-eyed man whose name was probably Scott and who would likely kill her when he got home.

After another ten minutes, she'd had about as much quiet contemplation as she could stand. There was an elaborate stereo system in the living room and she walked over to it. The power button made a bunch of lights come on, which was a good sign. But no sound. The complexity of the system turned out to be a plus—taking her mind off everything else for another few minutes as she tried to figure it out. Finally, she was rewarded with the strains of Bruce Springsteen's "The River."

Perhaps the most depressing song ever written.

A tablet attached to the system contained a playlist and she decided on one with the self-explanatory title *Elvis*.

It was a significant improvement until it was joined by the hum of a garage door going up. She froze in the middle of the room, listening to the door go silent for a moment and then descend again.

After about another thirty seconds, she spotted the shadowy figure walking toward the refrigerator. It seemed like he hadn't noticed her, but when he turned back to the kitchen island with a piece of pie in his hand, he spoke.

"I love this record. My parents used to play it when I was a kid."

He was still wearing black fatigues but the balaclava was gone, revealing a handsome face and close-cropped blond hair. The gun strapped to his thigh was hidden by the cabinets but the dried blood on his sweater was visible even in the dim light.

"I like it, too," she heard herself say.

"So, you can build a fire. Can you cook?"

She nodded.

"Go to it, then. I'm gonna hit the shower."

When he reappeared again, he was wearing jeans and a gray sweatshirt. No visible weapon, unless you counted the wine bottle in his hand. Not that he'd need one if he decided to get rid of her. She'd met enough men like him during her training that she knew with great precision what he was capable of.

"I found some canned clams and linguini. So, I made pasta."

"Perfect," he said, sounding vaguely relieved. "I was afraid you'd make Russian."

He slid the bottle toward her across the counter. "It's from my cellar. I think it's supposed to be good."

"You don't know?"

"Not really. A friend of mine gave me a list of what I should buy." He pointed to the sweater she was wearing. "In fact, that's hers."

Voronova grabbed a couple of glasses and an opener off a rack and started working on the cork. She had a thousand questions that she didn't really want to know the answers to. Better to just keep her mouth shut and pour.

He took a sip, shrugged, and then downed half the glass.

"He wasn't there."

"You mean Alton?"

"Yeah. It doesn't look like anyone's been in that house for a while."

The silence stretched out between them, with only the sound of the fire, "Heartbreak Hotel," and boiling water to keep it from becoming oppressive. Finally, she waved a hand around her at the house. "This isn't what I expected."

"No?"

"No. At worst, I figured a CIA dungeon. At best maybe a cage in some government bunker."

"We turned the Agency's dungeons into racquetball courts a while back and the government's bunkers are really crowded. Mitch hates crowds."

"Mitch?" she said, taking a sip of wine. The

anonymous woman's good taste apparently wasn't limited to sweaters.

"You met him earlier. Leather jacket? Kind of humorless?"

She swallowed another—this time much larger—gulp of wine at the memory of him. "I tried to contact the FBI but you can't get anywhere near their building. And I was about to get on ham radio and broadcast everything I knew. I had a script and everything. But then my house got attacked."

"Yeah, I know."

The alarm on the stove went off and she nearly dumped her drink all over herself. It was a narrow save, but she managed to put it down and start preparing a couple of plates.

He dug in like he hadn't eaten in a week while she took a position on the stool across from him. It was hard to determine his age exactly. His skin had seen a lot of sun and wind over the years, but his eyes were sparkly and he had an easy smile that seemed sincere.

She was still picking at her first few bites when he finished and leaned back to contemplate her. The smile, she noted, had disappeared.

"Mitch is coming over to talk to you."

"Okay," she responded, looking down at her food.

"He can come off as a bit . . ."

"Dangerous?" she offered.

"Yeah. But the truth is that he just likes to get from point A to point B in the most efficient way possible."

She nodded and spun a little pasta on her fork.

"So, here's my advice to you, Sonya. Don't lie. And don't get longwinded or start trying to answer questions he hasn't asked you. Right now he thinks of you as a Russian operative who was following orders. He doesn't have a personal problem with you. Don't give him reason to develop one."

"And if he does?"

He refilled his glass and took a swig. "Look, I'm sure you're really good at your job and at manipulating people. But you're not going to play us off each other. This isn't good cop, bad cop. It's bad cop, worse cop."

"So, you'll kill me if he asks you to?"

"He won't ask. Mitch is capable of doing his own wet work."

"But if he does?"

"Then you're going to end up under my lawn."

"Thank you for your honesty."

The smile returned. "Try to relax, Sonya. You don't seem stupid and none of us really blame you for this. We've all been on the wrong end of fucked-up orders. Just play it straight, okay?"

They were almost through the bottle of wine when the front door opened. Reluctantly, she turned to watch the man approach. If she was going down, she wasn't going to do it cowering.

"Do I smell food?" he asked.

Scott pointed to the stove. "Linguini and clams. Dig in."

Mitch—his last name was still a mystery—piled some food on a plate and joined them at the island before dumping what was left of the wine in a water glass. She watched him eat, and tried to walk the tightrope between staring and avoiding eye contact. While he and Scott might be in the same business, they seemed very, very different.

He was through his food in less than a minute and went back to the stove to get seconds.

"What's Russia's involvement in this?" he asked while he fished the rest of the pasta from the pan.

When she spoke, she discovered her mouth had gone dry. "None. John Alton contacted us and I was sent to meet him with orders to evaluate whether he could do what he said he could."

"Is there beer?"

"In the fridge," Scott said.

He dug out a bottle before coming back to the island.

"What was your conclusion?"

"That he was credible."

"And that's what you told your superiors?"

"Yes," she said, deciding that she no longer felt any loyalty to Moscow. In fact, fuck them.

"And their reaction was what?"

"That they weren't interested but that they weren't going to do anything to stop it. I was told that they were going to cut off all contact with the subject and I was ordered to forget all about it."

"How did you know where he lives then?"

"I knew what he looked like and stumbled across a picture of him on the Internet. After that, I kind of couldn't help myself. I started researching him."

"And?"

"It was just stuff in the public record. You know, until I broke into his house."

He stopped eating and looked directly at her. "You broke into his house? Back when he was still living there?"

She nodded.

"Did you find anything?"

"Not really. I tried to clone his hard drive, but he came back partway through the process."

"Do you still have what you recovered? Is it in your apartment?"

She shook her head. "It's on my phone. Upstairs."

He and Scott exchanged a look that suggested they were reading way more into this than there was.

"Before you get too excited, I had to yank the cable out while it was still backing up and that may have corrupted what data managed to transfer. Plus, it was encrypted and Apple FileVault is no joke. I threw everything I had at it and came up empty."

CHAPTER 37

"I think I'm going to keep her."

Rapp leaned against the back wall of his kitchen and focused on Sonya Voronova as she stirred a steaming pot and chatted with Claudia.

"She's not a pet, Scott. She's a Russian mole."

"What do you want me to do? Kill her?"

Rapp took a pull on his beer. "I'd be lying if I said it hadn't crossed my mind."

"Come on, Mitch. She got backed into a bullshit situation by the president of Russia. And she tried to make things right. It's more than most people would do."

"Then throw her back. Fill her backpack with some provisions and tell her to hit the road."

"She'd die out there."

"Better than you waking up one day with your throat slit."

Coleman shrugged. "What can I say? I like hot, dangerous women. And don't pretend you don't. Between Claudia and Donatella, it's a miracle you're still breathing."

Rapp shrugged. "It's your jugular. Do what you want."

The doorbell rang and Claudia shouted to her daughter without looking up from the elk roast she was slicing. Less than a minute later, Anna appeared with Marcus Dumond in tow.

Kennedy had wanted to set up a face-to-face and the obvious meeting place was Rapp's house. It was almost dead between Langley, where Dumond was camped out, and the West Virginia bunker where she was now living full-time. A satellite connection would have been a hell of a lot more convenient, but no one was one hundred percent certain it was secure anymore. Or if it would even work.

"Real food," Dumond said, leaning over the roast and peeking into the pots on the stove. "You must be Sonya. I'm Marcus."

Voronova shook his hand sheepishly before turning her attention back to cooking. She seemed to think her survival was directly linked to her being useful and blending into the furniture. Not entirely wrong.

"Come on!" Anna said, grabbing his hand again. "I've got a puzzle upstairs I can't finish. You're really good at those. I'll bet you can get it done before Dr. Kennedy comes. We've still got a few minutes. Come *on!*"

Anna's ETA on the CIA director turned out to be a little optimistic and she'd barely dragged him past the refrigerator before the bell rang again. Rapp started for the front of the house as Claudia called after him.

"The food will be ready in about an hour, Mitch."

"Can you bring it to us?"

"Absolutely not. We're going to pretend we're still civilized people and eat in the dining room. You're going to need a break by then anyway."

He nodded. No point in starting a dispute he was destined to lose. "Don't forget to send something out to Irene's security detail. They're going to want to stay on the fence line and I'm guessing they haven't had a decent meal in more than a week."

"This was worth the trip," Kennedy said. "I was starting to forget what normal life was like."

The fireplace was roaring and there was an open bottle of red wine on the coffee table. Dumond and Coleman had already helped themselves to generous portions and were parked on the couch. Rapp poured her the minuscule splash that she tended to like in these types of meetings.

"You look tired," Coleman said, not bothering to hide his concern.

"I'm fine," she said, sinking into a chair with her glass in hand. It was an obvious lie, but there wasn't much to be done. The island of calm that she'd constructed at the CIA was below the waves at this point. And she was drowning.

"Where do we stand?" Rapp said, falling into a chair across from her.

Kennedy took a cautious sip of her drink and a satisfied smile crossed her lips. She savored it for a moment before answering. "The FBI's gone through John Alton's house, but they didn't find anything. It had already been broken into and emptied out when they got there. We're looking to find the people who ransacked the place, but I'm not hopeful that we'll turn up anything useful. His phone is still connected to the network, but we haven't been able to trace its location. He's too smart to make a mistake like that."

"But you think he's behind this?" Rapp said. "That Voronova's telling the truth?"

"The circumstantial evidence is strong," Kennedy responded. "He's one of the only people in the world with the know-how and access to do something like this, and now he's disappeared. We've also discovered that he has legal residency in Mexico. We're trying to find out if he owns property there, but that's easier said than done."

"But what's the motive here?" Coleman said. "Why would he do something like this? What's in it for him?"

"The FBI profilers are talking to people who knew him and a picture's starting to emerge. Basically, Alton's socially isolated, feels no compassion for others, and has extremely powerful delusions of superiority. He feels that he hasn't gotten his due from society, from women, from his employers . . . And now he's looking to make everyone pay."

"So, a brilliant psychopath who's probably doing tequila shots at his beach house in Mexico right now."

She stared into her glass thoughtfully. "Maybe. Probably, in fact. But the profilers think there's a chance he's still here."

"Here in the US?" Rapp said. "Why?"

"They think he'd want to see this happen up close. That watching Mexican news reports wouldn't be . . ." Her voice faded for a moment. "Personal enough."

"That's great, but America's a pretty big country."

"True. And that's where Marcus comes in."

Rapp turned to him. "The data Voronova pulled from Alton's hard drive. She said it wouldn't be easy to crack."

"That's an understatement," Dumond said. "We're talking about a partially completed data transfer from a heavily encrypted disk that she didn't eject properly. It isn't like the movies where you—"

"—try a few passwords and you're in," Rapp said, completing his sentence for him. "I've been hearing this from you since you took the job. But there has to be *something* you can do. You've got the full attention of the US and Europe. And with China's export business collapsing, I'm guessing they'd help you out, too."

"Look, all I've been able to do is completely

decrypt the disk, download all the usable data, and send it to our analysts at the FBI. Beyond that, my hands are tied."

Rapp frowned, unsure he understood what he'd just heard. Kennedy smiled and came to the rescue.

"I imagine Marcus has been rehearsing that line all day."

"Not *all* day," he said, grinning. "But for pretty much the whole drive over."

"You're saying you did it?" Rapp said incredulously. "Already? How? You've always said that getting into Apple's stuff was virtually impossible—that even *they* can't do it. Are you telling me that a guy smart enough to bring down the entire US power grid used his dog's birthday as his password?"

"Not exactly," Dumond said. "We called the CEO of Apple to see if there was anything they could do to help us. We expected him to say *no* like usual, but that didn't happen. It turns out that when they're losing a billion dollars a day and thinking they might starve to death, they suddenly remember the back door they built into their encryption."

"You've got to be kidding."

"Nope. Took 'em less than five minutes."

"Is there anything we can use?"

"We don't know yet," Kennedy said. "Despite the corruption and the fact that Sonya had to shut down the transfer prematurely, there's a lot of data to sift through—everything from old credit card receipts to pornography. The bottom line, though, is that staying in the US during this isn't a trivial matter. You know that as well as anyone that he'd have to set up a secure location. And if that's the case, the hope is he's left some trail to it."

"And what if he hasn't?"

"Responders are very close to exhausting what few supplies they have access to and the water systems in our major cities are on the verge of failing in rapid succession."

"Is there a plan to handle that?" Rapp said.

Kennedy stared into the flames reflected in her glass. "None at all."

CHAPTER 38

Near Linden
Virginia
USA

The recording playing over the stereo in Claudia's Tesla X ended and instead of switching to the next, Rapp just let silence descend. It was a couple of hours before dawn and he was navigating the vehicle using a night-vision monocular attached to a combat helmet. A little ridiculous, but necessary.

Four days ago, Irene Kennedy and Marcus Dumond had been able to get to his house without too much difficulty. But the situation was worsening exponentially—just like TJ Burton had promised. Being on the road in a functioning vehicle was completely different now than it had been only ninety-six hours ago. Without a military escort to protect him from America's increasingly desperate citizens, stealth was critical.

In truth, it would have been better not to be on the road at all, but that wasn't an option. He'd been ordered to attend a meeting at the Seneca bunker and, despite a fair amount of effort, hadn't been able to get out of it. The purpose of the meeting was a mystery, but he was starting to suspect. And if those suspicions were right, he was going to personally put his foot in the president's ass.

Rapp finally reached for the car's touchscreen to start the next installment in a series of radio segments that had been compiled by the CIA. A moment later, the voice of Jed Jones came on. The subject matter wasn't the nutritional value of insects or the art of not shitting near your water source, though. In recent days, Jones's wildly popular show had taken on a darker tone.

Still nothing from the government. Six days since I asked the head of FEMA to come on and explain himself and not a fucking peep. They're too busy running the same public service announcements they were the day the lights went out. And that's bullshit. There are reports of more and more people taking to the streets and why wouldn't they? Because they don't want to miss the government's latest prerecorded messages saying they should stand by for more information that never comes? Let me just tell you this. I'm having off-the-record conversations with soldiers out there who aren't sure what their operating parameters are anymore. That different commanders are making different calls. They're scared shitless that tomorrow they're going to be ordered to open up on their fellow countrymen—hungry people who just want to know what the fuck's going on.

The recording paused for a moment before switching to another CIA-curated episode.

I hear people out there saying that a bunch of foreign countries are going to bail us out. That we bailed them out more times than we can count and even our enemies need us. We're the largest economy in the world and we're connected to everyone. But I've been talking to other radio operators all over the world and I can tell you that help ain't coming. We live in an interconnected world and America was the biggest piece. Yeah. That's true. But think about it. Take us out of the picture and every other country in the world is flailing around trying to plug the hole.

Another brief pause and another episode switch.

Where's the president? Where's his cabinet? Kicking back in some bunker watching America go down the toilet. Doing nothing. Saying nothing. You know what we should all start watching out for? The disappearance of hot young girls. Seriously, if you've got a good-looking eighteen-year-old daughter, keep her hidden. 'Cause the geriatric bastards running this country are going to need some quality tail to help them repopulate after you're dead.

Rapp spotted a broken-down SUV in the middle of the road and eased silently around it.

At least we know where the congressmen are.

They're at home being protected and provided all the creature comforts. If you're cold or hungry, maybe that's where you should go looking for supplies? I mean, why not? We're—"

Rapp shut off the radio and let out a long breath.

Fuck.

Returning his full attention to the hazy green of the road, he accelerated to the edge of what night vision would allow. He was still an hour and a half out and already running ten minutes behind schedule. Instead of pushing the pace, though, he wondered if he wouldn't be better off turning around. This wasn't going anywhere good.

After about fifteen minutes of nothing but the sound of tires on the asphalt, his phone began ringing over the sound system. Not Claudia calling to check up on him, though. He wasn't that lucky.

"Hello, Irene."

"It looks like you're running a little late."

"Worse than that, I was just thinking about spinning it and going home."

"So, you've listened to the recordings I sent you."

"Yeah."

"We found where he's transmitting from some time ago but we let him keep broadcasting. He was a largely positive force that could say things the government couldn't. Now that seems to have changed."

"Still a free country," Rapp said. "He can say what he wants. Particularly when people are dying and the government's running PSAs about planting a garden."

"He's inciting violence against government personnel. That's pushing free speech a little far."

"He's pointing out that the incompetent, corrupt assholes who did this to them are living large, while they starve. Why shouldn't they take what some senator or congresswoman has? Why shouldn't they attack the bunker you and the president are holed up in? Hell, why shouldn't they show up on my doorstep? The American people pay us to keep this kind of thing from happening and we fucked up."

"That's why you've been included in this meeting. We're going to have to move to phase two and the president wants to hear from people he trusts."

"Phase two? What the hell is phase two?"

"That's what we're going to try to determine."

"Let me tell you something right now, Irene. I'm an assassin. For better or for worse, I own that. But I'm not a murderer. If the president wants me to put a bullet in some amateur DJ for speaking too much truth, he can go fuck himself."

There was a brief silence over the line before she came on again. "Let's leave that discussion for another time. It's not actually why I called."

"No? Then what?"

"We found something interesting on John Alton's hard drive. It'll probably turn out to be nothing, but we're not in a position to be choosy about what we follow up on."

"What is it?"

"A fragment of a delivery notification for some construction materials. We weren't able to recover the complete address, but the FBI's been able to piece together a probable location."

"Are they sending a team?"

"Yes, but they're a little more than two hours out."

"What's that to me?"

"It just so happens that you're currently within forty miles."

The proximity alarm woke Alton from a dream and he muffled the dull wail by pulling a pillow over his head. It had become an almost daily occurrence that always seemed to happen at the crack of dawn. For some reason, the deer were migrating across his property and every time they did, they got picked up by his motion sensors. The only consolation was that they were probably fleeing desperate, starving people chasing them with wooden spears. Why wooden spears? Why not? It was a great mental image.

He considered getting up, but not because of a bunch of flea-bitten pests. Because the shit was really starting to hit the fan. The effect of

America's collapse on the rest of the world was far greater than even his most optimistic estimates. And the government's ability to handle that collapse was far worse. He'd at least expected a healthy dose of panic, and some world-class demagoguery. But what he was getting was paralysis.

Pathetic.

Having said all that, Armageddon would still be happening an hour from now. And Jed Jones's morning doom-and-gloom show wouldn't come on for another two. No point in leaping out of bed just yet.

He was almost back to sleep when the pounding started. At first, he thought it was part of an oncoming dream, but no such luck.

"What?" he shouted.

"There's someone out there," came the answer from the other side of the door. Alton always kept it locked while he was sleeping. The Arabs seemed to be under control, but they were a shifty bunch. Best to be careful.

"It's just another deer, dumbass."

"It's not a deer. We can see it on the monitor."

Alton swore quietly as he rolled out of bed and pulled on a tracksuit. After sliding into a pair of slippers, he walked across his luxurious sleeping quarters and yanked the door open.

Feisal Ibrahim was standing on the other side and Alton brushed past him on his way to the control room. Inside, he found the two other Arabs studying the computer screen on his desk.

"Get out of the way," he said, falling into his chair and looking at a shadowy outline moving through the starlight. He switched to night vision and zoomed, pulling in tight on the figure. An adult male, with a distinct limp and a gloved hand holding the front of his coat closed. A stocking cap obscured his hair and he had a scarf wrapped around the lower portion of his face.

"This is what you woke me up for?" he said, pointing to the screen. "Some half-starved scavenger?"

"How can you be sure that's who he is?" Ibrahim said.

"I can't be sure. But what do you want me to do? Go out there and shoot him? What would be the point? When he finds out there's nothing here, he'll move on."

"And if he doesn't?"

Alton rose from his chair. "Then come and wake me up again. But until then, keep it down, okay?"

CHAPTER 39

The frozen dirt road led to an expansive clearing and Rapp limped into it. He was pretty well covered up due to the cold, but it had been pointed out to him that he had a unique way of moving that was easy to spot. The unsteady gait was a remedy for that and, frankly, not all that hard to feign. His left knee was beat to shit, just like the rest of him.

A sky full of stars and a half-moon provided enough light to see that he was in the right place. The burned ruin of a house and undamaged barn perfectly matched the overhead images the Agency had sent him.

He spotted movement out of the corner of his eye but immediately identified it as nonhuman. Probably a deer. Continuing forward, he focused on the former home site. Not that there was much to see. The brick fireplace and a few charred walls were all that was left standing. An uncomfortable reminder of his Chesapeake Bay house. And of the wife and unborn child who had died there.

It was possible that there was an intact basement beneath the rubble, but it wouldn't exactly be the most comfortable place to rubberneck the end of the world. The barn would be a less oppressive accommodation, but probably a little too obvious.

Sooner or later, someone would take interest in it and what useful supplies it might contain.

Rapp knew nothing about profiling psychos, but it was hard not to second-guess the FBI guys. Why would someone as smart as John Alton want to hole up here when he could be sipping umbrella drinks in Mexico? The profilers got more right than they got wrong, though, and the truth was that Rapp couldn't figure out why people did half the shit they did. The only thing he was absolutely certain of was that his species was a few cards short of a full deck. Maybe more than a few.

He turned toward the barn, listening to the frozen weeds crunch beneath his boots as he approached. The main doors were closed, but a smaller door in the side was being pushed gently back and forth by the wind. He retrieved a flashlight from his coat and turned it on, entering cautiously and sweeping the beam around the cavernous interior.

For the most part, it was what he'd expected. Shovels, rakes, a lawn tractor with various accessories. Some stacked lumber and a pile of unsplit firewood. The exception was a six-wheeled military-grade cargo truck. Rapp recognized it as similar to ones he'd piloted over the years, but with a faded logo on the door that suggested it had once been used to fight wildfires. The canvas walls that normally enclosed the cargo area had been swapped for steel and all the glass was covered with heavy screening.

A quick examination suggested that the vehicle had seen better days. The tires were all flat, the upholstery in the cab was rotting, and the exterior was covered in a thick layer of dust. The overall impression was of a forgotten vanity restoration project. Rapp opened the rear doors and aimed his flashlight inside. Empty, but formidable. Whoever added the steel carcass to the back hadn't cut any corners.

A closer inspection of the tires revealed that, while lacking air, they were actually in pretty decent shape. Not much wear and no visible dry rot. A few seconds crawling around beneath the chassis turned up no obvious fluid leaks and revealed an auxiliary fuel tank that looked custom. He banged on it with the flashlight, producing a hollow ring that suggested it was empty. But huge. Gassed up, the thing would probably have a range of more than a thousand miles. He slid out and was tempted to look under the hood, but the FBI guys would be there soon and they'd piss themselves over everything he'd touched.

Rapp ascended a set of stairs along the back wall, finding that they led to a door that looked like it had been kicked in. Passing through, he found himself in an apartment that felt recently constructed. The beam of his flashlight bounced off granite counters, stainless steel appliances, and furniture that bordered on luxurious. Nice, but definitely not designed with survival or security in mind. Flimsy door, no obvious power generation, and no evidence that it had ever been stocked with supplies.

He turned off the flashlight and took a seat on the sofa, examining the space by what little moonlight could filter through the windows. What now? Get back on the road to his meeting with the president? Execute a radio personality who had started running his mouth a little too hard? Phase two, whatever the hell that was? Maybe Jed Jones was right. Maybe Rapp would be sent out to scour the country for young girls to keep the powers-that-be entertained while the country burned. Probably not, but it was hard to imagine something like that wasn't coming. Maybe not until Phase Three, but certainly no later than Phase Five.

Rapp heard the vehicle before he saw it. Like him, the FBI team was driving with headlights off to avoid attracting attention. Unlike him, they'd gone with a traditional gas motor.

The horizon was starting to hint at dawn, just enough to erase the stars to the east but not enough to wash out the darkness surrounding him. When the vague outline of an SUV became visible, Rapp walked into the road and directed it into a gap in the trees.

Randall Sikes stepped from the passenger seat, grabbing a down jacket and slamming the door. "You're always one step ahead of me, Mitch. Have you been up to the site?"

"Just came down."

They shook hands as three thirtysomethings piled out of the vehicle and went around back to get their gear.

"Did you find anything?"

"A military transport truck that's probably worth looking over and an empty apartment above the barn, but that's it. I didn't want to do anything too obvious in case I was being watched."

"And I assume you didn't touch anything."

"Absolutely not."

Sikes laughed. "Okay, we'll walk up now and do a low-key overview of the place. Get an idea of what we want to concentrate on and whether it's worth bringing in a drone with infrared. I've been told to keep everything nice and calm. If we find this little bastard, it's been made crystal clear that we can't even mess his hair up. In fact, the director called him the most important man in the world."

"I'd like to do a hell of a lot more than mess up his hair," Rapp commented, and then motioned to Sikes's people. "Is this all you've got?"

"Nah, we have a security team on the way with some heavier equipment, but they had to stop at a gas cache to fill up. They'll be along in ten minutes or so."

"So, you're good without me, Randy? I'm late for a meeting with the president."

"The president? Well, la-di-da. You've come a long way from your days of getting slapped around by Stan Hurley."

"Maybe too far."

"Yeah, take off. We got this."

Rapp slapped him on the shoulder and started toward his car. "Do me a favor and find something I can use, okay?"

"We'll do our best. Mitch."

Rapp put on a pair of sunglasses as the rising sun turned blinding. He didn't like being out on the road during the day but there wasn't much choice at this point. He'd hoped his detour would allow him to miss his meeting, but the president had pushed out the time to compensate for Rapp's late arrival.

A sharp corner forced him to slow and, as he did, movement became visible in the treetops to his right. He hammered a foot down on the brake and was thrown forward as the car's computers fought to maximize traction.

The tree, probably a good foot and a half in diameter, fell across a choke point in the road, making it impossible to maneuver around. He managed to stop before the front bumper impacted but not before the hood got crammed beneath thick branches. Not good. He was already in the doghouse for rolling his eyes when Claudia bought this thing to save the environment and now the front end was going to be scratched to shit.

He glanced in the rearview mirror and, as expected, a similar tree fell about thirty feet behind. Through the branches ahead, a man was visible approaching with an AR-15. Another appeared from the woods about twenty feet back, holding a hunting rifle of some kind. Based on their tactics—or, to be more precise, the lack thereof—it was likely that they were more accustomed to prey of the four-legged variety.

Rapp reached for his Glock as his mind played out what was about to happen. Throw open the door. Stay behind it and shoot back at the man who had taken an indefensible position in the middle of the road. Drop and roll beneath the dense branches of the tree. The man in front would fire, but he'd be panicked at seeing his companion go down and, in all likelihood, would just punch a hole in Claudia's windshield. Then Rapp could come up through the branches and take aim. Range would be around fifteen feet. Clean shot between the eyes. Total time elapsed? Ten seconds at the most.

As the man behind grew in Claudia's side mirror, it became clear that "man" was an exaggeration. The kid was no older than seventeen and bore a noticeable resemblance to his partner in crime.

Father and son.

Rapp's hand moved away from his weapon and instead he used it to open the door. Abandoning his earlier plan, he just slowly stepped out onto the road.

"Morning."

"Don't move," the man in front said. He was gripping his rifle like a holy relic as he climbed awkwardly over the downed tree. Rapp ignored the kid behind. He'd follow his father's lead and, unless they were complete idiots, they'd be reluctant to shoot. The crossfire they'd inadvertently created was as likely to kill one of them as it was him.

A few moments later, they were both in front of him with weapons trained on his chest.

"I'm sorry, but we need what you got."

They were wide eyed and seemed vaguely confused. Clearly this wasn't who they were. A few weeks ago, they would have been more likely to stop and help clear the tree than put it there.

Rapp nodded and walked to the back of the vehicle, opening the hatch and pulling out two milk crates.

"There's some food in there and a little clean water. I've also got a sleeping bag and a stove with a couple fuel canisters, if you can use it."

Their eyes went down to the crates and then returned to Rapp. The father spoke first.

"This isn't my only kid. I've got two daughters and a wife at home."

"I understand."

"What about the gas in the car, Dad?"

Rapp shook his head. "It's electric and I need it."

"Maybe we could hook up the battery and use the electricity."

"Like I said, I need the car. And there's nothing you can do with it that's worth killing or dying for."

Rapp reached into the back and retrieved a rope that he held out. "Now, tie this end around the tree. We need to get it out of the road. I'm running late."

CHAPTER 40

"Meeting with the president, my ass," Randall Sikes said under his breath. Rapp was probably sitting in front of his fireplace eating one of those sheep that ambled around his neighborhood.

As forecasted, clouds were forming fast and the wind was picking up. Widely spaced snowflakes swirled around the clearing, sticking to the exposed skin on his face and blurring the horizon. His people had wandered around the interior of the barn, halfheartedly picked through the debris of the house, and were now strolling around the wet fields. The idea was to keep things casual for now. His backup had been delayed by one of the trivial fuckups that had once been fairly rare but were now becoming hourly occurrences. Until they arrived, he and his people would just play the role of run-of-the-mill scavengers.

Thus far, they'd found precisely nothing. A burned house, a broken-down truck, and an empty apartment. Not that he was surprised. The lead he was following was almost comically thin, but it was all they had. So, while wandering around in the cold wasn't his idea of a great time, it beat standing by helplessly while the country collapsed.

He stalked back to what was left of the house

and nudged a charred two-by-four with the toe of his boot. When his backup arrived, they would finally be able to kick this thing into gear. While he was skeptical that there was anything to find, missing something due to lack of effort was unacceptable. First order of business would be a bulldozer to clear all this debris and see if there was anything under it. The second would be a flyover with infrared cameras to check for hidden patterns that might suggest power generation, water collection, or anything else.

Unfortunately, that kind of activity was bound to attract the attention of the locals. Maybe he could get the military to set up an aid station down the road as a diversion. What he didn't need was a bunch of desperate civilians trampling everything in sight and trying to siphon the tanks of his equipment.

He was about to walk into the woods to make a call when one of his people starting shouting and waving her hands over her head. Sikes slid a finger across his throat to try to get her to take it down a notch, but it didn't work. The three kids he'd brought with him were all technical wizards, but none had much field experience.

Thankfully, when he started jogging in the woman's direction, she stopped waving and instead dropped to her knees. By the time he reached her, she had brushed a dusting of snow from a large flat rock embedded in the ground.

"What?"

"This," she said, tapping the rock excitedly.

"I'm not following you, Kate."

"I'm ninety percent sure this is one of those panels from Williamson Solar."

"What are you talking about? It looks like rock."

She nodded, removing her pack and retrieving a shovel from it. "Williamson makes superefficient solar collectors designed to blend into the environment. Most of them look like roof tiles and wood siding, but they also make ones that look like rocks so you can put them in your yard. They're still superexpensive so not many people have them yet, but they're amazing technology."

"I appreciate your enthusiasm, Kate, but I'm still pretty sure that's a rock."

Another one of his people ran up and looked down at her. "What's going on?"

"I think this might be one of those Williamson solar panels."

"Really? I've never seen any of their stuff in person."

Sikes spotted his last team member approaching from the east and tried to wave him off. Not only because this was likely a waste of time, but because he didn't want them bunching up. Meanwhile, Kate was digging the end of her shovel under one edge of the rock. A moment later, it popped out of the ground, revealing a smooth back with wires connected to it.

"You've got to be kidding me," Sikes muttered. "Kate, whatever I'm paying you, you're worth it."

She grinned. "I know, right?"

"What are they doing?" Ibrahim said, leaning forward and concentrating on the screen.

"Shut up," Alton responded.

The young woman was on her knees with a shovel as an older man looked on.

"Do you have supplies buried there?"

"I said shut the hell up!" Alton shouted.

Another man came up behind her—three of the four people out there were now centered on that one spot.

"Fuck, fuck, *fuck!*" Alton said.

"What is it?" Ibrahim said, sounding increasingly alarmed. "Tell me what she doing?"

Alton's stomach was churning to the point that he was in danger of spewing his breakfast all over his keyboard. He'd spent the better part of a hundred thousand dollars and untold hours placing those panels and wiring them to the board in his bunker. They were responsible for the vast majority of his power and now one of them had been found. But not by some hungry group of rednecks wandering by. That's how these people were trying to portray themselves, but it was obvious bullshit.

"Tell your men to get their weapons," Alton said when she pried up the panel.

"What?"

"Those are government agents. We have to kill them and get the fuck out of here. Now!"

Ibrahim hesitated for a moment, but then ran back down the passageway, shouting in Arabic. Alton started to hyperventilate and for a moment he thought he was going to pass out. His heart was racing to the point that he felt obligated to check the monitor on his wrist. One hundred and thirty beats per minute. Well below the threshold he'd set, but it didn't matter. His chest felt like it was going to explode.

The older man crouched and reached toward his ear in a motion meant to look innocent. It was anything but.

"The old one!" Alton screamed, leaping from his chair. "In the green jacket! He's got a phone!"

One of the Arabs was already coming up the narrow corridor with an assault rifle. He collided with the ladder and started climbing at what looked like a full sprint. When Alton turned back to the screen, the man depicted on it was talking, but it was unclear if it was to the people around him or if he'd succeeded in connecting a call.

"Do it, you stupid son of a bitch! Do it now!"

A moment later, the sound of a gunshot echoed through the tight space and the man pitched forward into the mud.

Kate Reynolds heard the shot but didn't even have time to react before her boss fell. She grabbed the back of his coat and tried to roll him over but he shoved her hand away.

"Run."

Her two companions had anticipated his advice, taking off in separate directions and trying to retrieve their weapons from beneath layers of insulated clothing. Not that it would do much good. Sure, they carried guns like all FBI agents but, with the exception of Sikes, they never used them. They were glorified technicians. Experts in things like communications, computers, and—in this case—solar panels.

"Run," he said again, but this time so quietly she could barely hear him over the wind. Despite the bullet in his back, he'd manage to get his weapon free and was aiming from where he was lying on his side. The sound of it when he fired broke her from her trance.

She had to get out of there. But not without him. Kate grabbed the collar of his jacket and began dragging Sikes backward. He shoved her away with a burst of strength that caused her to lose her grip and fall backward into the mud. This time his voice was a little stronger.

"I'm already dead, Kate. Now run!"

Whatever he said after that was drowned out by shooting coming from the west. It was then that she spotted two men who had appeared from nowhere in the ruins of the house. Muzzle flashes lit up the dull gray of the clearing and she saw David jerk. He managed to stumble a few additional steps and then went down, rolling awkwardly across the wet ground. A moment later, she heard a dull slap in the mud to her right.

Sikes was firing again and somehow his aim was still good enough to make the men attacking them dive for cover. With no other choice, she ran crouched toward the trees. With every step she waited for the bullet that would end her life, but it never came. She burst into the woods, immediately ducking behind a tree and clawing for her weapon. A moment later it was hovering in front of her face, gripped by shaking gloved hands.

The shooting had stopped but she wasn't immediately sure what that meant. Likely nothing good. There was no way Sikes had taken those men out with a handgun—they were too far away and he was too badly injured. Confirmation of that hypothesis came a moment later when shouts rose above the wind.

Not in English, though. In something that sounded very much like Arabic.

She wanted more than anything to go back. To help. But what good would it do? Sikes was either dead or dying. David was down in open terrain. And she had no idea what had happened to Greg. Maybe he'd made it to the woods, too.

Calling for backup would have normally been the first order of business, but that was impossible. She was nowhere near high enough on the totem pole to have access to what was left of America's communication network. Her phone was sitting at home with a dead battery. It had been for more than two weeks.

In the end, there was no logical decision to be made other than to do what Sikes had told her. Swallow her terror, set her guilt aside, and run.

She peeked around the tree to make sure no one was coming after her and then took off, weaving through the forest at as fast a pace as she could manage.

The grade kept getting steeper, causing her lungs and legs to feel like they were on fire, but keeping her from running in circles. She was forced to slow when she started to stumble but managed to keep putting one foot in front of the other.

There were no more shouts or gunshots. Nothing but the rustling of the branches, the rhythm of her footfalls, and ragged sound of her breathing. She crested the slope and the terrain became easier, allowing her to increase her speed. She made it another ten yards before she began to hear footfalls that weren't hers. Still well behind, but judging by their increasing volume, coming fast. When she reached a section of ground that was fairly flat, she dared a quick look back.

The distance between them was probably no more than twenty-five yards and the man didn't even look tired. His stride was long and steady, seemingly unaffected by the terrain. When she faced forward again, she could see that the trees were becoming increasingly sparse. No cover. No help coming. And legs that felt like molten lead.

With no other option, she stopped and spun, drawing her weapon and getting a shot off at the man now inside of fifteen yards. It went wide and she saw him raise his right arm, revealing a weapon that she hadn't noticed but that had probably been in his hand the whole time.

The muzzle flash came with an impact that made her feel more numbness than pain. She saw empty branches, snow, a cloud-covered sky. Then nothing.

"Come on!" Alton shouted. "Two more!"

He flinched when the sound of gunshots made their way into the barn, but didn't have the luxury of worrying about them. Instead, he returned to prying up floorboards and tossing them aside. Across from him, Ibrahim was doing the same.

Finally, they freed all the ones necessary and Alton opened the hatch hidden beneath. He grabbed the end of a rubber hose and dragged it to the truck. After sliding it into the tank, he turned on an electric pump that would fill it from an underground container.

"The battery!" he said. "Do you know how to install it?"

Ibrahim nodded, lifting it from the hidden storage area and teetering toward the front of the vehicle. Alton grabbed another hose, this one attached to an underground compressed air tank, and began filling the tires. He was almost finished when one of the other Arabs entered through the bay doors and spoke briefly to Ibrahim.

"Where's the other one?" Alton yelled from behind the truck.

"The woman escaped into the woods," he responded. "My man is chasing her."

Shit.

They were FBI. They had to be. Somehow they'd found this place and sent a team. More would come. And if that bastard got a call off before he was shot, it would be sooner rather than later. In a few minutes, they might be pulling out of that barn and into a swarm of attack helicopters and SWAT teams.

"Go into the bunker," Alton ordered. "Start bringing up any crate marked with a red X. Do you understand me? A red X. Those are the ones I set aside in case I had to run."

Ibrahim translated his orders in Arabic. The calm tone of his voice was infuriating. These sons of bitches didn't give a fuck what happened to them. Hell, they'd be pigs in shit if they could go down trading bullets with a bunch of government agents. Calm tone or not, though, the man turned and started running toward the bunker.

Prick.

Alton checked his heart rate monitor as he finished airing up the tire. One hundred and forty beats per minutes. Still fine, but he'd have to keep an eye on it. The smart move would be to just disable the system. But Feisal wasn't stupid. If he found out it was no longer functioning, Alton would find himself with his throat slit in a matter of seconds.

Making history tended to generate strange bedfellows and this was no exception. He trusted these ISIS nutcases about as far as he could throw them, but he also needed them. Even if it was just to stop a bullet.

"When you're done with the battery, go help him," Alton called. "I'll back the truck up to the hatch as soon as I can. And if your other guy isn't back by the time we're ready to go, he's getting left here."

"The girl won't be hard to catch," Ibrahim said, slamming the truck's hood. "He'll be back. And then we'll be on our way."

CHAPTER 41

Warming temperatures had turned the snow to rain and brought the cloud layer down on top of Rapp. He was forced to slow, leaning over the steering wheel to try to pick out detail on the side of the road. The turn couldn't be much farther but, in these conditions, it'd be easy to miss.

In the government's West Virginia bunker, the president's meeting was going off without him. Rapp had been an hour out when Kennedy called and told him that the Bureau had lost contact with Randy Sikes.

Not that this should have been a problem. When Rapp left him, backup was supposed to be arriving within a few minutes. Unfortunately, the security team was stranded at a government gasoline cache that turned out to be empty. The Bureau had fuel on the way, but it wasn't going to get there anytime soon. Once again, Rapp had been the closest available operator.

The turn ended up being easy to find—but for reasons that caused his gut to clench. There were two muddy streaks visible where a vehicle with massive tires had pulled onto the asphalt. Rapp spun the wheel and started up the unmaintained track, struggling to avoid the deep ruts made by what he suspected was the military transport he'd seen in the barn.

Even fighting with the terrain, the electric vehicle was almost silent. Rapp took advantage of that, getting to within a hundred yards of the clearing before ducking into the forest on foot. He moved quickly with his Glock in his hand, but suspected it wouldn't be necessary. Whatever had happened there was long over.

He stopped at the tree line, peering through the branches to confirm that the tire tracks he'd seen did indeed originate in the barn. More telling, though, was an outline lying to the east of the buildings. Clearly human but, through the mist, impossible to identify.

Fairly sure he wasn't walking into an ambush, Rapp broke cover and ran toward the motionless figure. Crouching next to it, he found himself staring into the frozen expression of someone he'd known for almost twenty years. Sikes had been a hell of a good man and now he was dead because of some careless math at a refueling station.

The winter conditions made footprints easy to pick out and he examined them, reeling through what he remembered of the FBI team. An African American with a bright red parka. A young woman with a blue down jacket and matching headband. A skinny blond kid with glasses and a wool coat that nearly reached his knees.

The one in the red parka wasn't hard to spot. He'd been standing next to Sikes at some point and it was a simple matter to follow his tracks to where he'd fallen. The other male team member blended in a little better, but Rapp finally managed to pick him out to the south in a similar condition.

He would have liked to confirm that they were dead, but it was going to have to wait. Another set of tracks—small, widely spaced prints—led to the trees. The woman. Moving fast.

The rain was coming harder and he could feel it streaming off his nose as he penetrated the trees. She'd made it this far and the cover might have been enough to save her.

With no idea what her name was, he couldn't call out to her specifically.

"I'm Randy's friend!" he shouted, moving up the slope as quickly as the intermittent nature of her tracks would allow. "The guy with the Tesla. If you can hear me, come out!"

He repeated some version of that call a few times before he spotted her lying on a carpet of dead leaves. The wound in her chest and eyes staring into the rain made checking for a pulse a waste of time.

Fuck.

He turned and ran back to the clearing, cutting north in order to come out just above the kid in red. Getting any closer than twenty-five yards turned out to be unnecessary—half his head was missing. The one in the wool jacket had less obvious wounds. His glasses were lying a few feet away and white fingers were still wrapped around his weapon. Rapp crouched and put a hand on his neck, confirming what he already knew.

He used a zigzag search pattern that took him to the barn and then past it to what was left of the house. Four distinct sets of tracks, all originating from the ruin. Two led straight to the barn while the other two—both moving much faster—belonged to the men who had engaged Sikes's team.

The truck had been backed out of the barn and into the charred rubble. The groove the men had trampled suggested they were loading supplies and made finding the bunker entrance fairly easy.

There was a voice emanating from it and Rapp reached his gun hand through the opening before peering inside. Dim LEDs illuminated a metal ladder descending to a narrow concrete passage. The voice continued, unintelligible, but now recognizable. Jed Jones going off on another of his antigovernment rants.

Rapp slipped silently down the ladder and made a quick pass through the space. One side of the barbell-shaped bunker had an incongruously luxurious bedroom and what looked like a high-tech control room. The other consisted of a bathroom and a storage area that had been partially—and hastily—cleaned out. The fact that there were three sleeping stations on the floor supported his analysis of the footprints outside. Alton and three men. At least two of whom could shoot straight and move quickly over difficult terrain. A makeshift prayer rug in the corner provided another clue.

His satellite phone couldn't get a signal underground and he was forced to exit into the rain to connect.

"Hold on a second," Irene Kennedy said. "I'm in with the president."

A few seconds of silence passed before she came back on.

"Are you there?"

"Yeah. Tell Darren that his people are dead."

"Dead? What happened?"

"Alton had a bunker under what was left of the house."

"But he's not there now?"

"No. He took off in a military transport vehicle. It looked like an MTVR set up as an armored troop carrier. Kind of rusted but still the standard green and it's probably got a thousand-mile range. There was an old logo on the doors that had something to do with fighting forest fires. I can't remember exactly. But you're looking for four men. I'm guessing at least two are Arab, probably three. They headed north on the paved road that cuts in front of Alton's property. If you figure Randy's team got up here about two hours ago and the time it would take for the Arabs to kill them, load the truck, and go, they can't have been driving for much more than an hour. An hour fifteen at the most. That doesn't give them a lot of options."

Kennedy didn't respond.

"Irene? Are you still there?"

"I'm here. But finding them isn't going to be as easy as it should be. There are a lot of unpaved roads in that area and not all of them are reliably mapped. The weather's going to make searching from the air impossible and we have very few ground resources that we can bring in quickly. The federal government's concentrating its people and equipment on the urban areas, where eighty percent of people live. And local governments don't have fuel or manpower."

"What the hell are you saying to me, Irene? That isn't a priority?"

"Of course it is. But look at what's already happened. Randy's backup isn't there because they're stuck at an empty fueling station. That's not an isolated incident, Mitch. Those caches are few and far between, and they're not particularly reliable. Also, putting people on the road in civilian vehicles—or even patrol cars—is risky because they're being attacked."

Rapp opened his mouth to argue, but then remembered that exact thing had happened to him only a few hours ago.

"We can't make any more excuses, Irene. I've got four dead FBI agents out here and our one chance to put this thing right is probably within a forty-mile radius of where I'm standing. You know Alton has a plan for this. If we don't get him before he makes it to a safe haven, we might as well get on the emergency broadcasting system and tell people to start eating their neighbors."

"Understood. What's your situation? Do you have the ability to try to track him?"

Rapp let out a bitter laugh when he realized that, for all his protests, he was in the same stupid situation as everyone else.

"For about a hundred and fifty miles. Then I'm dead by the side of the road."

CHAPTER 42

Jed Jones was playing over the truck's radio, but he seemed to have forgotten about the national weather forecast that he did around that time of the morning. Instead, he was arguing with some static-ridden idiot about the popular conspiracy theory that Israel was behind the blackout. Alton turned the volume down and stared blankly through the windshield.

His meticulously constructed plan had devolved into chaos. From now on, his life—or, just as likely, death—would rely almost entirely on blind luck. Were government resources in sufficient disarray to prevent them from mounting an intensive search while they still knew his general location? Would the Arabs he was saddled with remain focused on his survival or would they martyr themselves at the first opportunity? Would the heavy overcast continue or would clearing skies allow the authorities to use search planes?

How long could he count on luck? None of this was supposed to have happened. He'd gone over every detail a hundred times. How had they found that place? And what else did they know?

Images of what the government would do to him if he was captured began to reel unbidden through his mind. The leaked pictures of Muslim detainees at Guantánamo Bay. Cheesy action movies he'd seen that involved CIA interrogations. Even a documentary he'd once seen about the Spanish Inquisition. The urge to vomit became overwhelming but he managed to fight it back.

Focus.

He had to concentrate on what he was doing. On escaping. He'd anticipated emergencies. In fact, he'd planned for almost this exact situation. But it had always seemed so remote. Coming up with ways to beat everything the government could throw at him had just been part of the fun. Part of the game.

He looked at the tablet in his lap and scanned the map depicted on-screen. He'd created it himself after extensive exploration of the area in a 4x4 purpose built for the project. All roads were coded to provide information like whether they appeared on widely available maps, in what conditions they were passable, and what average speeds they would support. GPS satellites were still functioning, but he was reluctant to connect out of concern that his device could somehow be tracked. Instead, Alton was forced to count crossroads and estimate mileage based on the truck's questionable odometer.

It took almost another thirty minutes, but he finally spotted an overgrown unpaved road to the left.

"Slow down," he said to Ibrahim, who was behind the wheel. "This might be it."

The Arab did as he was told, pumping the massive vehicle's brakes as Alton scrolled to a photo of the road entrance. It had been taken on a sunny, midsummer day, but after a few seconds of study, he was able to match up a fallen tree lying across a boulder.

"Yes!" he exclaimed. "Turn here."

Even with the powerful engine and six massive tires, the truck struggled to climb the steep two-track. They'd made it no more than fifty yards before Alton spoke again.

"Stop here."

He jumped out of the cab and went around the back to open the steel doors. "Grab shovels and get out. We need to cover the ruts we made where we turned off the road and camouflage the entrance."

Ibrahim translated and the two men inside grabbed the necessary implements before running back down the muddy slope. Alton watched until they disappeared from view, then looked up at the sky. Still completely socked in.

The cold penetrated his jacket and he found himself unable to stop thinking about the bunker they'd just left. Its warmth. The luxurious bed and state-of-the-art video game setup. The collection of top-shelf liquor. All gone now. Instead, he was standing in the rain with three Arabs who'd like nothing better than to see him dead. The most hunted man in the history of the world.

"Where are we going?" Ibrahim said.

"Shut up."

The Arab fell silent. But not for long.

"The balance of power has shifted a bit, don't you think, John?"

It occurred to Alton that it was the first time Ibrahim had used his name. "What do you mean?"

"The road—even this road—is a dangerous place to be. Particularly in this weather. It wouldn't be very comfortable to be left here, would it?"

"No, it would suck," Alton said, and then held up a wrist to reveal the heart rate monitor strapped there. "For both of us. I wouldn't make it through the night and you'd get to watch all the lights come on."

"Then it seems we're partners in this. So, let me repeat my question. Where are we going?"

It was a delicate subject to navigate. Alton's natural instinct was to lie, but he couldn't come up with anything that was even vaguely believable. And, in light of that, maybe it was time for some truth.

"About three hundred miles southwest of here. I have an emergency cache of food, electronics, fuel, and weapons. We need to get to it."

"Your signs are very clever, but it's likely they have a description of our vehicle."

The "signs" he was referring to were vinyl US Army logos that he'd placed in all the appropriate places on the truck. It would now look more or less like all the other military vehicles he assumed were still traveling the roads. Ibrahim's concerns were well founded, though. The camouflage wasn't going to count for much if the government managed to pull its shit together.

"The weather's cooperating and we can stay on obscure roads for a while. The government isn't going to have a lot of resources that they can bring to bear out here in bumfuck. At some point, though, I agree. We'll have to find another vehicle. Probably sooner rather than later."

"To what end? To drive around back roads in pursuit of what?"

Alton finally turned and looked the man directly in the eye. "You owe me, Ibrahim. I've done for you what your beloved Sayid Halabi couldn't. I've killed America. The difference between you and me, though, is that I don't want to die along with it."

"What *do* you want?"

"I want to go to Mexico and disappear."

Ibrahim didn't react other than to wipe the rain from his eyes. The dead expression on his face made him look disturbingly like the other two.

"So, here's the deal," Alton continued. "You get me across that border and I'll write you a greatest hits list—the most critical infrastructure that's still intact, along with details on how to best take it out."

"And you'll disable the heart rate monitors?"

"I'll toss them in the garbage on my way to the beach and you can go to your reward without a care in the word. In what used to be America, that's what we call a win-win."

CHAPTER 43

Near Seneca Rocks
West Virginia
USA

The third time was the charm. Rapp had finally made it to the government's bunker seventy-two hours after finding the bodies of Randy Sikes and his team. The crowding was about the same, but the smell had gotten significantly worse. Added to the sweat was now an undercurrent that suggested a problem with the sanitation system.

The conference room he was directed to was probably thirty feet square and packed with people. It looked more like an oversold rock concert than any meeting he'd ever been to.

Rapp forced himself inside, slipping left with his back against the wall before stopping barely clear of the doorjamb. Over the years, he'd developed a serious aversion to crowds and not having room to maneuver. The closer he could stay to the exit the better.

Unfortunately, the relative comfort of his position didn't last long. The president entered, grabbed him by the arm, and pulled him along as he fought his way through the bodies. The conference table, previously invisible, was full of the usual suspects. Two seats were still available—one at the head and another next to Irene Kennedy.

"You finally made it," she said as he sat.

Before he could respond, the president started to speak.

"I think everyone here has been briefed on what's happening. We found John Alton and he escaped at the very high price of four FBI agents. The Bureau's been going over the site and I'll turn it over to Darren Phillips to tell you what they've found."

The normally well put together FBI director looked like he hadn't showered in a week and was almost unrecognizable without his impeccable suit. He pushed up the sleeves on the sweatshirt he was wearing and stood.

"Alton had a bunker under a burned house. It won't be a surprise to anyone that it was pretty well thought out—water, power, supplies, communications . . . We've been through it with a fine-toothed comb, but haven't come up with much that can help us. There were fingerprints of four separate people, which matches the number of distinct footprints we found. John Alton, Feisal Ibrahim, and two others we can't identify. Computers were all completely wiped and there's no way to retrieve that information. We estimate that they had enough supplies to keep four men going for about six months. Some of that was transferred to a truck they used to escape. Because Alton has legal Mexican residency, we're assuming he's heading south and we've been looking for him on the road. So far with no luck."

"There's basically no traffic and it's a huge vehicle," the president said. "How is it possible you can't find it?"

"We have a detailed description from Mitch, but it's not a lot different than hundreds of military transport vehicles on the road. The weather keeps getting worse, which makes it impossible to use aircraft, our resources are pretty much depleted, communications are pretty much wrecked . . . And there are more potential routes than you'd think. Also, we have to carry out this search very carefully. We can't just start shooting at any truck we can't positively ID as being one of ours. Alton has to be taken alive and unharmed or there's no point to any of this. The personnel qualified to carry out an operation like that don't grow on trees. Particularly now."

"But you're bringing more in."

"Everyone we can from every agency we have. But, obviously, the more time it takes, the more options Alton has. Every minute that passes, our search area gets bigger and the probability that he's switched vehicles gets higher."

The president leaned back in his chair and let out a bitter, exhausted laugh. "So, we've got a guy driving a truck big enough to see from space on virtually empty roads and we can't find him."

"We're doing our best, sir. And I have to point out that you can't see him from space because of the—"

"Clouds," Alexander said, finishing the man's sentence. "But clouds do happen on this planet, Darren. Right? They've been floating around up there for millions of years."

Phillips didn't seem to know how to respond, so he remained silent.

"Any other ideas?" the president said. "Anything at all? Because, believe me, I'm listening."

The room fell silent, but after a few seconds Kennedy spoke up. "Mitch and I have been talking about this problem and we think there might be another way to attack it."

"I'm all ears."

She turned to Rapp. "You're an expert in survival, Mitch. And you saw this coming. How did you prepare for it? And by that, I mean how long did you supply your house for?"

"Based on the information I had, I figured a worst-case grid attack would take about a year to shake out."

"Then you're saying you laid in supplies to hold you for a year."

He shook his head. "Two is one, one is none."

"So, you doubled it. Two years' worth of food for you, Anna, and Claudia."

"Yeah."

She turned back to the president. "We think that John Alton made the exact same calculation."

"I thought you said he had supplies for four men for six months."

"We don't think he originally planned on having those other men there."

"That seems like pretty wild speculation," the FBI director said. "He may have just planned to go to Mexico as soon as the fireworks were over. Living underground for a year—even with nice linens and good food—isn't trivial."

Kennedy looked around her. "Is the person who led the search of Alton's bunker here?"

An unseen woman's voice answered from somewhere in the crush of people. "Yes! I'm here."

"Based on what alcohol had been consumed so far, how long would the supply have held out?"

There was a lengthy pause. Rapp couldn't see her but suspected she might actually be punching numbers into a calculator. Finally, the answer filtered to them. "About two years."

"So, six months' worth of food and two years' worth of booze," Kennedy said.

"And Muslims don't drink," the president added.

"With due respect," Darren Phillips said. "So what? Maybe he decided he needed protection. Or he had plans for those ISIS pricks."

"I don't think so," Rapp said. "I know these people. Hell, I'm the one who shot Feisal

Ibrahim's brother in Syria. ISIS doesn't protect people. They kill people. And Alton should be number one on their hit parade. They know full well that if we capture him, he might help us. The other thing that doesn't add up is why they're just sitting in that bunker with their thumbs up their asses. It's not the way they work. They don't hang around a comfortable bunker playing video games while their brothers in arms martyr themselves. Allah's watching."

"Could they have been planning a secondary attack?" the president said.

Janice Crane, from the Department of Energy, responded. "As much as I hate to say this, there's no point. They've already won."

"Okay," Alexander said. "Then what?"

"The main weakness terrorists have is that they want to die for their cause," Rapp said. "And the secret to beating them is to make sure they get that opportunity."

"How?"

"We want to provide them a target," Kennedy said. "Preferably one complicated enough that they need Alton's help to plan the attack."

"To lure them into a trap," Alexander said.

"Yes. And to make sure that Alton continues to be valuable to them. Because when he's not, Mitch and I are confident they'll kill him."

"Can it be done without interfering with the Bureau's efforts to find the truck?"

“Absolutely,” Kennedy said. “We’d coordinate with Darren every step of the way.”

Alexander leaned back in his chair, considering what he’d just heard. “I like the idea of giving them a reason to keep Alton alive—assuming that he still is. The rest seems far-fetched, though. Basically, a long chain of speculative links that, if only one fails, the entire theory fails. Is that really how you want to spend your time, Mitch?”

Rapp just shrugged. “My calendar’s wide open.”

CHAPTER 44

South of Stanley
Idaho
USA

"On schedule."

Charlie Wicker was the last of the team to check in over Rapp's earpiece. The diminutive sniper had been charged with covering six miles of completely wild mountain terrain on foot—a journey that including scaling a cliff covered in a thick layer of ice and crossing a lake where the layer wasn't so thick. Fortunately, he'd grown up a few hundred miles to the east and this landscape was indistinguishable from his backyard.

"Roger that," Rapp said over his throat mike.

He started moving forward again through almost eighteen inches of new snow. A storm had descended on the West two days before, dumping enough precipitation to finally put out many of the fires still raging across the region. According to forecasters, the system would persist for another couple of days. Good news for the country, but bad news for him. Visibility was crap and the accumulation was probably more than an inch per hour. On the bright side, temperatures had risen to around twenty. Manageable even to a desert fighter like himself. But not comfortable.

He finally hit the tree line, turning on his night-vision gear to allow him to safely navigate through the dense evergreens. It would take another hour or so to reach the acre of private land that was his objective. It was a good three miles up the side of a mountain from the nearest dirt road and a good ten miles from the closest patch of pavement.

By the time Rapp reached what was supposedly his target, the fingers he had wrapped around his M4 carbine were starting to get numb. But they were in better condition than his feet. The only reason he could be certain those were attached was the nearly inaudible thump of his snowshoes. He took off his pack and put it on the ground before lying on top of it.

"I'm in position," he said into his throat mike.

Scott Coleman, Joe Maslick, and Wick all called in ETAs. Between seven and twenty minutes.

"No rush," Rapp said. "Stay silent."

Maybe no rush at all. From where he was lying, it seemed that the intel he'd been provided was bad. Through the trees and falling snow, he could see a small clearing that was bounded on one end by a steep, scree-covered slope. And that was it. The Air Force said that detailed photography had been impossible because of the angle, but it looked more like it had been impossible because there was nothing to take a picture of.

Rapp rose, leaving his pack and staying just inside the trees as he skirted the clearing. If he'd spent the last few hours freezing his ass off so he could assault a pile of broken rock, someone in Langley was going to wish they'd never been born.

He was almost to the slope that defined the eastern edge of the clearing when he spotted a horizontal shadow that seemed a little too straight to be natural. Rapp slowed and used his light-sensitive peripheral vision to examine it.

A latrine.

Nothing fancy—basically, a board with a cutout attached to a tree. But functional. He came up alongside it and looked down into the hole dug to catch waste. It appeared to be in regular use.

"I'm in position above the target," Wick said. "Looks like this is the place."

"How so?" Rapp responded.

"There's smoke coming out through a natural filter up here. You know, like the ones the Viet Cong used."

Rapp nodded to himself. When they holed up underground, the Vietnamese channeled their smoke through layers of branches and leaves. A shockingly effective way to cover up cooking and, in this case, heating.

"Roger that. Is there an entrance up there?"

"Not that I can see."

"Okay. I'm on the east side of the clearing. Scott and Mas. Forget the positions I designated for you. Come to me. Wick, stay put."

All three acknowledged and Rapp crouched to wait and try to get some feeling back in his hands.

It was déjà vu all over again. Except this time instead of sitting around getting snowed on in North Carolina, Rapp was lying on his stomach and getting snowed on in Idaho.

The thin camping mattress beneath him and the evergreen branches piled on his back kept him from freezing, but only barely. Fortunately, he was also generating warmth with fantasies about what he was going to do to John Alton when they finally met. Right now, Rapp was torn between the battery acid and piranhas. Maybe it was possible to combine the two. An acid bath full of flesh-eating fish. Probably not biologically feasible, but an attractive image nonetheless.

From his position, he couldn't see the sunrise, but nearly imperceptible shadows were beginning to appear in the snow. Hopefully, they'd be accompanied by warming temperatures. The display on his watch was reading fourteen degrees.

"I've got something," Maslick said over the radio.

Rapp didn't respond, instead concentrating on contracting and relaxing his muscles to loosen them up. He might need to move fast.

"You're not going to believe it," Maslick said, not bothering to hide the admiration in his voice. "This guy's not fucking around. There's a hidden door built into the rocks . . . Two people coming out. A kid about Anna's age and a woman. She's carrying a single-barrel shotgun like she knows how to use it. Hammer's not cocked."

Rapp heard their footsteps and a few seconds later they entered his limited field of vision. The young girl was wearing a camo parka, insulated ski pants, and a hat with ear flaps. Her mother was similarly dressed, but a lot more attentive. She scanned the woods smoothly as the girl began undoing her pants and dusting snow off the plywood toilet before climbing on.

When the woman turned her back to give her daughter a bit of privacy, Coleman made his move. It was always a pleasure to watch him work and this was no exception. He appeared behind the girl like a ghost, clamping a hand around her mouth and nose, and carrying her away. The only evidence that she'd ever been there was a barely visible line of urine leading into the trees.

"Come on, Karen," the woman said. "It's freezing out here."

When there was no response, she turned back

toward the makeshift toilet. Her expression shifted from annoyance, to confusion, and then to fear.

"Karen? Honey?"

She took a hesitant step forward, clinging to the shotgun but still not cocking it.

"Quit messing around. You're scaring me."

A couple more steps took her in front of Rapp. He rose to his feet and came up behind, yanking the weapon from her hands and slipping an arm around her throat.

She went stiff as he leaned into her ear. "I work for the government, Julie. I'm not here to hurt you or take what's yours. I just want to talk."

Despite Rapp's significantly improved way with children, the girl was nearly paralyzed with terror. He was wearing her mother's coat and hat, and was carrying the shotgun in one hand while clinging to Karen's with the other. It was doubtful that they were being watched, but better safe than sorry. He kept his head down and tried to move in a way that obscured the fact that he was pretty much dragging the girl across the snow. Not exactly an Oscar-worthy performance, but it would likely be enough to fool even an HD camera setup. People tended to see what they expected to see.

They arrived at the rocky slope and he nudged the girl forward. At this distance, the door seams were visible, but he had no idea how to open it. That was her job.

The tears running down her cheeks glistened in the sun breaking on the horizon, but she did as instructed. The door—basically a steel hatch with rocks glued all over it—swung open on well-maintained hinges. Mas was right. This guy wasn't fucking around.

Inside, low-power LEDs illuminated walls hewn from the earth and reinforced with concrete. Supplies were stacked everywhere—food, weapons, clothing, tools. Pretty much everything necessary to ride out the apocalypse in style.

A familiar voice became audible somewhere ahead. "What do y'all want for breakfast? I'm leaning towards hash. Objections? Speak your piece now."

Rapp kept hold of the sniffling girl as they moved through the narrow space.

"Is that you I hear boo-hooing, Karen? What, did your butt get cold? You gotta harden up, girl!"

They came to an arched opening and Rapp stopped in it. He released the girl's hand but she just stood there, unsure what to do.

"Hash sounds good to me."

Jed Jones spun, but then froze when he saw his wife's shotgun aimed at him. He glanced down at his daughter to confirm she was all right and then locked eyes with Rapp.

"You're not from around here."

"Nope."

"Government?"

"Yeah."

"Here to shut me up? To put me and my family in a hole out in the woods?"

Rapp lowered the weapon. "I'm here to ask for your help."

"Where's my wife?"

"Outside with my guys. You mind if they come in and warm up?"

"Do I have any choice?"

"It's your house, Jed."

The silence stretched to about ten seconds before he responded. "Sure. Why not?"

Rapp leaned the shotgun against a wall and activated his throat mike. "We're clear here. Come in."

A few moments later, the sound of the entrance door opening again reached them.

"Is there somewhere we can talk?"

Jones nodded and pointed back through the archway. When he walked past, he patted his daughter on the head. "We're good, kiddo. Tell your mom to make everyone something to eat."

He led Rapp into his homespun radio studio—a desk stacked with electronic equipment, a mike, and set of headphones. He sat in a chair next to a series of handwritten notes hung on a wire and pointed Rapp to a folding chair in the corner.

There was little doubt that he had a weapon hidden somewhere in the clutter, but it wasn't worth worrying about.

"So, what's the government want so bad that they sent you here? For me to start toeing the party line? Tell everybody that Uncle Sam's going to save them if they just stay inside and remain docile?"

"No."

"Then what?"

"We've figured out who did this. A little prick named John Alton, with the assist of some ISIS fighters."

"John Alton," Jones repeated slowly. "An American?"

Rapp nodded.

"Why?"

"It doesn't really matter. What does matter is that he knows *how* he did it. He knows what infrastructure's been damaged, how to get back into the power company computers, and everything else our people need to fix this thing."

"But you can't find him."

"He's on the run. Hopefully, still somewhere on the road between Virginia and Texas."

"What's it to me?"

Rapp dug a piece of paper from the pocket of his jacket and held it out. "This is a general list of talking points. You can deliver them however you want. We know Alton listens to you and there's a good chance he'll keep listening out on the road."

Jones's brow furrowed as he scanned the paper. "Is this true? Are you going to be able to get the power back up in south Texas?"

"No."

"So, it's bait?"

Again, Rapp nodded. "I know these ISIS guys as well as anyone. If we tell them we're fixing this thing, they're going to try to stop us."

Jones leaned back in his chair, contemplating the paper in his hand. "If I say this on the air, a lot of desperate people are going to start moving south. The road's not a safe place to be and what they're going for is a mirage. I'll be sending some of them to their deaths."

"Yeah," Rapp agreed.

Jones continued to stare at the script in his hand. "If this Alton guy is smart enough to pull this off, won't he be smart enough to spot a trap?"

"Maybe. But we're not sure how much control he has. ISIS will follow him as long as he's helping them bring down the country. But telling them to stand down when the power's coming back on in Texas is something completely different."

"This sounds like kind of a Hail Mary, man. You're asking me to send thousands—maybe tens of thousands—of people on a trip to nowhere based on not much."

"I can't argue with that," Rapp said. "But can I tell you something off the record?"

"Sure."

"They're gonna die anyway. The government's still in the early stages of just assessing the damage. Nobody's even *talking* about fixing anything yet. Optimistically, we're looking at seeing some isolated pockets of power coming up in three months—mostly around solar and wind farms. And then another five before you see the cities starting to light up. Rural areas aren't even on the agenda."

"We can't survive that long, man. There won't be anyone left to use the electricity."

"That's pretty much FEMA's assessment, too."

Jones took in a deep breath as the scent of canned hash began to reach them. "Okay. I'll do it. But I want something in return."

"What?"

"If you catch this asshole and eventually put him in an electric chair, I want a front-row seat."

Rapp stood and held out a hand. "You got my word."

CHAPTER 45

Near Prestonsburg
Kentucky
USA

"You're not going to believe this, but I finally shamed those pissants in Washington into contacting me. They wouldn't let me record the conversation because, as we've already established, they're pissants. But I've spoken personally to TJ Burton, the head of FEMA. And, to be fair, he didn't actually sound like a pissant. He sounded like a smart guy who gives a shit about the American people and who can't remember the last time he slept."

"There," Alton said, over the sound of Jed Jones's voice on the radio. "The dirt road just ahead."

Ibrahim turned the massive truck off the rural highway and Alton let out a long breath he hadn't been aware he was holding. Thank God he'd spent so much time gaming scenarios and creating maps to deal with them. The trip to Kentucky had been done creeping along muddy mountain roads, backtracking, and taking random detours. But it had worked. They'd only seen three other vehicles on the road the entire time—two civilian and one military transport not much different than the one they were driving. Passing by the latter had damn near given him a heart attack, but instead of the desperate firefight he'd expected, the soldiers inside had just waved solemnly. Clearly government communications were still a kluged-together mess. But for how much longer? There was no question that in some hidden government bunker, an unprecedented manhunt was gaining momentum.

"Stop at the edge of that pullout."

The Arab obeyed and Alton got out into the damp fog that he likely owed his life to. The two other ISIS men jumped from the back and waited for his orders. They weren't happy about it, though. And they didn't bother to hide it.

"Get the shovels and follow me," Alton said, walking into the trees.

By design, he hadn't put the cache far from the pullout, nor had he buried it very deep. Other than a few hunters, he couldn't imagine why anyone would ever come up here. And even if someone did, they wouldn't be looking for a buried treasure consisting mostly of freeze-dried food and fuel.

Using natural landmarks, he finally found the root- and rock-free patch of dirt he was looking for. "Dig here. Top off the tank and put the supplies and whatever diesel's leftover in the back."

Alton returned to the relative comfort of the truck's cab, grateful to still have his Arab slaves.

While their presence had serious drawbacks, what he didn't want to do was spend the next hour of his life digging in the rain. A partial twist of the ignition key got the radio going again as Ibrahim climbed in the driver's-side door.

"Not going to help them?" Alton asked.

"There are only two shovels. And I want to hear what the FEMA director said."

"—and short is that things aren't going so great. The government wasn't prepared to defend against an attack like this and they weren't prepared for the aftermath. That's two bad mistakes back-to-back and you're the ones paying for it. Having said that, who's ultimately responsible? Us. Because we're the ones who insisted on electing complete fucking scumbags and driving all the good people out of politics. But that's a rant for another day. So, with the bad news out of the way, let me move onto some good news coming out of Texas. Apparently, they have their own grid that's separate from the rest of America's. Why? I have no idea. Maybe because they're fucking Texans and can't just do things like everyone else. In this case, though, it works for us. Their grid's smaller and simpler, and their weather's good enough that people don't have to climb through four feet of snow to inspect the damage. Burton fed me a lot of technical shit, but the bottom line is that he thinks they're going to be able to start bringing Texas back online next

week. They've already got a number of individual power generation plants ready to go and it's really a matter of repairing the damage to one major substation before they can start routing electricity to a few major cities. Not that he's saying it's going to be easy. I guess they're having to scavenge equipment from all over the country . . ."

"Could this be true?" Ibrahim said.

"Shut up," Alton replied, notching the volume knob a little higher.

"The initial goal is to get power back to the southeastern part of the state. The water's been out in Houston for two days and that's one of the biggest population centers in America. More important for the rest of us, though, is where southeast Texas sits. Not only is it on the border of Mexico, which will allow overland transport, it's on the Gulf. If they can get those docks running again, they can start bringing in supplies twenty-four/seven from the rest of the world. And that's the ballgame. It's still going to be a horror show of a year, but it'll be enough for us to get our shit together . . ."

Alton leaned back in his seat, staring through the windshield as Jed started warning people against packing their suitcases and trying to walk to Texas.

"Could this be true?" Ibrahim repeated.

It was a good question. The Texas grid was indeed simpler and the weather *had* been cooperative. There was a major substation outside of Bryan that was critical to Texas in general and to Houston in particular—which was precisely why Alton had put so much effort into overloading it in as devastating a way as possible. Was it plausible that the damage hadn't been as extensive as he'd planned? The short answer was yes. There was just no way to control for all variables. Something as simple as the power company having taken that substation off-line for maintenance during the attack could have saved a significant portion of its capacity.

"It's possible," Alton admitted finally.

"What can we do?"

Another interesting question. The answer, of course, was the same as before: get him safely across the Mexican border. But the Arabs' interests were obviously different.

"My take is that it's a pretty optimistic report, Feisal. Even if they can get the power up in southern Texas, the benefits are going to be pretty marginal. Water isn't just out in Houston, it's out in major cities all over the country. Plus, the idea that you can supply three hundred and fifty million Americans with what they need to survive from charity coming through Gulf ports is ridiculous. Even if all this is true and things go perfectly for the government, you're still talking about millions of Americans—probably tens of millions—dying. That's more than the Civil War, more than the Spanish flu, more than World War—"

"But they have a chance," Ibrahim said. "And when you give the Americans a chance, they tend to succeed."

Alton nodded and considered his next words carefully. Again, though, he decided there was no good reason to lie. "It could also be a trap. Maybe there's nothing at all going on in Texas. Maybe they just got the DOE to come up with the most plausible story they could think of and now they're waiting for us there."

"But it could also be the truth," Ibrahim countered.

It really was mind-boggling. These assholes just refused to take the win unless they could die in the process. In truth, though, maybe he was getting to the point where that worked for him. Whether it was a trap or not didn't much matter if he refused to stumble into it.

Some scraping and banging drifted from the back of the truck and Alton glanced in the side-view mirror. One of the Arabs was loading a couple of five-gallon jerry cans.

"There's no reason for us to fight about this, Ibrahim. We can both get what we want."

"How?"

Alton picked up the tablet containing his maps and drilled down into the files. Finally, he pulled up a folder filled with schematics and photos of the Bryan, Texas, substation.

"This is it. The only substation in southwestern Texas that fits the story that Jed just told. I can give you all the intel you need—how to get there, the most effective way to attack—you name it."

"And what do you want in return?"

"I think you already know the answer to that. I want you to escort me to a predetermined point on the Mexican border where I've arranged a way to get across."

Ibrahim looked down at the tablet for a few moments and then got out of the cab. Alton watched in the mirror as he spoke at length to the two men outside. The discussion eventually turned heated, with one of the men jabbing a finger violently in the direction of the cab.

Alton sat quietly, debating what to do. Stay out of it or take charge? Finally, he decided on the latter. There wasn't shit they could do to him as long as he was wearing the heart rate monitors and now wasn't the time to let these morons start thinking for themselves.

He opened the door and jumped down into the mud. "What's the problem? Are we going to get the hell out of here or are you going to stand here all day running your mouths?"

The two enforcers glared at him with the crazy jihadist gleam that he'd come to expect. Ibrahim, on the other hand, maintained his calm.

"They point out that the Mexican border is still more than two thousand kilometers away.

During that journey, we could be captured by government forces or even attacked by desperate civilians. Any of these events could lead to you being killed or at least elevating your heart rate to the point that it triggers your monitors. Then everything is lost."

"Yeah. That sounds about right."

One of the two men either understood enough English to follow Alton's meaning or just picked up on his tone. He lunged, but Ibrahim managed to stop him.

"Careful," Alton said, taking a step back. "Right now, I'm the most important man in the world. To you. To the Americans. To everybody. Just two thousand kilometers to go and all your problems are over."

The man backed off and Ibrahim spoke again, obviously struggling to keep his voice impassive. "My men suggest that you disable those monitors in return for our solemn word before God that we will do everything in our power to see you safely to the border. As Muslims, it's an oath we take very seriously."

Alton tried to stifle his laughter but even standing there in the rain with the entire world breathing down his neck, it was impossible. "You might take it seriously but I sure as hell don't. Now get the rest of that fuel and food on board and let's get the fuck out of here."

CHAPTER 46

North of Birmingham
Alabama
USA

John Alton shoved his hands deeper in the pockets of his jacket and took a few steps forward. The change in position continued to provide him with cover while allowing a better line of sight through the bushes. Not that there was anything to see. Just an empty highway and the tree-lined shoulder on the other side of it. The cloud cover was starting to thin, turning a dire situation potentially disastrous. To the south, he could already see intermittent patches of blue sky.

For the thousandth time, he tried to figure out how the hell this had happened. What could have possibly led the government to his bunker? He'd been so careful. Meticulous. Perfect. The fact that he was standing there in the middle of nowhere Alabama with the cold seeping into him seemed impossible. Like a nightmare that he would soon wake from, screaming and drenched in sweat. Like when he was a kid.

Blue sky would bring search aircraft and that had forced them onto the main road three hours ago. It was critical that they find a new vehicle before the overcast dissipated and they were hard to come by on the back roads they'd been limiting themselves to. Which had kind of been the point.

Since turning onto a more major thoroughfare, they'd seen a number of civilian vehicles, none of which had the necessary capacity or range. Much more interesting—and terrifying—had been the military convoy they'd spotted being escorted by a tank. A fucking tank! You knew the shit had hit the fan when the mobile artillery came out.

Their luck had improved about an hour ago when they'd passed a Red Cross truck that resembled a midsized U-Haul painted white. Plenty of capacity for supplies, four men, and it ran on the diesel they were carrying. The only problem was the Humvee escorting it and the armed soldiers it contained.

Even with that drawback, the Arabs had decided it was their best shot. But they weren't happy about it. Even Ibrahim looked like he wanted to gut him like a fish. Every second he spent out on the open road increased the chance of him being captured or killed.

All the better reason for them to quit fucking around and get him safely over the Mexican border.

Alton squinted through the disconcertingly bright sunlight, searching for his truck that they'd hidden among the trees. Nothing. He knew it was only a few feet off the road, but the Arabs had done an impeccable job of camouflaging it. Hopefully, their competence would continue. Because if not, he was probably fucked. Fully, royally, irretrievably fucked beyond all recognition.

Calm down, John.

He forced himself to slow his breathing and even closed his eyes for a moment. If his ability to think succumbed to panic, things weren't going to go well for him. He was a genius. He'd brought down the most powerful empire since Rome. He'd accomplished more than almost anyone in history. All he had to do was stay cool and keep his mind sharp.

No matter how Zen he managed to be, though, it didn't change the fact that if the Arabs blew this, his situation would turn untenable. He'd be left standing in the woods with nothing but the clothes on his back. At that point, he'd have no choice but to finally return Janice Crane's calls and start bargaining. A complete fucking disaster, but the American government was desperate. The politicians would do whatever was necessary to go from being villains in the eyes of their constituents to being heroes.

Alton heard the approaching vehicles before he saw them. Shading his eyes, he scanned north, finally picking out a subtle flash of white. It grew in size and detail until he could make out the Red

Cross logo above the truck's cab. A few more seconds passed before he spotted the Humvee lagging about fifty yards behind.

The adrenaline began to flow despite the fact that he had no involvement in what was to come. In fact, he didn't even know exactly what to expect—Ibrahim and his men had done their planning in Arabic before depositing him there, out of harm's way.

The Red Cross vehicle passed without incident and Alton refocused on the Humvee behind. It was almost even with him when his truck burst into view. The Humvee had no time to maneuver and slammed into the rear quarter panel at probably fifty miles per hour. The force of the impact was sufficient to spin the truck one hundred and eighty degrees and, more important, flip the Humvee onto its roof. Alton watched it slide across the asphalt, spraying sparks.

A moment later two shots sounded in quick succession. Alton redirected his attention to the Red Cross truck as it swerved right, rocking onto two wheels. His heart leapt dangerously when it swerved onto the soft shoulder and began plowing through the saplings at its edge. In the end, though, the vehicle remained upright as it coasted to a stop. One of the Arabs ran around to the driver's side, aiming his rifle at the window for a moment before opening the door and dragging a body out.

The sound of shooting started again, this time right in front of Alton. The other Arab was lying in the road, firing at the men trapped in the Humvee.

And then it was over.

They'd done it. They'd actually fucking pulled it off.

Alton started running toward the road, but then slowed when he remembered the heart rate monitors strapped to his wrists. By the time he came into the open, phase two of the Arabs' admittedly well-wrought plan was in motion. The bodies of the Red Cross people had been hidden in the forest and a tow rope was connected between his truck to the overturned Humvee. After collecting weapons from the corpses inside, the Arabs moved both vehicles into the trees.

After that, it was a flurry of activity as they transferred supplies to the Red Cross truck and topped off the tank from the jerry cans they'd been carrying. When done, Ibrahim closed his two men in the back and got behind the wheel. Alton climbed in the passenger side and they pulled out onto the road.

The whole thing couldn't have taken more than ten minutes and left no evidence beyond a barely noticeable gouge in the asphalt.

Maybe Allah really was on their side.

CHAPTER 47

Near Bryan
Texas
USA

"That's the last one we could reasonably get," Janice Crane said, pointing to an approaching semi with a massive transformer on its flatbed. Rapp watched it divert to a makeshift parking area and take its place among other trucks carrying similar cargo.

He shaded his eyes as he scanned the lot, watching the sun reflect off the equipment there. Crane and her engineers had put a lot of thought into what machinery was being brought in, treating the repairs to the massive substation as if they actually had a chance of succeeding.

A few hundred yards to the west, countless people were at work—cutting out transformers damaged by Alton's attack, making modifications to accommodate replacements, and running new transmission lines. The hope was that even if Alton figured out a way to examine the project in detail, he'd see something that looked entirely viable. Right down to Janice Crane pulling sixteen-hour shifts and sleeping in a trailer alongside a bunch of construction workers.

Rapp turned his gaze to the road leading into the work site. It was the only access and it weaved through various stands of low trees. The closest stand was sparse enough to provide a good view of the replacement transformers awaiting installation but dense enough to create a choke point.

"Do you think it'll work?" Crane asked. There was an edge of desperation in her voice that wasn't surprising. She was the one responsible for hiring Alton and inadvertently giving him the keys to the kingdom.

"You know him. What do you think?"

"That he's not going to be easy to trick. He's a genius in every sense of the word and knows more about America's grid than anyone on the planet."

"Sometimes long shots are the only shots you have left."

"What about the FBI and the military?"

"They're doing what they can, but it's a big ask. We assume he's headed to Mexico and that he has stashes on various routes, but there's no way to be sure. Also, one or more of those stashes could have included another vehicle but—"

"There's no way to be sure," she said, finishing his sentence.

"Yeah. And resources are hard to come by. Most of the computers the government relies on to track people are off-line. So is the local law enforcement manpower we'd normally rely on." He pointed to the blue sky. "The weather's cooperating, though. We've got aircraft operational but it's still a lot of territory to cover."

"What about catching him when he tries to cross the border to Mexico?"

"Low percentage. He's not going to use a legal checkpoint and the Mexicans aren't exactly prioritizing our problems."

"So, this is it," she said. "America's last stand."

Rapp let out a long breath. "Yeah. This is it."

"Is this actually functional?" Rapp said, crouching in the dirt road to examine a heavy cargo net partially buried in the dust. Unable to pick up much detail in what little light was filtering from the construction site, he reached down and ran his finger across one of the nylon straps.

"As far as *you* know," Scott Coleman responded.

"That's not what I want to hear."

"I'm just screwing with you, Mitch. We've tested it like five times. Unless Alton shows up in a battleship, we're good." He pointed to the trees on both sides of the road. "The net's attached with springs and activated by remote. Hit a button and it deploys. When a vehicle impacts it, the springs reduce the force. Plus, we've dug up the road a little so you can't drive very fast along this section.

"How fast is not very fast?" Rapp said.

"Depends. I mean, if he had a trophy truck stashed, we might be in trouble. But even a pretty capable SUV would be flat out at twenty miles an hour."

Likely not enough to injure the driver or passenger, but Rapp still had his fingers crossed that Alton was a seat belt wearer. Fortunately, he seemed like the type. Seat belts. Hand sanitizer. Toilet seat covers whenever he was forced to use a public bathroom . . .

"So, we're ready."

"I think so. My guys are in position. We've got drones overhead looking for any suspicious traffic coming our way. The car-catcher—or whatever the hell you want to call it—is ready to rock. The only question is whether our guest of honor is going to show."

Rapp stood. "All right. Good."

"I can't help noticing that every time we talk, your enthusiasm's faded a little more."

"It's because every time we talk, I've thought of another five reasons that this isn't going to work. Alton doesn't want to come here. He's carried out his plan and now he just wants to get across the border. I'm starting to think Darren Phillips was right and this is a waste of time. Maybe I invented this whole op because I didn't want to sit around my house while my country implodes."

"Maybe you're right. Maybe that little prick doesn't want to come here. But those ISIS guys do. They want to go up in a ball of flame big enough for Allah to see."

"Yeah, but what's Alton's role in that? I mean, there's one road in and a bunch of obvious equipment. Drive in and blow it up. Do they really need him to plan that out for them? Enough to risk leaving him alive?"

"You're just a ray of sunshine tonight, Mitch."

He just gazed into the shadows created by the work lights illuminating the substation.

"Any final orders?" the SEAL asked.

"Yeah. Everyone wears full body armor and I don't want to hear any complaints about the weight. No weapons except Wick, who's overwatch. He's the only one authorized to fire, and then only if it's somehow in defense of the tangos. We take them alive. Period. If it comes down to them dying or us dying, it's us. Clear?"

Coleman flashed a grin. "Let's suit up."

CHAPTER 48

Near Columbia
Mississippi
USA

The darkness had closed in, providing Alton a sense of security that he knew was an illusion. The stars were visible above and that meant the government was up there somewhere. Scouring every highway, side street, and dirt track. Dedicating billions of dollars' worth of technology for one purpose and one purpose only. Finding him.

"Continue," Feisal Ibrahim said over the hum of the Red Cross truck's motor. Alton ignored him, instead focusing on the tiny points of light above. Searching for any sign that one of them was hovering at a distance that could be measured in feet instead of light-years.

"I said continue!"

The sudden volume and sharpness of tone snapped Alton from his stupor. He looked over at the Arab perched on the console between the seats and then beyond at the man behind the wheel. Finally, he returned his attention to the tablet in his lap and the image of the Bryan, Texas, substation it contained.

Alton took a deep breath and started back into

the narrative he'd let fade a few moments before.

"I still think it's better to stay on back roads even though it's slowing us down. We have plenty of fuel and the government can't cover everything. Not with their supply chains falling apart and riots breaking out in the cities. At the pace we're going, I figure we're about seventeen hours from where you need to drop me in Laredo. Once I'm there, I'll make contact with the people who are going to get me across the border."

"And once you've made contact, you'll turn off the heart rate monitors."

"I already said I would."

"What if you get caught?"

"In Mexico? Not a chance."

"I imagine you said the same about your bunker in Virginia."

Alton frowned in the light of the dashboard. The problem with Feisal Ibrahim was that he wasn't stupid.

"I'm not going to blow sunshine up your skirt, man. If I get caught, you know as well as I do that I'm going to wheel and deal with whatever I've got not to end up with a CIA cattle prod shoved up my ass. But it's not going to happen. The American government's resources are thinner and thinner every day. At the rate this thing is accelerating, there's not even going to *be* an American government in a few weeks. Not one anybody would recognize anyhow."

"Unless they get the power back on in Texas."

"I doubt they can and, even if they do, it won't do as much good as they say. But it's a moot point, right? You and your guys are going to take care of that little problem after you drop me off."

Alton fell silent and gazed into the darkness beyond the truck's headlights. Seventeen more hours. That's all he needed. For this thing to hold together seventeen more hours.

"Continue," Ibrahim said.

Alton used a finger to zoom the image on the tablet. "The substation only has one access road, so that's your option. The good news is you probably won't have to go very far up it—"

"I don't understand."

"Then shut up and I'll explain. Unless something went very wrong in the execution of my cyberattack—and I find that hard to believe—the transformers highlighted in red are completely melted down. There's no way they can be repaired. The takeaway here is that you don't want to get suckered into trying to break something that's already broken."

"Then what?"

"Think about what they need to accomplish here, Ibrahim. If the transformers can't be fixed, then they have to be replaced. And that's not a small job. These things are huge and made to order for every station. The government's only hope is to bring in the handful of transformers that have any chance at all of fitting. And that's going to work in your favor."

"How so?"

"Because, unless I miss my guess, those replacements are already on-site," Alton lied. In truth, he was increasingly convinced that this was a trap. But what was it to him? Once he was across the Mexican border, he'd be perfectly happy for these three pricks to incinerate themselves.

He recentered the image on a lightly treed, relatively flat piece of land on the southwest edge of the facility. "If it were me, I'd store them here. And if that's what they've done, you've got an easy target. Don't worry about the substation itself. Worry about the replacements. If you destroy those, you destroy any chance they'll get that facility going again."

"What if you're wrong? What if they're already in place?"

"I seriously doubt they've had time for that, but if they have, your job gets real hard real fast. Beyond the fact that they're going to have security, there are going to be a lot of workers milling around—electricians, engineers, welders, whatever. And it's going to be hard to differentiate between damaged units and replaced units."

He drew a few crude numbers on the satellite photo with a stylus. "If they've already got transformers in place, then attack them in this order. They're the most critical and hard to replace."

When Ibrahim was finally satisfied with his understanding of the operation, Alton went back to studying the sky. It was a suicide mission, but that seemed to work for everyone. And, as an added bonus, if the government really *had* figured out a way to get Texas running again, these assholes would throw a serious wrench in that plan.

Five or so minutes passed in blessed silence before a hatch leading to the cargo area opened. The man on the other side spoke at length in Arabic before sliding the hatch closed again.

"What was that all about?" Alton asked.

"He's finished inventorying the Red Cross supplies."

"And?"

"Mostly medicine that we don't have any use for. He also asked if we wanted food. I said we did."

Kind of a long conversation to get across not much information, but at this point Alton didn't care. A quick glance at the time reading out on one of his heart rate monitors suggested they were down to sixteen hours. Sixteen hours before he connected with the coyotes he had on retainer and got shuttled across the border. Then he'd get the Lexus he had in storage on the Mexican side and take a leisurely cruise to his house on the coast.

A few minutes later, the hatch opened again and the man handed them some MREs. Alton ate in silence before returning his attention to the window.

With a full stomach, he realized how tired he was. It was becoming increasingly difficult to keep his eyes open and he finally gave up. When he finally drifted off, he did so to visions of palm fronds and umbrella drinks.

Alton awoke slowly, feeling strangely numb. And not just his limbs from the uncomfortable truck seat. Everything. His mind, his chest, the eyelids that didn't seem to want to fully open.

When they finally obeyed, the daylight pouring through the windshield was almost painfully bright. They were stopped in front of a modest brick house with peeling window frames and an ancient satellite dish on the roof. Overgrown grass stretched out in every direction, dead-ending into a dense tree line after a few hundred yards.

Ibrahim and one of his men were walking up the cracked driveway but only made it about halfway when a confused-looking man appeared at the house's front door. Not so confused that he didn't have a shotgun in his hands, though.

As Alton's brain cleared, the scene turned

increasingly strange. Both of the Arabs were wearing Red Cross jackets. The man with Ibrahim was the one from the back, not the driver. He was still behind the wheel, focused on what was happening outside, but occasionally glancing in Alton's direction.

Ibrahim began speaking, gesturing casually in the general direction of the truck. As he did so, the man in front of him began to relax and nod.

It was then that Alton realized that he was no longer in the passenger seat. He was sitting on the console where Ibrahim had been, held in place by a seat belt strapped awkwardly across his torso. How had he gotten there? Why couldn't he remember?

The man who apparently lived in the house began following Ibrahim toward the truck, never even catching a glimpse of the knife that penetrated the base of his skull. Alton continued to look on, but didn't feel the expected thrill or surge of adrenaline. He remained mired in dull confusion as the two Arabs sprinted toward the house.

"What . . ." Alton started, his voice sounding strangely distant. "What are we doing here?"

The man in the driver's seat didn't react, staying focused on what was happening outside. A few moments later, Ibrahim and his companion reappeared, giving the thumbs-up. The driver reacted by unbuckling Alton's seat belt and dragging him from the cab.

He couldn't seem to get his feet under him and when he finally did, they wouldn't support his weight. Was he sick? Had they been in an accident that injured him? Ibrahim ducked under his free arm and helped support his weight as they started toward the house. The world began to swim nauseatingly and Alton's peripheral vision went blank. Then everything went dark.

Consciousness came back in flashes. A moldy ceiling shedding plaster. Blood splattered against floral wallpaper. The body of a woman leaking the contents of her skull onto a shag carpet.

He tried to sit up but failed. Too ambitious. An attempt to roll on his side was met with more success, but he felt himself jerked back into his initial position after only a few inches. Confusion turned to fear. And then that fear grew into terror—or at least the closest thing to terror his muddled mind could conjure.

He came to understand that he was naked and that his wrists and ankles were bound to the bed he was lying on. The heart rate monitors he wore were still operational and various charging wires led from them to a battery backup unit on the floor.

He tried to shout Ibrahim's name, but the sound that came out was more of a desperate groan. Still, it was enough. The Arab appeared in the doorway a moment later, looking down at him for a moment before sitting in a chair beside the bed.

"Do you understand what's happened?" he asked, leaning in close.

"No," Alton managed to get out. "I—"

"Then let me explain. Ahmad is a medic trained by the Saudi Army. And when I told you the pharmaceuticals in the Red Cross truck were of no use to us, that wasn't entirely true. In fact, it was filled with all kinds of interesting sedatives and painkillers."

"But . . . But you—" Alton stammered.

"I know. I know," he said soothingly. "We promised to drive you to the Mexican border under clear skies on roads increasingly patrolled by the government. And when we had no choice, we were fully prepared to do that. But the drugs in the truck provided a much better option. Ahmad is confident that he can keep your heart rate between fifty and a hundred beats per minute without a problem. The house has a number of solar panels and generators that will keep your electronics charged indefinitely. And between the food we had with us and the food we found here, Ahmad can keep you alive for at least another five months. At that point, I don't suppose it will much matter if your files are uploaded to the government. As you've pointed out, it's unlikely that America's government will even exist at that point."

"You don't have to do this," Alton stammered. "I swear that if you let—"

"But we *do* have to do this, John. You'll lie here like this for the next five months—drugged, wallowing in your own excrement, and increasingly covered in sores. And when the food finally runs out, Ahmad will stop giving you the drugs you'll have become so reliant on. And when you're fully conscious again, he's going to slowly—over the course of many days—skin you alive."

CHAPTER 49

Near Natchitoches
Louisiana
USA

"There!" Ibrahim said, pointing through the windshield at an abandoned pickup truck by the side of the road.

Despite warnings from both the government and the wildly popular Jed Jones, there were already significant numbers of people trying to make their way to Texas. Hope—likely misplaced—was forcing them from their homes and onto the road. As he and his man got closer to the state's border, they saw an increasing number of people walking, riding bicycles, and even a few on horseback. Some had started their journey in family vehicles that had eventually run out of fuel, forcing them to leave them behind.

"Do you want to stop, Feisal?"

It was an excellent question. They were concerned that the Red Cross truck could have been reported overdue and might have become a target for the authorities. Further, it lacked maneuverability and four-wheel drive, which would likely be necessary to navigate the road leading to their target. And, finally, they no longer needed the vehicle's capacity. All supplies had been left in Mississippi to be used to keep John Alton alive for as long as possible. The only things in the back of the truck now were jerry cans full of diesel and improvised explosives.

"Yes," Ibrahim said finally. "Stop."

They pulled to the side of the dark highway and he jumped out. It was the fifth time they'd tried this in the last two hours and thus far they'd been unsuccessful.

Initial indicators were good—the driver's door was unlocked and the vehicle took the diesel they were carrying. It was the last requirement that had stymied their previous attempts.

Feisal reached around the steering wheel and felt a surge of adrenaline when his fingers found a key still inserted in the ignition. He turned it and, praise Allah, the dashboard lights went on.

It was a late-model vehicle, well cared for based on the condition of the body and interior. The only discernible problem was the fuel gauge that read empty.

"This is it!" he shouted as he ran to the back of the Red Cross truck and opened it. His man came up next to him a moment later, grabbing a container full of diesel and taking it to fill the pickup's tank. As he did so, Ibrahim began transferring the other jerry cans to the vehicle's bed. Once fueled and loaded, he went back to the Red Cross truck for two final things. The first was an explosive vest he'd built from materials found at the house in Mississippi. The second was a bomb that would go in the back of the pickup with the spare diesel.

Everything from now until the end of their lives in a few hours would be a game of improvisation. It was impossible to know how either of their martyrdoms would play out, making flexibility key. They had no intelligence regarding the current level of security at the Bryan substation. No idea if the general population had deduced which facility it was and descended on it in search of food, security, and information. In truth, they had no idea if it was all an elaborate trap. In the end, though, it didn't matter. Whatever happened, they would strike one last blow against the Americans and join their comrades in paradise.

Rapp checked his watch, a normally simple act made unwieldy by the head-to-toe body armor he was wearing.

2 a.m.

A quarter mile up the road, Janice Crane was still awake, directing the phony substation repair. Work lights and the flicker of welders reinforced the illusion and provided enough illumination for less precise operations like repositioning equipment and digging trenches for new transmission lines. It was all designed to make the target irresistible, but also had the potential to attract desperate locals. It hadn't happened yet, but it was a headache that was undoubtedly coming.

Meanwhile, he was entering what felt like hour one hundred of sitting propped against yet another tree.

The wait didn't leave him with much more to do than think. A little too much, probably. With every sweep of the second hand, he became more convinced that this was a waste of time. That Alton was either dead or had gone to ground in Mexico.

That the little prick had won.

And not just won. Won big. World financial markets were imploding. China was suffering increasing unrest and even riots as the economic growth they relied on collapsed. Latin America had gone into survival mode, taking the body blows that they'd become good at absorbing over the years. Canada was fully focused on disaster relief to the parts of their country that were connected to the US grid and could provide little assistance beyond staging US aircraft. Russia was getting hit much harder than they'd expected as commodity prices collapsed. Other than Africa, which was less closely linked to the US economic engine, Western Europe was probably weathering the storm best. Their situation was still pretty dire, though, and there wasn't much they could do to help their old ally.

So, where did that leave the country he'd spent his life bleeding for? Fucked, according to the top secret report Irene Kennedy had forwarded him. According to a group of economists that included two Nobel laureates, the United States would be down to about the population of Peru in a year. The middle would empty out, with its surviving citizens huddled in cities near the coasts. Scavenging would be the primary industry—stripping everything that was no longer being used and selling it at bargain basement prices. Cars, furniture, electronics . . . It'd all be there for the taking. In fact, a number of European agencies were already working with US museums to move out priceless objects before people just started wandering off with them.

Second question: Where did that leave him?

For better or worse, probably fine. He'd spent most of his career operating in violent, collapsing countries. Hell, he'd probably live long enough to see the Washington metro area return to its agricultural roots of a century ago.

Good thing he'd been so halfhearted in putting the brakes on Anna and Scott Coleman's budding livestock business. Act three of his life was looking like it would be his farmer period.

"We have an incoming vehicle. Southbound on twenty-one. About fifty miles out."

The voice coming over Rapp's earpiece was

unfamiliar—not one of his people. Probably an Air Force drone operator.

"Can you identify it?" he said over his throat mike.

"Civilian pickup. Arkansas plates. We're working on getting what information we can."

It wasn't the first. There were way too many people on the road chasing the illusion he'd created.

"Roger that. Keep me advised."

In all likelihood, that would be the end of it. The truck would pass by before the government could find a working computer capable of providing the name of the owner. Rapp crossed his heavily armored arms over an equally well-protected chest and closed his eyes again.

The same voice woke him again about thirty minutes later. "The pickup's still on course to you. It's owned by Jason and Cynthia Brixton from Pine Bluff, Arkansas. What records we can access say they're a family of four—two kids ages eight and nine. We don't want to get too close with the drone, but there appear to be only two adults in the cab."

"Is it possible the children are laid out in the back seat?" Rapp said.

"Possible, but we're betting against it."

"What about cargo?"

"Five-gallon jerry cans. Quite a few of them, but we can't get an exact count."

Normally, that would set off alarm bells—a potential car bomb. But in this environment, carrying extra fuel wasn't exactly unusual. Still, it was a civilian vehicle driving in their direction with the wrong number of passengers and a bed full of flammable liquid. Not enough to prompt him to drag himself to his feet, but enough to keep him from nodding off again.

"They've just turned southeast on twelve-eighty," the voice said.

Rapp responded immediately. "Repeat that. Confirm that the target has turned southeast on twelve-eighty."

"Confirmed. It's heading in your direction."

And in roughly the opposite direction as before. It was hard to come up with a good reason for anyone to divert onto that relatively minor road unless they had a specific destination in mind.

"How far to the turn that'll bring them in front of us?"

"Seven miles," was the response.

"Bruno, you're on twelve eighty. What are you seeing?"

"Nothing yet, but they should be closing in on my position."

Rapp stood, using the tree behind to help him overcome the weight of his armor and stiffness in his knees. Bruno McGraw came back on the comm a moment later.

"Two men. The one in the passenger seat is

pretty bulky. Can't tell if it's clothes or he's just fat. He does have a pretty impressive beard, though."

"Suicide vest?" Rapp said, feeling the front of his helmet to ensure that his goggles were still perched there.

"Could be, but it's impossible to tell."

Two more miles. In order to get to the substation, they'd have to turn right in two more miles.

He moved through the trees, stopping near the edge of the dirt road just behind the hidden cables snaking across the ground.

"Turn," he said quietly to himself. "Turn."

"They've diverted off twelve eighty," the drone operator said after a few more seconds. "Coming in your direction."

"This could be it," Rapp said over his comm. "Heads up."

He could see a map of the area in his mind. After a little less than a mile, they'd come to the dirt road leading to the substation. If they made that turn, there was no longer any question.

"They're slowing . . ." the drone operator said excitedly. "That's it, gentlemen. They're on the dirt."

"We're up," Rapp said, crouching. He instinctively reached for the Glock strapped to his thigh, but stopped before touching the grip. Instead, he went for a hammer lying on the ground. “Everyone remember the mission. These assholes get taken alive. There are no other considerations.”

The drone operator came on in the midst of Rapp’s men acknowledging the order. “He’s turned his headlights off and we’re estimating his speed at just over twenty miles an hour.”

“Roger that,” Rapp said.

The truck became audible a few seconds later, but he still couldn’t see it. Finally, a vague outline materialized, moving along the road as fast as the surface would bear. Rapp focused on his breathing and got into a position resembling a sprinter crouched in a set of starting blocks. He needed to cover the few feet to the vehicle before the Arabs knew what hit them. As much as he wanted to take them alive, they would be just as anxious to ensure the exact opposite outcome.

Rapp remained absolutely still, knowing he’d be invisible if he did so. The pickup continued to approach, unable to increase its speed in the intentionally roughed-up road, but also unwilling to slow down. It fishtailed slightly when it hit a particularly egregious set of artificial potholes and three seconds later it was in front of him.

The crack of the cargo net activating sounded like a gunshot. If the driver saw it, there was no indication. The truck impacted without so much as a brief flash from the brake lights.

As promised, the net stretched, absorbing much

of the force before dragging the vehicle back a few feet. Rapp activated a powerful lamp on his helmet and lunged forward, crossing the short distance to the driver's door.

The glare off the glass was bad, but not so bad that he couldn't make out two figures in the front seats. No one was evident in the back, but it was impossible to confirm that was the case with one hundred percent certainty. Not that it mattered. He couldn't do anything about it.

One of his hands hit the handle of the door at the same time the other swung the hammer into the window. As expected, the door was locked and the glass spiderwebbed but held. He shoved it inward with a gloved hand, but it didn't come completely free, blocking his access to the lock switches.

Nothing was ever easy.

Rapp threw himself partway through the window frame, squashing down the glass with his armored chest as the driver pounded him with clenched fists. He managed to unlatch the seat belt and a moment later was dragging the man back through the opening.

The passenger was reaching for something in his pocket—hopefully a gun, but Rapp doubted his luck would be that good. He managed to get the driver clear of the vehicle and spun, putting his own body between the terrorist and the vehicle.

The blast lifted him in the air, and he struggled to keep hold of his prisoner, finally losing contact when they slammed into a tree. Rapp was vaguely aware of the stench of diesel and that flames had engulfed one of his arms. Whether it was his left or right, he wasn't entirely sure. The concepts of direction and gravity became increasingly vague as his eyes tried to focus past the cracks in his goggles.

Somewhere he heard the unmistakable sound of a fire extinguisher, but it wasn't aimed at him. He was confused as to why for a moment but then remembered. The mission. His survival was irrelevant. The men in the truck were all that mattered.

Something heavy landed on top of him. Another armed body. More shouting. Something about fire. Was he on fire? Oh, shit. That's right. He was.

Another extinguisher became audible, this time accompanied by the sensation of its contents billowing around him. Then nothing.

CHAPTER 50

Rapp jerked awake to the stench of smelling salts. He immediately scanned his surroundings for threats, but there were none. The room was small, windowless, and white. The man leaning over him had a stethoscope hanging around his neck and Scott Coleman was standing against a wall.

With no immediate danger to confront, Rapp took a moment to assess his condition. The pounding headache was the worst of it. A close second was the pain in his side where he'd been shot. The hospital gown he wore was stained with blood but, in the context of his career, not that much. Surprisingly, the arm that he now remembered had been on fire slotted in at a distant third.

"What's our situation?" he managed to get out through a throat that felt like it was full of sand.

"You're okay," Coleman said. "Mild concussion from your flight trajectory being interrupted by a tree. The body armor and flame-retardant suit saved your ass."

"What about Mas?"

Joe Maslick had been carrying out roughly the same task, but on the passenger side.

"His guy was wearing a suicide vest. That was the source of the explosion. Not super high tech, but enough. Mas saw it coming and managed to duck down behind the door, but he still landed about sixty feet into the woods. We had to chopper him out."

"Is he going to make it?"

"He's in surgery now, but they say he'll be fine. You know Mas. He's like shower mold. You just can't kill him."

"What about the guy I pulled out."

"It was Ibrahim. His back got burned pretty bad, but nothing fatal. He's conscious in the next room over."

Rapp lay back carefully, letting out a long breath. "It worked. I can't believe it."

"You and me both. Someone up there's looking out for us."

A scream filtered through the thin wall to Rapp's left and he squinted over at it. "Is someone already working on him?"

Coleman shook his head. "Just the docs cleaning up his burns. I told them they couldn't give him any painkillers."

Rapp stopped in front of the door, now changed into jeans, cowboy boots, and a sweatshirt. He still felt like a dump truck had backed over him but a couple of Excedrin had dampened the pounding in his head. He took a deep breath, plastered a casual expression on his face, and pushed through the door.

"How you doing, Feisal?"

The man was lying facedown on a hospital bed with wrists cuffed to the rails on either side. There was a doctor in surgical garb hovering over him, carefully placing bandages on his back. Where the Arab's skin was still visible, it looked like a medium rare hamburger.

The doc looked with alarm at the two men invading his sterile space. "You need masks and gowns. The risk of infection is—"

"He's not going to live that long," Rapp said, taking a seat in a folding chair next to the bed. Feisal examined him through half-closed eyes that slowly widened.

"You know who I am?" Rapp asked.

"I know," he said, managing to spit hard enough to hit Rapp in the leg. It wasn't the first time. Or even the hundredth. Swimming pools could be filled with the amount of terrorist spit he'd been the target of over the years.

"Where's John Alton?"

The doctor, after his momentary confusion, went back to bandaging the man's back. Ibrahim was making a effort to hide his agony, but wasn't fooling anyone.

"We killed him," he said, his voice dripping with pain and hate. "We slit his throat like an animal and left him to bleed."

"Where?"

"What?"

"Where did you leave him to bleed? I want the body."

He didn't respond.

"Don't be stupid, Feisal. We know Alton was the brains behind this and that he had no reason to tell you how he did any of it. If he's dead and you can prove it, we have nothing else to talk about. I'll put a bullet in the back of your head and dump your body in the woods. If you want to fuck around, though, you've got an ugly future to look forward to."

"I don't remember," he said, through gritted teeth. "It was alongside the road."

"What road? How far off it? Did you bury him or just dump him? And how long ago? It's pretty warm out. I might be able to smell him. Just give me a ballpark and we'll finish this."

His silent stare gave Rapp hope. While it was hard to figure out exactly what Alton's status was, he was now pretty sure he hadn't been killed. Why, though, continued to be a mystery.

He picked his feet up and rested his boots on the man's injured back. The high-pitched shriek that emanated from him was loud enough to make the doctor take a hesitant step back.

"We both know you're bullshitting me, Feisal. If you'd killed him you'd want to rub my face in it, right? You'd want me to stand over his rotting body knowing my last hope was gone. So, let me ask you one more time. Where is John Alton?"

"We . . ." Ibrahim gasped. "We wanted to kill him. But he ran. He escaped."

"Escaped?" Rapp said. "What? On foot? Let me guess, he said he was going to the bathroom and did the old slip-out-the-window trick. Is that what you're telling me? Okay. But then what? He jumped in an Uber and drove off while you guys stood around holding your dicks?"

"Yes . . . No. He—"

Rapp shifted his feet into a more comfortable position, eliciting another scream from the man. This time he also lost consciousness.

"Wake him up," Rapp said to the doctor.

The man hesitated. "I . . . I don't want to be part of this. I—"

Scott Coleman moved from his position against the back wall and clamped a hand around the back of the physician's neck. "You heard him."

The smelling salts that had worked so well on Rapp worked equally well on his prisoner. The CIA man put his feet back on the floor and leaned forward. "So, you were telling me he wanted to cross over into Mexico. What then?"

The pain and sudden return to consciousness made it impossible for Ibrahim to track where their conversation had left off.

"Yes!" he coughed out. "We took him. To the border. He had people there to escort him across."

"Where? Tell me where you took him to cross. Describe it to me. Was it in a city? Which one?

Or was it out in the desert? Near what? Details, Feisal. I need details."

"Laredo. Near there."

"Where's your other man?" Rapp said, suddenly changing the subject to further confuse him.

"What? What other man?"

"You had two men with you when you left Virginia."

"In the truck."

"No, they tell me it was only the two of you in there."

"I . . . I don't know."

Rapp placed his feet on Ibrahim's back again and again he lost consciousness.

"We could be here for a while," Coleman said.

It was a fair observation. The secret to successful interrogations was having information that the subject didn't know you had. In this case, Rapp was just swinging in the dark. There were a hundred lies the man could tell and he wasn't anxious to spend the next six months chasing them down.

They'd have to get systematic. Create a careful line of questioning, take notes on everything that was said, cross-reference them . . . Ibrahim wasn't going to just roll over and give them what they wanted. And in his current physical state, there was only so hard they could push.

"Go track down a pen and some paper, Scott.

And Doc—if you had any other appointments today, you should probably cancel them."

Six hours.

Rapp walked back through the door and fell onto the bed he'd awoken in.

"You all right?" Coleman said.

"Get Irene on the line."

The former SEAL dialed and put his satphone on speaker. Kennedy's voice came over the tinny speaker a moment later. "Scott. Where's Mitch? Were you able to get anything from Ibrahim?"

"I'm here," Rapp said, throwing a forearm over his eyes to block out the light. The hammering in his head was starting to get worse again. "We got what we could, but I'm not sure how much it's worth."

"Tell me."

"I'm more or less convinced that Alton's alive and that he's with Ibrahim's remaining man."

"What about a location?"

"There's a rural house in Mississippi that came up a few times."

"You think he could be there?"

"Maybe. We pulled up satellite photos and Ibrahim described it well enough that I'm sure he's been there. But is it where he left Alton? I don't know. Why would he? Hell, why are they even keeping him alive? It seems stupid and Feisal's not stupid."

"But neither is Alton. If I were him, I'd be telling them that there was more I could do. That if they kept me alive, I could shut down any attempt to get the power back on."

"Maybe," Rapp admitted. "But my sense is that there's something Ibrahim's not telling us. He's obviously been pretty well trained in interrogation techniques and he's mixing enough truth with his lies that it's hard to tell them apart."

"But, in the meantime, we at least have something. A target in Mississippi," Kennedy said.

"Yeah . . ."

"Do you disagree? You don't sound sure."

"I don't like charging into situations I don't understand, Irene. We've got one shot at this and our track record so far has been shit. Maybe we should think about putting surveillance on the Mississippi property and let the experts at Langley take a crack at Ibrahim."

"I'm not going to be able to sell that to the president. I know you haven't had time to track the details of what's happening in the rest of the country in the last twenty-four hours, but it's not good. The water's going out in one major city after another. We've lost control of Detroit and have actually moved most government forces out of there. We're bringing water into Houston in tankers but the only thing holding that city together is the story we concocted about getting the Texas grid back running. It's going to collapse into chaos in the next few days. That's the fourth most populous city in America. Casualties are skyrocketing, Mitch. Tomorrow—and I mean tomorrow alone—we're expecting one hundred and eighty thousand deaths due to thirst, violence, and lack of medical care. And we're getting to the point that starvation is going to become a significant killer. The president will say that there's no more time to be conservative."

"What if I say no?"

"Then he'll send someone else. And that would significantly increase the chance of the mission failing. I'm sorry, Mitch, but our options have run out. You're the best in the world at this. Please. Think about how you can make this happen. Now, I have to go update the president. Call me back."

The line went dead.

There was a moment of silence and then Coleman started to laugh.

"Did I miss something funny?"

"You're the best in the world at this," Coleman said, imitating Kennedy's steady tone. "Are you kidding me? You're the *worst* in the world at this. You are, without question, the worst person in the world at not killing people. A few months ago, you wanted to shoot your plumber in the knees over some problem with your garbage disposal. And none of us can figure out how your dentist is still alive."

His words were intended to be a joke but, like all good jokes, there was a kernel of truth in them. Rapp wasn't a hostage rescue expert. And the property in Mississippi had clearly been selected to provide open views in every direction. Ibrahim's man would be watching and would likely kill Alton if he saw anything even slightly out of the ordinary. Like a bunch of heavily armed operators strolling up the driveway.

"Ideas?" Rapp said.

Coleman picked up the phone and scrolled to the overhead photos of the target. "One mistake and it's game over."

"Then we don't make any."

"I dunno, Mitch. What are we talking about here? Anything we do has to have a pretty high probability of success, right? And I don't mean ninety percent. I mean ninety-nine point nine nine percent. So, tunnel in from the trees, drill into the underside of the house and pump in gas? Seriously, that's the most plausible thing that springs to mind."

Rapp didn't respond, instead just lying there with his arm thrown over his eyes.

"What about you, man? What are you thinking? Is it even doable?"

He considered the question for almost a minute, spinning every possible scenario over in his mind.

"It's doable," he said finally. "But maybe not by us."

CHAPTER 51

Near Columbia
Mississippi
USA

Elizabeth Dawson stepped on a dry branch, struggling not to wince when the loud crunch echoed through the woods. Instead, she added to the cacophony by trudging through a carpet of dry leaves instead of taking an easy route around them.

If her men could see her now, they'd die laughing. And it wasn't just the fact that she was clomping through the woods like a herd of drunk cattle. She was doing it in a pair of form-fitting jeans, a pink down jacket, and a knit hat with an enormous white pom-pom. Better than the getup she'd been forced to wear on the plane in Granada, though.

She'd taken a ton of shit over her naturally blond hair and ample chest during her years in the military. But that had quieted down a bit after she'd been ambushed with a group of Marines in Afghanistan. She'd ended up in charge, been shot twice, and gotten everyone out alive.

It was no surprise that her commanding officers had taken notice and a few shiny medals had accompanied some additional respect. What *had* been a surprise was that someone else had taken notice as well. And that someone else was Mitch Rapp.

That's right. Mitch *fucking* Rapp.

When his people had called about that crazy-ass Spain op, she hadn't hesitated for a second. And now here she was again. This time he'd called her personally. She'd been summoned to the base commander's office, put on a secure phone, and you know whose voice was on the other end? Yup. Mitch *fucking* Rapp.

The sky was dead clear and afternoon temperatures were climbing. That, combined with the down coat, class III body armor, and Walmart backpack, was making her start to sweat. Hopefully, the makeup artist who had beautified her that morning was right about the durability of his materials.

It didn't take as long as anticipated to pick up a glimmer of gold ahead. She adjusted her trajectory, focusing on keeping her gait natural as she headed toward it.

Despite having been told about what to expect, the woman coming into focus seemed completely . . . wrong. Dawson had always gotten a lot of looks from passing men, but this chick was on a whole other level. She didn't need makeup or a flashy pom-pom on her hat. Her chestnut hair flowed luxuriously over a shiny jacket that was cut just above a perfect, denim-encased ass. The blue of her eyes stood out even at a distance, hovering over a nose that was as flawless as her butt. The bitch even had rosy cheeks.

Those gorgeous eyes followed her approach, absorbing everything they saw in a way that was a little dead. Or maybe just hopelessly unimpressed.

"Sadie?"

The young woman just nodded and started in the direction of the target. Her gait wasn't particularly efficient, though the furry boots at the ends of her twiggy legs weren't exactly designed for backcountry travel. The mesmerizing way her hips swayed, though, suggested she probably didn't have to walk very often. Men would be killing each other to give her a ride.

Dawson went after her, coming alongside, but remaining silent. There were a number of questions she'd like to ask, but it was pretty clear that Sadie wasn't the type to answer them. So, with America's very existence on the line, she'd be going into this op backed up by someone who looked like she'd break in half if the wind gusted.

Victoria's Secret agent.

Dawson suppressed a smile at that. It made the fact that she was now absolutely certain she was going to die more palatable.

They came out onto the long dirt drive about a quarter mile from the target, turning north and heading up it in silence. Dawson had no idea if her new partner was carrying a weapon but she herself had been provided with nothing more than a small syringe hidden beneath one of her backpack straps. Not much of a substitute for her M4, but understandable given the mission parameters. Her orders were that none of the tangos were to be harmed. Even if she had to take a bullet for one of them.

The house came into view and she studied the façade. The only photos she'd seen were overheads, but they looked to be pretty accurate. The interior layout, on the other hand, was a complete unknown.

Dirt turned to cracked pavement and they walked up the driveway toward the front door. Flimsy wood painted blue with no glass or peephole. After a brief pause, Sadie balled a well-manicured hand and pounded on it.

No response.

She tried the knob.

Locked.

The next move was obvious. If they were who they were portraying themselves to be—two desperate women on their way to salvation in Texas—they'd assume the place was empty and break a window. The chimney on the west side suggested it was a good place to warm up and there might be a few scraps of food the owners forgot when abandoning the place.

Sadie picked up one of the rocks delineating the edge of the driveway but before she could throw it, the front door was jerked open. Dawson felt a dull surge of adrenaline as she watched the shotgun-wielding man step onto the porch. Dark complexion, thick beard, eyes full of hate.

The plan was simple, but also a little loose. It would have been virtually impossible for Rapp and his team to get anywhere near the house without being made. Understandably, they were concerned that this Arab asshole would kill John Alton at the first sign of trouble. So, they'd subcontracted the job to someone better qualified to take advantage of Arab men's greatest weaknesses: their misogyny. The average Middle Eastern male found it impossible to see a woman as a threat. Particularly two young American hotties. It was a blind spot she'd taken advantage of a number of times overseas. And it just needed to work one more time.

Sadie's face lit up as she walked toward the man. Her voice came out excited, but with just a hint of relief. It was like she'd become a completely different person. Exactly the person she needed to be.

"Thank God's someone's home! We're on our way down to Texas and need to get off the road before it gets dark. It's not safe."

She made it to within about five feet of him before he raised the shotgun and aimed it directly at her face.

"Hey, man. It's just the two of us," Sadie said, stopping and holding out her hands in a call for peace. "We don't even need any food if you don't have it. Just a little time by the fire and a sofa to sleep on. Tomorrow morning, we'll be on our way. Did you hear? They think they're going to be able to get the power back on in Texas. It's going to be incredible."

Dawson was familiar with the man's expression from her time in the Middle East—he didn't speak much English and was only catching about thirty percent of what was being said. Her tone continued to be dead on, though. As unthreatening as a basket of kittens.

"Go!" he said, confirming Dawson's suspicions about his language skills. "Nothing for you!"

Sadie kept talking and she was persuasive as hell, but he just wasn't having any. As the Blues Brothers had been fond of saying: he was on a mission from God.

The few feet between them might as well have been a mile and there was still no sign of their primary target, John Alton. They had to get close enough to make a move and at this point that wasn't going to happen. He needed a little more persuasion. Preferably something that could be understood with kindergarten English skills.

Maybe it was time to leverage another of the weaknesses shared by Muslim males: opportunities to get laid were few and far between.

When Sadie finally fell silent, Dawson walked up and planted a kiss on her mouth. And not just a peck. A long, sensual one that, thank God, she played along with. In fact, she had quite a gift.

Finally, Dawson pulled away and turned back to the man with an expression that was crystal clear. If he let them inside, they'd be happy to let him join.

Unfortunately, his reaction was to just stare at them with a slightly furrowed brow. Maybe it wasn't his language skills after all. Maybe he was just a fucking idiot.

Finally, the Arab adjusted his aim to Dawson's chest and shouted again in his broken English. "Go! Get away."

With no other option, she began backing away from Sadie, making sure the man tracked her with his weapon. This was it. The moment of truth. America was imploding and Mitch Rapp was watching. What was she going to do?

The shotgun was a double-barrel 12-gauge. Even with the body armor she was wearing, it'd be a bad day to get hit from this range. Unless he went for her face, in which case the durability of her makeup would *really* be tested.

She could see Sadie in her peripheral vision. Since the man was no longer paying attention, her expression had gone dead again. She was impossible to read, but Mitch Rapp had chosen her and he didn't work with the second string.

Right?

Dawson swallowed hard and then charged straight toward the barrel of the shotgun. A split second later, it went off. She thought she'd completely exhaled before lunging, but the force of the blast found some remaining air to knock out of her. As she was thrown backward, the crazy supermodel collided with the man. She wrapped her legs around him, snaking one hand over his mouth and nose while using the other to slam a syringe into his neck. He staggered left, unleashing the other barrel across the empty driveway just as the back of Dawson's head hit the ground.

The Arab crumpled, but Sadie landed catlike on her feet and darted through the open front door. Dawson tried to get up but there was no way in hell. It felt like someone had jumped on her chest and the ground where her head had hit was rock hard.

A few seconds later, three men sprinted past and into the house. The fourth, a blond man with a SIG, crouched to cover her and the team that had led him. Shouts of "clear" broke the silence and then Sadie's voice rose above them.

"In here!

"He's alive," Sadie said. "But it looks like he's unconscious."

She stepped aside, revealing a bed with John Alton firmly secured to it. He was completely motionless and Rapp would have assumed he was faking if it hadn't been for a nightstand lined with pharmaceuticals and the overwhelming stench of feces.

Much more interesting were the wires leading from beneath the quilt covering him to a large battery on the floor. Rapp carefully pulled back the blanket, not sure what to expect.

The charging cables were connected to two separate heart rate monitors, one on each wrist and each with a corresponding chest strap. Both units were familiar to him and he'd actually trained for a while with one of them. What he didn't understand, though, were the homemade electronics modifying the straps.

He checked the digital readout on one of Alton's wrists. His heart rate was reading fifty-nine beats per minute. The other unit said the same.

"What have we got, boss?" Bruno McGraw's voice from behind.

"Heart rate monitors connected to something I can't figure out. He's got high and low alarms set. My guess is that if he hits one of those limits, something happens."

"Like what? A booby trap? Maybe the ISIS guys put it on him so he couldn't run?"

Rapp shook his head. "Seems like a lot of trouble for a guy who doesn't look like he's going anywhere. Call Marcus. This is his wheelhouse, not ours. In the meantime, nobody touches anything."

"Roger that."

Rapp turned and walked back outside. The Arab was still unconscious on the porch, now flex-cuffed. In the yard, Coleman had Elizabeth Dawson on her feet. The hat and down jacket were on the ground and the former SEAL was helping her out of the body armor.

"You all right?" Rapp said, lending a hand.

She nodded and managed to whisper, "Yes, sir."

"It was a solid play," Rapp admitted. "I'd have bet money on it working."

"Never that easy," she breathed.

"Never that easy," Rapp agreed.

CHAPTER 52

The scene had completely transformed. The goal was to maintain blackout protocols so as not to attract attention, but it was a challenge. In the starlight, Rapp could make out three choppers in the clearing surrounding the house—one of which was a tandem rotor transport. Security personnel had been posted in the woods and the main road to the east had been barricaded in the unlikely event that someone might drive past.

Inside the house, everything seemed to finally be moving in the right direction. Marcus Dumond and his team were trying to figure out the purpose of Alton's heart rate monitors. Medical personnel had pronounced him reasonably healthy, but were keeping him sedated for the time being. And, finally, Coleman was in the back room, working on the Arab.

Rapp took one last breath of the cool, clean air and then headed back inside. The confined space had gotten fairly crowded but he managed to push his way to the kitchen, where some food had been brought in. He crammed a ham and cheese sandwich in his mouth and was about to wash it down with a warm Coke when he heard a voice behind him.

"I'm not getting anywhere with this guy, Mitch."

Rapp struggled to swallow as Scott Coleman, spattered in blood, entered.

"Has he said anything at all?"

"Nada. If we hadn't heard him out on the porch, I'd be wondering if he isn't deaf and mute."

"Keep trying," Rapp said. "But don't do any permanent damage. We'll take him back to Langley. See what they can do."

The former SEAL nodded and disappeared again, grabbing a sandwich as he went. Rapp was about to rip open a bag of potato chips when Dumond appeared in the doorway.

"We're as ready as we'll ever be."

Rapp emptied the bag into his mouth and nodded.

The room Alton was lying unconscious in had taken on the look of a high-tech medical facility. There was a clean adjustable bed, a monitor reading out Alton's vital signs, and IV set up. The stench of human excrement was gone, but it was unclear whether that was because they'd cleaned him up or because he'd been wrapped in lead blankets similar to the ones used for X-rays.

"Is he still good?" Rapp said to an Army doctor who was the only other person authorized to enter the room.

"Fine. We got the blood tests back, so we know what he's been given and in what amounts. Nothing dangerous. The IV's a sedative, fluids, and some nutrients."

Rapp nodded. “Marcus?”

“Like we talked about, he’s wearing two commercially available heart rate monitors. There are low alarms set at zero and high alarms set at one hundred and sixty. All this is connected to a heavily modified satellite phone that’s wired to the chest straps.”

“Why?”

“I don’t know exactly. What I can tell you is that he’s set it up so that if one of those alarms goes off—basically if he dies or gets too amped up, the satphone activates.”

“You’re saying it makes a phone call?”

“Could be. Or an email. Or a text.”

“Could it do something like trigger a bomb?”

“Anything’s possible, but probably not. The satellite it’s connected to is completely under government control and only very select users—like you and, ironically, him—are still authorized to use it. Some random phone connected to a bomb would have been kicked off a long time ago.”

“So, if I’m hearing you right, this setup can’t do anything but make a call or send data to people who are still on the network. So, basically critical government personnel.”

Dumond shrugged. “Yeah. To put it in Mitch Rapp–speak: It’s a phone. It can do phone stuff.”

“Okay. What’s that call or data going to be about?”

"Hell if I know. The data's encrypted and cracking it isn't going to happen anytime soon. Unfortunately, that leaves us only one option."

"Which is?"

"Set off the alarms and see what happens." He pointed to the lead blankets. "That's what those are for. We've deauthorized him on the network, but I don't want to take chances. The signal can't penetrate."

"You're sure."

"Alton is one brilliant son of a bitch, but even he can't break the laws of physics."

Rapp stared down at the unconscious man for a few moments, trying to process what he'd heard. "Do you think the Arabs put those things on him or did he do it himself?"

"My hunch is that he did it himself. But I can't guarantee it."

Rapp pulled up a chair and sat down next to the bed. "So, if something bad happens to him, the phone makes a call to someone on the network."

"Or sends data."

"Or sends data," Rapp agreed. "An accomplice?"

"That's the obvious answer. But why? To come and save him? To notify him or her that he's dead? What would be the point?"

They could sit here and speculate all day but, in the end, Dumond was right. There was only one way to know for sure.

"Doc. Can you bring him around?"

"Of course,"

Rapp watched the man work and a few moments later Alton's eyelids started to flutter. After another minute, he was looking around the room, dazed.

"How are you feeling?" Rapp said.

He didn't answer immediately, continuing to study his environment while his mind came back online. Calculating.

Interestingly, when he looked in Rapp's direction there was a flash of recognition followed by fear. Not exactly a new experience for the CIA man but, in this case, unexpected. The only time Alton had laid eyes on him was at that meeting in Maryland.

Or was it?

"Who are you?" he finally blurted. "The government? Thank God. Thank God you're here. They were keeping me in this bed, drugging me—"

"You're all right now," Rapp said, playing along. Clearly Alton had already managed to devise a story to save his ass. It'd be interesting to hear what it was.

"Why were they holding you here?"

"They're the people who did this. They forced me to help them. I'm John Alton. I was a consultant for the Department of Energy. They knew that if I got away, I'd go straight to the authorities."

"Why didn't they just kill you?"

"Because they thought they might need me if the government managed to start fixing things." He paused. "Oh my God. Texas! Two of them are going down there to try to destroy the repairs to the grid. You've got to warn them."

Rapp leaned back in his chair, impressed. To come up with a solid story like that under the circumstances showed some serious mental horsepower.

"Well, you're safe now, John. And thanks for the information. We'll send a security detail to Texas right away. More important, though, is that the power companies need to know how to get back into their computers and we need to know exactly what damage was done."

Alton avoided looking at him, instead examining the straps securing him to the bed and then lying back. Calculating. Always calculating.

"Sure," he said finally. "Of course."

"Great," Rapp said. "But one last thing. What are the heart rate monitors for?"

Alton took a few seconds to answer. "I don't know what you're talking about."

Rapp tapped one of the chest straps with his index finger.

"I . . . I don't know. I've never seen that before. They must have put it on me while I was unconscious."

"Interesting," Rapp said.

"What?"

"The docs tell me that, based on the condition of your skin, you've been wearing them for a long time. Weeks at a minimum. Maybe more than a month."

Alton finally met Rapp's gaze, holding it for a moment before refocusing on the ceiling again. That magnificent brain of his was undoubtedly reeling through the entire history of this thing. What Rapp could plausibly know. What he didn't. How the government had found him. And, finally, how he could craft all those elements into the perfect lie.

"You don't believe me," he said finally.

"I just want the power back on, John. And my understanding is that you're the man who can do it."

"I can, you know."

"What?"

"I can have half of the country back up and running in a week. Three-quarters in a few months. By summer, this could all be a memory."

"Then this is the beginning of a beautiful friendship."

"Is it? What happens after?"

"After what?"

"After I bring the grid back online."

"I don't know. Maybe you get your old job back. Obviously, we need the help."

Alton didn't respond for almost a minute.

"I'm not stupid, you know."

"You've made that crystal clear."

"You believe I'm responsible for all this and once I give you what you want I'm fucked."

"I think you're being a little paranoid, John. Besides, even if this was all your idea, I doubt a guy as smart as you would leave a trail that'd hold up in court."

Alton smiled. "Why don't I believe you?"

"I don't know, John. Trust issues?"

His condescending smile broadened. The effects of the sedatives had cleared enough for him to once again believe he was the smartest guy in the room. And maybe he was. But it was Rapp's room.

"What's your name?"

"Mitch."

"How about I make this work for both of us, Mitch."

"I'm all ears."

"ISIS did this. And you caught them, punished them, and got the lights back on. The American people love to hate Muslims. They'll eat that story up. Somebody like me just complicates the narrative. The sheep don't like things that are complicated."

"No?"

"Don't be stupid like them, Mitch. Make yourself the biggest hero in US history. You want to be a senator? Piece of cake. The White House probably wouldn't be out of reach, either. I mean, you're the man who saved the life of every voter in America."

"I have to admit that I like where your head's at," Rapp said. "I'd look pretty good behind the *Resolute* desk. But I'm guessing you want something in return. Can I assume that it's for us to let you loose in Mexico? That's where you were headed, right? Mexico?"

"You're smarter than you look."

"Thank you."

"Sure. Fine. You want to cut through the bullshit? Let's do it. You're right. The plan was Mexico, but I think that's out the window now. Obviously, you'd be able to get to me there. I'm thinking Cuba. Just drop me in Havana and let me disappear. Once I'm settled and I'm sure there's no one tracking me, I'll give you all the information you need to turn the lights back on."

Rapp nodded slowly. "There are a lot of people dying out there and the government's desperate. I imagine they'd take that deal."

"Then call the president and offer it up."

"I hate to call the president without answers to all the questions he's going to ask. And I can tell you that he's curious about those heart rate monitors."

"Forget the fucking heart rate monitors!" Alton said, his voice rising to a frustrated shout. "How many people have died just while we've been talking? A thousand? Two thousand? Who are you anyway? Some FBI guy? What's that saying people like you have? You're way above your pay grade? Get the president on the phone. It's time for the big boys to talk."

Rapp didn't respond. Finally, the silence stretched out long enough that Alton felt compelled to fill it.

"Okay! You win. You want to know what the heart rate monitors are for? They're for this exact scenario. If you kill me or torture me, it launches a secondary attack."

"What kind of secondary attack?"

"Fuck with me and find out, asshole."

Rapp wondered. If he'd been in Alton's position, he'd have been a hell of a lot more afraid of ISIS than the remote possibility of being captured by the government. And if those heart rate monitors were going to set off a secondary attack, wouldn't Feisal Ibrahim have wanted that to happen? He wouldn't even have had to kill Alton. Just get his heart rate up. But no. They'd done the opposite. They'd kept him alive and sedated. As if they didn't want those heart rate limits hit.

"Marcus," Rapp said. "What kind of secondary attack could he be talking about?"

"None that I can think of. The power's either off or it's not. You can't have it, you know, more off."

“You have no authority to make this kind of a decision,” Alton said. “Now, get the president on the phone.”

Rapp just shook his head slowly. “The curiosity is killing me, John. I’m sorry, but I’ve just gotta know.”

Rapp felt a hand on his shoulder, shaking him awake. When he opened his eyes, Scott Coleman was looking down at him. “Marcus says he’s ready.”

He pushed himself into a sitting position on the moldy carpet. “Did you talk to Irene?”

“Yeah. She agrees with your hunch and the president thinks the risks are acceptable. You’re a go.”

Rapp walked back into the bedroom and closed the door behind him. Alton’s expression suggested that his earlier confidence was starting to fade. He wasn’t panicking yet, but the monitor displaying his vital signs suggested he was on the way.

“So, you’re set?” Rapp said, dropping onto the chair by the bed again.

“Yeah,” Dumond replied. “Everything’s hooked up and tested. The sending unit on his chest will get picked up by our receivers under the lead blankets, but won’t go any farther. We’re good to go.”

“Get the president on the phone!” Alton

shouted. “I can fix this! Every minute we sit here screwing around, people are dying!”

“Yeah, but how many more are going to die while you’re negotiating your golden parachute and disappearing into Cuba? And how can we even be sure you’ll hold up your end of the bargain once you’re gone? Seems like you’d want to keep the US weak so we wouldn’t have the resources to come after you.” Rapp looked over at Dumond. “Am I good to get his heart rate up?”

“Knock yourself out.”

“Wait!” Alton said. “You want to know what will happen? I’ll tell you. The secondary attack will be on your nuclear power plants. You won’t only be in the dark, you’ll be dealing with a cloud of radiation that’ll cover the whole country.”

“Marcus?” Rapp said.

“I’m not worried. All the plants are off-line and it’s not like you can get them going again with a phone call. Besides, like I said, he’s been kicked off the network and he’s lying under a bunch of lead.”

Alton glared at the young African American and he glared back. “You’re not the only person in the world who understands technology, asshole.”

“So, you’re confident,” Rapp confirmed.

“Yeah. I say we go for it.”

Rapp dug a lighter from his pocket and grabbed Alton’s right hand.

"What are you doing? Stop! You can't—"

His words turned to screams when Rapp flicked the lighter to life under his forearm. The vital signs monitor showed a steady increase in heart rate to one hundred and forty but then it plateaued. Rapp released the man's hand, allowing him enough freedom of movement to get his arm away from the flame. He chased it, moving the lighter in a way that caused Alton to thrash wildly in an effort to keep away from it.

One hundred and fifty-two. Still short.

"We could probably just take off the straps," Dumond pointed out. "That'd be the same as his heart rate going to zero."

"I know," Rapp responded, pulling a tactical knife from the sheath on his hip. Alton saw it and tried to pull away, but there wasn't anywhere for him to go. Rapp was about to shove the tip under the man's thumbnail, but then changed his mind. Someone had done something similar to him once in Syria and, for some reason, it was all about the material. Sure, steel hurt. But wood was a whole other level.

He kept an eye on the vital signs monitor as he carved a piece off the chair leg and began fashioning it into a spike. Alton's heart rate rose to one fifty-four while Rapp whittled.

"Stop!" he said, beginning sob. "Please stop . . ."

"You want to know something?" Rapp said as he put the finishing touches on what now looked like a six-inch-long splinter. “That FBI agent you gunned down at your property in Virginia was a friend of mine. We’d known each other for twenty years.”

He grabbed Alton’s thumb and rammed the chunk of wood up under the nail.

The man’s shrieks were exacerbating Rapp’s headache, so he clamped a hand over his mouth and watched the monitor.

One fifty-six. One fifty-eight . . .

One sixty.

“It’s transmitting,” Dumond said.

“What? It’s transmitting what?”

“Hold on. Wait . . . Wait for it . . . Okay, it’s still uploading, but I’ve got a complete file.”

“And?”

“I can’t believe it.”

“What?”

“You were right.”

EPILOGUE

South of Stanley
Idaho
USA

It was one of those rare days that it was hard to find anything to complain about. Temperatures in Idaho had hit the mid-eighties and the mountains were a deep green capped with what was left of that winter's snow. Best of all, the sun-heated hood he was lying on didn't belong to the loaner AMC Pacer he'd been expecting. Instead the commander of the Mountain Home Air Force Base had rolled out his 1971 Caddy and handed over the keys.

Peace and quiet weren't things Rapp got much of. In truth, they weren't things he'd really pursued. At that moment, though, sitting by that particular rural road, he wondered if he shouldn't start making more of an effort.

Life in the United States was slowly getting back to normal. The electricity was flowing everywhere but a few remote rural enclaves, but at nowhere near its former levels. The damage from the attack and the subsequent fires were going to take a long time to fully repair, making rolling blackouts and brownouts part of daily life. Casualties had been buried and honored. The new president was ensconced in the White House, busy passing out blame for what had happened. Upgrades to grid security had bogged down in politics, corruption, and partisanship, setting the country up for a similar attack in the future.

Hopefully far enough in the future that he'd be long dead when it happened. Once was enough.

In the meantime, there was a light breeze, an eagle floating overhead, and nothing but the sound of rustling trees and the river behind him. Later that evening, he'd be back in Virginia, where Claudia and Anna would join him for some grilled burgers, a round of lawn darts, and maybe a mindless movie. The worldwide recession caused by America's temporary fall from grace had calmed the planet down. No one seemed to have the time, resources, or energy to make trouble and Rapp was using the lull to relax and heal his injuries.

The sound of a motor became audible to the south and he jumped down to the asphalt, taking off his sunglasses to be more recognizable. The pickup slowed. Then it sped up. Then it stopped on the shoulder about fifty yards ahead. Finally, after sitting there for almost a minute, it backed toward him.

"I've stayed one hundred percent on script," Jed Jones said as he stepped out.

"I know."

He seemed unwilling to get much closer than fifteen feet. "All the government's talked about is ISIS. There's never been anything about that Alton asshole."

The distance forced him to nearly shout, but it didn't matter. Other than the eagle, there wasn't anyone around to hear.

"We've been holding him and forcing him to help us in a way that's . . ." Rapp's voice faded for a moment. "Well, let's just say it's not strictly legal. And that's not a story the politicians want out in the wild."

"So, what are you doing here? I've kept my mouth shut just like you told me. Was that a mistake? Have I become a liability?"

"Relax, Jed. You've lived up to your end of the bargain and I'm here to live up to mine. Now, get in your truck and follow me."

"I don't understand," he said warily.

Rapp just slid behind the Caddy's wheel and pulled out onto the road. Langley had preprogrammed the GPS on his phone and he followed the directions as Jed reluctantly climbed back into his truck and followed.

The road Rapp eventually turned onto was rougher than he'd been led to believe, forcing him to slow to a crawl in order to avoid rock chips. The Caddy handled itself admirably, though, and after forty minutes they dead-ended into a berm that denoted the wilderness boundary. There would be little reason for anyone to go beyond that point. Vehicles and hunting were prohibited, and trails were nonexistent.

Rapp walked around to the trunk and slid a key into the well-oiled lock. Jed approached hesitantly but then stopped dead when the lid opened to reveal John Alton's hogtied form inside.

"Oh, shit! Is that him?"

"That's him," Rapp said, ripping the duct tape off the man's mouth. It started running almost immediately.

"What are you doing? Where am I? You can't do this to me! I have a right to a trial."

"That's a lot to unpack, but let me take a shot. I'm getting rid of you. We're in Idaho. I can actually do whatever I want. And as far as your right to a trial goes, I don't see any lawyers around."

Rapp pulled a switchblade from his pocket and cut the ropes holding the man.

"Get out."

Alton suddenly seemed extremely comfortable in the trunk that he'd fought so hard to stay out of. Rapp was forced to grab him by the hair and drag him to the ground. He tried to make a break for it back down the road, but six months in solitary, eight hours secured to an aircraft seat, and another five in the trunk hadn't done much for his running ability. He barely made it ten feet before tripping over a rock.

"I'm not sure I understand what's going on here," Jed said as Alton struggled back to his feet.

"You don't remember what you asked me in return for your help?"

His eyes narrowed for a moment, but then a light dawned. "I said if you caught him, I wanted to be there when they fried him."

"And here we are."

"Hold on, now, man. That's not how the government works. They don't just give someone like this to one guy and let him drive away in an old Caddy."

"I'm surprised at you, Jed. It's actually exactly how the government works. The higher-ups want things done but they don't like to get their hands dirty."

Alton finally made it to his feet and Rapp shoved him toward the end of the road. He was a genius—something confirmed by everyone who had interrogated him—but this situation was so far from his world that even his supercharged brain couldn't grasp it. He just stumbled forward in silence.

Rapp glanced back at Jones. "You coming?"

After fifteen minutes, Alton was having to rest at regular intervals. The sweat pouring down his face was mixing with tears as the reality of his situation started to sink in. He leaned against a tree and spoke for the first time since they'd left the car.

"I can help. You still need to secure the grid. If I could do this, someone else can, too. I'm the only person who can make sure the country never has to go through this again."

"You were already paid millions of dollars to do exactly that," Rapp said, shoving him forward again. "And it didn't work out so well."

"But now you can control me," Alton countered as they moved into a dense stand of trees. "I'm not asking for freedom. Put me in a secure location. You don't even have to connect me to the Internet. But I can help. I can."

"Let me think about it," Rapp said.

After another fifteen minutes of listening to Alton's increasingly desperate rundown of his positive qualities, they came to a rock outcropping that overhung what looked like a low cave. Probably no more than two feet high and three wide, but deep enough that the back was inky black. A body hidden there wouldn't be found for a thousand years.

"End of the trail," Rapp said.

Five feet ahead, Alton stopped short. "What do you mean?"

"Was I not clear?"

"You can't do this. I have a right to a lawyer. A trial. You can't just murder me out here. You can't."

"We've already been through this," Rapp said as he screwed a silencer to the end of his Glock. "Hundreds of thousands of people are dead, John. Mostly old ones, weak ones, sick ones. And I don't remember you being too worried about their right to due process."

He seemed frozen to the ground, mouth moving but with no sound coming out. It was Jed, suddenly faced with the reality of what was happening, who spoke in his place.

"I think he might be right, man. Is this legal?"

"It's sanctioned," Rapp responded.

"That's not really an answer."

"Welcome to my world, Jed. Do you want to be here for this or do you want to go back to your truck?"

Alton had fallen to his knees and added begging to his sobbing. One positive thing Rapp could say about the Islamicists was that you usually got a pass on the blubbering.

"I appreciate that you're a man of your word," Jones said. "But I was picturing more of a prison viewing area and a lethal injection table."

"I understand."

He started back the way they'd come and Rapp waited until he couldn't hear his footsteps anymore before using his weapon to indicate the black maw of the cave.

"You like the dark, right?"

"Please!" Alton screamed, putting his hands in front of his face.

The round went through his right palm and struck him just above the bridge of the nose. His head snapped back and for a moment he seemed suspended by some unseen force. Then he just pitched forward onto his face.

Books are produced in the United States using U.S.-based materials

Books are printed using a revolutionary new process called THINKtech™ that lowers energy usage by 70% and increases overall quality

Books are durable and flexible because of Smyth-sewing

Paper is sourced using environmentally responsible foresting methods and the paper is acid-free

Center Point Large Print
600 Brooks Road / PO Box 1
Thorndike, ME 04986-0001 USA

(207) 568-3717

US & Canada:
1 800 929-9108
www.centerpointlargeprint.com